S

In the
It...

CA...
MA... ...AYO
CATHERINE GEORGE

MILLS
BOON
&

Published in Great Britain 2013
by Mills & Boon, an imprint of Harlequin (UK) Limited,
Eton House, 18-24 Paradise Road, Richmond, Surrey TW9 1SR

IN THE ITALIAN'S BED © by Harlequin Enterprises II B.V./S.à.r.l 2013

Bedded for Pleasure, Purchased for Pregnancy, The Italian's Ruthless Baby Bargain and *The Italian Count's Defiant Bride* were first published in Great Britain by Harlequin (UK) Limited.

Bedded for Pleasure, Purchased for Pregnancy © Carol Marinelli 2009
The Italian's Ruthless Baby Bargain © Margaret Mayo 2008
The Italian Count's Defiant Bride © Harlequin Books S.A. 2009

Special thanks and acknowledgement are given to Catherine George for her contribution to the International Billionaires miniseries.

ISBN: 978 0 263 90570 0
ebook ISBN: 978 1 472 00143 6

05-1113

Harlequin (UK) policy is to use papers that are natural, renewable and recyclable products and made from wood grown in sustainable forests. The logging and manufacturing processes conform to the legal environmental regulations of the country of origin.

Printed and bound in Spain
by Blackprint CPI, Barcelona

BEDDED FOR PLEASURE, PURCHASED FOR PREGNANCY

BY
CAROL MARINELLI

Carol Marinelli recently filled in a form where she was asked for her job title, and she was thrilled, after all these years, to be able to put down her answer as 'writer'. Then it asked what Carol did for relaxation, and after chewing her pen for a moment Carol put down the truth—'writing'. The third question asked—'What are your hobbies?' Well, not wanting to look obsessed or, worse still, boring, she crossed the fingers on her free hand and answered 'swimming and tennis'. But—given that the chlorine in the pool does terrible things to her highlights, and the closest she's got to a tennis racket in the last couple of years is watching the Australian Open—I'm sure you can guess the real answer!

Carol also writes for Medical Romance™!

CHAPTER ONE

'GUESS who's coming tonight!'

Emma smiled at the excitement in her mother's voice as Lydia Hayes replaced the phone receiver.

'Half of Melbourne are coming!'

The party was all her mother had spoken about for the past few weeks, Emma's father's sixtieth birthday, and the intimate dinner they had initially planned had swelled to marquee proportions! Every inch of their sweeping bay view home had been commandeered to maximum effect, with the marquee open to reveal Port Phillip Bay in all its glory, and even the weather had obliged, with a clear sky allowing for city views. The dance floor had been laid, the band was setting up, caterers were milling, and Lydia was rattling with nerves as the hour approached. But the telephone call had, momentarily at least, halted her nerves.

'We've got an unexpected guest!' Lydia clasped her hands in delight. 'Go on, Emma, guess who.'

'Mum…' Emma wailed, wrapped in a towel and painting her toenails. Having spent the day helping her mother prepare, she was already racing against the clock to be ready.

'Just tell me.'

'Zarios!'

A smudge of red nail varnish streaked across Lydia's little toe. Pulling out a cotton bud, she dabbed at the area, refusing to let on that it mattered a jot that Zarios was coming tonight.

Oh, but it did.

Zarios—the single word that sent a tingle up every woman's spine. A man who didn't need to use his high-profile surname to be instantly recognisable.

His scowling but effortlessly beautiful face often appeared in the gossip columns. His reputation with women was appalling—so much so that it was a wonder, after so many blistering articles written on the man, that any woman might even *consider* getting involved with him.

Oh, but they did—over and over they did. And without fail it always ended in tears—or, to be more exact, the woman's tears.

'Why?' Curiosity got the better of Emma, and, screwing back the top on her nail varnish, she just couldn't stop herself asking.

Their fathers might be best friends, but why would Zarios D'Amilo even entertain the thought of coming to her father's celebration? Shouldn't he be sleeping with some supermodel on a Saturday night? Or crossing the equator on the way to some exclusive star-studded function? Certainly not on his way to celebrate Eric Hayes's sixtieth birthday.

Rocco D'Amilo had arrived in Australia nearly half a century ago, at eleven years of age. The son of Italian immigrants, he had been teased and goaded in his first hellish days at school. Unable to speak English, his lunchbox full of smelly meat, he had been an easy target, until Eric Hayes, who had suffered his own share of teasing in his time, had blackened the eye of the ringleader. The unlikely pair had been firm friends ever since.

Rocco had started out his working life as a builder, Eric as a real estate agent, and they had remained in touch even when Rocco had taken his young bride and new baby son back to Italy. They had been best man at each other's weddings, godparents at christenings, and their friendship had been the support Rocco needed when his young wife had walked out on her husband and four-year-old child.

Eric had done well for himself over the years and a few wise property investments meant his family lived comfortably. He had followed the 'worst house, best street' rule, and had bought a rundown home on a rundown acre in an exclusive beachside suburb, refurbishing it slowly until it gleamed with the same majesty as its view. Rocco, too, had achieved success, both here and in Rome, yet it was his son Zarios who had turned the family business into the empire it was today. His father's strong work ethic, combined with a private school education and a brilliant brain, had proved a dizzying recipe for success.

Zarios had emerged from university with big plans, which he had rapidly implemented, turning the modest but successful building company into a global property and finance company. D'Amilo Financiers had multiple branches throughout Europe and Australia and was stretching its golden fingers ever further across the globe. Now, with Rocco's retirement imminent, Zarios was expected to officially take the helm.

If only he would behave!

'He's on a final warning!' Even though there were only the two of them in the room, Lydia spoke in a loud whisper. 'Your father was telling me that apparently the board are sick of Zarios's caddish ways. They're uncomfortable with the prospect of him being the majority shareholder…'

'That's up to Rocco, surely…?' Emma frowned.

'Rocco's fed up with him, too. He's given that boy everything, and look how Zarios repays him. If the rest of the directors band together…' Lydia's voice lowered another octave '…and it sounds as if they might now. If the rumours that Zarios has split up with Miranda are true—she was his one saving grace.'

'They were only going out four months!' Emma pointed out.

'Which is a long time in dog years!'

Oh, how they laughed at that.

Emma's parents infuriated her at times—most of the time, in fact. The blatant preference they had for Emma's brother Jake, the way they repeatedly dismissed her career choice, as if by being an artist she didn't have a real job, and yet she adored them. Her mother was, and always had been to Emma, the funniest woman she knew.

And wrapped in a towel, doubled over in laughter as her mother hooted with mirth and the early evening sun dipped lower over the bay, drenching the living room in gold, somehow, on some level, Emma knew that this moment was precious.

She could have had no idea how precious, rich and good life was that gorgeous summer evening. No idea how many times she'd find herself playing it over and over again.

'Come on!' Dabbing her eyes, Lydia hurried her daughter up. 'Where on earth can I put him?'

'He's staying the night?' Emma's eyes widened at the very thought of Zarios D'Amilo sleeping here in this house.

'Yessss!' Lydia hissed, the joking well and truly put aside now, as her already high stress levels rocketed. 'I knew Rocco was—but Zarios! He'll have to have your room!'

'He jolly well won't.'

'We can hardly give him the trundle bed in the study—Jake's squeezed into his old room, Rocco's in the guestroom…Zarios will *have* to have yours. Come on, it's time to get dressed,' Lydia said, refusing to debate the point, buoyed at the prospect of having such a high-profile guest. 'My friends are going to simply *die* with jealousy—can you imagine Cindy's face when she finds out? You did buy something nice for tonight, I hope?'

'Like a bridal gown?' Emma said, firmly tongue in cheek.

'Well, he *has* broken up with Miranda!'

Emma's sarcasm was entirely wasted on her mother. Lydia Hayes had spent her married life clinging on to the middle rung of the social ladder, and was determined that her children would rise to the heights she had never achieved.

'Australia's most eligible bachelor is joining us to celebrate your father's sixtieth birthday, Emma. Surely you're just a little bit excited?'

'Of course I'm excited.' Emma smiled. 'About Dad's birthday…'

'Get ready, then,' Lydia chided, and then, wincing

slightly, massaged her temples. 'They'll be arriving soon…'

'Mum, calm down.'

'What if they're expecting something spectacular?'

'Then we'll wheel out Zarios!' Emma smiled again, but her mother was past jokes. 'They're expecting a birthday celebration, which this *is*,' Emma said, walking across the lounge and taking her mother's hands from her temples and holding them. 'They're coming to see you and Dad. That's all that matters.'

'Jake's not even here yet!' Lydia trilled. 'My own son can't make it on time. Do you think he'll have remembered to order the pastries for breakfast?' Emma could hear panic once again creeping into her mother's voice and moved quickly to avert it.

'Of course he'll have remembered. You go and sort out fresh sheets for my bed, and I'll go and get ready. *And*,' she added with a wry smile, 'I'll give my room a quick tidy!'

Her bedroom was exactly the same as it had been seven years ago, when she'd left home to go to university to study art. Emma loved coming back and staying in her old room, amongst her old familiar things, but this evening she eyed it somewhat critically, wondering what Zarios would make of the paintings that adorned the walls, the curtains she had tye-died herself when she was twelve, the tatty overfilled bookshelves and the dressing table laden with childhood photos.

Emma had always intended to wear *something nice* for her father's special night. Her tiny broom cupboard of an art gallery was in Chapel Street in Melbourne, and as well as her gallery the street boasted an array of designer boutiques. Slipping on the cerulean blue dress, Emma wondered what on earth had possessed her. It had caught her eye in the window—the shade of blue almost a replica of the view of the bay from her parents' balcony. The price had been an instant dissuader, yet the assistant had suggested Emma at least try it on. Staring at her reflection, Emma let her teeth worry away at her bottom lip as she wondered if it wasn't just a bit too much.

Or too little!

An inch shorter than she would have preferred, it clung provocatively in all the wrong places. Her bottom surely appeared massive, and her breasts as if they had instantly gone up a size, where the feather-light wool caressed her figure, only loosening its grip at mid-thigh, then hanging innocently, yet flaring as smoothly as a trumpet bell as she walked.

It was, quite simply, divine.

Worthy, Emma told herself as she pulled a shoebox from her case, of the horribly expensive strappy sandals she'd bought to go with it. Worthy of the hours of buffing and polishing her body had endured—and her first visit to a tanning parlour.

Running her ceramic straighteners for the final time over her long blonde hair, she stopped worrying her bottom lip and applied a final layer of lipgloss instead, thanking the gods who had looked after her these past days, who must have known that Zarios D'Amilo would be coming tonight, and had, unbeknown to Emma, insisted that she look her best for the embarrassing task of facing him again after all these years.

Emma picked up one of the photos on her dressing

table and stared at the wedding group. Even though it was ridiculous, even though it was only a photo, still she blushed as she looked into Zarios's serious dark eyes.

She'd been nineteen…

A young and extremely naive nineteen-year-old, she had been dressed up like a vast pink blancmange, as bridesmaid at Jake's wedding.

Zarios had been invited. He'd only been in Australia a few weeks back then, and his accent had been so heavy and rich Emma had struggled to understand his words—except she could have listened to him talk for ever. Put simply, he had been the most stunning man she had ever seen. The whole wedding had passed in a dizzy blur until finally, dutifully, he had danced with her. And because it had been Zarios D'Amilo holding her, and she'd had rather too much champagne, Emma had promptly fallen in lust.

Shoving the photo in a drawer, she turned it face-down and covered it with the drawer's contents, then slammed it closed. The last thing she wanted was for Zarios to see it—for Zarios to recall her exquisitely embarrassing mistake. But even with the photo safely tucked away Emma was struggling to beat her blush, struggling to banish the image of the two of them dancing that night. Zarios had lowered his head to say something and stupidly, blindly, she'd misinterpreted the action, closed her eyes and, lips poised, waited expectantly for him to kiss her.

Even six years on she burnt with the shame of the memory.

Could still hear his deep, throaty laugh as he'd realised what she thought he had intended.

'Come back when you're all grown up…' He'd smiled

at her and patted her bottom as the music had ended, merrily sending her on her childish way. 'Anyway, my father would never forgive me.'

He'd probably forgotten, Emma consoled herself.

With all the women he'd dated, as if he'd remember a teenager's clumsy attempt at extracting a kiss. Anyway, she was six years older now and light years wiser—she could see a man like Zarios exactly for what he was: a player.

She certainly wouldn't make the same mistake again; she'd be aloof and distant, Emma decided, practising an aloof and distant look in the mirror. Maybe she should wear her hair up? Emma thought, piling her long blonde hair on her head and seeing if it made a difference, then deciding against. Maybe she should just make a joke about it, laugh the whole thing off…

Maybe she should tidy her room!

Her mother joined her, and the embroidered quilt was hastily replaced with crisp white linen as Lydia ran around the room removing stray bras, mascara wands and tampon boxes. Folded towels and washcloths were placed at the end of the bed, along with a little bar of Lydia's expensive soap, and a jug of water and a glass was put beside the bed, covered with a little linen cloth.

'It's mineral water,' Lydia assured a bemused Emma as she arranged the jug with precision. 'Should I put out a little snack for him?' she worried. 'Is there anything else you can think of?'

'A box of tissues?' Emma nudged her mother, making Lydia giggle again. 'Legend has it he can't go twelve hours!'

But even if she could make her mother laugh and

relax just a touch, as she stared out at the bay Emma felt her throat tighten when she heard a helicopter approach and knew it was him. As comfortably off as her parents and their friends might be, only the D'Amilos would arrive for a party in a helicopter. She watched it hover for a moment, could see the marquee flapping, the grass flattened by the whirring blades, and then…

She knew she was holding her breath, because the window had stopped misting over, and she knew as one well-shod foot appeared, followed by an impossibly long leg, that it was *him*.

The view only improved from that point.

Zarios helped his father down, then, having ducked under the blades, they strolled across the lawn, too used to their mode of travel to give the helicopter even a backward glance as it lifted off into the sunset.

He was wearing black dress pants and a fitted white shirt, and like a prize thoroughbred being paraded before the race he had a restless energy, a glossy, groomed appearance, that had Emma's stomach fold in on itself as he tossed his head back and laughed at something his father said. For just a moment, an embarrassing twinge, Emma was sure he saw her. Those black eyes had glanced up as if he knew he was being watched, and Emma stepped quickly back, as if burnt.

'Emma!' She could hear her mother's shrill summons and, taking a deep breath, she steadied herself. 'They're here! An hour early and they're *here*!'

'Questi sono i miei buoni amici.' As they walked across the lawn, again his father reminded him how important these people were to him.

'You believe too much of what you read!' Zarios laughed. 'I *am* capable of behaving occasionally. Anyway, I fear it will be slim pickings at a sixtieth birthday bash, Pa!'

'Zarios…' Rocco was serious. It had seemed like a good idea for him to bring Zarios. Fresh out of a relationship, Zarios had that gleam in his roving eye that spelt danger—and if Rocco could avert scandal at this precarious time, then he would. Ah, but had it been wise to bring him here? On the short flight over Rocco had remembered the wedding, the instant attraction that had flared between his son and Emma Hayes. He had warned Zarios off that night—and thankfully the warning had been heeded. But Zarios was six years older now, and way past taking his father's advice. 'You remember their daughter, Emma?'

'The good-looking blonde?' A smile flickered across his face in instant recall. Things were maybe looking up for tonight after all. 'Actually, I do.'

'She's grown into a very attractive woman…'

'Splendid!'

'Attesa!' Rocco called for his son to slow down, pulling out his handkerchief and mopping his brow.

'Are you okay, Pa?'

'A little chest pain…' Rocco took a pill from a little silver box and placed it under his tongue. 'Nothing I am not used to.' He *did* have chest pain—perhaps not enough to merit taking a pill, but if the sympathy card would help Rocco was only too willing to play it. 'You know I think the world of Lydia, but you know how she loves to spend—and, well, it would seem that Emma has the same tendency…'

'It is fortunate I am rich then, no?' Zarios joked, but his father wasn't smiling.

'Eric is worried…' It was only a small lie, Rocco consoled himself. In fact he hadn't lied, he told himself, just implied… Surely it was better to put Zarios off now, than face Eric after his son had broken his daughter's heart?

And he would, Rocco thought wearily, mopping his forehead again before folding his handkerchief and putting it back in his pocket. Zarios *would* break her heart.

'Don't get involved with her, Zarios.' Rocco resumed his walking. 'It would be far too messy.'

'You're early!' Eric, as laid-back as his wife was neurotic, didn't worry about things like guestrooms and final layers of lipgloss, instead he was simply delighted as Rocco came through the door, and hugged and embraced his lifelong friend in the effusive Italian way. Zarios stood slightly back.

'We wanted some time with you before the other guests arrived.' Rocco beamed, offering Eric a lavishly wrapped gift. 'Hide that and open it tomorrow.'

'The invitation said no gifts!' Lydia scolded, but she was clearly delighted that he had. 'Zarios—we're *thrilled* that you came.'

'It is good to be here.'

His accent was still rich, his voice low and deep, and Emma could feel the tiny hairs at the back of her neck stand on end as she came down the stairs, attempting to maintain her distant and aloof look, watching as he kissed her mother on both cheeks and then did the same with her father. His black eyes met hers.

'Emma. It's been a long time.' His smile was guarded, and in a split second his eyes took in the changes. The short cut she had once worn had long since grown out, and her hair now hung in a heavy blonde curtain over her shoulders. Her once skinny, overactive body had softened and filled out since then, too, and her feminine curves were enhanced by the soft drape of her dress— a dress that swished around her slender legs as she moved. Zarios was surprisingly grateful for his father's warning, because without it the night might have taken a rather different direction.

She had always been pretty, but she was stunning now!

'It *has* been a long time.' She walked down the last two steps and hovered on the bottom one, but still he had to bend his head to kiss her on the cheeks. As he did so, he smelt her—*again*. His body flared in surprised recognition as his lips dusted her cheeks. How nice it would be, Zarios thought wildly, to give her the kiss he had denied her so many years ago.

Had denied *himself*.

The others moved forward, leaving them alone for just a moment, each lost in their own thoughts.

'You are looking well.' He frowned slightly. 'How long has it been since we've seen each other?'

'A few years?' Emma shrugged, refusing to acknowledge she knew the exact length of time, down to the month! 'Four—maybe five?'

'It's not that long…' Zarios shook his head as they headed through to the lounge. 'It was at your brother's wedding.'

'That was five years ago…' Emma smiled. 'Actually, it was six!'

'Come through,' Lydia scolded. 'Emma, get our guests a drink.'

At that moment one of the hired help arrived with a hastily filled tray of champagne. Emma grabbed one for herself before Lydia shooed her away.

'A real drink!' Lydia hissed to Emma out of the side of her mouth.

'Whisky?' Emma checked. That was what Rocco always had when he came over. 'And a small dash of water?'

'She has a good memory.' Rocco beamed.

'Zarios?' Emma deliberately forced herself to look him in the eye. 'What would you like?' Black eyes held hers, and she could have sworn there was just a fraction of innuendo in the pause that went on for just a beat too long. The torch she had carried for him over the years flared brightly as his eyes held hers, no matter how she tried to douse it.

'Whisky.' He added no please or thank you to his order. 'No water.'

And as easily as if he'd flicked a switch she was lost.

Pouring the golden liquid, she could see her hand was shaking. She hadn't exaggerated the memory of him. He *was* as lethal and as potently sexy as he had been all those years ago—and as arrogant and rude, Emma reminded herself. Handing him his glass, trying and failing not to notice the brush of his fingers against hers, she crossed the room and sat on the sofa, as far away from him as possible.

The cat soon found the mouse.

He sat beside her, just a tiny bit too close for her liking. There was no contact, none at all, but she could feel the heat from his body, feel the weight of him, the ancient springs in the leather couch tilting her just a fraction towards him.

He invaded her space—but perhaps that was his trick. No one watching could testify to intrusion; you had to be beside him, or looking at him, to feel it. Taking a sip of her champagne, she wished she had chosen whisky, too—wished for something, anything, strong enough to douse the nerves that were leaping like salmon in her chest.

'I take it Jake and his wife will be coming tonight?'

'Just Jake.' Emma gave a tight smile.

'They have twins now, don't they?' Zarios checked, watching her closely, seeing the brittle smile on her face slip into a more relaxed one as she described her niece and nephew.

'Harriet and Connor—they'll be three in a few weeks' time.' On cue her brother arrived, bustling into the room.

'Darling!' Lydia practically fell on to her son's neck, the lateness of his arrival immediately forgiven. 'It's *so* good to see you.'

'Sorry, sorry…' Jake beamed. 'The traffic was an absolute nightmare.'

'On a Saturday?' Emma couldn't help herself.

'The football's on!' Lydia beamed. 'The city's hell around this time—it's just wonderful you made it, darling. You did remember the pastries for tomorrow…?'

There was a tiny, appalling pause as Jake's fixed smile slipped just a fraction, his frantic eyes darting to his sister. Lydia's mouth opened in horror mid-sentence. Emma was almost tempted not to intervene, to refuse to save the day yet again for her brother and let them see that the *one* thing, the one thing he had been asked to contribute, had proved too much for him. But, as Jake well knew, she couldn't do that to her parents.

'Oh, I forgot to tell you, Mum—the bakers rang to confirm Jake's order. They'll be here first thing.'

'Oh, Emma!' her mother snapped. 'You could have let me know!'

'Where is Beth?' Rocco frowned, voicing the question Lydia had clearly hoped he wouldn't. 'And where are the twins? I was looking forward to seeing them again.'

'Tonight's for adults only.' Lydia beamed again, but there was a rigid set to her lips.

'Why?' Rocco had been single too long, and missed the warning signs flashing from Lydia's eyes to simply drop it. 'Children are part of the family…they should be here…'

Surprisingly, it was Zarios who saved the day.

'Oh, come on, Pa…' Zarios gave a thin smile, and Emma was sure there was just a flash of contempt as he halted his father—could hear the slight drip of sarcasm in his expansive deep voice. 'Surely you remember how hard it is settling little ones to bed at a family function— and all those things you have to remember to bring?'

'Absolutely!' Lydia nodded furiously. 'We'll see the twins next weekend—oh, and Beth, of course…'

'Don't worry.' Zarios gave Emma a tight smile as the conversation drifted on. 'My father is a master of the "don't do as I do, do as I say" school of thought.'

'Meaning?'

'Nothing.' He took a slug of his whisky before concluding, 'It does not matter.'

Oh, but clearly it did!

He dismissed her frown with a shrug. 'It is strange

seeing my father in this setting—looking forward to seeing little children and catching up with friends. Usually the only time I socialise with my father is at work events…'

'And family—'

'No.' He cut her off, and she winced at her own insensitivity—her parents *were* Rocco's family. 'It is strange to see him amongst a family.'

She had always known that once his mother had left Zarios had been raised at a boarding school; her mother had told her how hard poor Rocco had had to work, jetting between the two countries to keep up with the fees, and how devastated poor Rocco had been when sometimes he couldn't get back to see Zarios.

Only then did it dawn on Emma—really dawn on her—that, as difficult as it might have been for *poor* Rocco, how much harder it must have been on his son.

CHAPTER TWO

STILL, Zarios didn't appear to be dwelling on it.

If he was here under sufferance he didn't show it—laughing at Eric's jokes, and making Lydia blush at every turn with his smouldering smile.

Suddenly the hour had arrived, and the small party moved into the marquee as the band started playing and the guest numbers began rapidly multiplying. Zarios was quickly cornered by Cindy, a good-looking blonde who was a good friend of her mother's. Emma knew she had to be nudging fifty, but years of botox and bulimia were serving her well tonight. Well, good luck, Emma thought, actually glad of the reprieve.

Zarios unsettled her.

Unsettled each fibre of her being.

Every flicker of his five-star reputation was merited. The question as to how any woman could dismiss such a heartbreak reputation had, for Emma, been well and truly answered—up close he was intoxicating.

Emma suppressed a smile as Cindy laughed a little too loudly at something he said, her hand resting on his arm as she spoke intently—she was welcome to him.

'Can I talk to you later, Emma?' Jake came over,

waving to a couple of geriatric aunts and smiling as if for cameras—just as he always did.

'Sure!'

'Away from everyone…' he added, and Emma's heart sank.

'Why?'

'Don't be like that.' Jake sighed.

'Are you going to pay me for the pastries?' If she sounded petty, it was with good reason. *If* Jake paid her maybe there would be nothing to worry about—maybe she *was* being surly for no reason.

She truly hoped that was the case.

'Look, I'm sorry about that.'

'Jake, it was the one thing Mum asked *you* to organise. What if I hadn't ordered them?'

'But you did!' Emma could have sworn there was a belligerent tone to his voice, but he quickly checked it. 'Here…' He pulled out his wallet and thrust her some notes. 'Thanks for organising them. I'll catch up with you later.'

'Can I ask what it's about?'

'Not here, okay?'

Not here, where everyone might find out that you're less than perfect, Emma thought savagely. But of course she didn't say it, just gave him a nod and bit hard on her lip, close to tears all of a sudden as Jake walked off.

'Jake.' Zarios raised his eyebrows in greeting as Jake brushed past, he'd seen the exchange and Jake must know it. The polite thing to do would be to ignore it, but Zarios couldn't be bothered with being polite. Shrugging off Cindy, he offered a friendly enquiry as Jake approached. 'Is everything okay?'

'All good!' Jake grinned, but his cheeks were red, his eyes following Zarios's gaze to his sister. 'Just family stuff. You know…'

'Not really,' Zarios answered.

'Just…' Both men stood watching as Emma slipped the money into her purse. 'Well, it's difficult for Emma. You help out when you can, you know?'

Yes, Zarios knew—and he knew now he should leave well alone. But his curiosity was well and truly piqued, and when a coo of delighted glee swept around the party as waiters and waitresses walked through with silver trays laden with finger food Zarios found himself making his way back to Emma.

'You're looking worried.'

Emma forced a rapid smile. 'I've no idea what my mother's cooked up for tonight.'

'Well, she's surpassed herself.'

Knowing how important keeping up appearances was for her mother, Emma was relieved to hear it. Glancing at the tray a waitress offered, she expected the usual variation on a theme. But a *real* smile formed on her full lips as she realised that for the first time, where the politics of entertaining were concerned, had listened to her own heart.

'Oh!' Emma blinked at the tray laden with tiny little sandwiches. The bread as thin and as light as butterfly wings, yet it was crammed with the strangest of filling choices for such an important function.

Jam.

Vegemite.

Salami.

Prosciutto.

All beautifully presented, of course, but as she bit into them the familiar flavours brought a gurgle of laughter to Emma's lips. She got the joke.

'Your father and mine used to swap their school lunches.' Zarios grinned, too. 'I can remember my father telling me the first time he tasted your father's sandwiches. He thought they were the most disgusting thing he had ever tasted—and your father thought the same of his. Within two weeks they were trading lunches.'

'My dad insists he was the first Australian to really appreciate a sundried tomato—he was eating them daily long before they were popular.'

'He was,' Zarios agreed. 'He was also a friend to my father when no one else was. He's a good man.'

'He is.' Emma smiled. 'Which is why you'll have to excuse me. I ought to socialise…'

'You are.'

'I mean…' Emma was flustered '…with aunts and things…'

'I'm sure your father would rather you looked after a guest who doesn't know anyone…'

How dangerous was that smile, just curving on the edge of his full mouth?

'It's not fair to leave me on my own.'

'I'm sure Cindy would be delighted to keep you company!' *Ouch!* Emma could have kicked herself for letting him know that she'd noticed.

'Cindy only wants me for my body!' He leaned forward, his voice dropping an octave. Cool and confident Emma was not. Her face burned at the near contact, her toes curling in her sandals at the feel of his breath on her ear. 'And I will not let myself be used!'

'As if.' Emma laughed, jerking her head back, but the laugh came out too shrill. The effect of him so close was devastating.

'Anyway, I am under strict instructions to behave tonight…' Again he lowered his head—just as he had a moment ago, just as he had six years ago—and again her body demanded a kiss. 'I think Cindy has an issue with her age…' His Italian accent was thick, his words curious rather than mocking. 'Which puts me off.'

'Her age?' Emma checked, struggling to sound normal as he pulled her ever closer into his personal space.

'No, the fact that she has issues…' Zarios smiled. 'I am too much of a bastard to remember to be reassuring.'

God, he was gorgeous. Wicked and bad, but funny, too! Pulling her head back, holding out her glass for a waiter to top it up, Emma was sorely tempted to ask for the ice bucket to douse herself in.

He was thoroughly good company, and if his conversation was laced with innuendo, not once was he sleazy. And, Emma noticed with a shiver of nervous excitement, despite his arrogance it was with great skill and surprising kindness that he deflected the numerous attempts from women to garner his attention.

For tonight at least his sole focus was on her.

Her mother *had* excelled herself—and for Emma it really was a wonderful party. The mixture and the number of guests was perfect, the food delicious and the drinks plenty. Zarios continued to be good company, and had it not been for Jake, following her into the house and colliding with her as she came out of the toilet, it would have been perfect.

It wasn't good news—but then it never was with

Jake. As he led her to the study to *talk*, and as Emma listened to all he had to say, the sense of foreboding that had been her companion for a long time where Jake was concerned gave way to sheer incredulity at what he was asking of her. There was no way she could help him.

'Jake, I don't have that sort of money…'

'You could get it, though!'

'How?' Emma's eyes widened. 'You're talking about a six-figure sum.'

'Your flat's worth way more than you paid for it, Emma.'

'Why would I pay off your debts…again?' she couldn't help but add. She'd helped him out in the past and had never been paid back. She had chosen not to pursue it, but this was a ridiculous amount Jake was now asking for. 'Why would I take out yet another loan to help you?'

'Because if I don't get this sorted Beth will leave. Listen, Emma…' He dragged a hand through his hair. 'She hasn't worked in years, she moans about money all the time, and yet she does nothing to help out…'

'She's got two-year-old twins!' Emma pointed out angrily. 'Surely that's work enough?'

'Emma.' He dropped his voice so low she had to strain to catch it. 'Don't tell Mum and Dad—I don't want to worry them—but we're having problems with the twins…' As Emma bit on her lip, he continued. 'Behavioural problems. That's one of the reasons we didn't bring them tonight. Beth has no control—she can't even manage to get them dressed before lunch. You don't know what it's like, living with her. She doesn't lift a plate, she's at home all day and I'm still having to pay for a cleaner… Emma, if you don't help me and I lose the house, you can guarantee I'll lose the twins, too. Can you imagine Mum and Dad…?'

'You have to tell them, Jake,' Emma pleaded. 'You say it isn't gambling this time?'

'It isn't!' Jake promised. 'Just a lousy call on the stockmarket. Emma, it would kill Mum and Dad. They're so…'

'Proud?' Emma spat, because at this very moment she hated him—and hated, too, how easily her parents were fooled by him. Jake the golden boy. Jake the one with the *real* job. Jake who had given them the twins. Poor, responsible Jake, with his moody, depressed wife.

If only they knew.

'I'm due for a massive bonus at the end of June. If I don't tell Beth about it, I can pay you back then.'

'Lie to her again, you mean?'

'Help me, Emma.'

'I'll think about it.'

'Emma, please.'

'I'll think about it!' she said again, and it was the best she could offer.

Upset, worried, she marched out of the study, trying to get her head together before she faced the party that was still going on.

'Hey!' Zarios stepped back as she practically collided with him.

'Sorry…' Emma gave a quick shake of her head. 'I wasn't looking where I was going.'

'I'm trying to find where they put our cases. My father needs one of his tablets.'

'Of course.'

Flustered, Emma led him to the guestroom, her mind reeling too much from Jake's confession for her to be embarrassed at being alone upstairs with Zarios.

'They're not here.' She scanned the bedroom. 'They must be in my room…where you're sleeping,' Emma added as he followed behind.

'How very open-minded of your parents!'

'Daughter not included!' Emma gave a tight, distracted smile as she flung her bedroom door open. 'There they are. I'd better go down—the cake should be coming out soon.'

'Are you okay?'

No, she wanted to scream, but knew she couldn't. She just gave him a worried, confused nod.

'I'm fine.'

'If you want to talk…'

'Why would I talk to *you*?' Emma challenged. 'I hardly know you!'

'That can be sorted.' He gestured to the bedroom, but on turning back to her immediately Zarios shook his head at her stunned expression. 'I meant we could talk in private here…'

Only a fool would walk into a bedroom with Zarios and expect conversation! But for a second she was tempted.

Tempted to push his arrogant, testosterone-loaded body into the dark space. Tempted to be daring and wicked and reckless and…her rabid mind flailed as it tried to come up with the word—*bad*.

To for once be irresponsible—and, yes, very, *very* bad.

Only it wasn't Emma.

'As I said.' Ever the dutiful daughter, she gave him a brittle smile, then turned on her new and starting to rub high heels. 'They'll be bringing out the cake soon.'

* * *

She wished they *would* bring out the cake.

There was the most appalling lull—but only Emma seemed to notice.

The dance floor was still heaving with couples, the tables filled with chatting and laughing groups, but despite her best efforts to join in with a couple of conversations it was hard going.

Dutiful Jake was chatting up the old aunties and making them laugh, and Cindy's eyes had shot knives when Emma had attempted to join a group of women. All in all she'd left it too late to suddenly join in with the others. Everyone was settled in to their little cliques, making her feel like a wallflower. Then Zarios returned.

'Looks like you're stuck with me.'

He took her by the wrist, then led her to the dance floor without asking.

Which was a wise move on his part. Because had he asked, she would have declined—not because she didn't want to dance, but because of how much she did.

He held her loosely at first, swaying to the heavy beat as she willed her heart and breathing to slow down. The second they did, he pulled her closer.

Was it his looks or his status that made him so appealing? Emma begged to know as his arms snaked around her back. And was it just his reputation that held her back? All she knew was that it was a dizzying combination—want and trepidation, curiosity and nervousness, all there fizzing in each cell of the body he was holding.

'I don't like cake...' Zarios smiled down at her '...which gives us more time for dancing.'

'Oh, but my mother thinks of everything,' Emma quipped. 'I'm sure there'll be a fruit platter.'

'Forbidden fruit, perhaps?'

'I'm far from forbidden.' Emma gave a wry smile as her mother danced past them and practically fractured her father's rib as, none too subtly, she pointed out the lovely couple dancing, clearly delighted at to how well they were getting on. 'My mother lives for the day we might get together.'

'While my father shudders at the thought.'

All the ingrained insecurities of her childhood, all her mother's deepest fears seemed to seep into her pores. But as his hands spread around her waist and he pulled her just a fraction closer, Emma realised she'd misinterpreted him.

'He has told me many times that, though he would love nothing more than for us to be together… Well, he knows my reputation. He says he would not be able to look at your father if I were to hurt you.'

Her blue eyes jerked to his, her mind screaming for her to be quiet. But the words were out before she could stop them.

'Then don't.' It was the most blatant flirt—the most blatant acknowledgement of their attraction— but she recovered quickly. 'Anyway—given you're seeing Miranda…'

'We broke up.'

'I'm sorry.'

'I'm not.' He didn't miss a beat, either in dancing or flirting, his repertoire as sleek and practised as the body that moved with hers. 'Maybe we could have coffee or dinner when you are back in the city—somewhere away from our families' eyes…'

'Perhaps…' Emma nodded, trying to shrug, trying to pretend it didn't matter.

Oh, but it did.

'Is that a yes?'

'Yes…'

'I will ring.'

'Sure.' Somehow she managed a casual smile, but her heart was soaring as he pulled her in closer.

'I like your scent.'

'It's just…' She shrugged, tried to be casual, but for the life of her she couldn't remember the perfume's name. 'I got it for my birthday.'

'I meant *your* scent,' he corrected her, which made her cheeks burn.

She'd never been held like this. He was barely touching her, and they were barely moving, yet it was positively indecent the sensations he evoked. Her internal barometer had shattered, common sense scattering like tiny balls of mercury, irrecoverable as he pulled her right into the circle of his arms. His breath was hot on her ear and suddenly she wanted him to lick it—he didn't. Lowering his head just a bit further, till she could feel his mouth just inches from her neck, she fought the urge to repeat her mistake of yesteryear. She wanted to turn her face to his like a flower to the sun, to receive the sweet reward of his mouth on hers.

It was a relief when the music ended—a relief to stand apart from him in the darkness as the room broke into song.

Eric smiled broadly as a vast cake was wheeled in, blazing with sixty candles. Still Zarios held Emma's wrist, his hot fingers wrapped tightly around her flesh as she sang along. Then the candles were blown out and the tent was plunged into full darkness. Tonight she finally received what she'd longed for all those years ago and for way too many moments in between. Finally Emma was rewarded with the prize of his mouth on hers.

Even a vivid imagination couldn't adequately prepare her for the thoroughness of his kiss, the shocking feel of his tongue sliding into hers, the way his body enveloped hers. He tasted like manna, his scent potently male. It was a thrilling, decadent kiss that she *absorbed*—a kiss during which he pressed himself so hard into her she could feel the dangerous thick length of him. It was a kiss so consuming that it triggered a dangerous chain reaction—one that made her forget to breathe, forget to think, forget even herself.

If the entire embrace lasted only ten or maybe fifteen seconds it was just as well. Because any more and she'd have come there and then. His timing was impeccable, though, and by the time the last cheer had faded, before the cameras had stopped flashing, his mouth had released hers. She had to peel herself off him and stand in lights that were suddenly blazing. No one had seen them, all eyes were still on her father, yet she felt as if the spotlight was suddenly on *her*—that surely everyone knew what had just taken place. She felt as embarrassed, almost, as if they'd been caught making love—hell, she felt as if they *had* been making love. Her panties were damp with arousal, her nipples erect and throbbing beneath her soft dress; so exposed was her want, surely everyone could see it?

What did this man do to her?

She could see Rocco's eyes narrowing in disapproval, and her mother's questioning frown as she saw the glow in her daughter's cheeks.

Zarios *was* dangerous.

Bad and dangerous—yet irresistible.

It was nearly 2:00 a.m. by the time they all got to bed, and Emma was exhausted.

Peeling off her dress, only in reverence to its price tag did she bother to hang it over a chair in the study. And apart from a lethargic brush of her teeth, the rest of her nighttime routine went to pot. Climbing into the trundle bed in the study, Emma listened to the familiar sounds of the family home—her father coughing, the stairs creaking as her parents went to bed, the bark of a possum in a tree outside. It should have been soothing and familiar, and she was so tired she should have been asleep in a matter of seconds, but she was too aware that Zarios was *in situ*—that tonight he lay in her bed.

How she wished she were there!

Every creak of the floorboards, every turn of a tap, had her staring into the darkness at the door, terrified that he'd come in.

And she was shamefully, bitterly disappointed when he didn't.

CHAPTER THREE

EMMA didn't know what to do.

The sun wasn't up yet, and the silence of dawn was attempting to soothe her as Emma strode along the beach, her head racing at a thousand miles an hour after an angst-riddled sleepless night.

Damn Zarios for being so irresistible.

And damn her for being so willing.

Anyone might have seen him kissing her and pressing himself into her last night. If the lights had come on even a second earlier... Emma simultaneously cringed and soared at the memory, viewing it as if through parted fingers, wanting to see it, yet horribly embarrassed all the same.

He was a playboy, Emma told herself, walking quickly now. A bored playboy, stuck at a party he probably hadn't wanted to attend. A restless, oversexed male who'd been looking for diversion, for amusement—and she'd provided it.

Well, no more.

He'd be gone after breakfast and that would be the last she'd see of him.

Unless he called her!

Still, it wasn't just Zarios and his potent sex appeal that had her head spinning as she strode angrily through the still dawn. Damn Jake, too, for ruining her father's birthday for her.

If only her parents knew.

If only they knew the thin ice he perpetually skated on. Oh, their parents had helped Jake out a couple of times—when the stockmarket had supposedly taken a tumble, and when the twins were first born and Beth had been hospitalised with depression—but unbeknown to them she, too, had helped. Emma swallowed down the flutter of unease at the thought of the credit card account she had opened to bail him out, the personal loan she had taken… Each time Jake had promised he'd pay her back; each time he had sworn it would be the last…

…and each time he had lied.

Emma stared out at the grey morning, willing the sun to come up and shed some light on what she should do.

She didn't have the sort of money Jake needed.

Possibly she could get an extension on her mortgage. She'd always been so careful. She had lived frugally throughout her student years, even managing to set some money aside from casual jobs, and her father had found her a modest flat near where she rented the gallery—a flat that had increased in value. But her paintings weren't doing so well. She was still too new, too little known. Because of helping Jake she'd had to cut back on advertising, had had to forgo the promotional nights at her gallery that might draw in the customers.

Emma gulped. Why *should* she help him? If she gave him this money Emma knew that she'd never see it again—which should make saying no incredibly simple.

Only… She could almost feel the sting of her mother slapping her cheek all those years ago when, after another of Jake's so-called cries for help, Emma had voiced the same question. Why couldn't he *cope*?

'He's ill, Emma!'

Closing her eyes, she could see her mother's lips—pale, furious lips that had been spitting at the edges as she spoke. The slap had been less shocking than the fury that had accompanied it—her mother had been appalled at the question her seventeen-year-old daughter had raised.

'You should try and be more understanding!'

That had been their sole conversation regarding Jake's illness—no discussion, no acknowledgement. The memories of those black days had been filed and tucked away, by unspoken rule never to be opened.

But, try as her mother might, the lid was peeping open.

And, try as Emma might, this time she might not be able to stop it.

To swim alone on a deserted beach that was still draped in darkness broke every safety rule that had been in-grained into Emma from the moment she could walk and had toddled on little fat legs to the water she adored. Only Emma truly wasn't thinking—her mind was solely consumed with her brother and his prob-lems. As Emma stripped down to her bra and panties all she sought in that moment was a clear head—a break from her frantic thoughts.

The water was delicious—refreshingly cold as she plunged in. There was nothing better than swimming in the ocean—the weightlessness, the pull of the waves, the invigorating feel of salt water on her skin and the bliss of escape. Here, Emma knew, she was just a speck in the scheme of things, and the vastness of the ocean soothed her mind, her panic abating as her body tired.

She had swum a long way out.

The first fingers of fear tightened around her heart as Emma stared back at the grey beach, her legs moving as she attempted to tread water, and at that moment terror seized her. She could see rocks moving alongside her even though she was trying to stay still, and felt the very real force of a seemingly benign ocean as it rapidly pulled away her from the shore.

She was caught in a rip. A fast-moving channel of current that ran perpendicular to the beach. She knew not to fight it—knew she could never swim against it—but the foolhardiness of her actions caught up with her. The vastness of the ocean that had moments ago soothed her scared her now.

He didn't want to go back.

Even though he had spent only twelve hours away from the city, Zarios actually felt as if he had had a break. Walking along the beach, the sun just starting to appear on the horizon—it was bliss to have the place to himself.

Last night had been nice, watching his father and Eric talking, and for once he had been able to relax and enjoy a pleasant evening without worrying about Miranda, about work, or the board's decision.

He was almost tempted to accept Lydia's offer to stay the entire weekend—to cancel his other engagements and to just get off the treadmill for a little while.

Except he couldn't.

It seemed everyone wanted a piece of him these days—everyone demanded their pound of flesh. It wouldn't even enter their heads that he really *needed* a weekend off—naturally they'd assume the worst.

That Zarios D'Amilo was boiling towards yet another scandal.

Oh, his father was upset—furious, in fact, that things hadn't worked out with Miranda, that another teary story would no doubt hit the magazines in a week or so, at a time when the D'Amilo name could least afford it. Zarios knew he had *tried* to make it work with her, but her behaviour had been becoming more and more bizarre. With each passing week she became more possessive, more demanding, till nothing bar a proposal of marriage would convince Miranda that he wasn't cheating on her. And though it might have soothed Miranda and might have appeased his father and their fellow directors, Zarios had refused to be pushed.

Once again, he hated how he had been judged.

Despite the scathing words that were written about him, despite his heartbreak reputation, he actually *loved* women—loved the rush that came at the beginning of a romance, that moment when he actually believed she might be the one who was different. Zarios went into every breathtaking relationship wishing over and over that this time he'd found her—that this time he'd met the one.

Picking up a stone, Zarios skimmed it out to the water.

The one!

'*Hah!*' He shouted out the word as he skimmed another stone.

There was no such thing as *the one*! He picked up a

handful, skimming them angrily now. Take Emma, for example. Had his father not warned him about her problem with money? Had he not seen it with his own eyes and heard it directly from Jake?

Well, she might have had him convinced for a while, but not for long, Zarios thought savagely. Never for long. Over and over he was proved right: women wanted only one thing—well, two if he was being accurate. And the second he was happy to provide for free!

He refused to be as blind as his father—a man who still loved the woman who had shamed him, who had walked out on her husband and child without a backward glance.

A woman who wanted to creep her way back now that his father was ill and about to retire… Well, she'd have to get past Zarios first. From his shorts he pulled out a letter, read again the needy words he had intercepted, then wrapped it in a stone and tossed it out to the ocean.

She was too late!

Thirty years too late. And if his father couldn't see that, then he was a fool.

For a moment he thought he was seeing things. Squinting out into the grey pre-dawn ocean, he saw a flash of something white. His heart stilled in his mouth as he saw it was a hand, and realised with dread that someone out there was in trouble.

His first instinct was to dive in, but Zarios fought it. The person was a long way out, and a clear head was what was needed here. Behind him was the lifeguard's shed, but he found it was locked. Soon he knew the first surfers would be coming, but for now it was down to him alone.

He was running before his plan had actually formu-

lated in his mind. Already he was acting on it, running
the length of the beach, scanning the slippery low rocks
ahead, while whipping his head around every few seconds to the water, making sure he didn't lose sight of
the swimmer.

The panic that had gripped him when he had realised
it was a person out there in trouble had abated now.
Zarios was running on pure adrenaline, focussing just
as he did at work, only on the task in hand and not upon
the stakes. It was a formula that had served him well.

Don't slip.

He told himself that as he reached the rocks. Just get
to the mid-section.

She was still treading water.

She.

He pushed that thought aside as he navigated the
sludge and seaweed, dragging in two large lungfuls of air
as he calculated the distance and realised he was as close
on land as he could get. Aware of the rocks, he lowered
himself rather than dived in, kicking off with a powerful
front crawl, looking up every now and then, keeping his
eye on his target, feeling the power of the water beneath
the relatively calm surface as he neared her.

Just like that she was gone.

A glimmer of fear crept in then—a first glimpse that
he was too late. A frantic, urgent second of negotiation
cluttered his mind. If he'd just run faster, swum
quicker…if he dived under now… And then she resur-
faced, blue eyes frantic, mouth open, arms flailing. For
the first time in his life Zarios tasted pure, unadulterated
fear. It seized him as if someone had touched his insides:
this fury, this panic at what had nearly been lost.

What still could be lost.

He grabbed her, pulled her into the crook of his arm and lay on his back. Then with every ounce of strength he could muster he kicked and propelled his body back towards the rocks, swimming across the rip. Someone must have been really looking out for her, because just when his body was tiring a surfer, who must have seen the action from the beach, was there, helping her onto his board. The two men worked in silent unison to bring her to the shore, where she knelt in the shallows, coughing and retching and just so very, *very* lucky.

'*Stupido!*' He was beyond furious. Between dragging in lungfuls of air and coughing out half the ocean, still he managed to loudly point out first in rapid Italian and then in English what a fool she had been. Whatever language he spoke, the message was blatantly clear. '*Voi idiota stupido!* Swimming alone…'

Emma was kneeling in damp sand, coughing, shivering, too terrified to be grateful—too shaken to yet relish being alive. Instead of filling her hungry lungs she could only manage tiny shallow breaths. The panic that had gripped her in the ocean was nothing compared to her realisation of the fragility of existence. Of the thoughtless action that had nearly cost her life.

'Okay, mate…' Surfer boy must have seen it all before, because, though breathless himself, he was incredibly calm. 'She knows she made a mistake. You did the right thing, letting the rip carry you,' the boy reassured her as Zarios stood there silently fuming. 'You can't swim against it.'

Her breathing was slowing down now, delicious

oxygen creeping into every exhausted cell. Each and every breath was like a refreshing glass of lemonade, and she relished each one.

A little posse had formed—mainly lean, bronzed surfer-types, and an elderly woman who was walking her dog, all standing around her as she shivered in her bra and panties and in her own misery. A blanket was produced from the surf shed, and Emma was grateful for its heavy, musty warmth as it was wrapped around her shoulders.

'Did you take in a lot of water?' the surfer asked.

'No! I was just tiring. I'm fine now…'

'Maybe we should get you looked at?'

Emma shook her head. 'I just want to go home.'

She remembered to thank him, although Zarios actually remembered first, shaking his hand and then wrapping an arm around Emma's shoulders before leading her up the stony path to her parents' house. He even smiled and thanked the elderly lady when she rushed up, having retrieved Emma's clothes.

'Don't tell Mum…' Her teeth were chattering so violently she could hardly get the words out. 'I don't want to ruin the weekend.'

'You nearly took care of that…' He stopped himself from ramming home the inevitable point. 'Let's just hope they're not up yet…' His voice faded again.

Despite the early hour the marquee was already being taken down. Lydia was trilling her orders, anxious to get the place in shape before the champagne breakfast.

'What about in here…?' He pushed open the doors of the summerhouse, a pretty white room where her mother read and her father escaped. Leading her to a daybed, he sat her down, then set about locating a towel, taking the musty blanket from her shoulders and wrapping her in its soft warmth. 'We'll get you dry, and then you can get dressed and back to the house…she won't know.'

'You won't tell her?'

'On one condition.' He gripped her upper arms, his face stern and serious. 'You have to promise me that you will never do anything like that again.'

'I won't.'

'*Christo*, Emma…' His eyes burnt into hers, anger creeping back in. 'What possessed you?' He was drenched, his black hair almost blue, droplets of water still on his wide shoulders.

'I don't know…' She couldn't give a sensible reason. She'd grown up by the beach—knew the rules. Knew, knew, *knew*… 'I just wanted to clear my head. I'm just worried…'

'About what?'

She wanted to tell him so badly. In fact, she almost did, but even as she opened her mouth, she shook her head. Jake's gambling and the filthy, complicated mess he had created were just too big and scary to face, let alone share.

'I can't say.'

'You could.'

'I can't.'

'Okay, don't worry about it now…' His hands were stroking her through the towel, moving to her back, drying her off, then moving down to her legs. The floor was littered with sand. 'Let's get you dressed and inside.'

And then it *really* seemed to hit him. Zarios paused mid-stroke, bemused eyes looking up to hers.

'You could have died!'

Oh, there was no better warmth than his arms. Fiercely, he had pulled her from the daybed into his embrace, and kneeling he held her, held her, *held her*, as if checking that she was still there. And, Emma thought, being held was so much better than being told off—just feeling his heartbeat in her ear, his warmth imbuing her. For a full five minutes he held her, and whether it was adrenaline that propelled them, or just the sheer exhilaration of finding out just how sweet and precious life was, it felt entirely right that he kissed her.

It was the most thorough, expert and welcome kiss of her life. His mouth claimed hers, pressing hard into her shivering one, warming her as his body scooped her in. Kneeling, facing her, he devoured her with his mouth, kissing her harder and harder as though he still had to prove that she was really there, pausing for a second and then possessing her mouth again.

Just absolutely the best a kiss could be. Like a balm to her wounds. The horror that had consumed her simply faded. The soft stroke of his tongue, his taut body against hers, obliterated everything.

No kiss had ever moved her like this. She had thought last night's effort wonderful, but it had only skimmed the surface of what his mouth could do. His touch seemed to flick a trigger, unleashing in her such *want*. He was pushing down the straps of her bra, his mouth still pressing on hers, his rough and unshaven and utterly delicious jaw rasping her cheek. His skilled fingers impatiently unhooked her bra and tossed it aside. Her frozen and exhausted body was warming and waking beneath hands that massaged her full breasts as still he kissed her.

'I thought I'd lost you when you went under…'

He was talking as if he loved her, and her head was spinning with his words. He spoke as if they were, as if they had once been lovers. The world was spinning in a strange fast-forward, in recognition of some future time. Everything aligned as she knew, without it being said, that they were going to make love. The passion, the emotion that ripped through them, was inexplicable, almost, but utterly, utterly right. Kneeling still, they pressed so hard into each other it hurt—a hurt that reminded her she was alive!

As he kissed her cheeks, her ears, her eyelashes, and gently tugged at her panties, Emma remembered that she had nearly died. And nearly dying was a very, very good reason to start living, she told herself, as both of them stood just long enough to dispose of their few pieces of clothing.

And *this* was living!

She'd expected the frenzy to continue, but Zarios slowed things down. As they sank to their knees he rested on his heels, devouring every inch of her with hungry eyes, one single finger tracing the length of her body. She quivered under his scrutiny. Pathetically grateful she'd taken her panties off when she'd had a spray tan, Emma was agog with terror as she watched him harden to his full, impressive length. Her stomach curled inside as his fingers moved down and slowly stroked her damp blonde curls.

'All night I thought of you.' His knees parted hers, the dark hair on his legs scratching against her thighs, pushing them apart until he exposed her. He began to stroke her slowly.

Unable to stop herself, Emma admitted the same. 'I thought of you, too.'

She was having trouble breathing for entirely different reasons now.

'I thought of this.' He slid a finger inside her, the nub of his thumb working her clitoris. 'And then I thought of this...' He lowered his head and suckled on her nipple, the rhythmic sucking matching his handiwork.

Her head arched back as he worked her, and in a moment of weakness again she admitted the same. 'I thought of this, too.'

He was huge—worryingly so, excitingly so. Her head was back down, watching as her fingers instinctively reached for him as if they belonged to someone else. She began to stroke him in the same slow motion with which he was stroking her. She could see his mouth still suckling her breast, but she gazed down beyond it, one greedy finger taking the silver pearl of moisture from his tip and massaging it into the soft velvety skin that belied the strength beneath.

'Attente!' His voice was thick, the words spoken between greedy mouthfuls. 'Be careful.'

And then he looked up, warning her, offering her an out. But her voice, when it came, was absolutely sure. 'I don't *want* to be careful!'

It was all the confirmation he needed to go on, and, oh, the bliss as he guided her onto the daybed. She braced herself for his weight, but it never came, his fingers instead working their magic, sliding deep inside her as his erection hovered at her entrance. She was a frenzy of sensation, a bleating mess of indecision, wanting him to go on, but wanting him to come in. She could hear the sounds of her own moisture as he massaged her deeply, as he made sure beyond doubt that her tight space was oiled and ready to accommodate him. And thank heavens he did, because even with his lavish attention, even with a body that was cooing and aching to be filled, she felt a sudden pain when he entered, a delicious hurt as he filled her. The heat was building as he pushed so hard inside her, so deep within her, she could feel the bruise of her cervix.

She was coming, biting his salty chest, wrapping her calves around his muscular back. Still he bucked inside her, the throb of her orgasm gripping him, but it didn't match his strength because he pushed her on.

'Zarios…' She wanted him to stop, was almost scared that he might continue. Her twitching body was surely spent, but still she could feel him swell further, feel the more urgent, reckless staccato rhythm of his thrust, and she was coming again, her orgasm more intense than she could have ever dared to imagine it might be. Her hands were two balled fists of tension on his back. Unfurling her fingers was an impossible task as every muscle in her body twitched in spasm as she received him, felt a shudder of tension rip through him, and then the warm melt of him on her.

And then he kissed her.

His tongue was strangely cold as his lazy kiss brought her round, welcoming her back to a world that was brighter, and somehow very different.

'If I swim out again will you rescue me?'

'That is not funny.'

'Well, *that* wasn't a very good deterrent.'

'I might not be here next time to save you…'

As he looked down at her Emma realised that his eyes, though they looked black, were actually the darkest deepest indigo, more purple than blue, and a colour she wanted to capture and recreate with her brush. Only, even with her artistic prowess, she wasn't sure she could do the colour justice.

'Although I would like to be there.'

And she knew he wasn't talking about swimming—knew, because at that moment they were so close words were hardly needed. A new language was forming, and their minds were meeting with the same force their bodies had and blending just as perfectly.

'I'd like you to be there.'

'Let's get you back to the house.' He held her tighter as he spoke. 'This weekend cannot be about us. I want your father to enjoy his celebration.' He kissed her very slowly. 'Emma, this is big.'

A rather facetious comment was on the tip of her tongue, given the length of him on her thigh, but Emma restrained herself. Her mind was simply being kind, using humour to deflect the seriousness of his words for a moment. What they had just found was monumental.

'I know.'

There was nothing to joke about.

'We need to be very sure, and we need to get our heads around things ourselves before we share this with our families.'

Oh, he was right. If there was even a hint of romance today, the whole dynamics of the weekend would shift.

They had to get used to things first, before they revealed their feelings to the world.

There wasn't a flicker of question or doubt in her eyes as she stared back at him.

For that moment at least, she absolutely trusted him.

'There you are!' Lydia smiled when, a considerable time later, a rather bedraggled Emma appeared. 'We were about to send out a search party.'

'I was enjoying a walk.'

'And the water!' Lydia frowned at the knot of wet hair trailing down her back.

Given that it was now after eight Emma could be a touch honest. 'I had a swim—I couldn't resist.' Emma flushed, her heart thumping as, not for the first time, she realised just how disastrous the consequences might have been had Zarios not saved her. Thankfully Lydia was too wrapped up in preparing for the champagne breakfast to question her further. 'Do you need me to do anything, Mum?'

'Get changed, darling!' Lydia scolded, pulling out of the fridge the vast bowl of Strawberries Romanof that Emma had yesterday painstakingly prepared for the occasion without comment, then twittering with delight as she pulled back the cloth on the basket of rolls and pastries that had thankfully been delivered.

'He's gone way over the top, as always…' Lydia tutted at the contents. 'But then, that's Jake!'

The shower was bliss—warm water washing away the salt, her body burning still from Zarios's attention. Massaging conditioner into her hair, Emma closed her eyes and revelled in the sheer wonder of being alive, every nerve in her body tingling as she recalled his hands and mouth on her. Her heart was fluttering with excitement, and she cradled her knowledge like a treasured gift—scarcely able to comprehend that in just a few short hours everything had changed.

She dressed in pale khaki shorts and a white cotton halter neck, quickly blowdrying her hair and then tying it back in a loose ponytail, before adding just a little make-up. She joined her family and the D'Amilos out on the decking. Today was more intimate—just immediate family, which Rocco practically was, and of course Zarios.

He smiled as she entered, just a brief smile, but it confirmed every last thing she was feeling.

There was an exhilaration about her that perhaps had something to do with surviving a near death experience, or perhaps just the sheer pleasure of being with her family, all combined with the giddy recall of Zarios's lovemaking. For Emma it truly was the sweetest time, every second relished as she sipped on Bucks Fizz and listened to her father's laughter, saw her mother's face flushed and pretty with the relief that the her beloved Eric's birthday had gone so well. He was opening his gifts, smiling at the slippers, the tankards, at an expensive pair of binoculars for his beloved bird-watching, and then frowning at Rocco's gift.

'A phrasebook?'

'For when you come to visit me at my home in Rome.' Rocco waved away Eric's protests as he opened a travel itinerary along with two first class tickets. 'When Bella left—when I was on my own—every week you rang me, every week there was a letter, and every time I came back to Australia to check on my business here not once did I sleep in a hotel. You, my friends, were always there. Now it is time for you to eat at my table—for you, Eric, to take your wife to what is surely the most beautiful city in the world,' Rocco finished, wiping tears from his eyes as he told the couple the true value of their friendship.

Well, nothing was going to top that!

'Here, Dad.' Emma found she was biting on her lips as she handed her father her gift. An oil painting, it was of the beach scene from their house at late afternoon. Normally in her paintings Emma always left faces blank, so the people who bought her pieces were able to place themselves in the image—it was the signature mark of her work. Except in this one, amongst the families and children playing on the beach, unmistakably there were her parents, smiling and relaxed as they walked hand in hand along the beach they had loved for so long.

It had taken her days to paint.

But it had been weeks of thought that had drained her.

'It's lovely, darling.' Eric gave her a suitable smile as he studied her work for, oh, around ten seconds, before kissing her cheek.

'You and Mum are there…' Emma pointed to the figures in the scene.

He pulled on his glasses and peered more closely. 'So we are!' Eric beamed, then took his glasses off and kissed her on the cheek again. 'Thank you, darling.'

He put the painting down on the floor beside the mountain of other presents, then peeled open the gift Jake and Beth had bought, crowing in delight at a bottle of champagne Emma could have sworn she'd given them as a gift when the twins were born, and holding up the two department store champagne glasses that accompanied the bottle as if they were made of the finest crystal.

'That's for you two to share,' Jake said, and smiled, 'when the party's over. Happy birthday, Dad!'

Emma found she was biting hard into her lip as her mother oohed and ahed, kissing Jake and telling him he was so thoughtful. Her fingers were clenched, and in an effort not to say anything, not to spoil things, Emma actually sat on her hands, telling herself she was being unreasonable. Her father *had* been delighted with her present. She was just being sensitive, that was all, because Rocco was nodding at the lovely champagne and Zarios was busy with his mobile phone. She was surely just being childish. But was she the only one who could see the glaring disparity between how she and Jake were treated? Blinking back sudden pathetic tears, Emma was glad of the diversion of her own phone bleeping. Picking it up from the table, she frowned slightly when she saw that she had a message from Zarios.

Don't sulk!

She suppressed a smile as she texted back.

Do you blame me?

As she hit 'send', the sound of his phone bleeping at the opposite end of the table sent a fizz of excitement through her—especially when she saw that he was texting again.

I liked it.

She was about to text back her thanks, but she had another incoming message.

I want you.

Two spots of colour burnt on her cheeks as her phone bleeped again, and Zarios told her exactly how *much* he wanted her. She was blushing like an eighteen-year-old—*felt* like an eighteen-year-old as her mother's frown scolded her for spending so long on her phone.

'Could you get some more orange juice, Emma?'

'Of course.'

She fled to the kitchen, embarrassed yet exhilarated, as jumpy as a cat. She trembled as she pulled open the door of the fridge. It wasn't just that he was sexy—though he was, Emma thought, gulping icy air from the fridge—it was that smile, that lazy smile that just made the world pause, and the intensity of his eyes when they held hers.

And instinctively he had known how much her father's dismissal of her work, however unwitting, had hurt her.

Never had a man read her more skilfully.

It was as if he'd versed himself in her thoughts—like an extension to her mind.

He *got* it!

Got the crazy make-up of her family and the fact that

they could make her smile, make her laugh, even as they drove her round the bend.

'Need a hand?'

He didn't wait for an answer. His hot palm was between her legs, running lazily the length of her thigh, and she rested her head on the freezer door to steady herself, simultaneously revelling in his touch and tensing at the thought of anyone walking in.

'Zarios...' She turned to face him, to warn him off with a brittle expression, to tell him this was neither the time nor the place—but he'd beaten her to it. He was smiling down at her, pulling out cartons from the fridge and feigning such utter innocence that if her thighs hadn't been on fire she'd have sworn she'd imagined the whole thing.

Zarios had been confused by her parents' reaction to the painting—had been confused by the gift as well. From the way Lydia had spoken, and from the information he had gleaned over the years, he had assumed Emma's hobby had simply been indulged by Lydia and Eric.

But with one glance he'd seen her talent.

A real talent that should be nurtured and applauded, not tossed amongst a pile.

He was lying, and they both knew it, when he tried to say the right thing. 'I know how it looked out there,' Zarios said as he picked up some jugs from the bench, 'but they *are* proud of you!'

'I think you're talking to the wrong sibling.' She snipped open the juice and poured it into the jugs. 'They're proud of the one with the *real* job and the fancy car—the one who gives them grandchildren...'

'You're incredibly talented.'

'That doesn't always sell paintings!' She hadn't meant to say anything, but the financial pressure Jake had heaped on her fledgling business was just too much to bear, and unwittingly, just as her mother did when stressed, Emma put down the carton and massaged her temples for a moment.

'Business not going too well?'

'Just a few money worries at the moment; it will pick up,' she said, doing just that to the juice. But his hands caught hers, making them let go of their contents.

'Tomorrow?' Zarios said, stunned by the comfort saying that single word gave him.

'Tomorrow,' she agreed, taking a deep breath, and then another rapid one, as he deeply kissed the nape of her neck. He kissed it so hard that when she fled to the loo moments later she could see the bruise he had left, which had her pulling out her ponytail and arranging her hair to hide it. She had been angry with him at the time, and yet was surprisingly grateful later.

Grateful, because when everyone had gone, when the chopper had long since lifted into the sky, and her parents had read through the cards for the hundredth time and all that was left was the tidying up, it was almost impossible to fathom what had taken place.

She checked her phone for the hundredth time, willing a text to appear, telling herself it didn't matter that there wasn't one—he was at a christening; he'd told her he'd speak to her tomorrow…

Later, having undressed for bed, exhausted, she brushed her teeth, and then, lifting her hair, saw again the smudge of purple bruise. She shivered, running her fingers over the only tangible evidence of what had taken place. Emma clutched the memory of it to her like a hot water bottle as she curled up in the same bed Zarios had slept in last night, slid under the weighty warmth of a duvet that still held his scent and let memories caress her exhausted body.

Remembered the bliss of being in his arms.

Willed sleep to come so that soon she could greet the morning.

CHAPTER FOUR

'COME with us, darling,' Lydia said again, as Emma read the morning paper. 'We're going to drive along the coast and have a long, lazy lunch…'

'I really can't, Mum.' Emma shook her head. 'I haven't been at the gallery since Thursday.'

'Surely one more day off won't hurt?' Lydia pushed.

Oh, but it would. A buyer had been in twice the previous week, looking at her paintings, and Emma knew that a closed sign on her shop too many days in a row would soon temper his interest. And then there was Jake to deal with.

She jumped with nervous excitement as her phone shrilled, dismayed and panicked to find that it was just Jake—wanting to know her answer, wanting to know what time she was getting away so that they could talk.

'I need to be at the shop.' Emma filled her cup from the pot and added sugar. 'Anyway…' she smiled as her dad walked in and pinched Lydia's bottom '…you two don't need me sitting in the back seat spoiling your fun. You've got a trip to Rome to plan!'

'I can't believe Rocco was so generous!' Lydia clapped her hands in delight at the prospect. 'I just can't believe he did that.'

'I can…' Eric slathered butter on his toast. 'He's always wanted to show us his home town, and I think, with his retirement coming up and everything…' he paused for a pensive moment '…he's probably wondering how he'll fill his time.'

'I know how *I'd* fill it!' Lydia shook her head in wonder. 'He should be off on a cruise. The women would be lining up for him, with his pots of money…and he's a nice man, too,' Lydia added, more as an afterthought.

'You're incorrigible!' Eric laughed, but his expression was serious. 'He's a *very* nice man who happens to still be in love with his ex-wife.'

'Then he needs to get over her!' Lydia said, unmoved. 'You know I love you, Eric, but I wouldn't wait thirty years.'

'She wouldn't wait thirty minutes!' Eric winked at his daughter, peeling off the front and sports pages of the newspaper, as he always did. 'Have you had a good weekend, darling?'

'I had a great time,' Emma enthused. 'Everyone did!'

'You're sure?' Lydia checked. 'Did you hear anyone actually *say* that?'

'Everyone had a ball…' Emma's voice trailed off as she turned the page, everything freezing as Zarios's face suddenly stared out at her from the newspaper. He wasn't alone.

He was with Miranda.

The regular Monday gossip column, telling what had happened with the rich and famous over the weekend, was causing more than a vague stir of interest as Emma read the words below the photo.

The rumoured break-up of drop-dead gorgeous financier Zarios D'Amilo and his model girlfriend Miranda Deloware (pictured yesterday, wearing an exquisite Kovlosky gown), seems to be just that: a rumour.

Appearing together at the christening of Elizabeth Hamilton (see p42) there was no mistaking that they were very much a couple. A source close to the pair hinted there might soon be the sound of wedding bells.

Sorry, gals…it would appear Zarios is very much spoken for.

'I thought as much…' Lydia tutted as she peered over Emma's shoulder. 'Any woman would be mad to get involved with him.'

'That's not what you said on Saturday.'

'I hadn't spoken properly to Rocco then. Zarios is the incorrigible one! He's got the morals of an alley cat, apparently; he'll say anything to get a woman into bed. Really, I can see why Rocco's hesitant to just hand everything over to him.' She stabbed at his image in the paper. 'Zarios doesn't know the meaning of the word *commitment.*'

Somehow Emma managed to be normal.

Somehow she managed to kiss her parents goodbye and thank them for a wonderful weekend as they headed off for their drive along the coast.

She wasn't even angry as she clipped on her seatbelt and headed for her own long drive home, still hoping that he'd ring, that her phone would bleep and it would be Zarios, offering some sort of an explanation.

Pulling up at her flat, Emma felt her heart leap as she

saw him standing at her door, glad—so glad—that she hadn't rung and blasted him with accusations.

He gave a very thin half-smile of acknowledgement as she parked her car, then walked towards him, and Emma felt her heart sink at the grim expression on his face.

'Hi.' Refusing to be needy or jealous, refusing to let him know she'd even *seen* the newspaper, Emma let him into the hallway then up the steep steps towards her flat. She certainly wasn't going to make this easy for him—if he was still with Miranda then he could tell her so without assistance!

'I've been waiting for you…' He couldn't meet her eyes; he followed her through to the kitchen. 'May I?' He gestured to the sink and Emma frowned as he poured himself a glass of water and downed it in one gulp. For someone who had had so much practice in breaking women's hearts, he sure looked nervous. 'As I said, I've been waiting for you.'

'Well, I'm here now!' Emma kept smiling, *deliberately* kept smiling, even though her heart was shrivelling. Just yesterday she'd been in his arms. Little more than twenty-four hours ago she'd been foolish enough to glimpse a future with Zarios in it—and now she knew, just knew, he was about to break her heart.

What an idiot she was to believe him.

What a blind, trusting fool.

'Your brother asked me to come…'

'My brother?' Emma frowned. What on earth did Jake have to do with all this? Unless he'd been asking Zarios for money… Emma's blood chilled at the very thought.

'He's at the hospital…' Zarios ran a tongue over very

pale lips. 'We thought it better that I came and told you rather than the police…'

'The police…' Tiny needles prickled at her scalp, along her arms. Her eyes shot to his, seeing the very real anguish there. 'What's he done?' Frantic images dotted her mind. Oh, she'd known Jake was worried—in deep trouble, perhaps—but from the serious note in Zarios's voice, from the grey tinge to his skin and his reticence, Emma knew that this was serious. 'What's happened to Jake?'

'It's not Jake.'

Her hand flew to her mouth as she thought of Beth, the twins… 'What the hell has he done?'

'It isn't Jake, Emma…' Zarios swallowed hard. 'It's your parents.'

'My parents?' She shook her head. Nothing he was saying was making sense. 'What are you talking about? I just left them.'

'There was an accident on the beach road…'

She was already turning for the door, desperate to get to them, only Zarios was pulling her back.

And she knew why—knew as he pulled her into his chest what was coming next. Only she didn't want to hear it. Struggling like a frantic cat in his grasp, she was desperate to get away, to flee, to run, rather than be held and face the truth.

'Emma, they were killed outright.'

CHAPTER FIVE

HIS arms were the only thing that stopped her falling as everything in her world went black.

In the horrible shrinking vortex which she'd entered, for a moment there was nothing. No sound, no thought, no gravity. Just a spinning sensation of doom that coated each cell in its rapid black welcome, then expelled her to another side—a side where, no matter how she pleaded and wept to go back, there was no escape.

On the most horrific day of her life he was there beside her, this strong pillar of support. In fact, Emma was so bewildered that she didn't even realise till much later how much she must have leant on him that day.

And that evening, too.

She had let him drive her back to her parents' home and there lead her to her bed, where she had woken just that morning when everything had been so normal. He had sat on the chair beside her whilst she had drifted in the twilight zone between rest and sleep to a place of vague awareness, and somewhere between darkness and dawn she remembered.

'Miranda…'

'Shhh…' The loose lips of a liar might once have

soothed her, but she was beyond comfort now, beyond pain—beyond anything, really.

'Are you two back together?'

'We'll talk in the morning.'

'Are you back together?'

The endless silence before he spoke was louder than his words.

'Emma, it's complicated….'

'Yes or no?'

There was the longest pause. 'Yes.'

Which still didn't answer her question. It was unfathomable to her that after the most breathtaking lovemaking, after all that had been said, he could within a matter of hours simply walk away.

'Is she pregnant?' It was an arrogant question, but it was all she could think of, all that could rationalise such a rapid demise.

'No.' Zarios looked her in the eyes and lied. Lied because they *had* to be over. Lied because he wouldn't do it to his child—could never let it be said, even to himself, that it was the only reason he was with its mother.

'Miranda and I have been together a long time— four months,' Zarios added. And Emma suddenly felt as if her mother was in the room with her, recalling the sun-drenched evening and how they had laughed. The perfect answer was there for the taking, but she chose not to use it. 'Emma, what happened that morning…'

He closed his eyes; she could see his face screwed up in concentration as he tried to find the words, but rather than wait for his paltry summing up, she found words for him.

'Was just a bit of fun.'

He frowned before he opened his eyes again. Clearly her response was the last thing he'd been expecting, but Emma was hurting so badly that there was plenty to go around, so instead of humiliating herself, instead of letting him think she'd once wanted him, she told him otherwise. She was more than willing to grate off a piece of her raw bruised heart and let him sample the pain— let him take a sip of the humiliation he'd force-fed her.

'Emma, you know that's not the case.'

The acrid bitter taste of humiliation was choking her. She had lost not just her parents that day, but the man she'd glimpsed loving, too.

'Oh, come on, Zarios, my mother would never have forgiven me if I hadn't at least attempted to flirt with you.' She stared through the darkness towards him. 'The great Zarios D'Amilo, coming to my house for a party. My business almost in tatters. It would have been almost criminally irresponsible for me not to at least *try*…' And there it was, the tiniest swallow in his olive throat that told her that maybe, just maybe, he believed her. It was enough to make her go on. 'So you went back to Miranda—oh, well, you can't blame a girl for trying. Anyway, you know how the saying goes—rich men are like buses; if you miss one, there will be two more following shortly behind.'

Silence hissed in the air. Emma knew she had gone too far, but it was too late to attempt retrieval, and right now she simply didn't care.

'Just leave, Zarios.'

'You shouldn't be on your own.'

'Then I'll ring someone I want to have here.'

'Well—' his voice was crisp and businesslike, but the

contempt in his eyes would surely stay with her for ever
'—I'm glad we both understand each other.'

'Me, too.'

It was Zarios who had the final word.

'I wouldn't waste your time on your artwork, Emma.
After your performance in the summerhouse you should
try your hand at acting. For a minute there I actually
believed you were different.'

CHAPTER SIX

PRIVATELY Emma had often wondered how Jake would cope in a real crisis—the answer had surprised her.

He had dealt with everything—and not just the practical—had offered endless support as Emma struggled just to function. He had dealt with the rapid sale of her parents' house when, two days after the funeral, a generous offer had come up to buy it, furnishings and all. And Jake had offered wise counsel when, on a particularly unbearable night, she'd confided to him what had happened with Zarios.

'You're best out of it, Em…' He had held her hand and said all the right things. 'Whatever he's got going on with Miranda is just to keep the board of directors happy—it will be over in a few weeks.'

And he had been right.

Two weeks before the board's decision and Zarios was again in the newspapers—but for all the wrong reasons.

She'd read about him—unable to help herself— with a morbid curiosity, scanning the magazines and newspapers.

D'Amilo Financiers shareholders were bracing themselves for the announcement, its share price hovering as the financial world held its collective breath and awaited details on the company's new direction. For a while Zarios had managed to behave. Emma had winced at every photo of him walking hand in hand with Miranda, hopping on a plane and joining her in Brazil on a photoshoot. His spin doctors had been working overtime, almost managing to convince the world that Zarios D'Amilo had changed—that this leopard now wore different spots.

Till last week.

No comment had been offered from Camp Zarios when Miranda had been dumped at the eleventh hour, just two weeks short of his father's retirement. The papers were ablaze with the scandal, the share price had tumbled, and even the gossip magazines wavered in their dogged devotion to Zarios.

After all, Emma thought, her lips curling in distaste as she'd read on, what reputable magazine could favourably report on a man who would end a relationship when he found out Miranda was unable to bear children?

Zarios, as Miranda had tearfully revealed to the enthralled media, having sold her story for a record sum, had wanted a child, an heir, and had refused to commit to marriage until she became pregnant. Tests had recently revealed that she was infertile, and there were photos of the two of them coming out of the specialist fertility department at a top Melbourne hospital—Zarios looking boot-faced, Miranda in floods of tears.

And, Emma had noticed with loathing, he wasn't even holding her hand.

Jake had been right—she *was* best out of it. And then suddenly her brother had changed his mind.

Arriving at her door a couple of nights ago, grey and ashen, suddenly Jake had insisted that she went to Zarios for help.

Emma felt nauseous at the mere recollection of the desperate conversation she had shared with her brother that night.

'You *hit* Beth?' she had asked, appalled at her brother's confession.

'I pushed her…' Jake was as irritated as Emma was horrified. 'And she fell. I was just trying to get past and she was in the way. Look, Em…' in an attempt to soften her, Jake reverted to her childhood nickname '…how can I walk in now and tell Beth I've lost the house? She's already threatening to leave. Surely Zarios owes you after what he did to you? You can sweet-talk him into a loan.'

'He's not going to pay off your gambling debts.'

'Tell him it's for *you*! Tell him that your business is in trouble—tell him anything, just keep me out of it. He'd never agree for me. He knows our parents' house had been sold, that the money's practically in the bank—it's just till Mum and Dad's money comes through.'

'Even if he did give me a loan, which is highly un-likely, what are you going to tell Beth? How are you going to explain it in a couple of weeks' time, when you have to pay me back?'

'Things will be calmer then,' Jake said. 'If I tell her now, she'll walk. She'll take out a restraining order and I won't see the kids.'

'What if I go with you and speak to the bank? Maybe if you can sign a guarantee that the money's coming.'

'The guys I'm dealing aren't going to wait for the

bank to make up their mind, Em. I need…' Jake gulped
as he told her the appalling figure—he needed nearly
one million dollars by the close of business tomorrow.
'Every day that passes it goes up more…'

Those poor kids… Emma almost wept as she pictured Harriet's and Connor's innocent, trusting faces.
Poor Beth, too. God alone knew what *she* must be
putting up with.

What would her parents want her to do?

'I can't take this much longer, Emma.'

There was her answer. So now, with Jake's veiled
threat still ringing in her ears, for the first time since her
parents' funeral Emma dressed carefully.

But it took for ever.

Since their death it had felt as if her brain was working in slow motion. Her stomach was knotted in constant tension and the simplest decision took for ever to
make: which shoes to wear, hair up or down, even
whether to apply make-up—all required a mammoth
effort, one she didn't want to make. And she'd never
thought she would be making it for Zarios.

The putrid words of their last conversation still rang
in her ears at times. She hated what she'd said to him,
but hated what he'd done to her even more. She could
see clearly how he'd used her that weekend—she'd been
nothing more than a small diversion in an otherwise
boring weekend. Emma had played with the big boys,
she realised, and only had herself to blame for getting
well and truly burnt.

And now she had to face him. Had to swallow her
pride and ask the snake for help.

Which was easier said than done. His work life, as

Emma had found out when she had tried to contact him, was as capricious as his personal life—Rome one week, Singapore the next. He was flying from his office in Sydney down to Melbourne today, Emma had discovered on her third attempt to contact him, and surprisingly he'd agreed to meet her—or rather his secretary had arranged an appointment for 2:00 p.m. the following day, which had given her twenty-four hours to change her mind.

As if she had a choice.

She frowned at her dressing table as if it belonged to someone else, noticing that her hand was shaking as she stroked her make-up brush into powder. The two pink dots that appeared on her cheeks were just too much against her pale complexion and Emma wiped them off with a tissue, giving up on her face and grabbing her bag instead, clipping down the steep stairs of her flat. What the hell was the point of wearing make-up anyway? Nothing was going to disguise her humiliation—nothing was going to mask the shame of going to Zarios with a begging bowl in her hand.

'My appointment was at two.' Emma tried to keep the slightly desperate note from her voice. 'It's almost three now.'

The receptionist gave her a pussycat smile, which without words told Emma in no uncertain terms that she was more than capable of telling the time. 'Mr D'Amilo is an extremely busy man. As I've said, I'll inform you as soon as he's ready to see you.'

Not *that* busy!

Strolling through the lavish foyer, Zarios looked

completely refreshed and relaxed after his extended lunch. Maybe it had something to do with the company he was keeping.

A well-groomed brunette was beside him, hanging on his every word, laughing at whatever it was that Zarios had just said.

Emma had forgotten just how beautiful he really was. In the past few weeks, whenever her mind had drifted to him, or she'd read about his heartless, torrid break-up with Miranda, somehow her mind had managed to distort his image to almost devil-like proportions, marring his beauty perhaps to shield herself. But seeing him now, breathtakingly elegant in a charcoal-grey suit, his shirt gleaming white against his olive skin, there was no denying his beauty. He'd had his hair cut, those jet locks cropped closely to his head, which made him look more menacing and somehow more striking, if that were possible. Seeing him in the flesh even more than two months on had Emma's stomach curling—not at what she must now ask, but at what they had once shared.

When he spoke briefly to his receptionist, Emma was unclear whether she had let him know that his 2:00 p.m. appointment was waiting, because Zarios didn't even deign to give her a glance. Instead he headed towards the lifts and disappeared, leaving Emma more intimidated than ever at the prospect of what lay ahead.

It was another ten minutes till she was directed to his floor.

And another half an hour spent sitting in another waiting room—albeit a lavish one.

The groomed brunette must be his personal assistant, Emma realised, when she brought her an extremely welcome glass of iced water and peered at her from her desk when she thought Emma wasn't looking. Emma bit her lip as she awaited her fate, and then, with just an hour till the office building closed, the intercom buzzed and the snooty brunette finally gave her a nod. She was shown through.

'You wanted to see me.' There was no small talk, no apology for the delay. He curtly gestured for her to take a seat, his face utterly unreadable as tentatively she nodded.

'Regarding?'

He certainly wasn't making this easy.

'It's difficult…' Emma attempted.

'Then let me help you. We slept together approximately two months ago, and now you urgently need to meet with me—I can hazard a guess—'

'No!' Emma interrupted. The arrow he had shot had missed its mark, skimming over her shoulder surely to be forgotten. Except a sound resonated, a small hollow summons to tell her that somewhere it had hit a mark. But with a determined, irritated shake of her head she ignored it. 'I got my period on the day of my parents' funeral. That's not the reason I called.' Only now did he frown. Only now did he seem curious as to why she might be here. 'I wanted to see you about the release of my parents' money.'

'Of course!' Zarios gave a tight smile. 'Silly me for assuming otherwise!'

Emma ran a dry tongue over even dryer lips, embarrassment stinging every pore at his implication, regret-

fully acknowledging that after their bitter parting he
was right to think as he did. She forced herself to continue. 'The house has been sold…'

'I believe so.'

'The thing is…' She blew a breath skywards, but her
fringe barely moved; it was plastered to her moist
forehead. 'I need access to my share of the funds now.'

'Now?'

'Yes. Today.' She watched his eyebrows rise just a
fraction.

'Can I ask why you need money so quickly?'

'No.' She choked the single word out, then, clearing
her throat, said it more firmly. 'No. I'd rather not say,
but as soon as the sale of the house goes through I will
repay the money. It would just be a loan until then.'

'I can see that a lot of work has gone into your
proposal!'

His sarcasm, though merited, wasn't exactly helping. 'I realise it can't look good, me just walking in and
asking for money. But I have my reasons, and the inheritance—'

'I can't help you.' He interrupted her, shaking his head.

'Please.' She hated that she was reduced to begging,
but she had no choice. 'Zarios, please. You're the only
person who has access to that type of funds…'

'Not quite…' He flashed a mirthless smile. 'Have
you ever heard of banks?' Tears pricked her eyes as he
savagely continued. 'If you are so convinced it is just a
short-term loan, that in two weeks you can repay, then
you should have no trouble securing a bridging loan. Of
course a bank would want to know where the money
was going, why a twenty-five-year-old woman needs

access to such a sum of money at such short notice. Have you even *tried* the banks?'

She tried to say no, but the word wouldn't come out. Emma settled instead for a tiny shake of her head.

'Then am I right in assuming that is because you couldn't suitably answer their questions?'

Oh, *how* he must be enjoying this, Emma thought, the tears in her eyes drying as she stared at him across the desk, their mutual contempt meeting in the middle.

'Anyway,' he continued when she didn't answer, still holding her stare, 'even if I wanted to help you I could not.' He gave a dismissive shrug. 'There's a potential conflict of interest. I have excused myself from the board in regard to the execution of your parents' estate.'

'That's not what I'm asking…'

'I know that!' Zarios sneered. 'You are playing on the fact that we *once* slept together.'

'No!' Emma quivered. 'I'm pleading to you as a friend of the family.'

'Did you approach my father with your request?' Zarios snapped his very good point out. 'Of course not!'

'You know,' he continued bitterly, 'he said I was over-reacting when I removed myself from having any dealings with your parents' estate.' He stood up, clearly ending the meeting. 'Clearly I was right to follow my instincts.'

'You'll get it back…' Tears were streaming down her cheeks unchecked now. The thought of telling Jake, the thought of him telling Beth, the horrible reality of it all was unbearably close now, making her desperate. But her tears didn't move him. If anything they just compounded his disdain. 'I'll sign anything—the day the exchange happens you'll get the money back…'

'If you'll excuse me?' He glanced at his watch and pressed a button on his phone. 'I'm running behind schedule.' He smiled as his secretary opened the door, gave her a sort of wide-eyed look that acknowledged yet another tearful woman was leaving the building, and asked if she could please arrange that it was done quietly. 'Could you show Ms Hayes to the lift, please?'

As easily as that he dismissed her. His cold eyes made it clear there would be no further discussion, and the distaste was evident in the set of his face as he held open the door.

And who could blame him for what he must be thinking? Emma thought as the lift plummeted downwards—her parents were barely cold in their grave and she wanted her hands on their money with no questions asked, if that could possibly be arranged!

Clearly it couldn't.

She could feel her phone vibrating in her bag, knew it was Jake. For a tiny second she was almost relieved. Relieved that she couldn't help him. Relieved that the problem was no longer hers…

But then she heard his voice.

'Maybe Beth will understand…' Emma attempted as she told him the hard news. 'Maybe it's time to come clean, Jake—time to lay it all out in the open…'

'It's not what Beth's going to say that I'm worried about.' She could hear the fear in her brother's voice. 'Oh, God, what have I done, Em?' He was sobbing so hard he could barely get the words out. 'I can't face this! What are they going to do to me? What if they turn on her, on the kids? I'd be better off out of it.'

She was half walking, half running through the foyer.

She could hear the desperation in his voice and knew she had to get to him and turned, wild-eyed, when the receptionist stopped her in her tracks.

'Mr D'Amilo will see you shortly.'

Emma briefly closed her eyes in frustration before answering. 'I've already seen Mr D'Amilo.' She gave a very short smile, tempted to add, *for all the good it did*. She turned her attention back to her brother, but the receptionist persisted.

'I'm aware of that. Mr D'Amilo has asked that you wait while he considers your proposal further. If you'd like to take a seat, he'll send for you in due course.'

She had no idea what game Zarios was playing—the only thing she was certain of was that it was a game! How she would have loved to ignore the command to sit. But Jake was still on the line—or rather, Emma thought, Jake was at the very end of the line.

'Just hold on, Jake.' She put the phone back up to her ear. 'Just calm down. I'll sort out something. I'll talk to Zarios again.'

Despite the air-conditioning, sweat was beading on his forehead. Zarios felt as if his tie was choking him. Loosening it, he pulled open the top button of his shirt and tried to kick his stalled brain into some sort of action.

In an attempt to make things work with Miranda he'd relegated all the good things that he had shared with Emma to the recesses of his mind—had ignored the wonderful parts in the short life of their relationship and focussed solely on the death of it. He had replayed Emma's finishing words like a mantra every time his mind had wandered in that dangerous direction. But even if he had discounted their lovemaking, their passion, long before today, no matter how he had tried he hadn't been able to discount *her*.

And now she was back.

From the second he'd heard she was trying to make contact Zarios had been bracing himself—warning himself not to overreact, that if she did tell him she was pregnant he would stay calm… Except she wasn't pregnant.

Opening his office drawer for the first time that week, he pulled out the hand-sized teddy bear, with its smiling face and black button eyes, and managed to really look at it. He remembered the mawkish pride that had filled him when he'd paid for the little thing and had looked forward to sharing it with Miranda.

Just the thought of Miranda made his jaw clench.

The slurs, the innuendoes, the filth that had been reported this past week should have had him shouting the truth from the rooftops—should have propelled him to come out of his corner fighting. Except in the abyss of his pain the slights of the press had barely touched the sides.

Grief was the only thing that consumed him now.

A grief he couldn't understand and one he certainly couldn't explain—even to himself.

Resting his head in his hands, Zarios forced himself to breath evenly, to hold it together, to rise above it as he always did.

He had business to attend to.

And now, waiting downstairs, was the one woman who could possibly make his father believe that he had changed. Zarios's frozen brain was leaping into action now. He could even tell his father Emma was the *real* reason he had ended things with Miranda.

Stuffing the teddy back in the drawer, he slammed it shut, annoyed with himself for indulging in sentiment. The time for mourning was over.

Straightening his tie, he pressed on the intercom and told Jemima, his receptionist, to send her back in. After all…how could you mourn something that never even existed?

It was well after five before she was summoned. Way too late, Emma figured, for Zarios to do anything. The banks would have long since closed. Again the receptionist swiped her security tag for the lift and Emma headed to Zarios's floor. The only difference was that this time his snooty PA wasn't there to greet her. The sumptuous waiting area was empty, and Emma took a tentative seat, unsure what to do. She was also unsure what Zarios could possibly want with her now, so absolute had been his refusal to help.

She jumped slightly when his heavy office door opened and Zarios himself wordlessly gestured for her to come inside.

'You waited.'

He stood at the window, staring out at the darkening Melbourne sky that was thick with rain despite the summer month. Threatening droplets splashed onto the window and she knew that in a few moments, when he'd finished playing whatever his little game was, there was no doubt she'd be out there.

'I had no choice but to wait.'

'There are always choices.'

'Not always.' She took a seat uninvited, angry now. What choice had her parents had? What choice did *she* have now other than to sit and wait to see what the master had to say?

'You will have read about my break-up with Miranda?' He didn't turn to see her response; there was just a natural assumption that she had. 'My father and the board are less than impressed.'

As they should be, Emma thought, but didn't have the nerve to say it. Her voice was shaky when, after a moment, she found it. 'Is it true?' Emma swallowed. 'That you left her because she couldn't have your babies?'

'Why do you owe so much money?' Zarios countered, and when she didn't answer he gave a wry smile. 'We both have our own set of excuses, I am sure. When I first started working for my father it was a small company—building and refurbishing, here in Melbourne and in Rome. I found a property in Scotland—a castle that had the potential to be renovated into a top-class boutique hotel, ideal for weddings, that type of thing…'

Her head pounded with neuralgia. Why the hell was he telling her this? She didn't need a history lesson, she needed cash!

He must have sensed her impatience. 'Don't worry— I am as loath as you are to be in conversation. Believe me, this is not idle chatter!'

'Good.' She accepted the glass of water he poured, draining it in one gulp, not caring whether or not it was ladylike.

'For that to come to fruition we had to borrow, or bring investors on board. My father chose the latter option, and when the situation was repeated he brought in more investors. Ten years ago I was a year younger than you are now—twenty-four years old and still somewhat intimidated by father. The company was divided, with my father retaining a twenty-five percent stake, myself twenty-four. I strongly advised him to make his share twenty-six, mine twenty-five—are you still with me, Emma?' He must have seen her eyes glaze over, because he snapped her to rapid attention. 'Had he listened to me then, we would not be having this conversation now.'

'I can do the maths.' Emma gave a tight smile.

'Good—then you will know how important that two percent share is now, when D'Amilo Financials is worth billions. Once my father retires our directors want to rename it, and for my father's stake in the company to be spread between all the directors rather than passed to me—naturally, I am opposed.'

'What about your father?' Emma blinked. 'Surely it's up to him…?'

'He wants what is best for the future of the company, and on recent form he is not sure that is me. As he has said, whatever happens I am still a majority shareholder.' He registered her frown. 'My relationship with my father is not the same as the one you had with your parents. He is more a business partner to me than a parent.'

'What does this have to do with me?'

'My father wants to see me settled. He is unwell.'

The clipped tone of his voice told Emma he wasn't angling for sympathy, but no matter what she thought of the son, Emma cared about the father. 'What's wrong with him?' She watched Zarios's jaw stiffen, saw a flash of annoyance dart across his features at the invasive nature of her question. Finally he gave a brief, reluctant nod, before answering. 'He requires major heart surgery. His colleagues do not know—I would prefer that it stays that way.'

'Of course,' Emma responded. 'I'm very sorry to hear that.'

He neither wanted nor acknowledged her comment. Instead he moved swiftly on. 'This is why he is retiring so quickly. He was going to tell your parents about the surgery after your father's birthday. Given the seriousness of the matter, he is busy getting his affairs in order. He made it clear that if I toned down my behaviour, if I gave him reason to believe that I had changed, he would go against the rest of the board and transfer his stake to me. Miranda and I breaking up has almost put paid to that. However—' he gave a wan smile '—just when it seemed irretrievable a solution has appeared.' He gave Emma a black smile. 'He thinks the world of you.'

'He warned you *off* me!' Emma pointed out. 'I only wish you'd listened at the time.'

'He doesn't want me to hurt you, Emma!' His lips pouted and he blew her a mock kiss. 'Which is why we're getting engaged!'

'Please!'

'I've never made it official with a woman before…' He smiled at the novelty of his own treachery. 'It would go a long way to convincing him!'

'He'd never believe it.'

'You're too modest!' Zarios chided, his sardonic smile mocking her. 'Why, you're an excellent liar and a consummate actress, Emma! Personally, I'd *never* have taken you for a gold-digging whore!'

'Bastard!'

'Then we understand each other,' he drawled. 'You'll have no problem convincing him.'

'As if he's going to accept that we're suddenly together—' Emma shook her head. His proposal was too preposterous for words.

'Why wouldn't he?' Zarios interrupted. 'We will tell him the truth. We met up again after many years at your father's sixtieth birthday party and the attraction was immediate.'

Which *was* the truth, Emma conceded. But only so far!

'With all that has happened to you recently, it is no wonder things have moved so quickly. Of course it was hard, ending things with Miranda, but my feelings for you...' his eyes were black with malice '...were just impossible to ignore.'

'Why?' Emma blinked. 'Why does it matter to you so much? You're going to be rich either way...'

'Honour,' Zarios said. 'Look it up in the dictionary when you get home. You might learn something!'

'Honour amongst thieves, you mean!' Emma responded. 'You're asking me to lie to your own father, remember.'

'My father is too easily swayed by others—he has the Italian curse of worrying too much what others think.'

'It must have skipped a generation.'

'I have no...' he snapped his fingers as he searched for the word '...no doubt.' He shook his head, clearly not happy with his choice. 'No guilt...' Still he frowned.

'No qualms.' Emma stared coolly at him. 'The word you're looking for is *qualms*.'

'It was the D'Amilo name that made our current directors rich, it is my acumen that has lined their pockets, and it is *my* brain that keeps it that way. I have no *qualms* about fighting for what is rightfully mine.'

'Modest, too.' Emma's mouth twisted. She was way past even pretending to be polite now. She didn't have time for this. There was no way she was going to agree, and there was no way he was going to lend her the money. She should never have come back!

'I don't believe in false modesty,' Zarios continued. 'I am the best—it is as simple as that.'

He sat down then, and stared at her as if commencing a business meeting.

'I will transfer the funds you require into your account now; in return we will go to my father tonight and tell him of our plans.'

'And what happens when your father realises it was just a charade?' Emma asked scathingly.

'Who said anything about a charade?' Zarios frowned. 'We *will* be engaged.'

'But when it ends…' Emma flailed.

'It might not!' Zarios just laughed at her confusion. 'There is, after all, a high possibility we will get married!'

'Married…' She scooped up her bag. She had never heard anything more bizarre in her life. She loved Jake and would do anything to help him—well, almost anything—but a marriage of convenience with a snake like Zarios was way beyond the call of sisterly duty.

'You're hardly in a position to walk out,' Zarios called to her departing back.

'I'm in every position. You really think I'd marry *you*? After all you've done, the way you are, do you really think I'd want to be married to a man like you?'

'I never said that you *had* to marry me.'

'You just did.' Her fingers were reaching for the door handle. She was in absolutely no mood to decipher one of Zarios's cryptic messages—in no state to have her frayed emotions toyed with even for a little while longer.

'If you would let me finish—you will see you *do* have an exit clause.'

'An exit clause…' She blinked in anger and frustration at his businesslike terms. His utter disregard for the sanctity of marriage had never been more evident.

'Your parents' insurance payout, the funds from their house—all are due for settlement around the same time as the board's decision.' Warily Emma nodded. 'If you pay me back on the day you receive your inheritance you can walk away as soon as the board announces its decision.'

'That's all?' Emma frowned, turning around to look at him. 'I just have to pay you back?'

'That's it.'

'But what about your father?'

'I'll worry about that.'

'But it will devastate him…'

'You have delusions of grandeur, Emma. I don't think *devastate* is the word—I am sure we will all survive. Anyway, we are talking about a hypothetical situation—one I don't believe will transpire. As I said, I have every reason to believe we *will* be married.'

'Zarios, I will pay you back.' She couldn't really believe she was talking as if this was going to happen. 'You know what I'm due to receive, and I always pay my debts…'

'They *are* your debts?'

She swallowed, a dart of nervousness flashing in her eyes. Of course Jake would pay her back—she'd get it in writing this time, Emma decided. She'd get him to sign an agreement that he would pay her back in full on the day their parents' inheritance came through.

'You'll get your money.'

'We'll see.' Zarios smiled. 'Until I do, you will be my fiancée. You will move in to my home so that I can take care of you—or rather deal with the press and the questions…'

'I won't…' Emma flushed. 'I mean, there'll be no…'

'I don't understand what you are saying.' He flashed her an innocent smile.

'Oh, I think you do. I want to make it clear, *very* clear, that we won't be sharing a bed.'

'I think the cleaners might suspect something if my fiancée is sleeping in a separate bed. And, as I said, we will be at my father's this weekend. He found out his son had lost virginity many years ago…'

'Fine!' Emma trilled, her face on fire. 'But we won't be sleeping together.'

'You expect me to sleep on the floor.'

Bastard. The word hissed on her lips, but she swallowed it down. She knew he was goading her, knew he was going to make her say it—well, she would.

'There will be no sex—and I want an assurance from you that there will be no pressure.'

'Pressure?' For the first time that day she heard Zarios laugh. He actually threw his head back and laughed at her statement. But Emma stood her ground.

'You can add *that* to your precious clauses,' Emma spat.

'Why?' He stood up and walked towards her. 'Why waste my lawyer's time getting him to write up a rule that is only going to be broken?'

'It won't be.'

'And as for pressure…' He wasn't laughing now. 'Be careful what you accuse me of, Emma.'

He was in her face now, so close she could smell him even as she backed further towards the door. His dangerous gaze held hers, black fading to indigo, just as it had on the morning he had saved her. Only now it felt as if she were drowning again—drowning in this man who could blind her to his faults. She dragged her eyes downwards, but there was no solace to be had there. His full mouth was moving in on her as he warned her to choose her words more carefully, as he made a mockery of the one rule she had insisted upon.

'I have never, will never, pressure a woman.'

'Good.' Her voice was a croak, but somehow she got the word out. His hand was behind her now, lazily holding the door she leant against. There was not a shred of contact between them, but she felt as if he was inside her.

'Do you feel pressured now?'

His mouth was mere inches from hers, her mind was quailing, but her treacherous body flared in an instant recall of their one dizzy time together.

'You haven't answered the question…' Zarios said slowly. 'Emma, am I pressuring you now?'

'No.'

'Do you want me to kiss you?'

Yes.

She didn't say it, but the word snapped like a twig between them.

She wanted to forget, to escape…for just one moment. To forget this living hell and taste the heaven she had once witnessed. To accept the temporary relief his mouth would surely provide.

To be held instead of holding up.

He kissed her then, his mouth crushing hers. Except she was kissing him back with all her might, pressing her body into his as if she wanted to climb inside him to escape, revelling in the freedom that his touch, his kiss, his *being* somehow brought her. Oh, she was lost, lost, lost, and it was wonderful. She was back in oblivion and it tasted divine. His tongue stroked hers, extricated her from the hell of the past few weeks. *How* she kissed him back—biting on his lip, sucking his flesh, holding his head as he held hers. They were devouring each other with hot, angry kisses that soothed.

The ferocity of his erection pressed into her groin just wasn't enough. The incessant pressure of his mouth, the delicious probing of his tongue and the contentious feel of his hand pushing up her skirt, creeping along her thigh, was bliss. Yet it still wasn't enough! And he knew, *he knew*, because his fingers were hard on the soft flesh of her inner thigh. She parted them, just moved her feet a fraction, and still he kissed her, still his fingers crept higher, till they arrived at her sweet, welcoming moist warmth. As he slid his fingers inside her, his skilled hand dimmed reason. She pulled her head away from his kiss, biting on his shoulder or else she'd scream, knowing that in just a second she would come in his hand.

And then he stopped. His cruel withdrawal momentarily stunning her.

'As I said…' His free hand lifted her chin so he could

look at her, even as still he held her in the palm of his hand. 'I do not waste my time with rules I know will be broken.'

As he removed his hand, hers met his cheek. Tears, hate, shame and loathing—all were there in her aim. Not just for him, but for the betrayal of her own body, that even after all he had done still she could want him.

He didn't even flinch, just walked to his computer, four livid strokes where her fingers had been on his cheek.

Her phone was buzzing in her bag. Her body was twitching and confused at the withdrawal of his affection. Her mind was begging her to get out, warning her that she might as well make a deal with the devil himself rather than enter into this with Zarios.

And yet…

When everything had gone, there was nothing left to lose.

'I have one condition…'

'I thought we just dealt with that.'

'There will be no other women.' Emma swallowed hard. 'As long as this charade continues, as long you are engaged or married to me, there are to be no other women or the deal is off.'

He gave a surly shrug.

'I mean it…' Emma shivered. 'You are not to see anyone else. I won't be humili…' Her voice trailed off. It was a bit late for that.

'Fine,' he clipped. 'I am as good as my word—and here it is. If during our time together I sleep with another woman then you can walk away without owing me a cent. Now…' he turned his face to the screen to conclude the messy business '…can I have your bank details?'

'I hate what you did to me,' Emma said, just to be

sure he knew it. But Zarios was as unmoved as he was unimpressed.

'Your bank details, Emma?'

She hated herself even more for giving them.

CHAPTER SEVEN

'YOU'VE got it?' Jake was pale with relief. 'I can ring them…you can transfer it now…'

'Why don't I just deposit it into your account?'

'For Beth to see?'

'She's going to find out, Jake. Once the inheritance goes through, you're going to have to explain why there isn't any…'

'That's weeks away.' Jake shook his head.

'It's two weeks away, Jake. And you can deny it all you like, but this problem isn't going to go away. Beth *has* to be told.'

'I know that,' Jake shrilled. 'I know that. But I can't tell her now, Em. Not with the way things are. If Beth and I can just get past this… And anyway…' his face crumpled in despair '…I don't trust myself with that sort of money…'

'You're getting help?'

'I'm going to meetings every day… I haven't gambled in weeks.'

Her bank details jumped up on the screen and Emma swallowed, reeling at the balance, her fingers hovering over the keyboard as Jake read out his loan shark's details.

'You *have* to pay me back, Jake.'

'You know I will.'

'No, Jake, I don't.' She turned to face her brother. 'I want it in writing. I want the money you owe me to go directly into my bank account when the settlement goes through.'

'Are you saying you don't trust me?'

'I *don't* trust you, Jake.' After what she'd had to go through today, it wasn't hard to say. 'I don't trust you with money—I'd be an absolute fool to. I need it in writing.'

'Fine!' he snapped, ripping out a piece of paper from her printer and scrawling a note stating the sum that was being borrowed, and that he would pay her back at the time of their settlement. 'Satisfied?'

Emma took the piece of paper and placed it in her bag, hardly able to make out the digits on the keyboard as her eyes swam with tears. She knew the second she hit 'confirm' she was truly indebted to Zarios. For the next two weeks she was a pawn in the elaborate game he was playing—conning poor Rocco.

'Never do this again, Jake. I will *never* help you again.'

'I'll never ask.'

And he meant it. Staring into eyes that were as blue as her own, seeing the wretchedness in his features, the shame, the grief, the embarrassment, she knew that he meant it and reached out her arms to her brother.

'I'm so ashamed…' he sobbed. 'I hate myself more than you hate me.'

'I don't hate you, Jake. I'm just scared for you.'

'I miss them, Em.'

'I know.'

'They'd be so ashamed…'

'Don't think about that.'

'I'll make them proud.' He was a snivelling mess, his grief, his shame, his fear so raw, so real, that surely, *surely* this was his rock bottom? Surely this had to be the last time? 'I'm never gambling again. I'm going to make you proud—make Beth and the twins proud...'

'Make *yourself* proud, Jake.' She gave a tired smile as he glanced at his watch.

'I've got a meeting...'

'Then go.'

'How *did* you get Zarios to agree?'

'It doesn't matter.' Emma gave a thin smile. 'You've got the money.'

'Thank you.'

Jake wasn't the only one with an important meeting to attend. Staring out of her window Emma watched as Zarios's sleek silver car purred up to the kerb. She could almost sense that he knew the money had just been spent.

That she was now his.

That thought was confirmed when, instead of opening his car door, instead of walking down the path to her flat, Zarios gave a short burst on his horn that told her, as if she didn't already know, he was here.

That he had come to claim what he now owned.

'Emma!' Rocco rose from his chair and embraced her. 'It is good of you to come and see me...'

The house was just as it always was whenever Emma went there. Situated in the exclusive Melbourne suburb of Toorak. The door had been opened by Roula, Rocco's elderly housekeeper, and she had walked them through the home which was more like a vast mausoleum to his brief marriage—its walls and surfaces lined with images of their brief union.

Emma was shocked at the frailty of Rocco as he held her. In the few weeks since she'd last seen him he'd aged more than a decade, and Emma knew it wasn't just his illness he was suffering from, but a broken heart—he'd loved her parents, too.

'You should have told me you were bringing Emma over,' Rocco scolded his son.

'What, and spoil the surprise?' Zarios smiled.

'I am too old for surprises.'

'You're sixty,' Zarios pointed out, but it was hopeless. Age really was just a number, and despite his wealth, despite the trappings they afforded, the years really had ravaged his father.

'Emma is staying tonight,' Zarios informed Rocco. 'She needs a break, and there is also something—'

'You should have said—I will tell Roula to make up a room, that we have a guest…'

'There is no need to make up a room for a guest. Emma is family,' Zarios corrected him, and Emma noticed the slight swallow before he continued. 'Or she will be soon.'

A smudge of a frown flickered over Rocco's brow. 'You two?'

'Yes.'

'Are together?' Still Rocco frowned. 'Since when?'

'Since Eric's birthday.'

'But what about Miranda…'

'That is why I ended it with Miranda, Pa…'

'Why didn't you say?' Rocco's voice was bemused. 'Why did you let me think the filth in the papers was true?'

'We wanted to be sure…' Zarios took her hand and Emma realised he was as skilled a liar as he was a lover. 'Pa, we know how big this is, and we had to be sure. With everything that has happened these past few weeks, as terrible as they have been, it has helped us to make up our minds. I have asked Emma to marry me, and happily she has agreed.'

He would lie at his own father's grave, Emma thought, and then realised with a cold drench of horror that in effect she was doing the same: manipulating this wonderful man who, as Rocco's eyes sought hers for clarification, perhaps trusted Emma more than he did his own son.

'Is this true?' Rocco asked. 'You two really are engaged?'

She could feel Zarios's hand tighten around hers, attempting to provoke a response, but all she could manage was the tiniest nod.

'We are going to get a ring tomorrow…' Zarios filled in the long silence. 'We wanted to tell you before the papers got hold of it.'

'And you are happy?' Rocco asked, still more stunned than pleased.

Even when Roula, the housekeeper, was duly summoned, when champagne was poured and toasts given, there was a forced joviality about it all—and not just from Emma.

Rocco, she realised, was clearly choosing to reserve judgement—he was wary with his words, thin with his sentiment—and for the first time Emma glimpsed what Zarios had meant when he had said that his relationship with his father wasn't one she could understand. On the night his only son had announced his engagement, after a cursory glass of champagne and some rather strained small talk and stilted interaction between father and son, Rocco reminded Zarios of the time in Europe, and that he had an important call that needed to be made.

'I shouldn't be long.' Zarios glanced at his watch, and then to Emma, and for the first time she saw just a flicker of nervousness in his eyes. No doubt he was worried at leaving her alone with his father.

'Avetti is an important client…' Rocco waved him away. 'You will take as long as is necessary.'

Pensively, Rocco smiled over at Emma, once they were alone. 'You must have mixed feelings at a time like this?'

'I do.' Emma nodded, able to look him in the eye now, because for that second in time she was telling the truth.

'Come!' He stood up and gestured to a large dresser, where Emma joined him. 'I found this photo of your father and I just the other week, when I was going through some papers. You will not have seen it—I didn't even know I had it.'

She smiled at the image of two grubby little boys sitting on a wall, their knees grazed and dirty. It hurt almost too much to look at the image of her father, so she focused instead on Rocco. As dark as Zarios, but with a cheeky grin, there was a lightness about him Emma could never imagine in his son.

She was right—there in the another photo was Zarios, at eight or nine years old, refusing to smile for his school photo, looking as serious and as accusing as he did now.

'He hated boarding school.' Rocco interrupted her thoughts. 'I hated sending him. I thought I was doing the right thing by him at the time—it is a choice I regret.'

Hearing the wistful note in Rocco's voice, seeing his kind, tired eyes, reminded her so much of her dad it made her brave enough for an observation. 'You don't seem pleased, Rocco, about the engagement?'

'I am torn,' Rocco admitted. 'I love my son, but…' He frowned, more to himself than to Emma. 'Your parents meant the world to me. In some ways with them gone I feel more responsible towards you—almost as if you were a daughter. If I could forget for a moment that Zarios was my son, as much as I love him, I have to be honest— I am not sure he is what I would wish for my daughter…'

Which was hardly a glowing reference from a father, but it was said with more concern than malice. His eyes filled with tears as they came to rest on another photo. Emma followed his gaze, her throat tightening, because there, in contrast to the austere photo of his youth, was a very different Zarios.

A smiling, happy little boy, three, maybe four years old, running along the beach carrying a plastic windmill.

And there he was again, grinning and laughing, wrapped in his mother's arms, with a smiling Rocco looking proudly on.

A different Zarios and a different Rocco, too.

'You would never have met Bella.' Rocco picked up the photo and gazed at it fondly, then handed it to Emma. 'Our marriage broke up before you were even born.'

'She's beautiful.'

'She was…' Rocco smiled. 'She was also way too young to be married. She was just sixteen. Things were different in those days. The marriage was arranged by my grandparents—Bella was from my village back home. She came to Australia speaking no English.'

'As you did.'

'I was younger. I picked up the language more easily—and I had friends like your father to help me. Bella was just lost. I tried to make things easier on her, but she never settled. Now, when I look back, I think she must have been depressed after Zarios was born. But in those days we didn't really understand or talk about such things. I tried to make it work. We went back to Italy, but still she was unhappy.'

'So Zarios went to boarding school…?'

'And I came back here.' He nodded at the question in her voice. 'Here was the only place I could make the money to pay the fees and support my family, too…the lucky country!' He shook his head sadly. 'It didn't feel like it. I went back to Italy as often as I could, opened a business there, but here was where the money was being made. Of course I hoped his mother might be around more for him…'

It was unfathomable to Emma. She thought of her own happy childhood, of her parents who, even with their faults, would have moved heaven and earth for her, and wondered, just as her parents had over the years, how Bella could have excluded herself so totally from her son's life.

'More than anything I want Zarios to be happy. Always the hurt is there—always with Zarios anger. I want my son to find the love that has been missing for most of his life. You *do* love my son, Emma?'

Rocco's question was direct, his eyes so searching that she shouldn't be able to answer it. But, looking down to the photo she held in her hands, Emma knew she wanted to see Zarios happy, too. Wanted back what they had found that morning. Wanted the man she knew was there beneath the pomp and scorn. Wanted the merry dark eyes that danced in this photograph, that she was sure she had glimpsed that wonderful morning, to dance for her again.

There was no doubt she was indebted to him, and not just financially—he had saved her life when she'd nearly drowned, had held her hand when she'd identified her parents, had sat and offered quiet support that first long, lonely night.

Tears coursed down her cheeks, but not for the reason Rocco thought. Emma realised as she nodded, as she told Rocco what he wanted to hear, that she was actually speaking the truth.

She loved him.

She hated him, but somehow had loved him over the years—had loved him that one wonderful morning together—and despite all that had been said, all that was, all that could never be, still somehow she loved him.

'Then you will both be okay—love is what will see you through,' Rocco said wisely. 'Love is what was missing in my marriage. Not,' he added sadly, 'on my side. For my son to have asked for your hand in marriage, he must love you, too.'

Oh, she wished that this were true, that Zarios *did* love her, did want to rescue her from the hell of these past weeks.

Wished that it were that simple.

'You're quiet,' Zarios noted when finally they were alone and could let down the charade as the bedroom door closed behind them.

'I'm tired.' Emma sat at the dressing table and wearily attempted to remove her make-up while Zarios unashamedly undressed behind her. Tired was an understatement. She had been running on adrenaline since her meeting with Zarios, had been sitting on tenterhooks all evening as her head throbbed with a low-grade headache, and her mind was too tired to even attempt to make sense of what she had agreed to. 'Actually, I've got a headache.'

'Isn't it a bit early in our relationship to be making such excuses?' It was said so tongue in cheek and with such irony that as she caught his glance in the mirror Emma couldn't help but smile. But it faded. 'What *will* your dad say when he finds out?'

'What can he say?' Zarios shrugged.

Instead of the naked figure she had been sure she'd be sleeping with, he had pulled on a pair of black pyjama bottoms—only they did nothing to detract from his beauty. Even in the dimmed bedroom light she could see his reflection in the mirror, his body muscled and gleaming, the pants making him look like some martial arts expert, and just as toned and dangerous. Leaving on her panties, she pulled on a T-shirt and climbed into bed beside him. Turning off the light and rolling on her side, she braced herself for his onslaught—it never came. His breathing settled, and his body just relaxed beside hers as Emma lay twitching and restless, positive that the second she lowered her guard, allowed the heavy drape of sleep that was closing in to wrap around her, then Zarios would surely pounce.

Only he didn't.

The usual shot of adrenaline that had been her bed-

mate since her parents' death catapulted her awake at
4:00 a.m., but instead of sitting bolt upright and grap-
pling for the light switch, having to relive the nightmare all over again as she gulped down a drink of water,
an arm heavy with sleep wrapped around her, sliding her
across the bed in one easy movement. At first Emma
was so stunned she didn't resist, just lay in his arms, her
heart pounding. She was infinitely grateful for the contact, felt the fear seeping out of her as his solid presence
soothed.

'Go back to sleep, Emma.' His low voice growled a
welcome order as an idle hand stroked her hair, and she
wished she could obey—wished she could close her
eyes and desist. Only an unchecked niggle was scratching, reminding her of his distaste when she'd walked
into his office—of his first assumption as to the reason
she was there.

Wandering back into the forest, tentatively she
searched for that arrow he had aimed.

She had *definitely* had her period on the day of the
funeral.

Her body was spooned into his—Zarios's heavy arm
across her waist, his hand loosely dusting her stomach,
like any normal couple in bed. She struggled for a
second against his unwitting affection, but deep in
slumber, too comfortable to move, Zarios gripped her
tighter. Emma stumbled deeper into the wilderness,
locating the arrow and staring at a segment of her shattered heart. Tentatively she probed it.

She'd had her period that day, but it was six… She
screwed her eyes tightly closed as she did the maths. No,
it was eight weeks now since she'd had another.

'Dorme...' Zarios mumbled, pulling her closer towards him. 'Sleep now.'

It was easier to ignore it, easier to cover the remains with leaves rather than probe it with a stick, to just lie in his arms and do as he told her.

Even the lazy tumescence of his manhood that stirred as he dreamed didn't startle Emma. Instead the naturalness of it soothed.

Feeling him asleep but *alive* beside her, it was easy, too easy, to forget what had brought them to this point.

Maybe she was more like Jake than she realised. Because it was easier to forget about her problems than try to solve them—easier to just close her eyes and drift back to sleep, with Zarios there beside her...

CHAPTER EIGHT

DESPITE her mother's theories, even in her art student days wild parties hadn't been a regular feature on Emma's agenda.

But waking in Zarios's arms Emma got a taste of how it must feel to wake after a walk on the wild side. Every sin she had ever committed, and surely a few more to come, seemed to be laughing from the sidelines as she awoke in a strange bed, in the arms of the man she'd sworn away from.

'What time is it?' Zarios grumbled as she stirred awake beside him.

'Are we still engaged?' Emma winced, trying to do up the pieces of the jigsaw without the aid of a picture.

'We are.' His hot breath on the back of her neck somehow told her he was smiling. 'And, yes, you *do* owe me an obscene amount of money.'

As she rolled over to face him she hoped, actually prayed, for a whiff of bad breath, for something horrible and nasty to greet her—but her prayers went unanswered. It was Zarios! Just as gorgeous as yesterday, except he seemed to have grown a beard overnight, morning shadow dense on his strong jaw. The other change in him was that for once he was smiling—this was a far more relaxed Zarios than the one she was used to seeing.

And though sensibly she knew she should recoil, there was this lovely mesh of legs... Such a mesh that Emma didn't know where hers were, though she had a vague idea where his were, because she could feel the bit in the middle as it sort of rose to her groin to say good morning.

'Morning.' His eyes smiled their greeting just inches from hers. And she'd forgotten to notice his mouth—such a lovely soft, full lipped mouth—that was somehow on the same pillow...

'Morning.'

'You talk in your sleep,' Zarios said.

'You snore!' Emma countered.

'I don't.'

He didn't.

'Why are beds so much more comfortable in the morning?' Emma asked, after a few lovely moments of just lying there. 'I mean, you spend half the night trying to get comfortable, but in the morning, when it's time to get up...'

'Don't get up, then,' Zarios said, nudging the duvet up around them with his shoulder and then promptly closing his eyes.

There was a strange fuzzy logic going on in her head—she could feel his tumescent manhood between them, felt so warm and safe lying with him. It would be so easy to accept the lazy kiss she knew was coming, so easy not to deny the fierce attraction that was undoubtedly between them—but at what cost?

The pain of losing him to Miranda had her rolling on her back. Emma stared at the ceiling, hearing the grumble of his sleepy protest. How much easier it would be for him, how much more *pleasant* it would make it for him, to have her on tap these two weeks. And how appalling for her it would be when it ended—to face once more the obstacle course of getting over him!

It was with that in mind that she hauled herself out of bed and headed for the shower.

'How did you sleep?' Rocco asked as Roula poured the coffee.

'Very well!' Emma answered politely, smiling into her cup at Zarios's surly expression. He was clearly rattled that for once his impressive charm hadn't worked.

'So what are your plans today? You are going to get a ring? And then what, Emma? Will you be working, or…?'

'Emma's taking a break from work for a little while…' Zarios answered for her. 'Since her parents' death her painting hasn't been going well. She needs a break.'

'Good!' Rocco nodded. 'What about you, Zarios? You are in Melbourne this week, Singapore the next… You could do some shopping…' He smiled fondly at Emma, but again Zarios had it all worked out.

'We have the ball in Sydney. Emma will be preparing for that.'

'And then the board meets…' Rocco's eyes narrowed just a fraction as he looked over to his son, and for that fleeting moment Emma was sure he had worked their scam out. 'I spoke to your mother last night, Zarios.'

'You called her?' His words were like pistol shots, the ambient mood at the table suddenly plunging. 'Why?'

'Our son is getting engaged—it is right that she is told.'

'She lost her right to be informed thirty years ago.'

Incensed, he stood up. 'Why would you do that? Why would you even *think* to call her?'

'Actually, I didn't call her,' Rocco responded calmly. 'Your mother called me. You know she has been calling for the last few months…'

'Since she found out you were sick!' Zarios sneered. 'Can't you see what she is doing?'

'Is it impossible for you to believe she might regret what happened?'

'Yes,' came Zarios's curt reply.

'She wants to ring you tonight—to congratulate you herself.'

'Tell her not to bother.'

You need to forgive your mother, Zarios.'

'It's rather hard without even an apology from her,' Zarios said, standing up. 'Come,' he called over to Emma as he strode out of the room, 'we have to get going…'

'I thought you were staying the weekend?' Rocco said.

'I'm not staying to watch you being made a fool of—and I have *nothing* to say to your ex-wife!'

Rocco gave Emma a tight smile at the fading sound of Zarios climbing the stairs.

'It must be hard for him.'

'She has never had more children, and she has never settled down. She hates herself for what she did, but she was ill…. *Am* I a fool, Emma?' Sad, tired eyes searched Emma's for an answer she simply couldn't give. 'Am I a fool to believe she might actually be talking to me now because she cares?'

'I've never met her…' Emma said helplessly. 'Only you can answer that, Rocco.'

'You'd better go.' Rocco kissed her on the cheek, as

he always did, then cuddled her for a moment. 'He does need to forgive her, Emma. And not just for my sake—it is not good for him to carry so much hate in his heart. Talk to him…'

Which was an impossible task.

Any closeness that had been captured in the night had long since faded. Zario was driving back into the city as if the devil himself were chasing them, in absolutely no mood for a pep talk. Though she did try!

'He was right to tell her. I mean, if your father does believe we're really engaged, then of course he was right to tell her!'

'I don't give a damn what he told her,' Zarios cursed loudly, his hand lifting off the steering wheel as if he were swatting a fly. 'It is that he is even talking with the *puttana*…' He stared over at her appalled expression. 'You think I should not talk of my mother like that?'

'Yes! And I also think you're being a bit hard on your father.'

'You do, do you?'

They were sitting at traffic lights, Zarios beating a restless tune on the steering wheel, only talking again when the lights turned green and they were moving again.

'My father did what he had to do. There was no work in his village, and he had no family in Australia to help with me. I accept why he left me in Italy. But that woman he calls my mother…' Zarios shook his head. 'She has never been a mother, and it's too late to start now—way too late to start playing happy families just because my father is now sick. If he cannot see she is using him, then I am only too happy to point it out!'

'He deserves to be happy…'

'Emma!' Zarios snapped. 'If you were my *real* fiancée perhaps your opinion would be warranted. Unwelcome,' he added, 'but possibly warranted. But, given that you're not…'

They were pulling up outside The Casino, a valet parker making his way over, and Emma felt herself shrink into the seat.

'Why are we here?'

'To find you a ring,' Zarios answered, watching her closely as he spoke. 'To sort out your clothes and get your hair styled—we can do all that here. Is there a problem?'

Her heart was fluttering in her chest, her eyes wide as she watched the flurry of activity in the foyer. The Casino was a jewel in Melbourne's crown, hugging the Yarra River, and filled with lavish restaurants, designer boutiques and exclusive jewellers. And it was positively the last place Emma wanted to be. On many occasion she'd spent endless hours searching the gaming rooms there for Jake. Despite his alleged clean slate, still deep inside Emma couldn't relax—couldn't help wondering if Jake was here now, creating more debts.

'Do you have a problem being here, Emma?' There was an edge to Zarios's voice that she didn't understand.

'Of course not…' Emma tried to keep her voice light as her car door was opened, but knew she'd failed.

Zarios certainly made heads turn.

As they walked through the humming foyer, Emma could feel the glare of the spotlight his mere presence created. His aura caused people to frown as they tried to place him, or just to take a long, lingering look at a truly impressive specimen of man. Not that Zarios seemed to notice the stir he created. He merely dispatched Emma to a very exclusive beauty salon and had the nerve to tell the beautician what he was hoping she could achieve.

'Can I leave you here, then?'

Emma shot him a withering look. 'Tell me a time to meet you and I'll be there.'

'We will meet here,' Zarios said. 'And if you do finish early, please try and restrain yourself.'

She had no idea what he was talking about—just slipped into a gown while he went off and did whatever it was that people like Zarios did. Emma sat while her straight blonde hair was shot through with layers and caramel foils added. Then, when her hair was deemed suitable, her complexion that had been so ravaged these past weeks, from sleepless nights and too much crying, was given the attention it craved, along with the mammoth task of getting rid of the bags under her eyes.

Gone!

Staring in the mirror, waiting for Zarios, Emma could only marvel. Weeks of pain had been wiped away. Her hair was glossy and shiny, with chunky, angular layers giving it an up-to-date edge. The perfect hair and new make-up gave her a sophisticated air that belied the terrified, grieving child inside.

Zarios didn't comment when he came to collect her—his mood clearly hadn't improved, and neither had Emma's. She felt like a puppy being picked up from the kennel.

Humiliatingly, he paid the bill and then led her downstairs to a very exclusive jeweller, which looked, to Emma's untrained eyes, to be closed.

Zarios pushed on the intercom and growled out his name. It was clearly the abracadabra word, because the thick black glass doors parted.

'Mr D'Amilo…' A suited gentleman greeted them politely, ushering them to waiting chairs. An assistant entered with two glasses of champagne and an arrangement of chocolates, before the serious business of choosing a ring began. Emma hesitantly tried a couple on with the encouragement of the jeweller, as Zarios sat drumming his fingers on his thigh as he did when he was bored.

'They're all beautiful…' Emma gulped. 'What do you think?' Her eyes turned to his, silently pleading with him for some help, but his uninterest was embarrassingly apparent, causing Emma to flush in front of the jeweller.

'Does that one fit?' Zarios pointed to the one she was wearing.

'Don't worry about size—' the jeweller began, but Zarios's mind was already made up.

'I think my fiancée has chosen.'

He didn't even have to hand over his credit card! Zarios, Emma was fast realising, lived in the world of the seriously rich, where no money or signature was either exchanged or required. No doubt an invoice would be sent *somewhere* and dealt with by *somebody*.

As they stepped out Emma could feel tears stinging her eyes. Rather than letting them fall, she sniffed loudly.

'What's wrong?' Zarios said irritably.

'Could you have made it any more obvious in there?' Emma sniffed again, then checked herself.

'Made what obvious?'

'That we're not a couple—that we don't... It doesn't matter.'

'Clearly it does,' Zarios observed, then stopped walking, turning to face her. But they were blocking an aisle, and Zarios moved her out of the current to the entrance of a shop. 'How do you *want* me to be?'

'I'm just saying that in public...'

'Am I not affectionate enough for you?' There was a dangerous glint to his eyes.

'It's not that.' His face was so close she could barely breathe, her thought processes dizzied by his proximity.

'Would you rather I was more demonstrative?'

'No!' Emma shrilled. 'But if we are going to pretend, then at least you could look as if you care...'

'You confuse me, Emma.' His face was coming nearer so she backed away, leaning against the shop window. She was confused herself as to what it was she was saying, what it was that she wanted, but Zarios was rapidly enlightening her! 'You tell me to leave you alone, you dress like a gypsy for bed—and you certainly didn't want my attentions this morning—but now, suddenly, when I am observing your wishes, you accuse me of not being demonstrative enough.'

'We're supposed to be engaged...' Emma swallowed. 'We're supposed to look as if we're in love. Yet you snapped your fingers at me in the hairdressers, you couldn't have been less interested in the choice of ring, and you didn't even hold my hand!' Oh, what was the point? Shaking her head, she went to stalk off—but *now* he caught her hand and held it.

'Is that better?'

'No!' She stared down at their entwined fingers, at the obnoxiously large ring that had been placed there in the name of business only, unable to hold the tears back. 'I'm ashamed enough by what we're doing, even though I have my reasons for doing it…' There was a stoicism about her, despite the tears. 'But I'm not *that* good an actress, Zarios. If my real fiancé ever treated me or spoke to me in that way, I'd walk!'

'Fair enough!' For once it wasn't a flip comment. 'You're right—it does not look good—and for what it's worth, if you were *my* real fiancée, I'd expect you to walk… Hey…' he added as her tears fell further. 'My fiancée crying in the street is not a good look either.' But there was almost a smudge of kindness hidden in his pompous voice.

'They're tears of joy!' The irony of her words actually eked a smile from his haughty face. 'Just don't treat me like a lapdog…' Emma sniffed '…don't embarrass me further than I already am.'

He loosened his grip from her hand and with the pads of his thumbs wiped away the tears on her cheeks so tenderly it almost felt as if he meant it.

'Is that better?'

'Yes.'

'You're sure?' Zarios checked.

'Quite sure.'

'And if I did embarrass you in there…' his mouth lowered to hers, kissing her clamped unmoving mouth slowly and very, very surely as she stood there rigid '…then I was wrong.' He moved his face away just a fraction. 'I will remember to behave better in public next time.'

He was still just as appalling in private, though.

He ignored her request to stop at her flat and grab some things. 'You don't need them—you have nice things now!' Zarios said, pinging open the car boot once they had slid into the forecourt of a luxury five-star hotel.

'Where *are* we?'

'Home.'

She felt like a beggar girl as boxes and bags were hauled out of the boot by the bellboys, and King Cophetua led her by the hand briskly though the lobby, where they were whizzed to the Presidential Suite.

'You *live* here?'

'Sometimes,' Zarios said, dropping his jacket as he did so, and kicking off his shoes as he walked. He stretched out on the settee in the lounge, flicking a remote control. Instead of the television coming on, the drapes lifted to reveal the most stunning view out over the city and beyond to the bay. 'I divide my time between many cities. It makes sense to stay in hotels rather than maintaining several homes.'

Of all the surprises Zarios had thrown at her this was the one, however unwitting, that shocked her the most. Oh, it was luxurious—Emma had never stayed at such an exclusive hotel before, let alone in the Presidential Suite. At every turn it screamed luxury, and as she wandered through, Emma tried to take the details in: the deep sofa, the six-seater oak dining table with a lavish Australian native flower arrangement. The master bedroom was vast, opening into a sparkling marble bathroom, with racks lined with fluffy white towels, two robes hanging on the door just begging for someone to step into them—even soft white slippers patiently waited outside the luxurious two-person shower. Back she wandered, frowning as she realised there was even a small butler's kitchen, and the gnawing disquiet she felt multiplied as Zarios flicked through the room-service menu.

Staring out of the window, she saw Port Phillip Bay stretched like a horseshoe, and her eyes scanned the familiar landmarks that lined it: Brighton Pier, then along to Mentone, and ever on till they came to rest, as they always did, on the gorgeous tip at the end that seemed to be reaching out to embrace Queenscliff. The jagged edge that contained within it her family home.

This wasn't, as first she had thought, Zarios's home within a hotel.

This—despite its luxurious furnishings, despite the impressive artwork that lined the walls—*was* just a hotel room. A room that when Zarios left would be painstakingly prepared for the next well-heeled guest to stay.

Emma's eyes were so thick with tears that she could hardly make out her home now—but even if it was being sold in two weeks, even if her parents had gone way too soon, even if she was indebted to Zarios, still she was richer than he had ever been.

Even if she'd mourn them for ever, at least she'd had a family, and at least she'd had a home.

Which were two luxuries that Zarios had never been afforded.

CHAPTER NINE

'IT's just a dream, Emma.'

By unspoken consent it was the only time he held her. When nightmares crept in, so, too, did his hand, bringing her back to reality and then holding her for the rest of the scary night. It had never been discussed, and for that Emma was grateful. She was just surprised each and every night by just how *nice* he could be when he wanted—by the remarkable tenderness he offered at these times, and the infinite patience he was capable of.

But only at night.

Their first week together had passed in a blur of endless social functions as Melbourne's elite toasted the happy couple. Her days, though, had been long and lonely, while Zarios attacked his formidable workload, leaving Emma to rattle around the Presidential Suite like a marble in a tin.

Stretching in bed now, Emma glanced at the clock, her head pounding after another restless night.

'Morning!'

Emma jumped as she padded through and saw him at the table, dressed and ready for his day, lazily drinking coffee and flicking through his usual mountain of post.

'Sorry.' He grinned at her startled expression. 'Were you hoping I'd already gone?'

'Not at all.' Emma gave him a sweet smile, buttering some toast even though she didn't feel like it, shaking her head as Zarios picked up the coffee pot.

'I'll have tea.'

'Since when?' Zarios frowned. 'You *always* have coffee.'

'We've only been engaged for a week,' Emma pointed out.

'Full of surprises.' Zarios grinned again, but there was a glint to it which she chose to ignore. 'So, what are you doing today?'

'I'm not sure.'

'The tickets have arrived for next Saturday's ball—which reminds me.' Zarios glanced up. 'You need to get something to wear.'

'I have a wardrobe full of new things to wear,' Emma retorted, but Zarios wasn't listening. He just took a rather loud slurp of his coffee, which set Emma's teeth on edge.

'Sorry, darling!' Zarios said, which told her he wasn't. 'That's the awful sort of habit that should only slip in once you're safely married.'

'Which we'll never be!' Emma said, pouring her tea and adding a heaped spoon of sugar. She watched as Zarios ripped up an engagement congratulations card, which she could only assume was from his mother, and carried on with the rest of his mail.

'Oh, I don't know…' He slurped his coffee again, and Emma realised that he was toying with her. '*When* are you paying me back again?'

'Next Monday,' Emma answered coolly—refusing to

rise to whatever bait he was dangling, picking up a newspaper and reading the headlines.

'Good!' Zarios said, watching as she turned the pages, still too new to the game to be bored with the novelty of seeing her name in print. 'What are they saying about us today?' he asked.

'The usual…' Emma rolled her eyes. 'I'm your rebound from Miranda, a decoy for the board…' She scanned the words, more interested really in the picture. But it was the same one again! Zarios, Emma had fast realised, was always two steps ahead—the unexpected tenderness he had displayed outside the jewellers had been captured on film, and though he had denied it when Emma had confronted him, she was quite sure he had manufactured the whole thing just so that he could be photographed wiping away her tears of happiness and, as the paper had reported, sealing the deal with a kiss.

'This is a better picture of you…' Still reading his mail, almost distracted, he handed her another tabloid, neatly folded at an open page. Emma felt her insides turn to liquid. 'I think you're going into The Casino gaming rooms—I thought it must have been before last week, but your hair's already done. There's a small piece about you…' He wasn't *pretending* to be distracted now. He was staring over at her, his face loaded with contempt. 'It mentions that you looked as if you were crying when you came out…'

Zarios wasn't just two steps ahead, Emma realised, he was a whole street in front. This, Emma knew as she scanned the offensive article, was the *real* reason he was joining her for breakfast. She'd gone to The Casino looking for Jake. After numerous failed attempts to get through to him panic had gripped her, and Emma had headed to the one place she knew she might find him.

'I know how this must look…what you must think.' Emma ran a worried hand through her hair. 'But I don't have a problem—'

'Well, I do,' he interrupted darkly. 'I deal in people's money, in their investments, their savings… My fiancée staggering out of the gaming rooms isn't quite the image I'm hoping to portray.' She squirmed at his implication. 'I don't want your excuses, and I don't want your reasons—just know that I will not be shamed. Zarios D'Amilo's fiancée does *not* have a gambling problem— there will be an apology in the newspaper tomorrow. Don't make me call in any more favours again. Do you think you can stay away for one more week?'

When all she managed was a rigid nod, he said, 'Good. Don't think as my wife you will have access to limitless funds to feed your filthy habit.' Picking up his briefcase he turned to go, but thought better of it. 'I'm assuming that *will* be the case? I mean,' he added nastily, 'people don't usually come out of a casino crying when they've won!'

'You're so quick to think the worst…' She didn't have to justify herself to him—didn't have to beg his understanding or forgiveness for a crime she hadn't even committed. 'You're so sure that everyone's out for your precious dollar!'

'Remind us both again—exactly *why* are you here, Emma? Even before we got into this you told me yourself that was the only thing you wanted from me!'

'After you had gone back to *her*!' Tears stung her eyes as she veered towards the truth. 'You slept with me and then went back to *her*, Zarios. What did you *want* me to say? Congratulations? I hope the two of you will be happy—or the three of you, or whatever made you deem it necessary to just walk away?'

'Leave it, Emma…' Zarios warned, but she wasn't listening.

'You hurt me, Zarios, and I said those things to hurt *you*.'

'That morning…' His usually swarthy face was pale, his jaw so quilted with tension she could see the effort it took for him to form words. 'It was never my intention to go back to her. Miranda told me… I found out that she was…' He shook his head hopelessly. 'Leave it, Emma,' he said again.

Oh, but she wouldn't.

'She *was* pregnant?'

'No.'

'Did she have an abortion?' Emma flailed in the dark for an answer. 'Or lose the baby?'

'I've told you!' Zarios roared. 'There was no baby.'

'So it's true, then?' Over and over she'd tried to fathom an excuse for him—told herself that the papers had got it wrong, that the man she happened to love really wasn't that much of a bastard.

Except he was.

'I have every right to say those hateful things.' Through pale strained lips she told him her truth. 'I have every right to hate you—because you threw away what we had for no good reason. And Miranda has every right to hate you, too.'

'Leave her out of it.'

'Just as you did,' Emma spat, 'when she couldn't

provide you with children. Well, guess what, Zarios? You don't deserve them!'

Always Zarios had the last word—always there was a retort or a scathing reply—but not this time. His face was as white as chalk apart from his black angry eyes. He didn't even pick up his briefcase. He just walked towards the door. And if it hadn't been 8:00 a.m.—if she hadn't seen that he had been perfectly lucid just moments earlier—from his stagger Emma would have sworn he had been drinking.

'Zarios!' She called out to him but it was too late. The door had closed behind him without so much as a slam.

Emma was shaking—not just at the venom of her words, but at the effect they had had. She could feel nausea rising, and barely made it to the bathroom in time. Crouching, hugging the bowl, she was more sick than she had ever been in her life. The anger that had been aimed at him was now aimed somehow at herself, at her fury for not being able to accept that he wasn't the man she wanted him to be, was sure he could be.

After rinsing her mouth, Emma made her way back to the lounge, reading again the article that had led them to this row. Heading for the bin, she picked up the card he had tossed away.

The English wasn't great, but Emma was touched at the effort the woman had made.

Emma and Zarios,

It was with happiness I received the good news of your engagement.

Emma, I hope to meet you soon, to share in your joy.

Mamma xxx

What joy?

Emma stared at her luxurious surrounds and realised then that they counted for nothing—the trappings of wealth had done nothing to fade his scars.

Did Bella have any idea what she'd done?

'Well, that was a lot easier.' Blushing and uncomfortable, she attempted a smile as she closed his office door behind her. 'Your assistant didn't even ask me to take a seat.'

'What are you doing here, Emma?' His face was grey now rather than white.

'You forgot your briefcase!' she said brightly, dangling it on her finger. It was a pathetic excuse and they both knew it. 'Damage control, too…' she attempted. 'I thought it might look better if I show my face.'

'My staff knows better than to believe what they read in the newspaper—and, as I said, there will be a retraction and an apology printed tomorrow.'

'Do they work?' Emma sniffed. 'Because if they do, I'd like to try…'

'Let's just leave it.'

'I'm sorry for what I said this morning—about you not deserving children.'

'Can we forget about that, please?'

'Can we?'

'I just did.' He flashed a very on-off smile and Emma would have given anything to go back, anything to have him tease her or goad her—anything rather than this great aching distance that gaped between them.

'I thought we could go for lunch—'

'I have meetings.' Zarios didn't even let her finish. 'Why don't you go shopping…?'

'I don't want to go shopping.' If she sounded pet- ulant, it was from the embarrassment of having him politely refuse the olive branch she was offering.

'You need an outfit for the ball next Saturday. Our company is the major sponsor, and we will both be in the spotlight—it is an important event!'

'So what's the charity?'

'Scusi?'

He often did this, Emma had started to realise. If he was playing for time, his excellent English would curi- ously slip.

'Che cosa è la carità?' Emma said sweetly, in her phrasebook Italian, and Zarios raised an eyebrow. She then asked again. 'What's the ball in aid of?'

'A children's charity…' Zarios answered evasively, but there was just a hint of a smile on the edge of his lips as she played him at his own game. 'I assume. So, when did you start to learn Italian?'

'This morning,' Emma admitted. 'I knew you had no idea what the ball was in aid of.'

'Well, I will graciously concede the point.' He picked up his pen, wordlessly dismissing her, but Emma couldn't let it go.

'I was thinking…' she attempted. 'Tonight, when you get home, maybe instead of going out we could stay in…' She was blushing to her roots, as nervous as a teenager attempting her first flirt. 'We could order some- thing nice from room service…'

'Sounds nice…' she could hear the *but* coming even before he actually uttered it '…but I have to work late.'

'Zarios, I'm trying to say sorry here—'

'Emma, please…' He stood up to conclude their meeting, just as he had done the first time she was there. 'I have to get on.'

The only difference was that this time, when she walked through the foyer, the receptionist didn't call her back.

CHAPTER TEN

HE WAS driving way too fast.

For such a dangerous bend of road, Zarios should be crawling along, but instead he took each curve at break-neck speed, taking his hands off the wheel to fiddle with the radio station. Emma shrank back into the passenger seat, trying to tell herself that he did this every day, that he knew every last turn on the cliff road. She knew that every sharp breath she took just incensed him further, only she couldn't stop herself.

'You drive, then.' Zarios slammed on the brakes so violently that the car screeched to a halt. 'If you think you can do so much better…' He held his hands up in a supremely Latin gesture then climbed out of the car, slamming the door behind him, leaving Emma to take the wheel.

She could do this.

Glancing in the rearview mirror, checking the twins were safely strapped in, Emma gave Harriet and Conner a reassuring smile. 'We'll be there soon.' They didn't answer, just blinked back at her, their eyes huge and trusting.

She could do this, Emma told herself again, then

gently pressed her foot on the accelerator—only Zarios's car was way more powerful than her own, and she might just as well have stood on the pedal, because the car was lurching forward, shooting like a bullet from a gun, and there was nothing she could do. Her foot was jammed on the pedal as they shot over the edge and the salty ocean seemed to rise to claim them. The twins were screaming in terror and there was the sound of a baby crying, too. Emma attempted the same, only her voice was frozen within her, the building scream unable to get out…

'Emma.'

As she sat bolt-upright, dragging in air, she felt his arms wrap around her, his deep voice reassuring her, telling her again, as he had these past nights over and over, that she was safe.

'You're dreaming.' He pulled her back beside him, wrapped himself around her and stroked her arm. 'It's just a dream; you're safe, go back to sleep.'

Except she couldn't.

She hadn't seen him since their strained meeting in his office, hadn't even been aware of him climbing in bed beside her, but she was infinitely grateful that he *was* there. Her body trembled in the darkness as she wished that he would touch her, make love to her, take her away from her desperate thoughts for just a little while. But he'd been as good as his word and hadn't pressured her.

Even if sometimes she wished he would.

'You should see a doctor.' It was the first time they'd discussed her nightmares—the first time he'd done anything other than hold her.

'I don't want to take tablets.'

'Maybe just for a week or two,' Zarios pushed. 'You're pale, you're exhausted—please, just go to the doctor and tell him you're not sleeping.'

'I'll think about it.'

Her heart was slowing down now, her breathing settling, and he lay spooned behind her, held her till he was sure that she was asleep, his fingers coiling and then releasing a strand of her hair. He was resisting the urge to bury his head in it, or to wake her and demand that she stop wasting her life.

It was none of his business, Zarios reminded himself.

Whatever mess she was in—well, it was *hers*. In a little less than a week they would both walk away and never have to see each other again.

It killed him to even think about it.

He held her fragile frame against his, wanted to wrap himself like a shield around her and discount everything he had learnt today.

What had that counsellor on the helpline he had rung said?

That addicts were cunning and manipulative... Zarios's eyes were shuttered for a moment. He found it so easy to discount the brutal summing-up, when he was holding her in his arms.

He had been told that she first had to admit to the problem before Zarios could do anything to help.

'Emma?' She stirred into semi-wakefulness as he rolled onto his side and stared down at her. 'Nothing's ever too big that you can't tell me.'

He smiled as her groggy eyes tried to focus on his.

'If there's something worrying you it's better to face it.'

'I know,' she mumbled.

'And,' Zarios ventured on, 'if I can do anything to help, I will.'

'Even after this morning?' Her sleepy voice begged.

'Especially after this morning. Emma.' He was playing with her hair again, but this time it was her fringe, pushing it out of her eyes, feeling the damp stream of tears on her cheeks. He'd have given anything to lower his head and kiss her—would at that moment have given anything for her...

Which was the reason he didn't.

Pressure from any quarter, according to the counsellor, was the very last thing she needed.

CHAPTER ELEVEN

'No, there's no chance that I'm pregnant.'

Her GP glanced down at her rather obvious engagement ring, then flicked through Emma's notes. 'I see you're not on the pill.'

'There hasn't—I mean, we haven't—' Emma flushed purple. 'Not since Mum and Dad's accident.'

'Which was about eight weeks ago?' Dr Ross checked.

'Nine weeks now.' Emma gulped. 'I had my period on the day of the funeral.'

'And have you had a period since then?'

'No,' Emma admitted. 'But stress can affect that, and I'm not very regular at the best of times…'

'And you're vomiting?'

'Once or twice,' Emma lied, just a little bit. She could feel her stomach churning now, just from the smell of the coffee on his desk. 'But that's not what I'm here for—it's more about the nightmares—'

'Let's just get a sample…' her GP broke off her ream of excuses with a rather more practical suggestion '…and then we'll talk. I don't want to prescribe anything till we've covered all the bases.'

He was certainly thorough, checking her blood pressure and temperature, listening to her chest, feeling her neck, before unscrewing the little jar Emma had wrapped in tissues.

'Insomnia's a very normal part of the grieving process,' he explained—only Emma wasn't really listening. She was staring at the white card he had placed on his desk, at the moment of reckoning nearing. She watched him load the pipette, and the arrow she had for so long buried rustled from the leaves. Emma braced herself to face it. 'Sleeping tablets won't necessarily stop the nightmares,' the doctor went on, as two minutes seemed to drag on for ever. 'Would you like me to refer you to a counsellor? Talking things through might help…'

But it was pointless. Emma knew that. Oh, she had nothing against counselling, but there was no point going and them telling a counsellor only half of what was going on in her life.

'Emma…' The shift in his voice made her look up. He wasn't smiling, his face was emotionless and, Emma realised, it would remain that way until he had gauged her reaction. 'You're pregnant.'

'I can't be.'

'You are.' He pushed the little plastic card towards her—the pink cross on it told her she'd failed this test. But even if the evidence was irrefutable, even if at some level she'd already known that she was, still she tried to deny it.

'But I've *had* my period.'

'If you're sure about your dates, then it was probably breakthrough bleeding…that can happen in the first trimester.' Now he smiled—and it was a gentle smile that was kind. 'You *are* pregnant, Emma.'

'I can't be,' she said again, only in an entirely different context. 'I can't possibly be pregnant now.' Not by a man who didn't love her—a man she owed a small fortune to—a man whom, she was fast starting to realise, she mightn't be able to pay him back…

'Emma, accidents happen.' The doctor cut into her pleadings. 'You need some time to get your head around the idea. Now, I want to arrange some blood tests and an ultrasound, just to check your dates, and then we'll schedule an appointment to work out your options.'

She *had* no options.

She could feel the walls closing in, with every exit route blocked—could see his pen scribbling on pads—could hear him, talking about dates and LMPs and foetal sizes. She felt as if she'd suddenly landed in France, with only a schoolgirl guide to aide her, no accommodation booked and just a handful of coins. Completely and woefully unprepared for the journey.

'We'll get those tests done, and I'll see you in the next couple of days. Once we know your dates…'

She didn't hear anything else. Somehow, on autopilot, Emma paid for her consultation and made a follow-up appointment. Then, clutching her referrals, she stepped out into the bright afternoon and, for how long she wasn't sure, sat in the car, staring at the world rushing by at a million miles an hour as for just a little while hers stood still.

She tried to fathom Zarios's reaction—tried to fathom being bound to a man who would want his heir more than he wanted her.

She tried to fathom her own reaction, but that proved just as elusive.

Oh, she'd miss her mum for ever, but never as much as now. Leaning onto the steering wheel, she sobbed as if Lydia had died that very morning. Weeks of grief were no prelude to the pain that ripped through her now. They'd never see, never know, never hold their grandchild… And then her tears stilled. The sign that she'd begged for, pleaded with God for, had come—in the moment when she'd least expected it.

Loneliness lifted as realisation crept in—this little scrap of life, growing inside her now, had been conceived while her parents had still been alive; had been created on the day they had left this earth.

Surely that was no accident?

Sink or swim.

Despite her near drowning, only today did Emma actually understand the meaning of the saying.

Now, when life seemed to be falling apart, it was time to pull it together. There was no rescuer this time, no strong arms to haul her out of the water—she had to make it to shore by herself.

And she would.

If Jake was gambling again—and his avoidance of her attempts to contact him certainly hinted at that—then he wasn't going to pay her back. She'd have to pay Zarios back herself—and then, when she was no longer indebted to him, she'd work out what to do about the baby.

She'd have nothing. A surge of panic gripped her at the prospect, but she deftly knocked it aside. She'd have her baby.

She had talent.

Somehow they'd survive.

Turning on the ignition, Emma took in a steadying

breath, felt the wheel beneath her hands and the pedals beneath her feet, and for the first time since the accident started to take control.

She told herself, even if she didn't quite believe it yet, that she would be okay.

Because—for her baby's sake—she had to be.

'Jake.' Emma saw her brother freeze as he opened the door.

'Now's not a good time, Em. Beth's having a lie-down.' He looked over her shoulder and down the street, but Emma stood her ground.

'I know Beth's gone out.' Brushing past her brother, she walked into his home uninvited. 'I hear your house is on the market. Beth told me you're looking for something with a bigger garden, nearer the city… Oh, and she mentioned you want to take the twins to America, to Disneyland… Sounds expensive, Jake?'

'Beth's always talking things up.'

'You haven't told her, have you?' His silence said everything. 'Mum and Dad's house sale has gone through, the settlement's on Monday—when exactly *are* you going to tell her, Jake?' She could feel her stomach churning as still he didn't answer. 'Or are you not going to?'

'We need a change—a new start. You have no idea what we've been through…'

Instead of pleading he was angry. Instead of begging he was scolding—just as he always did when his back was to the wall. Emma realised for the first time that he blamed everyone but himself for the mess that he was in.

'You're engaged to Zarios D'Amilo. What do you need more money for?'

'It's a loan…' Emma shouted. 'I'm engaged to him till I pay back the loan…'

'Tell him you can't!' Jake shouted louder. 'He won't even notice it—Zarios can afford it.'

'Well, I can't. I lent it you, Jake, you signed an agreement…'

'So sue me,' Jake scoffed.

'I will!' Emma bluffed. 'And I'm going to tell Beth myself what's going on…'

'I'll never see the twins again if you do.' Jake eyeballed his sister. 'And neither will you—Beth's waiting for an excuse, any excuse, to leave. Go ahead,' Jake challenged.

She could hear the twins scampering up the path, Beth's key in the door.

'Tell her.'

'Tell me what?' Beth half smiled, half frowned as she walked in on them. 'Are you two rowing?'

'I'm just telling my sister—' Jake gave a tight smile '—that it would have been nice if she could have called round to tell us about her engagement, instead of us having to read about it in the papers.'

'Oh, leave her alone, Jake! I spoke to her on the phone—I'm sure Emma's got a million things to be getting on with…'

For the first time Beth was actually smiling, and there was lightness to her that, Emma realised, must have come when she'd finally known her marriage was back on track.

'Anyway, she's here now!' Beth picked up Emma's hand and gazed at the ring. 'It's gorgeous…' Beth wrapped her in a hug. 'It's so nice to have some good news at last. Come on, I'll make you a drink—and then I'll bore you senseless about our trip to Disneyland…'

It was at that moment that Emma realised she'd lost close to a million dollars.

'Where have you been?' Zarios asked, when finally she made it home.

'Don't worry, I haven't been kicking up my heels at The Casino…' Exhaustion seeped out of her as with a sigh she sat on the sofa as far away from him as possible. 'I was at my brother's.'

'I'm not checking up on you…I've been worried. You said you were going to the doctor.'

'Which I did.'

'Am I allowed to ask how it went?'

'He asked if I was stressed…' Emma gave an ironic smile. 'I said that I thought I might be.'

'Did he give you anything to help you sleep?'

'No. I have to have some blood tests…' She bent down to take off her sandals. A lousy liar at the best of times, she hoped her fringe would hide her blush. 'So I'm afraid you're going to have to put up with my carry-on for a little while longer. Sorry if I'm disturbing your rest!' she added as she sat up.

'I'm not worried about my rest,' Zarios bristled. 'I'm actually rather worried about you.'

Zarios was seriously worried, in fact.

And he felt seriously guilty, too!

Watching her fade before his eyes, hearing her crying out in the night, made something unfamiliar twist inside him—something that felt suspiciously like guilt. But he had nothing to be guilty for, he had told himself over and over—they had made a deal and she was being handsomely paid for a few weeks' work.

Staring over at her pale features, seeing that once smiling mouth grim now with tension, her head resting back on the sofa, her eyes half closed in exhaustion, he hated the mess she'd got herself into. But he couldn't, just couldn't, hate the woman. Couldn't not put her out of her misery.

'Emma?' She didn't open her eyes as he spoke, which made it somehow easier. 'I'm not going to force you to marry me…and I'm not going to hound you if you can't pay me back. You have helped me enough. The board are pleased—things are going well there. If we can just hold it together for a little while longer then that's enough. I don't want a loveless marriage any more than you do…' He watched as a tear slid out from under her eyelid, and wished he could reach out and touch her— wished it were the middle of night, when he was allowed to hold her. 'My mother didn't love my father—I have no desire to recreate history.'

He was trying to say the right thing, to do as the counsellor had said and take away as much pressure as possible, so why was she crying? Only he didn't have time to dwell. Taking a deep breath, Zarios said the hardest part. 'I rang up some places today—places that deal with addiction…' Now she did open her eyes, those bright blue eyes that had once danced and held his. They were tortured and confused now. 'When this is over, will you think about going…?'

She shot up from her seat, her head buzzing. Jake's cruel words, the doctor's diagnosis, all were just fading into the distance as she stared at the father of her child—

the man who had just admitted he didn't love her, had never intended to marry her.

'You've got it all worked out, haven't you? Ship me off to rehab, why don't you? Even your father will understand then why you had to end it…'

'Emma, please!'

She didn't want to hear it. He shook his head hopelessly, lifted his hand to wipe away a tear. She brushed it off.

'You have a problem…'

'*Jake's* the one with the problem.' She was through lying for her brother—just through with it now.

'Emma….' Wearily Zarios shook his head. 'When will you stop lying? Your father told me your business was going under, and I saw Jake give you money at the party. I spoke with Jake this evening and he confirmed it.'

'You spoke to Jake?!'

'Emma, I'm trying to *help* you.'

'Well, it doesn't feel like it!'

'This might.' He was angry now—angry at her denial, and hurt, too. This was the only woman he had truly put first—the one woman he had, hand on heart, offered to help. The million dollars didn't matter a jot— it was her refusal to acknowledge her problem that incensed him. 'I am flying to Singapore tonight. Hopefully things will be easier on you if I am not around. I'll meet you in Sydney for the ball on Saturday. If we can keep up appearances for a couple more days it would be appreciated. And then I suggest you read the brochures—and *really* think about getting some help.'

'Do you do it deliberately?' Emma asked, furious at the games he played, at how much he must be enjoying setting his trap and watching his victim squirm. 'Do you lie in bed thinking of ways to goad me, to put me down?'

'No…' Zarios didn't bat an eyelid as he stood up. 'I lie in bed at night thinking of you *getting* down…' He walked over to her and ran a finger along her cheek. He put his hand to the back of her head, his fingers knotting in her hair as he stared into her lying eyes, scarcely able to comprehend how much he adored her. 'I lie in bed thinking of you screaming my name. I lie in bed thinking of your legs wrapped around my head as I make you come so hard you beg me to stop.' He lifted her chin with one finger, raising her burning face to look at him. 'But then I remind myself we don't do that sort of thing, because Emma doesn't want to. Which is a shame…'

He dropped contact then, but she could still feel his hand, wished it were still there, wanted it there, wanted him to push her head down so she could kiss the erection that she knew was there waiting, wanted him to make her scream as he had described. She loathed the dignity that held her back as he picked up his suit carrier and headed out of the door. 'It might take your mind off playing the tables.'

The slamming of the door left her reeling, her body as raw, as inflamed, as if they'd just had sex—hot, desperate sex. She headed for the bathroom, lifted her hair and gulped water from the tap. But it did nothing to douse the fire. The cauldron of living with him—of lying in bed and not touching him—she had thought unbearable. But without him…

She'd thought he was trying to goad her. Now she realised he had actually been trying to help her…

She scanned the brochures, reading about the help he

was offering, and the words seemed to leap off the page.
She realised that with each denial she had, in his eyes,
reinforced that she had a problem. After all, her own
brother had told him as much.

Well, what did she expect? Emma thought with a
snort of scorn.

But Zarios…

The thought of this incredibly proud man acquiring
these, offering to wipe out her debts if only she sought
help… Somewhere inside she felt as if she were being
stroked. Somewhere in her heart she knew she was
glimpsing the real Zarios.

A man who would give anything to help her.

A man who had just admitted how much he wanted her.

A man she wanted, too.

CHAPTER TWELVE

LIVING in fear, Emma realised as she stepped out of the lawyer's office and onto the pavement, was harder than facing it.

Melbourne was delicious this morning, the trees that lined Collins Street giving off a bosky green haze, the heat from the pavement rising through her flimsy sandals, and Emma dipped into a side street café, ordering a large iced chocolate drink and sitting to sip on it, enjoying the simple moment.

Enjoying, for just a little while, the feel in her chest of the absence of fear.

She was doing the right thing.

Oh, any lawyer worth his salt would tell her that, but Emma knew she had been hearing the truth. Knew that, as hard as it might be to execute, the path she had chosen now to follow was the right one.

The only one.

She rolled her eyes at her bleeping phone—Zarios, who hadn't contacted her since he'd left, reminding her that her plane took off at two. As if she didn't already know!

In a few hours she'd see him again.

Only this time with honest eyes.

She would tell him her truth and listen as hopefully he told her his.

'Would you like to see the menu?' a smiling waiter offered, but Emma declined, glancing at her watch and realising she'd better get a move on.

These coming days were without a doubt going to be the biggest, scariest days of her life, but she'd prepared for it. Taking a deep breath, she doused the butterflies that were starting to dance.

It was time to get on with it!

Sydney was much the same as she remembered. The breathtaking view of what was surely the most beautiful harbour in the world matched her mood as the plane glided in.

The roads were as busy, the buildings as big, and the people in as much of a hurry.

And the luxury hotel Zarios was staying in, and where the ball would be held tonight, was as bland and as soulless as his Melbourne home.

She was sick of white bathrobes, Emma thought as she hauled herself out of another sunken bath.

She wanted red, Venetian Red, or Manganese purple—wanted to wrap herself in beach towels that still smelt of the beach and sunscreen, no matter how many times they were laundered!

And for the first time in the longest time she wanted to capture those colours. Wanted to dip her brush in bold primaries—wanted to squeeze out the oiled pigment and craft it into images that breathed and danced into life beneath her fingers.

And she would.

Drying herself with the safe white towel, smiling as her spray tan smeared the bleached cotton, she caught sight of her naked reflection in the vast mirror, for the first time seeing the very real changes that were taking place within her body.

Her breasts were swollen, and the areolae seemed to have doubled in size, and… She frowned down at her stomach. Oh, it was way too early for her to be showing, but there was a softness there, a sort of roundness, that reminded her that this wasn't her secret to keep, that a baby really was growing inside her and that Zarios had every right to know. And somehow, before this weekend was over, she had to find the words to tell him.

Her hands cradled her stomach as she imaged the little life growing in there—filled with love and wonder for the tiny miracle inside her. The fear and grief that had been her companions for so long now were replaced instead by hope—and not just for her baby, but for its parents, too!

She took for ever to get ready. The beautician and hairdresser the hotel had supplied to prepare her did a wondrous job. Tonight she wore her hair piled high on her head, her blue eyes shining bluer thanks to the glittery silver-kissed eyelids that matched her shimmering dress and shoes, while her throat and wrists gleamed with the jewels the sponsor had insisted she wore tonight.

But even when the beautician had gone, even when she stood more groomed and poised than she could ever have imagined, still there was work to be done!

Her shaking hands lit candles, hoping the dimmed lighting would hide her blush, hoping that Zarios wouldn't

roll his eyes at her pathetic attempt at romance and se-
duction.

She placed a hand low on her stomach for reassur-
ance—they had made a baby; there was at least one very
good reason for trying to make this work.

Except as the minutes turned into hours, as the
candles hissed their farewell and drowned in molten
wax, Emma felt more angry than foolish. It had never
entered her head that he mightn't come. Over and
over he had reiterated how important this night was,
but as the hands of the clock crept towards 8:00 p.m.,
Emma realised that Zarios's idea of important differed
widely from hers.

She was tempted not to answer the phone when it rang.

'My flight was delayed.'

'I checked on the Internet.' Emma refused to be lied
to. 'You landed over an hour ago.'

'We did,' Zarios agreed. 'And then unfortunately not
one but two passengers chose to be taken ill, in their
wisdom, and the plane was quarantined until a medical
officer could verify that the cases wasn't related.'

'Oh!'

'Was that a sorry?' Zarios asked.

'No,' Emma said tartly. 'That was a "you could at
least have rung!"'

'I was on another call, trying to appease Tania, the
charity's president…' He grimaced into the phone. 'For
the first time in my life I have a genuine reason for
being late, and no one believes me.'

'That's what an appalling reputation does, I'm afraid.'

He smiled at her tartness. 'Can I ask a favour?'

'No.'

'Can you go ahead without me? I will get changed at the airport as soon as my bags come through…'

'You *are* kidding?'

'No.' Zarios winced. 'There are pre-dinner drinks—Tania said that if you at least can put in an appearance the guests will accept that I am just delayed. I'll be there in half an hour—forty-five minutes at the most.' Pulling out his passport in preparation for Customs, Zarios did a very rare thing. 'Emma, I really am sorry.' He awaited her martyred sigh, frowning when it never came.

Instead came four little words. Only when they were said did he realise how much he'd longed to hear them.

'I missed you, Zarios.'

For the first time since puberty Zarios realised he was blushing. He was standing in the middle of a busy airport and blushing at the sound of her voice, worried he'd misheard, and terrified he might have misinterpreted, but prepared to take the plunge all the same.

'I missed you, too.' He flashed a very male smile at the Customs officer, to show he wasn't really that soft, but, hearing her voice again, he realised that he was.

'Can we talk, Zarios?'

'Please.'

'Properly, I mean.'

'I mean it, too.'

He'd chosen to drive himself to the airport, which with the benefit of hindsight had been stupid. No back of a limousine to dress in. Zarios had to slum it in the first class lounge, cursing like a sailor as he knotted his tie, frantic not that he was late, but to see her.

Every red light chose to greet him. A few Zarios chose to ignore.

Depositing his car, dashing through the foyer, he followed the arrows to the ballroom, consumed with the desire to be beside her. Except everybody wanted a piece of him. Crossing the floor, he felt like a bloody politician as he nodded and waved and stopped to make grating small talk. For now, only from afar could he see her.

She looked stunning. Her hair was blonder, her skin golden, the silver dress she had chosen to wear tonight breathtaking. There was an elusive quality to her that shone even from a distance, and it wasn't just Zarios who could sense it—like moths to a flame she held her audience, and the sound of her laughter was like music to his ears when he finally came up behind her.

She knew he was there—knew even before she felt the heat from his palm on the small of her back—and such was the delight on her face as she turned to greet him that for the first time in his life Zarios felt as if he were home, felt for the first time the simple pleasure of a loving return.

'Ah, my errant fiancé.' Her hand slipped inside his and he held it tightly. 'Glad you finally made it.'

'We hardly noticed you weren't here…' Even Tania, the president of the charity, appeared mollified by Emma's charms. 'Zarios.' She snapped into business mode. 'We ought to head over to the Governor.'

God, but he earned his stripes that night.

Chatting, laughing, drinking, eating—and yet all the while just wanting her, wanting the crowd to thin, resisting the urge to just grab her hand and take her up to their suite. But there was some sweet relief. When the endless dinner was over, when his speech had been executed, finally he could relax. Could wrap his arms around her on the dance floor and hold her again.

As they danced, as he held her as he had that first night, he was catapulted back to when it had been just the two of them, when it was about laughter and fun and fancy, being bound together for no other reason than that was where they wanted to be. So many nights he had wanted to call her, to apologise for his harsh words on leaving, to offer his help again—and he would do that, Zarios decided. Just not now. Not in a room where everyone was watching. For now he would just have to make do with the pleasurable option of holding her.

'If we had met for the first time tonight…' Zarios stared down at her '…if this was our first dance, what would you be thinking?'

'That I wish the night could go on for ever.'

'Anything else?' Zarios asked.

There were so many things she could have said, but in that slice of time there was only one thing she wanted. 'That I wish you would kiss me.'

That he *could* make happen.

Life was, Emma realised as his lips met hers, a series of kisses—some that mattered and some that couldn't be recalled. A mish-mash of hellos and goodbyes, of greeting and farewell, but sometimes, like this time, it was about existing.

This delicious human ritual, the blending of flesh, the sweet poignancy of sharing, was surely the part that mattered the most, which made one human—because only a kiss could truly forgive, and this kiss did that.

One kiss—the sustenance they needed to make it through the night—and then, much, much later, another kiss as they stood in the cool midnight air outside the hotel, waiting for the valet service to retrieve his car.

'Why aren't we going up to your room?' Emma grumbled. All night she had wanted to be alone with him, all night they had been aching to get away, and now that they had, now that their bed awaited, Zarios had moved the carrot.

'Because I want to take you home.'

As the car purred away from the city, through the hilly Sydney streets, she could never have guessed at his nervousness. Gates parted and the car slid into a garage, and as they stepped out Emma found that she was frowning, unsure as to why Zarios had selected a key and opened a front door.

It was the normality of it, Emma realised as she stepped inside. The normality of a key on a ring and Zarios letting himself in had momentarily dazed her—and never more than now, as she walked through the hall and into the lounge.

Oh, there was no doubt it was a luxurious property—the view alone took care of that, the ocean seeming almost touchable from the clifftop vantage point—but it wasn't even that that had her breath catching in her throat. It was the telescope set up beside the window, the low comfortable cushions, a book turned pages-down on the coffee table.

Zarios had been right.

This was a home.

'I don't get here often enough.' Zarios was flicking on lights, shrugging off his jacket, and instead of contemptuously tossing it on the floor for someone else to pick up, he actually hung it—if not on a hanger in the wardrobe, at least over the back of a chair.

'Progress!' Emma commented.

'Sorry?'

'If you keep practising, in a couple of days you might even manage to hang up a towel.'

'I only have someone come in once a week here—to stock up the fridge and keep the place ready for me. If I don't put it away myself…' He actually smiled as it dawned on him she was being sarcastic, and Emma found she was doing the same. Especially when he offered her coffee and actually made it himself.

'The view's stunning.'

The moon was waxing, just a couple of nights away from being full, and it lit up the inky water, catching the surf and highlighting it as it crashed to the beach. Zarios had slid open one of the vast windows, the Pacific Ocean was roaring its tune, and Emma realised that she was nervous. For days she'd waited for this moment, but now that it was actually here she wondered how to approach it—almost yearned for the anonymity of a hotel room, for the vagabond existence she had thought was his. Because here amongst his things, here in his home, Emma felt wrong-footed, embarrassed, almost, at her presumption that there was something she could offer him.

If Zarios wanted a family, then surely he would already have had one?

'Excuse me a moment…' she said, and she dashed to the bathroom.

There was a run in her very sheer stockings and Emma pulled them off. It was a relief to get out of her

Magic Knickers, too, to gulp some water from the tap, and then glance around at his things.

Zarios's things.

No glass bottles, no matter how fancy, filled from the vats belonging to a hotel, but *his* things. Cologne and shaving brushes… Funny that a box of cotton buds could make her smile, or thick brown towels and a book by the bath, which must have been dropped in it at one point because the pages were all wrinkled.

She tried to picture the room with baby lotions and nappies and a bath full of toys, but she couldn't. The heir he seemingly desired was a person in its own right, not a Band Aid to hold two people together.

She wished she could stop the clock, could pause the changes in her body long enough for them to work it out, long enough to establish the couple before the family.

Which was what she wanted to do tonight.

She'd put on weight.

Zarios watched her as she crossed the lounge room. Oh, he knew women too well to comment—knew she wouldn't believe him even if he insisted that he liked what he saw.

And he *did* like it.

Her legs were bare now, and still slender, but there was a roundness to her hips that suited her, and her breasts… Zarios found his tongue was on the roof of his mouth as he saw the swell of them, the sheer silver fabric accentuating swollen nipples.

There were so many reasons for her not to walk over to him—they needed to talk, needed to sort things out— except they needed togetherness more. It was as if some invisible thread were pulling her. The memory of his kiss was still alive on her mouth, and if somehow she could capture that, if somehow they could retrieve the closeness they had once shared, surely then they would be in a better position to sort things out?

Always he was beautiful—that was never in question—only tonight he was exquisitely so. His jacket was off, his tie loosened, his jaw dark, his cheekbones savage in the dim light and his dark eyes quietly watching. She wanted to bound up to him like a crazy puppy, or jump on his knee like a purring kitten, but instead she walked over.

'Come here.' He made the last few steps easy, caught her wrist and pulled her onto his knee. 'Come here so I can never let you go again,' he said. And if it was just about sex, if it was just about lust, why did he hold her for a full moment before kissing her? He pressed his face in her hair, as if her scent was enough, but only for a moment before the tension, the want that had simmered, eternally checked, infinitely controlled, was let loose in one savage motion—the hungry search for each other's mouth.

Greedy, greedy kisses that at first had nothing to do with pleasing the other, just satisfying one's hungry self—tasting, licking, sucking and confirming the other was real. His kisses were so potent, yet so desperate as mouths still entwined, he spun her round on his lap so she was straddling him. There was no choice but to hitch up her dress to accommodate his thighs between hers. His fingers grazed the bare flesh of her upper thighs, and she felt his low moan in her mouth as his fingers slid higher.

'Oh, Emma…' His hands cupped her bottom. 'You should have told me…'

A shocked gurgle of laughter filled her throat that he thought she had been walking around all night with no panties—but why spoil it when she was sliding down his zipper, freeing his delicious erection? She felt almost sick with want. His fingers were working her zipper also, his hands creeping in at the sides of her dress, the pad of his thumb working a nipple—till it wasn't enough, either for her or him. He broke the strap on her dress with mutual consent and then, capturing her breast in his mouth, sucked greedily as she pressed his length against her heat.

He lifted her buttocks the generous inches it would take to accommodate him, his mouth still working her breast, then came the heaven of him entering her. She could see him, sliding deep inside her, and it was the most erotic thing she had ever seen—his endless length teasing her, his hands moving her up and down more slowly than she would have preferred. But even if she was on top, it was Zarios who was in control.

'All the nights I have wanted you…'

'I wanted you, too…'

She was giddy with want, fighting his strong hands, wanting to move faster. But he wouldn't relent, each measured stroke deep inside coveting her, revealing the beauty of gleaming black hair against soft blonde curls. And still, even as she came, still he moved her slowly, wouldn't let her orgasm abate. He just ground her hips down to meet his, over and over again, till her body imploded, till she screamed out his name, till she was coming again. Only then did he let her move with wild abandon as he pulsed deep inside her, taking her closer to the edge than it was surely safe to do, then pulling her back when she was sure she was lost for ever.

'I missed you...' Still his kisses were urgent as he carried her to his bed a mesh of arms and legs, and she lay drunk on a cocktail of sensations. His slow deep kisses breathed life back into her and she kissed him again. It could never be so good with anyone but him. It was as though he could see inside her, could read her as if he *was* her.

'Can we make it?' Black eyes stared down at her. 'Could you forget the hurt, forget the past...?'

'Can you?'

'Yes.'

Oh, but it was too simple an answer—and her resolve to establish *them* before she brought in the rest of world faded with the caress of his eyes.

'Zarios, when I accepted the loan I thought there would be no problem. I mean...' Her mouth was impossibly dry. She was scared to trust him with her brother's secret, but scared not to. Scared not just because of the debt that would go unpaid, but scared for the future—because Jake was hurtling head-first into a pit of no return. Her parents were gone, and when her brother didn't pay her back their relationship would be gone, too. 'I wasn't honest with you when I asked for the loan...'

'It doesn't matter.' He shooed it away. But for Emma it did matter.

'It does...'

'It's money...' he kissed her mouth '...of which I have plenty. Forget about it.'

His mouth was toying with hers, numbing her panic, and when he kissed her like this she could kiss him for ever—because here in his bed, here in his arms, it was about so much more than a debt unpaid.

'I need your help.'

'You have it.' His tongue slid into her lips. 'Tomorrow we will sort out whatever trouble you are in. But tonight…'

Tonight was theirs. Tonight was about making love over and over, about lying in his arms afterwards and glimpsing a future she'd never dared to. A cot in the corner, their baby in bed beside them…

Sweet dreams were her visitors that night.

CHAPTER THIRTEEN

COULD they make it?

Walking in the surf, wearing one of his shirts and a rolled-up pair of his shorts, feeling the whip of water on her ankles, the salty spray on her face, her body deliciously tender from his attention, Emma relished the time alone as she tried to sensibly ask the question.

Yes!

Despite the damning evidence to the contrary, despite the appalling reputation that preceded him, somehow she knew he was better than that. That it wasn't a baby that would be holding them together when she summoned the strength to tell him—instead it was the love they'd shared last night that would bind them.

Climbing onto soft sandstone rocks, she hugged her knees as she gazed out, watched the early-morning swimmers race in the ocean pool, and shivered at the very thought. Yet there was no sight more beautiful than Coogee in the morning. Surfers waiting patiently in the distance for the wave that would carry them to the shore, lone joggers getting their fix of nature before they headed to their offices and computers.

All this she could have.

All this their child could have.

She could almost picture it—a child as blonde as herself or as dark as Zarios, laughing, running…

And Emma stilled.

Only her eyes moved—scanning, processing the colourful scene before her and trying to condense it into a grainy snapshot.

The same snapshot she had seen at Rocco's.

Of the slice of time when Zarios had been happy.

Craning her neck, she stared up at his windows, pondered the demons that haunted him, this most difficult and complicated man.

And vowed that together they'd face them.

The raised voices that greeted her as she pushed open the front door had her hesitating. The thick throaty sobs of a woman crying had every one of her hackles up. Miranda, perhaps—or another ex-lover come to plead for a second chance? All these thoughts whirred through her mind as she walked through the hallway.

All were laid to rest before she even got to the lounge.

Rapid words were being fired in Italian by Zarios.

The throaty sobs of their recipient told Emma they were brutal.

'Per favore…'

She was as beautiful as her son, her black eyes desperate, pleading with him to just listen, but Zarios was having none of it.

'Fuori!' He shooed her away as if she were a gypsy come begging, and when that didn't work, when she grabbed at his arm, he dusted her off as if she were some filthy fly. 'Out!' He bundled her bag in her arms, dismissing her so absolutely that Emma felt her blood run cold.

'Zarios…' She was torn, wanting to go after his mother but desperate to talk sense to him. 'She's your *mother*!'

'Mother?' He spat the word out. '*Puttana*, more like. Now she is back—now, when my father is near his grave, she decides she loves him, decides she made a mistake. It is thirty years too late…'

'For who?' Emma pleaded. 'It's not too late for your father—he never stopped loving her.'

'Then he's a fool!' Zarios snarled. 'All she wants is his money. It's all *any* of you want—' He stopped talking then, halted himself mid-sentence. But it was too late, the words were already out, his poison free. And she tasted it, glimpsed a future that was only as good as his most recent apology.

'I'll pay you back.' Oh, she would—she'd rather lose everything to Jake than be indebted to Zarios. 'On Monday you'll get every cent back.'

'Don't bother.' He stared right at her as he flung the final knife. 'We agreed that if I was unfaithful then you didn't owe me anything.' It hit her right between the eyes—the pain, the humiliation, all repeated—and she hated, loathed herself that she had let him do it to her again.

'You bastard.'

'Nothing's changed, then.' Zarios gave her a black smile. 'Go on—off you go…'

'Just like that.' She couldn't believe the callousness of him—that after all they'd shared last night he could so easily eradicate her, could loathe her so readily when so recently he'd adored her. 'Zarios, what about your father? The board?'

'I don't care!' Zarios roared. 'I don't care what they think any more. *I* am the one who made them rich—I am the one who lined their greedy palms. If they think they are better off without me then let them try.'

'You don't care about anyone.' She was scooping her stuff into a handbag, desperate to just get the hell out. 'You're so busy looking for the worst in people—'

'Where's the good?' Zarios interrupted. 'Tell me, where *is* the good?'

'I loved you!' Words that should had been said gently were instead hurled. 'I loved you right from that first night—but finally you've succeeded in convincing me that I was a fool.'

But fools still had feelings, fools still glimpsed paradise—and last night she had.

And she'd have given anything to reclaim it.

'I'm pregnant, Zarios.' She was trembling, shaking as she said it—hoping, praying, the words would slam some sense into him, would halt the row long enough so that they could at least talk. But he was unreachable.

For Zarios it was as if he were staring at Miranda, as if he were having his skull split with an axe. He had braced himself to be felled two weeks ago—he had never expected it today. Her last frantic attempts to salvage the situation made him sick to the stomach. So sick, he couldn't even look at her, struggling to even utter a single word.

'So?'

It was the cruellest of responses, and on behalf of their child she hated him for it. Yet there was a quiet dignity to her as she countered his poison.

'I'm letting you know just so you can't say I didn't tell you.'

'Put it in a letter from your lawyer.' Zarios shrugged. 'That's it?'

'Send me the bill…' Zarios jeered. 'But for now—get the hell out. You make me sick, just looking at you.'

He even had the gall to offer her his driver, but pale, nauseous, she declined, unable to even look at him, too numb even to be stunned at his sheer callousness.

'It's okay…'

She must have looked like a madwoman—dressed in his clothes, with bare feet and a sparkly handbag, and talking to herself.

Except she wasn't talking to herself. She was talking to their child.

Her child.

'We're going to be just fine, little one.'

Waving down a taxi, Emma asked to be taken to the hotel, then told the driver to wait as she grabbed her things, then headed to the airport.

It was *her* baby now, and Zarios could take her to court to prove otherwise.

He'd have to fight for the right to call it his now—he'd lost that privilege an hour ago.

CHAPTER FOURTEEN

'DOVE?' Incensed, furious, Rocco pounced on his son, demanding to know where he'd been. Thoroughly untogether, and reeking of brandy fumes, Zarios was present if not correct for the board meeting on Monday morning. *'Dove siete stato?'*

'Enjoying the fruits of my labour.' Zarios stared at his father. 'I work hard, so I play hard.'

'The paper says your engagement is over—'

'You believe the papers?' Zarios shrugged.

'You were to behave!' Rocco roared. 'All I asked was that for a couple of months you pulled your head in—instead you shame me. Engaged one minute, broken off the next—and what about Emma?'

'You were the one who warned me off her!' Zarios pointed out.

But Rocco refused to back down. He was so incensed he could hardly get the words out. 'Because I knew what you'd do! And now—now when my life's work is to be decided—you arrive *ubriaco*—'

'I am not drunk,' Zarios interrupted. 'I wish I *were* drunk—it would be easier to face those buffoons. Instead I will do it with a hangover! *You* should be the one doing this—you should be reminding them that *you* built this company, that this has been your life, this is what you chose over raising your child. And yet you let them walk all over you.'

'I will not be here soon. I am trying to make sure they accept you as their leader—that things—'

'Lead, then!' Zarios said. 'Lead me into the boardroom now and they can make their choice. But I will tell them what I am now telling you—I will *never* serve to appease!'

The blinds hadn't even been opened in the boardroom. Unshaven, dishevelled, and with bags under his eyes so heavy they looked like bruises, Zarios faced those who considered themselves his peers and smiled darkly at them.

'My father founded this company forty years ago—here in Melbourne. Now it is multinational, now it is a world leader—and now, when my father is due to retire, you question whether its name should remain D'Amilo. Now you question the leadership of the family that has enriched your lifestyle. There is no question.'

Zarios snapped open the blinds, drenching the boardroom in sunlight, and, despite his dishevelled state, somehow he was the most dignified of all of them.

'With the massive returns last year, while you were adding to your retirement fund or purchasing your beachside home, I, too, was securing my future.' He jabbed a finger at the office block beyond. 'In every D'Amilo boardroom around the world, if you look out of the window the view will be the same: I have secured prime office space in every city where this company trades, and I am telling you now that I can and I will take my family name and start again. And I will succeed—

because that is what the D'Amilo name means.' He eye-balled every one of his colleagues. 'You are either be-hind me one hundred percent, or you can sit at your desks and wave to me from this window.'

He didn't even wait for their response—just stalked out of the boardroom and back to his luxurious office, telling his assistant he was not to be disturbed under any circum-stances. Flicking off the lights, he lay on his leather sofa and tried to turn off his thoughts, tried not to go down *that* path. But at every turn the map led the same way, her face was the only thing he could picture. The only solace was sleep—at least in his dreams she was laughing.

'They are behind you.'

'Of course they are.' Zarios had shaved and changed, his hair was gleaming. He was utterly together.

'You are right.' For the first time ever Rocco praised his son. 'I am proud of you.'

'I will not let your company down.' Zarios accepted his compliment with backhanded grace. 'I may let my-self down at times, but it will never translate to our shareholders.'

'Your mother is coming back to me.'

As Zarios opened his mouth to tell his father exactly what he thought of that decision the older man got there first.

'Thirty years later in life than you, my son, I have worked out that I don't care what others think any more. Just as you will not appease them—I will not appease you. I love your mother. I have missed her for half of my life…'

'Can't you see she is just back now you are ill—now there is money?'

'Perhaps...' Rocco shrugged—the same shrug he had inadvertently handed down to his son. 'But is it better to die cold and alone in bed with your pride intact, or warm and caressed and believing that love exists?'

'What if she *is* using you, Pa?' They both knew Zarios wasn't talking about his mother as for the first time he begged his father's advice. 'What if you *know* she is trouble? What if you *know*?'

'Then you ask yourself if the good outweighs the bad.'

Oh, and it did. Closing his eyes, Zarios recalled Emma's scent, the sound of her laughter, and knew that he would lie for a week in the gutter with banshees wailing over him if it meant he could spend one night by her side.

'People don't have to be perfect for us to love them,' Rocco said. 'Emma is proof of that.'

'Emma?' Zarios frowned; they were supposed to be talking about *him*.

'You're the buffoon.' Rocco smiled. 'When will you get it in your head that Emma loves you?'

He would tell her.

Sitting at his desk, Zarios rested his head in his hands, his fingers bunching in his cropped hair as he prepared himself for the hardest task—to trust her, to forgive her, to tell her he was sorry.

He didn't care about the money, and he could help her with her problems—because what they had found, what they had shared, albeit briefly, was priceless.

'Zarios!' Jake knocked on his office door, his smile wide. 'Have you seen Beth or Emma? We were supposed to be meeting in the coffee bar opposite before coming to sign all the papers and tidy everything up.'

'Not yet…' Zarios dragged himself from his introspection and forced a smile, then glanced at his watch. 'There's still a while yet.'

'I can't get hold of Beth, that's all—maybe she's having trouble with the babysitter.'

'Maybe.' Zarios shrugged, because talk of babysitters and the like was a foreign language to him. 'Jake, I wanted to talk to you. When I rang you the other day about Emma—'

'Actually—' Jake gave a tiny grimace '—when we discussed Emma's problem—well, I didn't feel comfortable anyway. But given you were practically family…' He dropped the apologetic smile. 'And now you're not.'

'I still have your sister's best interests at heart.'

'Really?' Jake frowned in distaste. 'I think it would be better for everyone if you kept your distance.'

Which made sense, Zarios told himself. After all, Jake was just looking out for his sister—but he hadn't seemed too concerned moments before.

An uneasy feeling was building inside Zarios. Emma had said Jake was the one with the problem, and he'd dismissed it as her being in denial. Jake with the beaming smile and gleaming shoes. Jake with his fancy car and nice city lifestyle.

Jake with the depressed wife and out-of-control twins.

Damn.

His mind was racing, he was dialling her number, leaving rambling messages on her message bank. He attempted to filter their every conversation, trying to discard, dismiss, verify, trying to assimilate the facts…

Charging out of his office, he was just in time to

glimpse the meeting room door close, Zarios rueing the fact he'd removed himself from the management of their parents' estate. Pacing the floor like a caged animal, he wanted to be in there, wanted to be on the other side of the door, sitting beside Emma.

Emma halted her own pacing for a second and stared at her bleeping phone. There had been several frantic messages from Jake, asking where she was, and now Zarios had joined in—ringing her, texting her. Well, they'd all know soon enough.

'Thanks for coming…' Emma felt like the biggest bitch in the world as she let Beth into her tiny flat. 'Where are the twins?'

'I'm having them looked after today.' Shy, evasive, Beth declined a drink and then perched on the edge of Emma's sofa. 'You know, don't you?'

'Know?'

'That I'm leaving him today.'

Emma felt the thud as the rest of her world crashed.

'I'm not after his money.' Beth shook her head. 'He can have it—he can go throw it up the wall or put it on black—I just don't care any more…'

And Emma saw it then. If *she* had danced on the edge of Jake's addiction then Beth had lived in the full clutch of it. Here was a woman who was ready to walk away with nothing more than the clothes she was wearing and her babies—who deserved so much more.

'I love your brother…' Her tired, puffy eyes met Emma's. 'But as much as I love him I hate him. I know there isn't a good time to leave. I've tried…' great sobs heaved at her body '…but there was always something to get past first—the twins' birthday, Christmas, your dad's sixtieth, your parents' funeral—I keep waiting for the moment to be right. And it's not coming. Today,' she sobbed, 'he gets a million dollars. Please, God, today I can go…'

There was nothing she couldn't tell this woman, Emma realised as she put her arms around tired, weary shoulders—nothing she could say that would hurt her more than she already was.

'I know.' She felt tension, denial in her sister-in-law's shoulders. 'I know how hard this has been on you, and I'll do what I can for you and the twins. Beth…' She felt the mingling of grief and relief flood through her sister-in-law as she offered her support. 'I know about his habit. I've lent him my share of the inheritance…'

'More fool you, then.' Beth's voice was bitter, but Emma knew it wasn't aimed at her. 'You know you won't get it back?'

'I've hired a lawyer.' Emma's voice was shaking as she admitted to her sister-in-law what she had done. 'He's representing me today—Jake's just about to find out.'

As Jake marched out, his face like thunder, Zarios knew his hunch had been right. The nice-guy act had vanished and, not even acknowledging Zarios, he brushed past, banging his hand on the lift button, impatience in every cell. He finally gave in and took the stairs.

'You did the right thing!' Jed, one of the directors, rolled his eyes as the exit door slammed. 'Removing yourself—I don't think I've ever seen a nastier hand-over of assets.'

But Zarios wasn't listening. His eyes were looking over his colleagues' shoulder as the members of the meeting tripped out, desperate to see her, to offer his late support.

'Where's Emma?'

'She sent a lawyer on her behalf. The transaction went ahead, and then Jake was served with notice. She's suing him for the money he owes her, and all his assets have been frozen. He owes money everywhere.' Jed's lips were grim. 'Can't help but feel sorry for him, really. Not only did his pay-day not come, he's just found out that his wife's left him, too.'

Zarios could feel the blood pounding in his temples as realisation struck. The problem he had brushed aside when she'd tried to tell him, so sure had he been that the debt had been hers, had been her trying to help her brother. Ice seemed to be running through his veins and yet he was sweating, Zarios realised, as he recalled Jake's murderous expression as he left the office.

A man at rock bottom was a dangerous one.

'It's not his fault, of course…' Irony laced Jed's words. 'We're trying to contact the wife to warn her…'

But he was speaking to an empty space. Zarios was two steps ahead, jumping into the lift that had appeared, desperate to get to Emma—to warn her, to tell her, to protect her.

He could taste bile in his throat, the bitter, acrid taste of fear, and it was swirling in his stomach and rising as full realisation hit.

She had been telling the truth—and not just about her brother.

He ground the gears on his car as he wove through

clogged, grid-locked traffic, his mind frantic. He had to get there!

Zarios gave up on the car, depositing it in the middle of the street as angry commuters furiously sat on their horns. But he was running so fast, the blood so loud in his temples, he didn't even hear them. He had to get there—to protect not just the woman he loved, but the mother of his child.

'Open the door!' Emma could hear the door being pounded. 'You bitch, Emma. Open the door!'

'You didn't lock it…' Beth's eyes were frantic as her husband demanded to be let in.

'Go and hide in the bedroom,' Emma urged. 'I'll go.' Creeping down the steps, ready to turn the lock, she wasn't scared. She knew in her heart of hearts that Jake wouldn't hurt her, that he was angry, raging, but would never hurt her.

And then she missed a step.

The fall happened as the door flew open, and piercing pain shot through her before she even hit the ground. The anger in her brother's eyes faded into terror as he stared down at her.

There was the strangest sense of déjà vu as she awoke.

Zarios was sitting in the chair beside her bed, and her body was racked with a piercing sense of loss that she dared not explore.

'You're okay…' In a second he was beside her.

'The baby…' Her hands moved to her stomach, trying to fathom change.

'We'll know soon.'

His hot hand found hers as her lips and eyes moved downwards in a spasm of pain at the helplessness of it all. Her face crumpled as she remembered what had happened.

'Jake?'

'Don't worry about Jake.'

'Oh, but I do…'

'I know.'

'He didn't hit me.'

'I know,' Zarios said again.

'He wouldn't have—'

'Yes, Emma, he *would* have,' Zarios cut in then, clutching her hand gently as he made her face the unpalatable truth. 'He's already pushed Beth, and he *would* have hit you. That's what terrified him the most—the things that made him finally admit he had to get help. When he realised that he could have hit a pregnant woman—could have been responsible for the loss of your baby… You fell trying to lock your door on him. You have to stop making excuses for him, Emma.'

'He's my brother.'

'I never said you had to stop loving him.'

He was right. That much she had already decided for herself. Talking to the lawyer, choosing to take back control, to refuse to be manipulated, to own what was hers…none of it meant that she didn't love him.

'Where is he?'

'At a clinic.'

Zarios held her hand as if he was imparting bad news, but all Emma could feel was the flood of relief, and years of anxiety, of worry, of fear, lifted as Zarios uttered the words she had fought against yet longed to hear.

'It's for three months minimum—he agreed to go.'

'Rehab?'

'He will get rehab eventually, but for now they are dealing with his depression. Then he will get all the help he so desperately needs. It's a top centre. I have guaranteed...' He didn't finish. Somehow they both knew that it didn't matter—that this wasn't and never had been nor could be about money.

'How's Beth?'

'Beth is at my home in Sydney with her mother and the twins. She wanted to stay to see that you were well, but I wanted her out of the way while I dealt with Jake. She is very tired and she needs to rest. She has carried so much...'

'The baby...' she said again. She cared about Beth, but she cared about her baby more. Not a single thing could hold her attention till she knew the answer.

'Don't distress yourself.' He attempted to soothe her. 'You must rest. The doctor says you must not get upset. You'll be having an ultrasound soon, and we'll find out how our—'

She turned her head to face him. '*Our?* How come it's *our* baby suddenly?'

'I'm sorry, Emma. Sorry for not believing you...sorry for the terrible things I said. Sorry for the stupidity that made me nearly lose you both. When I saw Jake charging off for the first time in my life I tasted fear. I realised that I loved you.'

'No.' She shook her head on the pillow. 'I don't want to hear you say that you love me. Now, when you find out that I have been telling the truth, that I *am* having a baby, that I'm actually a decent person, you suddenly decide that you've loved me all along.'

'No!'

He had always been brutal in his honesty, so why, Emma reasoned, should she expect any less now?

'I have been doing my level best not to trust you and certainly to never love you—I didn't admit it to myself till today at one-forty-two p.m. For the first time in my life I listened to my father, and I realised that maybe being in love with a compulsive gambler, a self-confessed gold-digger, who had *told* me that she only wanted me for what I could give her, maybe wouldn't be so bad if at the end of each and every day I got to hold her.'

'I can never trust you.' Emma shook her head at the hopelessness of it.

It was too late.

'Never?' Zarios checked, and resolutely she nodded. 'Even if I told you that since that morning on the beach, since the first time we made love, I have not slept with another woman?'

'Please!' Emma managed a thin laugh.

'We'll need you to excuse us now!' A bossy, old-school nurse popped her head around the door.

She was the first woman Zarios had met who was impervious to his charms—because very clearly she told him that, no, he couldn't have five more minutes, that Ms Hayes was due in ultrasound soon, and after that needed her rest.

'Maybe just till the porter arrives?' It was Emma who asked—Emma who was told that she had two minutes, and that if she needed anything—the elderly nurse shot Zarios a venomous look—she was to ring the bell.

'You went back to Miranda—do you really expect me to believe you didn't sleep with her?'

'When I left you that morning I was fully intending to begin a relationship with you. I couldn't wait for the christening to be over so that I could call you. Miranda was waiting for me, though. She told me she was pregnant…' He frowned, as if just realising how very careless they had been that day. 'Until that morning with you I had always been careful, but I knew these things happened…'

'I thought she couldn't have children?'

'I don't know if she can…'

His voice was a whisper, a croak, his words confusing her. She opened her mouth to argue, to tell him she was tired of his lies, but she recoiled at what she saw. Zarios, who was always so together, always so ahead of the game, looked utterly destroyed. Grief was stamped on his face, and his mouth opening on words that wouldn't come out.

As the porter swished into the room with the trolley that would take her for the ultrasound it was Emma who asked again for one more moment—Emma who just didn't *get* what he was trying to say.

The door closed, and Emma knew that she had to listen without interruption. She wanted to rattle him, to shake him, for him to just *tell* her—except she had never seen a face so haunted with pain, and knew she couldn't rush him now.

'I was stunned…' Zarios shook his head as he relived it. 'I was thinking of you—of seeing you again on Monday—and suddenly Miranda was telling me she was pregnant, and that we must keep it quiet as she had some big work coming up. I was disappointed for you and me—for us.' His black eyes met hers. 'But I told myself that it had been one day, one night… I could not weigh that against a baby.'

She nodded—because that much she *could* get. 'Did you feel trapped?'

'No.' Zarios's answer seemed to surprise him as much as it did her. 'Emma, my mother left us because *she* felt trapped—she felt she was not a good enough mother and that I was better off without her. No matter her reasons, she was wrong. A poor parent is still that child's parent. I always promised myself that I would never do to my child what was done to me. I had never considered having a baby, yet when the idea presented itself I was happy. I was determined to do my best, to build a home… I fell in love with that baby within a minute of Miranda telling me.

'But we did not sleep together. I was still unsure— not about the baby, but about her. I told her I was worried that sex might affect the baby—a stupid excuse. She flew to Brazil for her photo-shoot and I joined her. But she wasn't taking care of herself. I arrived unannounced. She was drinking and smoking when I got there, taking laxatives—all the stuff she did to stay thin, all the stuff that drove me crazy when we were together. We argued.'

'I can see why,' Emma admitted.

'She accused me of being old-fashioned, of trying to police her…which I guess I was. When we came back to Melbourne I asked her to come here, where I have now brought you, to see the top specialist. She insisted on seeing her own doctor. She kept on trying to sleep with me, but I was angry. I wanted to be sure that the baby was okay. And then—' He started to run his hand through his hair then stopped, screwing his fingers so tightly together it must surely have hurt. 'I had never seen a scan—she had never let me come with her to the doctor. Finally, after an argument, she agreed to come here. I drove her and she kept the lie going right to the receptionist's desk.' His eyes were two deep pools of pain. 'There never was a baby. It was to get us back together. She was hoping she would quickly fall pregnant…'

'She never even was…?' Emma couldn't keep the shock from her voice.

'Which meant there was nothing to be upset about— nothing to grieve. Because it had never existed. Nothing had been lost. I was just a fool who for a little while had believed…'

'You're not a fool, Zarios.'

'I *loved* that baby.'

It was hard for men—that much Emma could see. Her body was a melting pot of hormones, of changes not yet visible, but her pregnancy was real just the same. All Zarios had had was Miranda's word—a word he had believed. And just as Emma loved her baby, just as she would move the world to make it right for the little life inside her, he had loved his, too.

Even if it had never existed.

'I'm sorry.' It wasn't her mistake, it wasn't her lie, but she truly *was* sorry. 'It must have been hell.'

'I found out there was no baby the week before you came to see me at my office to ask me for money. And when you told me that *you* were pregnant…' Zarios closed his eyes '…it felt as if it was happening again.'

'This one's real!' She tried to smile, tried to be brave— but what if she was wrong? What if it was already too late?

'I know.' He held her hand. 'And, whatever the outcome, this little one is loved.'

There was no delaying the porter this time. Emma climbed over onto the trolley, trying to fathom the mind of a woman who would lie like that—and trying to fathom Zarios's pain at being told that the little life wasn't just over, but had never even existed in the first place.

'Can he come with me?'

The bossy nurse was actually very kind. 'What do *you* want, Ms Hayes? Of course it's in all the papers that your relationship is over—and I don't want any of my patients feeling pressured...'

'I think I'd like him to come with me.' Emma swallowed, terrified of the outcome, but knowing now that Zarios was just as scared, too.

'Just some cold jelly on your stomach.'

It was routine to the sonographor. Oh, she was kind, but she was efficient and just a little bit distant—maybe she had to be? Emma thought. Having to regularly face parents whose dreams had been dashed.

'I want this baby,' Emma said, because it was imperative that she voiced it, that this little scrap inside her knew that it was wanted and loved.

'I know.' Zarios's hand was over hers.

'Do you want me to turn the screen away?' the sonographor offered, but Emma shook her head, feeling the probe move over her stomach, watching great black and white shapes swoop and swirl on the screen, clouds dashing in and out of focus, like travelling at speed through a tunnel.

And suddenly there it was….

Floating in its little universe, safe and unperturbed by the drama that had taken place, its whole chest a heartbeat that pumped and moved, their baby swung as if on some invisible trapeze, whooping and wriggling and very much alive.

'About ten and a half weeks…' the sonographor said, clicking away. 'Too early to tell the sex at this stage.'

'It doesn't matter.' Zarios spoke when Emma couldn't.

'I'll print off some photos.'

Those were the sweetest words she had ever heard.

Rest and more rest were the doctor's orders.

A slightly irritable uterus, a bruised lower back and an emotionally exhausted mother—there was nothing else he could prescribe.

Sitting in Zarios's car, pale, shaken, clutching her photo, Emma stared at a world that seemed just a bit brighter somehow. All the dirty secrets were out in the open now, and the world was a better place for it.

Jake was getting the help he needed and her baby was alive.

Closing her eyes, she rested against the passenger window, locked in a twilight world between waking and sleep, vaguely aware that the car-ride was taking ages, but too sleepy to question why.

She was imagining herself on the beach road, but in control now—her parents were riding safely along with her, no crumbling cliffs or murky waters, just the shriek of gulls and the delicious salty fragrance of her home…

The car door opened.

'We're here.'

She blinked, seeing her home, her family home, for the first time since the funeral.

And she wasn't so much in shock as he helped her up the stairs and into her familiar bedroom as simply at peace. There were no more questions.

The answers could wait till later.

She could hear banging, but she ignored it. Later— ages later—she was woken with grapefruit juice and toast by an unshaven, tatty-jeaned, strangely calm playboy, who stretched out on her single bed, watching her from its foot, his head on his hands, smiling as he watched her eat.

'You look better.'

'Thank you, Doctor.'

'You do.' He smiled over to her. 'However, I have taken an executive decision and told my parents that you are not up to receiving visitors just yet.'

She didn't say anything—scared she'd misheard, scared she might rush in on what was such a sensitive area—but Zarios was still smiling, a lovely self-mocking smile that quenched her thirst as much as the grapefruit juice did.

'At thirty-four years of age I now have a mother who thinks she can tell me what I should be doing—I am to feed you soup, apparently.'

'Sounds nice.'

'And we are not to have sex till the baby is here.'

'We'll listen to a doctor on that one.' Emma smiled.

'And I am to "communicate better", she has told me. Something apparently my father failed to do.'

'I'm beginning to like her.' Emma's smile faded;

suddenly she was serious. 'When did you buy my house, Zarios?'

'I put an offer in two days after the funeral.'

'You were with Miranda then.'

'I know.'

'Did you tell her?'

He shook his head. 'I cannot justify or even explain why I did it. I knew it would be tearing you up, having to go through things. I thought if I could just buy it as it was, maybe at some stage… I don't know…'

'You shouldn't have…' Emma gulped. 'On so many levels, you shouldn't have.'

'Don't make me feel guilty for not being open with Miranda—just know that it would never be the same with you. I tried so many times to close the door in my heart to you, and it kept springing open. I wanted to dislike you, to use you as I thought you were using me… Yet I couldn't.'

He was playing with her feet, which she'd always hated. In fact she couldn't imagine letting another person massage her soles or toy with her toes. But she let him.

'I want to see you happy, Emma.'

'I want to see you happy, too.'

'I *am* happy…now that I know you are okay.'

'So the board's decision went your way?'

'Naturally…' He smiled—a different smile, though, a smile she had never seen before, one that made her want to smile, too.

'What?'

'When you are ready to read the newspaper, you will find out that "in a surprising move", I, Zarios D'Amilo—' he spoke in the deadpan voice of a news reporter '—have declined the board's unanimous offer, choosing instead to amalgamate with associates so that I can spend more time with my family. That's you, by the way,' he added in his own voice. 'Just in case you hadn't worked it out. I know it is too soon now for you to be happy—that you haven't had a chance to mourn your parents and that these last months have been hell—but one day I am going to make you happy…'

Tears slid down her face. Only this time she didn't sniff them back. This time she just let them run un-checked, a salty catharsis showing that she didn't have to go it alone any more.

'I just miss them.'

'Of course.'

'I'm glad they never found out about Jake. I'm glad they died thinking he was doing okay. But I wish—I just wish they had lived to find out about *me*. That I'd had more time to make them proud. They'd have been so proud now. Not…' she gulped '…because of how rich you are. I know what I said, what my mother said…'

'They wanted you to be happy, to be secure, and now you are.'

'They don't know that, though. They don't know about the baby, about—'

'Hey.' Now he halted her tears. 'Do you think this is an accident?' His hand crept up to her stomach. 'Can you not see that this is their gift—their way of letting you know that they're okay? Of *course* they know.'

Oh, she wanted to believe that—so badly she wanted to.

'Come here.' He helped her out of bed, and on legs as wobbly as a foal's she was led to her parents' room. 'Look.'

She hadn't been in her parents' bedroom since before they had died, but there, above the balcony doors, was her painting.

'They put it up?' Emma blinked.

'They did,' Zarios lied, hoping she wouldn't notice the edge of the hammer sticking out from under the bed. If she did, he decided then he'd make something up.

It was a good lie—a white lie—and anything was admissible if it made her happy, gave her peace.

'Look closely, Emma.'

And she did.

Looked at the one piece of work in which she'd drawn faces. Her mum and dad, smiling, walking hand in hand along the beach. A laughing couple with a little girl and boy, running ahead. She'd known even as she'd drawn them it was Beth, Jake and the twins.

'How does this help?' She stared at the images her mind had created, and all it did was tear her apart. Every landmark she had known was gone for ever now. 'Beth and Jake are finished.'

'I would have thought so, too; yet she has rung me several times to enquire about him—where he is going, what his treatment will be.'

'It's too big to forgive…'

'I forgave you,' Zarios gently reminded her. 'Not that I needed to, as it turned out, but I *had* worked out that it was easier to forgive you than to lose you. Now, look closer, Emma.'

She frowned, scanning the picture, the surfers and the lady jogging, and the dog swimming in the ocean. Sometimes she hardly recognised her own handiwork, as if she disappeared into another dimension when she worked.

'Look!' Zarios pointed to a couple who were walking, the blonde lady smiling, the tall dark man beside her carrying a little girl on his shoulders, her dark curls dancing. 'That's us.'

'It's just a couple...' Emma protested, but Zarios was adamant.

Pushing her gently down on her parents' bed he held her in his arms as she stared at the picture she had painted—whether it was an image from her mind or a vision of the future she truly didn't know, but there was peace to be had in wondering.

'It's us, Emma...' He stroked the soft mound of her stomach, the gentle heat fading the last remnants of her pain, resting on their baby and telling it to stay for now where it was safe, that they'd meet it when they were all ready. 'That's our family.'

EPILOGUE

'ARE the twins ready…?' Jake's voice trailed off as he walked into the lounge and saw that his wife had company.

'Hi, Emma.' He gave an uncomfortable smile and Emma did the same. 'Zarios.' Jake nodded to his brother-in-law and Zarios nodded back. 'Congratulations.'

'Thank you,' Zarios answered. 'Beth just gave us your gift and card—it is appreciated.'

'You're welcome.'

'Do you want a drink, Jake?' Beth offered, but Jake explained that he couldn't stop. Emma thought that though to many it might seem strange that she and her brother were tonight guests in their late parents' home, on the one-year anniversary of their deaths, it didn't feel strange. It felt right.

Right that even if they weren't here still Eric and Lydia looked after their family—providing Beth and their grandchildren with a comfortable home during these long tumultuous months, a roof over Beth and her children's heads one thing she hadn't had to worry about as her life had rapidly unravelled.

'Well.' Jake gave a wooden smile. 'It's good to see you both—congratulations again.'

The tension was broken a touch as the twins ran into the living room, clearly delighted to see their father. A flurry of kisses and an exchange of bags ensued, as Jake collected his children for his access weekend, but as he turned to go he spoke again.

'Can I see her, Em?'

'Of course…' Emma held her breath as her brother crossed the room and stared down at his niece for the first time.

'Hey, little Lydia.' Jake stroked the petal of her cheek and Emma could see the flash of tears in his eyes. She hated how hard these months had been for him, and that he had lost practically everything—but she was proud of him, too, for turning things around. He had spent four months in rehab, then slowly entered the real world, and as everyone held their breath somehow Jake had held it together. Had found himself work, a flat, and had built from nothing a far gentler life than the one he had previously inhabited.

'Do you want to hold her?'

He did want, and cradled his tiny niece in his arms.

Emma could feel the tears trickling down the back of her nose, and was grateful that Zarios didn't take her hand—because any contact and she would have crumbled.

'You forget how small they are.' Jake looked over to his wife. 'Do you remember—?' He stopped talking then, regret etched on his features as he dragged his gaze back to his niece. Then a ghost of a smile dusted his features. 'It's a good job that you had a girl—I wasn't too keen on having a nephew named Eric!'

'Eric Rocco!' Zarios joined in with the thin joke

as Jake handed Lydia back to her mother. 'I am glad, too, that it was a girl.'

Emma was grateful, too, that Zarios didn't comment on the drive home—just drove quietly as she gazed out of the window, staring out at the view she would love for ever, before daring to voice what she was sure she now knew.

'They're going to get back together.'

'I think so.' Zarios didn't take his eyes off the road.

'What if he slips up? What if—?'

'We'll deal with it as best we can.'

We.

Which was so much stronger than I.

'Thank you…'

Later, much later, when Lydia was bathed and fed and had finished humming herself to sleep in her cot, when they lay exhausted staring at the ceiling, Emma said what she'd been meaning to and thanked Zarios—not just for today, but for the infinite patience he had shown with her family.

'I haven't done anything yet!' Zarios grinned.

'I know it's not been easy with Beth and Jake…'

'Hey, we've got *my* dysfunctional family next week-end…'

He could always make her smile, always make her laugh, always make her want him. His parents lived as if on extended honeymoon, and, as Zarios had pointed out on occasion, if Bella was holding her breath for Rocco to die—well, she was earning her inheritance. His father was the happiest, the healthiest, the youngest he had ever been.

'This year was the worst, and you're through it.' He held her so close she believed him—and tried to come to terms with the fact that the worst year of her life had also, somehow, been the best.

Seeds of hope were budding all around them—love and hope were beckoning from even the darkest of corners.

A chirrup from the cot had them both jumping.

Zarios padded across the floor and didn't even try to scold the twelve-week-old madam who, despite a clean nappy, despite being fed and burped and fed and burped again, had no intention of sleeping.

'Wide awake!' He held up his daughter and black eyes met black eyes, both equally entranced with the other. 'You're ruining my reputation…' He blew raspberries on her fat tummy, making Lydia giggle and coo, before placing her gently back in her cot, to stand the full hour it took before a certain little lady closed her eyes.

'Go to sleep,' he said when, on this most difficult night, Emma turned to him as, cold, tired and beyond exhaustion, he crawled in bed beside her.

'I don't want to.' Smiling, she kissed his full mouth.

She would never let him go.

Would never deny the comfort they brought each other.

She needed this reformed reprobate just as much as he needed her. And knew that, despite a cruel year, life was invariably kind.

After all, they had found each other.

THE ITALIAN'S RUTHLESS BABY BARGAIN

BY

MARGARET MAYO

Margaret Mayo is a hopeless romantic who loves writing and falls in love with every one of her heroes. It was never her ambition to become an author, although she always loved reading, even to the extent of reading comics out loud to her twin brother when she was eight years old.

She was born in Staffordshire and has lived in the same part of the country ever since. She left school to become a secretary, taking a break to have her two children, Adrian and Tina. Once they were at school she started back to work and planned to further her career by becoming a bilingual secretary. Unfortunately she couldn't speak any languages other than her native English, so she began evening classes. It was at this time that she got the idea for a romantic short story—Margaret, and her mother before her, had always read Mills & Boon® romances, and to actually be writing one excited her beyond measure. She forgot the languages and now has more than seventy novels to her credit.

Before she became a successful author Margaret was extremely shy and found it difficult to talk to strangers. For research purposes she forced herself to speak to people from all walks of life and now says her shyness has gone—to a certain degree. She is still happier pouring her thoughts out on paper.

CHAPTER ONE

FROM the first moment Penny looked into Santo De Luca's eyes she knew she was in trouble. They were the deepest, darkest brown she had ever seen, framed by long, silky lashes, set beneath a pair of equally silky black brows. And they appeared to be looking into her soul, trying to find out what sort of a person she was before she had even spoken.

It was impossible to ignore the rivers of sensation that flooded her veins, the way her blood ran hot, and the instant thought that she could be in danger. There was nothing to confirm this, just an impression, a feeling. The man was seriously sexy. 'Miss Keeling?'

Oh, hell, even his voice was sexy, coming from deep, deep down in his throat. Was there nothing about him that didn't set off alarm bells, that didn't stir her deepest emotions; emotions that she'd kept rigidly in check for a long, long time?

Penny nodded, feeling sure that if she dared to speak her voice would give her away. Never in her life had she felt such strong emotions at a first meeting, not when she didn't even know the man. Not when she was about to work for him. It was insane.

'You do have a tongue?' The voice had sharpened, still a low rumble in his throat but with an added edge, and his beautifully sculpted brows drew together over his eyes.

Such gorgeous eyes! Nevertheless his question had the desired effect. She snapped herself back into business mode. 'Yes, I'm Miss Keeling.' And she straightened her shoulders, standing that little bit taller. But even at five feet eight she still stood several inches below him.

'Do you look at all of your employers as though they're from a different planet?'

Penny wasn't sure whether he was joking or being serious. But just in case she kept her voice grave. 'Not as a rule, Mr De Luca.'

'So I'm the exception. Is there a reason for that?'

Not only did he look gorgeous but he also had a most attractive Italian accent. It raised goose bumps on her skin. And she wondered for a brief moment whether it would be advisable to work for a man who could do this much damage before she'd even got to know him. Perhaps she ought to turn and run?

'I… You're not what I expected.'

'I see,' he said. 'I'm not the normal run-of-the-mill father, is that it?'

Penny sucked in a deep breath. 'Normally it's the child's mother who organises a nanny, generally because she needs to go back to work—or whatever else it is she wants to do,' she couldn't help adding. She had worked for very rich women who preferred having a social life to bringing up their children.

'The agency didn't tell you that there wasn't a Mrs De Luca?'

'No.' She heard the surprise in her voice. Normally

she would have been given the background of the family and they would have wanted to see her prior to engaging her, making sure she was suitable. But on this occasion a nanny had been needed urgently.

'You come highly recommended.' He raised a brow as he said it, and Penny realised that she was hardly being professional. In fact she was acting completely out of character.

All because he was a strikingly handsome man.

'Though I'm beginning to have my doubts about whether you're up to the job,' he added crisply. 'Nevertheless I have a very important business meeting that I'm already late for. Come through to the kitchen and I'll introduce you to my housekeeper. We'll have a serious talk tonight.'

Up to the job! Penny took umbrage. 'Mr De Luca,' she declared, standing at her full height, staring him full in the face, 'I can assure you that I am more than up to the job, as you put it.' She thrust an envelope into his face. 'Here are my references, you'll see that—'

'Those aren't necessary!' he declared imperiously. 'I prefer to make my own judgement.'

And at the moment she was sadly lacking, thought Penny. She could hardly blame him; she had stood there like an idiot instead of ignoring his sexuality and being the truly experienced nanny that she was.

She had approached his house this morning with an air of excitement. The agency she worked for had stressed how important this job was. Mr De Luca was the head of the De Luca advertising agency—a global company—and if she pleased him it could work very well for them.

He lived on the outskirts of London in a huge mansion set in an amazing estate—it couldn't be called anything less, she'd decided, because after the electronically controlled gates had opened she'd driven through acres of woodland and gardens. To say she was impressed would have been an understatement.

And when she'd reached the house, well, she was truly stunned. Three storeys high, eight windows across. How many rooms was that?

'I understand your last nanny left you rather unexpectedly?' she questioned as she hurried at his heels through miles of corridors. Anyone would think they were in a race. His long legs were in danger of taking him away from her.

He wore a dark grey suit and white shirt, both Savile Row if she wasn't mistaken, but they did little to disguise the well-maintained body beneath. This man seriously worked out and she wasn't surprised, he'd need to be super-fit to work the long hours he did. She'd been told he left by seven every morning, and was always late getting home. It sounded to her as though he didn't see very much of his daughter.

'That is correct. And if you're having any ideas that this job isn't for you, then I'd be obliged if you would say so right now.'

He stopped so abruptly that Penny cannoned into him, taken aback when his strong arms steadied her and those mesmerising dark eyes locked into hers. She actually stopped breathing for a few seconds and gazed into those magical depths, then realised what she was doing and stepped back a pace.

Her nostrils were invaded by the most irresistible cologne she had ever come across. It was strong like the man himself, though not overpowering. It was subtly pervasive and she knew it would linger long after he had gone. 'I will naturally do the job to the best of my ability. I'm a conscientious worker, your daughter will be perfectly safe with me and—where is she, by the way? Don't you think we ought to be—?'

'Chloe's still in bed,' he told her fiercely. 'I saw no reason to wake her. My office hours are irregular to say the least, but Chloe needs routine, as I'm sure you understand. Emily, my housekeeper, will show you around and then I shall expect you to get Chloe ready and take her to school. I didn't see any luggage when you arrived, you do know that I expect you to live in?'

Penny inclined her head. 'It was a rush getting here this early,' she said, hoping to make her point. 'I planned on sorting my things out while your daughter's at school.' According to the agency his previous nanny had walked out yesterday. Though why he couldn't have taken a day off and spent time interviewing, Penny didn't know. At least it was her gain, and the salary she'd been offered was far higher than anything she'd earned before.

He muttered something under his breath in his native language and then resumed his race to the kitchen.

Emily was small and rotund and Penny imagined her to be in her mid-fifties. She had rosy cheeks and short grey hair and, judging by the way she looked at her employer, she clearly adored him.

Penny didn't realise how much his presence filled the massive room until he had gone. It was only then that she felt able to breathe more easily. Emily saw her relax and smiled. 'Welcome to the De Luca household. Mr De Luca's a wonderful man to work for. I hope you'll be happy here.'

And why was the housekeeper giving her more of a welcome than the big man himself? wondered Penny. 'Is he always so disagreeable?' she enquired. 'I got the impression that he wasn't sure I'd be any good at the job!'

'That's because none of the nannies he's employed before have lasted more than a few weeks.'

Penny frowned. 'Is Chloe a difficult child? Or is Mr De Luca the problem?' He was actually a big problem as far as she was concerned. Far too sexy for her peace of mind. Penny had never met a man who so instantly affected her senses. Even Max hadn't had this sort of effect on her, and she'd thought he had been the one.

Emily lifted her shoulders and let them drop again, slowly. 'Mr De Luca's a very fair man to work for. I should know, I've been with him for a very long time. It's the hours that people don't like. Most of the nannies before were all young with fancy boyfriends and they didn't want to be on duty twenty-four hours a day. It's understandable.'

'Is that what he expects?' asked Penny, widening her eyes. No wonder he'd offered her such a good salary. He wanted blood.

'He doesn't think, that's his trouble,' declared Emily. 'You just have to tell him if he puts on you too much. I do.'

But she was part of the fixtures, thought Penny. He wouldn't take it very kindly if she said anything. She was tempted to ask what had happened to his wife but felt it was too soon. Perhaps she too had been unable to put up with the long hours he worked?

'What time does Chloe normally get up?' she asked, glancing at the clock on the wall.

'Half past seven,' answered Emily. 'She's a slow

waker. Believe me, you'll have your time cut out to get her to school on time. I'll take you up there now.'

Santo couldn't get Penny out of his mind—even in the middle of his important meeting. She was nothing like any of the other nannies he'd hired. For one thing she had more to say for herself—which could prove interesting! He wasn't averse to verbal sparring; he liked a spirited woman. It had surprised him, that was all.

She had long, wavy blonde hair which, if he wasn't mistaken, was entirely natural, the bluest of blue eyes surrounded by amazingly long lashes, a tiny retroussé nose and beautifully shaped lips.

He had also noticed that she wasn't exactly as slender as some young women aspired to be these days—stick-thin did nothing for him. She had curves in all the right places and even thinking about the way her breasts had jutted against the thin cotton of her blouse made his testosterone levels rise.

He surprised himself by recalling these details. Surprised and dismayed. He didn't want to think of her in this way. He could do without such distractions. He had enough on his mind already.

But he did think of her and he was disappointed when he got home that evening and she was nowhere around. He'd been looking forward to talking to her some more, finding out what made her tick, what her hopes and aspirations were.

He'd not even thought twice about any other nanny the agency had sent him, but Penny Keeling was different. She was, without a shadow of doubt, a very intriguing woman and he was looking forward to getting to know her better.

* * *

After Penny had taken Chloe to school she returned to the flat she shared with a friend and began packing her bags.

'You do realise I'll have to find someone else? I can't afford this place on my own,' said Louise.

Penny nodded.

'You seem very sure that this is the right job for you. It's happened before, you know, and you've—'

'I'm sure,' answered Penny firmly. Why wouldn't she be with such a high salary? It was every girl's dream.

'De Luca, you say, that wouldn't be the Santo De Luca who's forever in the news, would it?' wondered her friend. 'The one who always has a glamorous girl hanging on his arm?'

'The very same,' Penny agreed and smiled at Louise's expression.

'No wonder you took the job. I'd do the same in your position!'

Penny grinned. 'I'm not a man-hunter like you, Louise.'

'Life's too short not to enjoy it,' answered her friend with a shrug. 'You picked the wrong man once, but hey, who's to say you'd do it again? You've been on your own for far too long.'

'You're incorrigible,' laughed Penny, shaking her head. 'And I'm off. I'll see you soon.'

Now it was late evening and she sat in her own private sitting room. A room that was luxuriously furnished with antiques and brocade drapes and had floor-to-ceiling windows overlooking the parkland. It adjoined her bedroom, and the other side of her bedroom was Chloe's room.

Chloe was adorable. A bright five-year-old, a chatterbox, and she'd already told Penny that she liked her better than her other nannies.

When Penny heard Santo's car she imagined him coming in and throwing his jacket on the back of a chair, pouring himself a drink maybe. She imagined his strongly carved face, the high cheekbones, the straight nose and the slash of his mouth. Would his features be relaxed or would the trials of the day still be imposed on them?

Had he eaten? she wondered, and then laughed at herself for even thinking such a thing. What did she care? Emily had cooked a succulent roast of beef with all the trimmings and Penny had eaten every last morsel. Even Chloe had cleaned her plate.

In most of her other placements Penny had cooked for her charges; it made a change to have a meal provided for her. She didn't know yet whether this was the norm. And if so, what was she to do with herself while Chloe was at school? There were definitely a few things she needed to discuss with Mr De Luca.

He had said he would talk to her tonight. Should she go down—or did he appreciate solitude after a long day at the office? She realised that she knew nothing about him—except that he stirred her senses like mad.

On the other hand, they really did need to talk. Even as the thought flashed through her mind a loud rap came on the door, startling her, making her jump, sending her heart into panic mode.

'Miss Keeling!'

Oh, that voice. That deep glorious voice!

Nerve-ends tingled and a flood of warmth filled Penny's body and for a few seconds she could do nothing. She couldn't answer, she couldn't even get up. It was crazy feeling like this about a man whom she'd only just met, and more importantly a man she was now working for.

But how could she hide such vast emotions? Supposing they showed on her face? How embarrassing would that be? For heaven's sake, she was a professional not some giddy schoolgirl with a crush on her teacher.

She closed her eyes and took a deep, steadying breath, and when she opened them Santo was standing in front of her.

'Were you ignoring me, Miss Keeling?'

Not ignoring; trying to prepare herself for the onslaught of her senses that she knew would take place. And it did! With his shirtsleeves rolled up, revealing sinewy forearms and his top three buttons undone so that her eyes feasted on smooth, tanned skin, skin that tempted her fingers to touch, to feel, to taste even, she could hardly get her breath.

'I wouldn't dare, Mr De Luca,' she answered, surprised to hear how strong her voice sounded; no hint at all of her inner struggle.

Straight black brows rose and dark, dangerous eyes locked into hers.

He didn't believe her and she could hardly blame him. She felt like an idiot now and pushed herself swiftly to her feet. 'I was actually just thinking of coming down to see you. You said you needed to talk?'

'That is correct,' he answered brusquely. 'But we may as well do it here.'

Before she could even bat an eyelid he had taken the companion chair next to hers. The two armchairs in the room were overstuffed and not entirely comfortable and she almost smiled when she saw Santo's expression.

'How can you sit in a chair like this?' he asked, shifting his large frame. 'I'll get them changed immediately.'

Penny guessed that all the rooms in the house had been furnished by an interior designer with no thought for comfort, only aesthetic beauty. And they were beautiful chairs. But…

'Come, we'll talk downstairs. I can't sit here.'

He strode from the room and Penny had no choice but to follow. She devoured him with her eyes as she did so, noting the way his shirt stretched across his broad, muscular back, the way his trousers were similarly taut over his behind and hips, emphasising once again his athletic physique.

Was she crazy for noticing all these things about her new employer? Was she heading for danger? Ought she to get out while the going was good? Or could she be strong enough to hide her feelings?

They were so out of character. She had never, in the whole of her twenty-seven years, felt like this about a man she hardly knew. A man who—according to her friend—had a fierce reputation for eating females for supper. And he certainly wouldn't appreciate such feelings from his daughter's nanny.

He led her into what had to be his private sitting room, a fairly small room with lovely deep black leather armchairs and French windows opening out on to a patio area filled with tubs of begonias in every shade of apricot imaginable. To one side was a hedge of honeysuckle and the sweet scent of it filtered into the room.

Penny inhaled appreciatively as she sat down. 'What a beautiful smell.'

'I enjoy this time of night,' he agreed. 'Everywhere's so peaceful. Would you care for a drink?'

Much as she would like one Penny shook her head. She most definitely needed to keep it clear. It was intoxicated enough with the sheer sight of him. 'You have a beautiful daughter, Mr De Luca.'

He nodded and gave a faint smile. 'Thank you. How did you get on with her?' He stretched his long legs out, crossing them at the ankles, looking totally relaxed for a change.

'We hit it off straight away. She liked me, I think; I like her. You have nothing to fear. I will look after her well.'

'I'm glad to hear it. She means everything to me.' He picked up his drink, which he must have left on the table when he had come to seek her, and Penny couldn't help noticing what beautiful, long fingers he had, how well-manicured his nails were. And for a very brief second she wondered what it would feel like to be touched by those fingers, to have them stroke her skin.

Simply thinking about it created a storm and it took an extreme effort to dash the thought away. Fantasising about this man was a dangerous occupation. One she would do well to steer away from.

'I need you to tell me exactly what my responsibilities are,' she said, stiffening her spine and hoping she sounded efficient and businesslike. 'I expected to have to cook for Chloe but it would appear your housekeeper does that.'

'Emily does all the cooking and washing,' he agreed, 'and I have cleaners who come in on a weekly basis. Obviously I'll expect you to cook for my daughter when Emily has her day off. To be quite honest with you, Miss Keeling, I'm not entirely sure what a nanny's duties are. I—'

He pulled up short, deciding against whatever it was he'd been going to say. 'Naturally I wish you to take care of my daughter's welfare, but when she's at school your time is your own. Which in effect makes up for your early mornings and late evenings. Do you have a boyfriend? Will you be needing time off?'

'Needing it, Mr De Luca?' questioned Penny, her blue eyes sparking dramatically. 'It's my right. No one works seven days a week.' Her tone was sharper than she'd intended. Possibly because of the way her senses were still all over the place.

'So let's say your hours are flexible,' he agreed. 'And if you do have a boyfriend I must ask that you do not bring him back here.'

Penny looked at him boldly, her chin high. 'As a matter of fact there is no one. But surely that was something you should have queried before you took me on?'

He gave a very slight lift of his shoulders. 'I'm new to this game.'

'So you're making up the rules as you go along?' she asked.

Dark eyes narrowed and a muscle jerked dangerously in his jaw. 'Are you questioning my values?'

Penny drew in a swift breath. 'Not if my job depends on it. But I'm sure you see my point?'

To her surprise he threw his head back and laughed. '*Touché*, Penny. I may call you Penny?'

Oh, goodness, the way her name rolled off his tongue! He said it like no one else. Made it sound different and—dared she say it—incredibly sexy. Of course, he didn't mean it that way, it was his accent that did it, but heaven help her, the inference was there.

'Yes,' she agreed but she didn't look at him. She looked out through the open doors instead, where she could see a myriad of dramatic colours in the sky. The sun had disappeared but its aftermath was other-worldly. As was the situation she found herself in.

Santo's male hormones were behaving badly. And it annoyed him because he didn't want to be attracted to Penny. He'd had girlfriends, yes, in plenty, in the years he'd been alone after his wife had left him. But nothing serious. They all knew it was just a game to him.

But Penny was different. For one thing she was his employee—and it was a cardinal rule of his to never mix business with pleasure. And for another, he sensed that she wouldn't be into casual affairs. He couldn't quite weigh her up yet but he had the feeling that she wouldn't settle for anything less than a serious relationship. When she met the man of her dreams it would be an all-or-nothing affair.

And what a lucky man he would be. She had to be every man's dream. Beautiful, smart, capable, interesting. He could think of plenty of adjectives to describe her. Sexy, provocative… He stopped his thoughts right there and tossed the rest of his whisky down his throat.

Standing up, he said, 'It's warm in here, don't you think? Shall we continue our talk outside?' Where there was more air to breathe! Where he could put more space between them.

Penny smiled her consent and jumped to her feet. 'You have an incredible place here, Mr De Luca. I'd love to explore your gardens.'

'Santo. Please call me Santo,' he suggested softly.

'I'd rather not; it's a little too informal for our situation,' she answered swiftly.

He noticed that her eyes had turned from blue to amethyst in the changing evening light. They looked softer and more vulnerable—and, dammit, he didn't want to notice these things. She was here to work, nothing else, and he'd be as well to remember it. 'I can't have you calling me Mr De Luca when we're on our own.'

'How about Signor De Luca?' she asked cheekily, and he was taken again by the flash in her eyes. She was so beautiful, all woman, teasing and flirtatious, whether she knew it or not. He guessed she didn't; she would probably be horrified if she knew what he was thinking. How he was interpreting her behaviour.

'Tell me about yourself,' he said, conscious his voice was even gruffer than usual. 'I really know very little— except that you come with impeccable credentials, and that you have no boyfriend,' he added with a twist to his lips. 'Where do you live, for instance?'

'I share a flat with a friend in Notting Hill. Or at least I did, I moved out today.'

'I see. Would that be a female friend?' The question was out before he could stop it. Even though she'd said that she didn't have a boyfriend.

'Are you prying into my private life, Mr De Luca?'

He was startled by her question until he saw the twinkle in her eyes again and managed a smile himself. 'I'm very curious. Do you have any family? Of course you do not have to tell me if you don't want to. But I always take an interest in my employees' private lives; I always enquire about husbands or wives or partners, because if there's a problem at home it can sometimes affect their work and then I can make allowances. I believe my interest helps improve working relationships.'

She looked at him disbelievingly for a few seconds and then she laughed, and it was such a musical sound that he felt like laughing too. He wanted to pick her up and twirl her around. He wanted to kiss her; he wanted to... He stopped his thoughts right there, berating himself for being fanciful. And he was grateful when she spoke.

'In that case, if it will improve our relationship, the answer to your question about my flatmate is that she is female.' And she slanted him another glance to see how he would take it.

He pretended not to notice.

'Do I have family?' she went on. 'My father died when I was Chloe's age. And my mother died a couple of years ago; she'd been ill a long time. But I have a twin sister who has a six-year-old and a new baby. I visit her often. I love the kids.'

All the time she'd been speaking they had been walking along a flagstoned path that led to the lake. It was a favourite place of his to sit and meditate—especially at this time of night. And he was looking forward to Penny's reaction.

It was not what he expected. When the vast expanse of water came into sight she gave a squeal of horror. 'Mr De Luca, you never told me about this. It's not exactly safe for Chloe. It really should be fenced.'

Never before could he remember feeling so deflated. And horrified. It had not occurred to him that it could be dangerous. He hoped none of the other nannies had ever let Chloe out to play on her own. He went hot and cold at the thought of what the consequences could have been.

'It will be done,' he declared. 'Immediately. *Mio Dio, sono un idiota.*'

'Otherwise,' said Penny, and he swore he could hear a hint of mischief in her voice, 'it's beautiful here.'

'It is especially beautiful at this time in the evening,' he answered. But he wasn't looking at the water, he was looking at Penny instead, and when she looked back at him with eyes so wide and so incredibly lovely he wanted to take her in his arms and kiss her—regardless of the consequences.

Penny saw the intent on Santo's face and knew that she had to act swiftly, or she too would give in to temptation. And how dangerous would that be? Her job would be gone and she'd never find another like it.

It had to be the incredible patterns of colour in the sky, reflected so perfectly in the water, that had done it. It was a place for lovers. It was a magical evening, everything still and hushed—and temptation was everywhere.

Not a place for an employer and employee. Unless she'd got it wrong and he hadn't been going to kiss her, but she couldn't be sure and she dared not take the risk. It would ruin everything, even though he was the most gorgeous man she'd ever met.

He wouldn't be after a serious relationship, just a bit of fun. And she wasn't up for that. She had many friends who would be—Louise, for instance. Friends who would tell her she was stupid not to go for it. Millionaires, billionaires, whatever, always lavished their girlfriends with expensive gifts. That way they didn't feel guilty when they dumped you.

Well, this girl wasn't for dumping. This girl wasn't going to enter into any kind of a relationship with him—except a purely professional one.

'Have you lived here very long?' she asked, deliberately moving a few feet away from him, pretending to watch a pair of ducks who'd broken the silence by squabbling on the other side of the lake.

He didn't answer her question. 'Why don't you have a boyfriend?' he said instead. 'A beautiful woman like you, I would have thought you'd have a whole string of them knocking at your door.'

Penny lifted her shoulders. 'I'm not interested in men. I'm a career girl.'

'You intend to be a nanny for the rest of your life?' he questioned, making it sound as though it was the worst thing she could possibly do.

'Why not?' she demanded.

'I cannot see it happening,' he declared dismissively. 'You're too beautiful to become an old maid. That is the right expression, is it not?'

Penny smiled and nodded. An old maid! It sounded so old-fashioned and not what she had expected from him.

'One day the right man will come along and you'll be swept off your feet. And before you know it you'll be married with a lot of little children of your own to look after. I'm sure that would be far more satisfying than looking after other people's children.'

'And you consider yourself an expert on that subject, do you? A man who needs a nanny to look after his own child.'

Penny saw him frown and knew she was out of order but for some reason the words wouldn't stop. He'd caught her on a raw nerve. She did want children; she'd thought once that she'd met the right man to give them to her. And ever since that disastrous affair she'd had doubts that there ever would be a Mr Right.

'Tell me, Mr De Luca, if we are being open and honest with each other, what happened to your wife? Did she leave you because of the long hours you work?'

The instant the words were out she regretted them. And when he spoke, when he answered her question, she wanted to turn and run. She wanted to wave a magic wand and make herself disappear. This was the worst moment of her life.

CHAPTER TWO

'MY WIFE is dead,' Santo told Penny coldly. 'And for your information I have no intention of ever marrying again.' Without more ado he began walking back towards the house.

For a few seconds all Penny could do was stare after him. She saw shoulders that were hunched and a stride that was not his usual determined one. She felt like hell. What a stupid, inconsiderate question to have asked. What must he be thinking?

She really had overstepped the mark and wouldn't be surprised if he told her to pack her bags and go. And she didn't want to do that. She must make amends. Hurrying after him, she said, 'I'm sorry, I didn't know. I wouldn't have asked if—'

Abruptly he stopped and faced her. 'And you didn't think it would be wise to get your facts right before passing judgement?' His tone was harsher than she had ever heard it, dark eyes unfathomable. A tall, proud man, incensed at the way he had been spoken to.

Penny guessed he was still grieving. It must have been fairly recent. Maybe that was why he worked such long hours, why he didn't seem to be giving his daughter the love and attention that she needed. He wanted to blot everything out and the only way he could do it was to work himself into the ground.

'I'm sorry,' she said again, feeling her heart bounce in her chest, feeling a raw kind of pity for him. She wanted to hug him—how ridiculous was that? She wanted to tell him that time would heal. She knew how heartbroken she'd felt when her mother had died.

But he didn't want to hear those words. He wanted someone responsible to look after Chloe. He had a business to run, he couldn't look after her himself. He didn't know how. He'd never had to do it. He was the breadwinner. The man of the house. The provider.

'Forget it,' he growled, and headed back to the house.

Penny didn't follow this time. She waited a few minutes before retracing her steps and then ran swiftly up to her room.

She couldn't help wondering what Santo's wife had been like. There were no photographs anywhere, nothing to remind him of her. Was that deliberate? Was he the sort of man who couldn't cope with death? Pretended it didn't exist? So many questions with no answers.

When Penny got up the next morning, not surprisingly Santo had already gone to work. She'd not slept well with thoughts of the way she had upset him last night, and as she got Chloe ready for school she gave the girl an extra-big hug.

Chloe looked so much like her father, with jet-black hair and big brown eyes—which were sometimes sad. Penny knew that the little girl must be hurting deep down inside, bewildered as well, because how could you really explain to a child of her age that her mother would never be coming back?

It wasn't for her to say anything, though. If Chloe wanted to talk, fair enough, but she had no intention of bringing up the subject.

After dropping Chloe off at school she did some shopping and visited her sister before going back to De Luca Manor—as she had privately named Santo's house. It was hard to believe that one man lived in such a huge mansion. Why? Unless he entertained a lot, or had done when his wife was alive.

At the back of the house was a row of garages—she'd been allotted one for her tiny car—and Penny was surprised to see Santo's sleek black Aston Martin already parked there. He was home! At this time of day? She glanced at her watch. It was scarcely lunch time.

'Where have you been?' he growled the second she entered the house. It looked as though he'd been waiting for her. His black hair was ruffled and she could imagine those long fingers running impatiently through it.

'I'm sorry,' she said, jutting her chin, resenting the inference that she should have been in when he arrived home. 'I didn't realise I had to keep you informed of my movements. Actually I've been to see my sister. You did say my free time was during the day.'

'I thought I'd take you out to lunch.'

Penny couldn't hide her shock. 'Me? Why?' A nanny lunch with her boss? It was unheard-of, especially with a man such as Santo.

'Because we didn't finish our conversation last night,' he answered. 'But if you'd rather not, then…' He lifted his wide shoulders in a careless shrug.

'I'm sorry about last night; I—'

Santo cut her short. 'The subject's closed. Go and get rid of your bags. We're leaving in ten minutes.'

Meaning he didn't want to talk about his loss. And she could hardly blame him. People dealt with their grief differently. Santo clearly wanted to shut his away.

Penny scurried to her room. It didn't seem right lunching with him, but who was she to argue? She ran a comb through her hair but didn't bother to change. She was already wearing a long brown skirt and a pretty peasant blouse, both fairly new purchases and perfectly suitable. All she did was change her sandals to a pair of high heels and with a touch of lip gloss and a splash of perfume she was ready.

Was her heart racing because she had rushed? Penny wondered as she ran lightly down the curved flight of stairs towards Santo, standing in the huge hallway. Or was it racing because she was about to dine with him?

The hall below was elegant and beautiful with a polished wooden floor and a centre table holding a bowl of sweet-smelling roses cut straight from the garden. There was a rocking chair in one corner and ornately framed mirrors on two of the walls.

But at this very moment she saw none of it; she saw only Santo's unsmiling face. Unsmiling but indescribably handsome. She couldn't believe that she was actually going out with him. In all her years of being a nanny nothing like this had ever happened.

On the other hand she had never worked for anyone like Santo before. This was a man apart. And because he was different her heart was hammering so hard that it felt painful against her ribcage.

When the agency had asked if she'd take this job she had said yes without any qualms. What they hadn't told her was what Santo De Luca was like. They hadn't said he was one of the richest men in the country. They hadn't told her that he was gorgeous-looking. They had told her nothing. Maybe if they had she would have run a mile. Or she might have been so intrigued that she'd have taken the job anyway.

Santo watched Penny as she descended the stairs; he watched each step she took. He looked at the way she pointed her toes, he looked at her slender ankles, at the soft material of her skirt as it brushed against her thighs. His blood whistled through his veins. He watched the movement of her breasts beneath the flowered cotton top and his heart missed a couple of beats. Then he looked up and caught her eye.

She was smiling.

She looked as though she was happy to go out with him. Which both surprised and pleased him. Last night he had spoken harshly and regretted it immediately afterwards. She had caught him on the raw.

One day he might tell her that he and his wife had been divorced for almost four years, that any love he had ever felt for her had been killed long before then. And that Helena hadn't even told him that he had a daughter! If he'd known he'd have helped out, he'd have got to know his daughter, he wouldn't be in the helpless position he was in now.

His feelings when he'd discovered the truth were of sheer disbelief and outrage. He'd found it hard to accept that she had done such a thing to him. He'd never realised how much she had hated him. Even thinking about it, reliving that moment when he made his discovery, twisted his guts.

Thank goodness for Penny. Fiery and spirited without the least interest in him, which made a refreshing change. He was so used to women hanging on to his every word, fighting to make themselves noticed, trying to trick their way into his bed, that Penny was like a breath of fresh air.

No doubt she thought him an uncaring father, but the truth was he felt simply helpless. He didn't know the first thing about bringing up children. He'd had no contact with kids since he had been one himself. They were a mystery to him.

'Good,' he said, 'a woman who doesn't take hours to get ready. I'm impressed.'

'I haven't changed, I hope I'm all right. We're not going anywhere too posh, are we?'

She seemed faintly worried and Santo smiled reassuringly. 'You're not to worry about anything; you look incredible.' Had he really said that? He'd have to watch himself. This wasn't a date. She intrigued him and he was looking forward to finding out more about her but that was all. Even then she didn't have to tell him anything about herself if she didn't want to.

Except that he wanted to know!

He'd summoned his chauffeur while Penny was getting ready and he led her out to the waiting Bentley, smiling to himself as her eyes widened, well aware that his wealth impressed her.

She slipped into one side, he into the other, and they sank into the luxurious cream leather. The light floral scent of her perfume was evocative, teasing his nostrils like nothing else. And he knew that forever afterwards this particular perfume would always remind him of her.

Penny was on edge, her hands clasped firmly in her

lap, her knees and feet together, her back straight. She hadn't expected the limousine and the chauffeur or she definitely would have changed. This was very alien, and she prayed that he wasn't going to take her somewhere equally classy.

'Relax,' he growled softly in her ear, 'I won't bite, I promise.'

Penny edged away, unable to stop herself, missing his frown but aware that he didn't approve. It was that infinitesimal stiffening of his body that gave him away. He wasn't used to a woman moving away from him, rather the opposite. Part of Penny, a large part, didn't want to move away. Heaven help her, but she wanted to find out what it would feel like to be held against his hard, hot body, bound to him by arms of steel, but she knew where such pleasures could lead. She was entirely out of his league; he would use her and then discard her, the way Max had done. And she had no wish to go through that again.

Men didn't have the same sort of feelings that women had. Their emotions weren't involved when they embarked on affairs. They could walk away at the end without getting hurt. Not so for the female sex.

'Where are we going?' she asked, and was horrified to hear the husky throb in her voice.

'To one of my favourite bistros.'

A bistro. That wouldn't be so bad. Her breathing got easier. 'Why aren't you driving?'

He gave one of his twisted smiles where his mouth went up on one side and his eyes crinkled at the corners, making him look almost boyish. 'Because of parking. You know what London's like.'

'We could have taken the tube.' And then she laughed

at his shocked expression. 'I presume you never take the tube anywhere?'

'Not these days,' he admitted.

Not since he'd made his fortune, thought Penny. She could have made some comment about his carbon footprint but she didn't. 'Actually it's nice to be driven like this,' she declared instead, giving a little bounce on her seat.

'I noticed your car was pretty ancient,' he said, still with that half-smile.

Penny shrugged. 'Nannies' salaries don't lead to new cars. Though,' she added daringly, 'if I stay with you long enough I might be able to afford one.'

'I'll buy you one,' he said at once.

Penny's mouth fell open and she stared at him. He'd said it as though it meant nothing. Which it probably didn't. Not to him. But hell would freeze over before she'd let him do that.

'You look surprised.'

'As indeed I am,' she replied. 'Why would you want to do a thing like that? My car's perfectly reliable. I don't need another one just yet.'

'So you're rejecting my offer?'

He actually looked offended, thought Penny. 'I am, most definitely.'

'Some of the nannies I've employed have not owned a car,' he informed her, 'so there's one in the garage bought solely for the purpose of ferrying my daughter around. You're welcome to use it.'

'No thanks,' said Penny promptly, 'but you can buy my petrol, I'll let you do that.'

Dark brows slid up. 'A woman with morals. A refreshing change. I like it.'

Penny wished her heart wouldn't thump so loudly; she was afraid he might hear it. 'There are a few of us left,' she tossed smartly, flashing him a sideways glance.

If only he wasn't sitting so close! There was space between them, yes, several inches in fact, but not enough. She could feel the warmth of him even with the air-conditioning, and her senses were attuned in a way that alarmed her.

She was tempted to edge towards the door but didn't want to give herself away. All she had to do was remember that this was a business lunch. They were going to discuss exactly what he expected of her where his daughter was concerned. Just that. Nothing else. Not themselves, nothing personal.

So why was she worried?

'You're still not relaxed, Penny.'

She jerked her head round. He was watching her. Those incredible dark eyes were smiling and she knew that he had sensed her unease. More than that, he'd seen how rigid her body was, how her hands were still locked. She could hardly believe herself. She was behaving in a totally alien manner. Usually she was brimming with confidence, nothing ever fazed her.

Except this man.

Damn! What did he have that was different—apart from great wealth, of course? But that shouldn't have made her feel like a dithering wreck. What he did have, in spades, was sex appeal. And it was this that was troubling her.

She had never encountered anyone like Santo De Luca before. Plenty of men were good-looking, were good company, were great guys, were fun, and some even thought they were God's gift to women. But

Santo was like none of these, he was in a different class entirely.

At school she'd been in the drama group and, although she'd done no acting since, Penny knew that she would have to act now as she'd never done before. So she smiled, and she shrugged, and she said, 'It's unnerving having lunch with your employer after only one day. I feel like I'm under the spotlight, as though I'm going to be interrogated. Am I?'

'We'll talk about whatever you want to talk about,' he answered easily, his incredible eyes locking into hers.

To Penny's relief the car slowed to a halt. But her relief was short-lived when they entered the bistro. An informal restaurant was her idea of a bistro. Tables on the pavement, tables inside with checked tablecloths, candles in bottles with melted wax down their sides, everything nice and casual.

This was nothing like it.

To begin with it looked expensive, terribly expensive. The room was large, airy and formal. Tablecloths were white damask, the tables spaced well apart; there were fresh flowers on them and the silverware gleamed. You wouldn't get a bowl of fries here, that was for sure. Foie gras and caviare looked more in keeping. But she held her head high and pretended that she was used to walking into such stylish places.

If only! One meal here would probably cost a whole week's wages.

Santo was greeted with a warm handshake and respect, making it evident that he was a regular customer.

'This isn't what I expected,' she said after they had been shown to their table.

'It's not to your liking?' he asked immediately. 'We can go somewhere else if—'

'It's not that,' Penny cut in. 'I expected something a little less formal. I wouldn't actually call this a bistro.'

'To me it's a bistro,' he said easily. 'It's very relaxed here. And the food, it is *squisito*.' He circled his thumb and finger. 'You will like it, I promise you.'

Why are you doing this? she wanted to ask. Are you trying to impress me? She hoped he wasn't after something else. Fancying him was one thing but she would never allow herself to be compromised.

But she was worrying for nothing. Santo was a gentleman. He discussed the menu with her, passionately, and their food was perfect in every way. By the end of the meal she was totally relaxed.

They had talked about anything and everything except themselves. She did enquire which part of Italy he came from, which she discovered was Rome, but he had noticeably clammed up at that point. She didn't dare ask whether he had parents still alive, brothers or sisters, and she'd posed no further questions. Though she couldn't help but be intrigued.

On the other hand he had found out that her favourite colour was brown. 'Brown?' he'd asked incredulously. 'It cannot be your favourite. I can see you in something sky-blue or aquamarine, something to bring out the fantastic colour of your eyes. Have you ever tried those colours?'

Fantastic colour of her eyes! What else had he noticed about her? It was a scary thought. She didn't like the idea of her employer observing something so personal.

'Most of my wardrobe is in autumn colours,' she

admitted, 'and this—' she spread her hands, looking down at the skirt she wore, and her cream blouse with its tiny brown flowers '—is one of my favourite outfits.'

The moment the words were out Penny regretted them. Her blouse had a drawstring neckline and sat quite low on her shoulders, and she had drawn Santo's attention to it. She could feel his eyes on her breasts, which to her dismay hardened and tingled, and she couldn't help wondering how it would feel to have his fingers stroke them. The very thought set her senses sizzling and pulses pounding and it was with an effort that she dashed it away.

Surely it was time they went. She couldn't sit here thinking these thoughts any longer. She glanced at her watch. 'I mustn't be late picking up Chloe.'

'And I must get back to work. I've enjoyed your company, Penny. I feel I know you much better now. It will be a pleasure allowing you to look after my daughter.'

'You could always pick her up from school yourself,' suggested Penny cautiously. 'She'd like that.'

But Santo shook his head. 'I have another meeting at three. Edward will drive you home. I can walk from here.'

'And will you be home before Chloe goes to bed?' enquired Penny.

'I'm not sure. Probably not. Say goodnight to her for me.'

'Chloe hardly sees you,' she told him. 'It's really not fair on her, the hours you work. It would be nice if you tried to make more of an effort to see her.' Then she clapped a hand to her mouth. 'I'm sorry, I shouldn't have said that. It's none of my business.'

'You're damn right it's none of your business,' he responded fiercely, his brown eyes losing the softness that had lingered during their meal. 'I wouldn't be where I am today and Chloe wouldn't have the life she does if I didn't work the hours I do.'

But you no longer need to, thought Penny, though she wisely kept the words to herself.

Amazingly, though, he wasn't late home. Chloe was in bed admittedly, but it was only a little after eight and Penny was sitting outside with a book on her lap. It was a warm balmy evening and through the trees in the distance she could see the evening sun glinting on the lake and she couldn't stop counting her blessings that she had been given this job.

Many of her friends would have found the solitude boring. They liked people and music and parties, but she was not missing them. Not yet at any rate. Or was it perhaps something else that attracted her—perhaps it was the man of the house himself?

She was sworn off men, so why she felt this pull towards Santo she had no idea. She'd met plenty of good-looking men in the course of her work and had felt nothing for them. Only Santo had made her senses run wild.

For a few seconds she closed her eyes and pictured his face. She could see him as he'd sat across from her at the restaurant. Those amazing dark eyes that could fill a woman with excitement without a word being said. Even thinking about him sent a burning sensation through her lower body, made her head fall back and the tip of her tongue moisten suddenly dry lips. Oh, hell, she thought, was this really happening?

'Penny.'

The voice was soft—and close! She was imagining it!

Then a hand touched her shoulder.

It was real!

'Penny, are you all right?'

'Santo!' Her eyes snapped open and without even realising it she used his name for the first time. 'You startled me. I—I didn't hear you come in.'

'Evidently,' he said, his rich, deep voice throbbing through her veins.

It was the sexiest voice she had ever heard. And she couldn't help wondering what it would be like if he were whispering words of love. She felt sure that it could quite easily make her climax without him even touching her.

What a crazy situation.

'What were you thinking?'

'Nothing,' she answered quickly. 'You're home early.'

His mouth twisted wryly. 'I took your advice. I thought I'd see Chloe before she went to bed, but it looks as though I'm too late.'

'You've only missed her by about half an hour,' Penny informed him, struggling for composure. At least talking about his daughter gave her time to rationalise her breathing.

To her dismay he pulled a chair close to hers and sat down. 'Then it's just you and me.' He looked relaxed for a change, younger, less severe, and because of the way she'd been thinking earlier it made her want to—to what?

Touch her fingers to his cheek, explore the contours? See what it felt like to be kissed by a real man. Lord, this hadn't happened to her since Max. She'd deliberately built a defensive wall and now it was crumbling fast.

She couldn't do this, she mustn't allow herself to once more fall for the wrong man. Santo wouldn't be

interested in her long-term. All he saw was a babysitter for his daughter, someone to take the weight off his
shoulders. And if he could enjoy the pleasures of her
body in the meantime—why not?

Now, where had those thoughts come from? He
hadn't shown the slightest inclination to want to kiss
her. But men were men. She knew that. Men took advantage of situations.

And her instincts proved correct when he leaned
towards her, when his mouth was inches away from hers.
She could see the pores in his skin, faintly smell cedar
wood, and the whites of his eyes were so clear that—that
she had to get away before she was lost in them.

Heavens! This wasn't really happening. It couldn't
be. She'd only been here two days. He wouldn't pounce
on her like that, surely? Risk the fact that he might send
her running.

And she was right. He gave a satisfied smile and then
sat back in his seat.

But she'd given herself away. She'd given him a
hold over her. He knew that he could take her any time
he wanted to.

'Excuse me, I think I'd better go and check on
Chloe,' she said, jumping to her feet. She was gone in
seconds, fleeing as fast as her legs would carry her, her
heart pounding. Letting Santo see how she felt had been
a big mistake. One he might take advantage of.

And she wasn't wrong.

She looked in on Chloe to find her sleeping like an
angel, a faint smile on her lips, her black hair, so much
like her father's, spread across the pillow. She was a
sweet child and Penny couldn't see why Santo didn't
devote more of his time to her, why he insisted on

working long hours and getting someone else to look after his daughter.

Leaving the nursery, her head down, her mind still intent on what she saw as Chloe's misfortune, Penny bumped straight into Santo. The sudden contact whipped the breath from her body and though his arms steadied her she felt as if her legs were about to buckle.

'What's the hurry?' he asked, concern in his voice. 'Is Chloe all right?'

Penny nodded. Everything was all right except these dangerous feelings flooding her system. A response that rocked her. Ricocheted a hot sizzle of awareness through every bone in her body.

'Then it has to be you—or me—or both of us?' His dark eyes filled with amusement and before she could guess at his intent, before she could protest or even draw breath, he lowered his head and captured her softly parted lips.

Penny had always known that Santo's kisses would be sensational; nevertheless she wasn't prepared for the whirlpool of exquisite pleasure that wreaked havoc inside her. The way her world began to spin until she felt sure that she would fly out into orbit if he carried on.

For so many years she had told herself that no man would ever get through to her again—and yet it was happening.

Now! And she had no control over it.

Santo had reached into the deepest recesses of her mind and turned it around so that she was once again a woman with needs that required satisfying, fully and deeply.

When he pushed open a door and urged her inside Penny realised they were in his bedroom. One tiny part of her mind railed against what was happening, the other exalted in the crescendo of feelings that were tipping her over the edge into a world where nothing else mattered except this moment in time.

And instead of fighting him she gave herself up to the erotic sensation of Santo's kisses, breathing his name against his mouth, feeling the fire he had ignited take hold until it consumed her whole body. There was no room for questions, for wondering what was possessing her, all she wanted was to give in to the heated feelings that ravaged her senses.

Santo led her over to the bed, pulling her against him as they lay down, lifting one powerful leg over hers, tucking her head into his shoulder. It was a big bed, deep and comfortable, and Penny closed her eyes, forgetting where she was and what she was doing. All that mattered was Santo's hot body next to hers, the throb of their passion that must surely be loud in the room.

With gentle fingers he traced the contours of her face. The urgency of that first kiss had gone; he was exploring now, gentle kisses followed his fingertips, and Penny relaxed against him, giving herself up to the magic of the moment, urging her body ever closer against his.

He found her mouth again in a kiss that shattered her senses, made her writhe against him and call out his name. She clawed her fingers into his hair and felt such a surge of emotion that it scared her. She hardly knew this man and yet here she was in his bed, enjoying his kisses as though he was the only man in the world.

With all the strength she could muster Penny pushed Santo away. This mustn't happen; she couldn't let it. It was the worst form of insanity.

CHAPTER THREE

TREMBLING all over, her blue eyes wide and accusing, she scrambled off the bed and glared down at him. 'Is this why your other nannies left? You couldn't keep your hands off them?'

'*Mio Dio!* You really think that's what I am like?' Santo's eyes turned jet-black as he unfurled himself from the bed, and his silence as he moved towards her with all the lethal grace of a jungle cat was more menacing because of it.

'So tell me it's not true,' she challenged, finding it difficult to breathe. 'Tell me you were kissing me because you found me attractive, and not because I just happened to be available and you were feeling horny.' She stood her ground, glaring into his face, trying to ignore the sensations still skittling around inside her.

'I don't remember you fighting me off,' he returned coolly. 'It seemed to me that the desire was totally mutual.'

Damn him! He was right, but she wasn't going to admit it, not in a thousand years. And since he hadn't confessed to finding her attractive she had her answer. And now she felt stupid, and because she felt stupid it made her even angrier. 'Trust a man to try to worm his way out of a situation,' she muttered, heading to the door.

But within seconds a heavy hand had her spinning round to face him. 'No one accuses me like that and gets away with it.' Black eyes pinned her and the savage fury pouring out of them twisted her stomach into knots and stiffened every one of her limbs so that she couldn't move had she wanted to.

'Our desires *were* mutual and you cannot deny it,' he informed her icily. 'If it was a guilty conscience that attacked you, so be it, but never, I repeat *never*, accuse me of doing something I am not guilty of.'

'So this is the end of it?' Penny said, facing him boldly, her spine straight, her head slanting defiantly up towards his face. 'Or should I be on my guard? Is it likely to happen again?'

'That depends on you.' He let her go, standing a couple of feet away, but his body was rigid, his arms folded across his broad chest, and his fantastic eyes were fixed unblinkingly on hers.

A quiver ran through her. She was here to do a job, not enjoy an affair with the master of the house. He'd thought she was fair game and she'd almost succumbed.

She felt sick even thinking about it. 'If it depends on me then I can assure you, Mr De Luca, that this will never happen again.'

He inclined his head. 'So be it.'

'So be it,' she flung back and this time when she marched to the door he let her go.

Santo smiled to himself as Penny left the room. It hadn't surprised him that she'd put a stop to their passionate embrace. In fact he'd been surprised that she'd let him kiss her at all. There was no denying that he'd

enjoyed the experience. She was temptation personi-
fied. He even began to wonder whether it had been a
good idea employing her.

The other nannies had been stiff and starchy, and
Chloe had hated them so much that she'd been a little
minx. But his daughter apparently adored Penny and he
knew very well that life in the De Luca household
would be much more stable with her there. So—for the
moment—he'd have to curb his hunger.

IT WAS the middle of the night and Santo heard Chloe
calling for her mummy. She'd had these bad dreams
ever since her mother had died, although they had got
further and further apart and he'd thought she was
finally accepting the situation.

Being a father didn't come naturally to him. He
always felt awkward when comforting Chloe and had
never been able to find the right words. He guessed it
was because he'd had nothing to do with her early years.

Now he leapt out of bed, pulling on a robe as he
crossed the room, and in seconds was at his daughter's
door. To discover that Penny was already there. He
watched in silence for a few seconds, marvelling at how
good she was with Chloe, how her words of comfort
came pouring out as though she were a mother herself.

Suddenly Chloe spotted him. 'Daddy, I had a nasty
dream. Penny made me feel better.'

He walked across to the bed, glancing at Penny, remembering the kiss—how could he not when it had
made his male hormones run more rampantly that he
could ever remember? Resolutely closing his mind, he
turned his attention to his daughter. 'Then I'm glad that
I found her, *mio bello.*'

Chloe held out her arms to him and he immediately hugged her, conscious as he did so of Penny watching him closely. It was the first time she'd seen any physical contact between them and her faint smile confirmed her approval.

'Daddy, can Penny sleep with me?'

Faint hurt pulsed through Santo. Why Penny? Why not him? He knew the answer before he had posed it: because he hadn't yet earned his daughter's love.

He looked at Penny, felt his gut twist into knots, a deep need rising like the devil incarnate, and knew that he had to get out of here before he gave himself away. 'If Penny doesn't mind.'

Penny gave him a curious look before she smiled at Chloe. 'Just for a few minutes, sweetheart.'

'I'll see you both in the morning, then,' said Santo as he left the room, but he knew as he lay in bed that he was in danger of making a fool of himself where Penny Keeling was concerned. He wanted her as he'd never wanted any other woman in his life. Because she was different? He didn't know. Because he knew she would never chase after him as many other women had done? He guessed that was true. There was a special quality about Penny. She had integrity as well as beauty.

Whatever had made her succumb to his kiss, it wasn't her normal pattern of behaviour. He felt sure of that. Her body would be given only to a man she was deeply in love with. And the fact that she had almost given in to him had scared her to death.

The best thing he could do was distance himself from her. And his saviour was the project his company was working on, a global campaign for a major company that had always eluded them—and they were so close this time that he was prepared to work twenty-four-seven to make sure he got the contract.

Penny knew that letting Santo kiss her, allowing her emotions to surface, giving way to them, allowing him to see that she was not immune to his kisses, had been a dangerous thing to do. Dangerous and exciting. It proved that the hurt she'd felt when Max finished with her was finally being laid to rest.

Max had been a big businessman too who could have his pick of any woman he wanted—just like Santo. She'd met him at a party and when he had singled her out, told her she was special, she had fallen head over heels in love. Their affair had lasted six months and she'd been expecting him to ask her to marry him. The shock when she discovered he was seeing someone else had made her sick.

She'd actually been warned that he got through women like other people drank cups of tea, but he'd told her that she was different and she'd believed him. She'd been too swept off her feet by his amazing good looks to realise he had said this to all of his dates. Just like Santo.

When Max had dumped her and declared that it was all over she'd been devastated, while he hadn't even seemed to care. She'd decided there and then that she would never allow another man to get through to her. And until now it had never happened. Until Santo.

Perhaps Santo's Italian origins had a lot to do with the attraction she felt for him. She would love to find out about his family and why he was living here in England. He was different in so many ways, and he had that attractive accent to go with the voice—which did her no good at all. He had somehow wormed his way beneath the thick skin she'd grown—and how! All in a matter of two days!

She guessed that all he'd want was an affair. He and Max were too similar for it to be any other way. But even though Penny could draw comparisons between Santo and Max, she had to admit that the men were actually worlds apart. Santo was a prince compared to Max and, even though she knew she had to stay away, still she felt drawn to him.

Penny tried to ignore the fact that she had needs too, which Santo had awoken. She'd have to be very strong in the days and weeks ahead to resist her seductive employer.

'Where are Penny and Chloe?' It was the following afternoon and Santo had come home from work early, only to find the house virtually empty. He'd not been able to stop thinking about Penny, about the way she had responded to his kisses—and then abruptly withdrawn, blaming him! Nevertheless he'd been looking forward to seeing her.

'At a birthday party,' answered his housekeeper.

'Without telling me? She's taken Chloe out without my permission?' He knew he was overreacting, knew instinctively that Penny was trustworthy. But the thought of her bonding too much with his daughter gave him a feeling he didn't understand and didn't want to examine.

'I'm sure Chloe will be perfectly safe,' said Emily calmly. 'Penny's a nice girl and Chloe's very fond of her. They've really bonded—not like some of the other women you employed.' Emily sniffed her disapproval.

'I know, I know,' he agreed. 'Maybe they weren't the best choices. Even so Penny had no right—'

'You weren't here to ask,' reminded Emily in her usual forthright manner.

'So where is this party?' he wanted to know.

'At her sister's. It's her niece's birthday.'

'And you have the address?'

Emily nodded. 'Penny gave it to me—just in case. I have the phone number as well.'

'Penny, there's someone here for you.'

Penny looked at her sister and frowned. 'Who is it?'

'Chloe's father,' informed Abbie uncomfortably. 'And he looks anything but happy.'

Penny widened her eyes. Santo! Home from work early—once again! And wondering what she'd done with his daughter presumably.

'Don't you think you'd better go and—?'

Before Abbie could finish the tall, imposing figure of Santo De Luca appeared in the doorway. 'A minute, Penny, if you please.'

Penny looked at her sister then at Santo, and she frowned. 'I didn't expect you to finish work this early.'

'Clearly,' he said coldly. 'And you didn't think to ask whether I'd mind you spiriting my daughter away to a stranger's birthday party?'

'It's not a stranger's, it's my niece's,' she retorted. 'And this is my sister.'

Abbie lifted her eyebrows. 'Pleased to meet you, Mr De Luca,' but she didn't sound it and she quickly moved away into the kitchen.

'Whether it's your sister's house or not,' declared Santo, 'I would like to be told when you're taking my daughter anywhere new. I came home to spend time with her and what did I find? That you were nowhere to be found.'

To spend time with Chloe! Penny doubted that very much, and she was hurt that he didn't trust her. Her chin tilted defiantly. 'I didn't find out there was going to be a party until Abbie phoned this morning. It was a last-minute decision and I thought Chloe would enjoy it—she hardly plays with any children her own age.' Seeing him again caused an eruption of awareness. Her whole body became stingingly sensitive and she prayed her hardened breasts wouldn't push against the soft fabric of her T-shirt and give her away.

'You could have phoned me,' he answered. 'You have my number.'

'You made it very clear that I was to call for emergencies only,' she tossed back. 'I hardly call a birthday party an emergency.' Damn her heart for beating so loudly, for reminding her that she was in grave danger.

'Regardless, I wish to know your movements. I didn't know what to think when I got home.'

'I told Emily.'

'Yes, and thankfully she told me. And that's why I'm here. Where is Chloe?'

'You're going to take her home?' questioned Penny disbelievingly. 'She's having the time of her life. Why don't you join us?'

She said it tongue-in-cheek, knowing full well that Santo would run a mile from joining a kids' birthday party. Not giving away how much he had surprised her, Penny led the way through to the garden where seven children were running around shouting and laughing and enjoying themselves.

Chloe was in the midst of it. She looked happy and animated and Santo felt faintly guilty for storming in like this. She was safe! He should have known that; he should have trusted Penny. Hell, he did trust her. He was frustrated, that was what it was. He'd come home early, yes, to spend time with Chloe because Penny had made him feel guilty, but he'd wanted to see Penny too and she hadn't been there. His disappointment had been acute.

And now he'd charged in here and discovered everyone playing happily and he felt like an idiot. Not that he let it show. He stood and unsmilingly watched the children—until Chloe saw him and came running across. 'Daddy, come and play hide-and-seek with me.'

But Santo couldn't see himself playing hide-and-seek with a whole bunch of kids. He smiled, at the same time shaking his head. 'I've come to take you home, Chloe.'

Her face fell. 'Not yet, Daddy! I don't want to go. It's fun here.'

And she hadn't had much fun recently! Losing a mother was no fun at all. He sighed and gave in. 'OK, ten more minutes, but that's all.'

She ran off happily.

He turned and Penny was standing beside him. 'Thank you for that,' she said quietly. 'I've never seen Chloe this happy.'

'She misses her mother,' he acknowledged.

Penny nodded. 'There's no one who'll take her place. But you should learn to relax more with your daughter—you might be surprised how much fun you'll have.'

'I think I would have more fun with you, Penny,' he growled, his voice lowered so that no one else could hear.

Penny felt her cheeks grow warm and the blood raced through her veins so swiftly that she felt she might faint. 'I thought we'd sorted that out. Didn't you promise never to—?'

'I did,' he acknowledged rapidly and fiercely. 'But aren't promises made to be broken?' His voice had dropped to a low, sexy growl, for her ears only, sending more agonies swimming through her veins

Heaven help her, *yes*! But it would be fatal and foolhardy. Her body wanted him so much that it hurt, but she was thinking with her heart and not her head. There had to be a modicum of sanity in all of this. And letting herself be sucked into Santo's world of sensuality would be insane.

'Maybe in your eyes, but not in mine.' Penny dared to look directly at him then wished she hadn't when the full force of those dangerous dark eyes immobilised her.

'You can't deny that you feel something for me,' he announced softly. 'Even here, now, you're wishing that we were alone somewhere, that our bodies were joined, that you could—'

Penny clapped her hands to her ears and hoped no one was looking, or else they'd be wondering what her peculiar behaviour was all about. 'I refuse to listen, Santo. I made a mistake, one that I'm not likely to repeat. I'd like you to go, please, I'll bring Chloe home in a little while.'

She felt as though her insides were unravelling, that soon she'd be no more than a heap of bones at his feet. She couldn't take any more of this. It was unreal. She caught her sister's eye and mouthed the word 'help'. Abbie immediately came across the lawn to them. 'Santo, I'd just like to say what a lovely daughter you have. She's a credit to you.'

Santo puffed up like any other proud parent and smiled warmly at Abbie. 'Well, thank you—er—Abbie, isn't it? Actually it's more credit to her mother than to me, but, yes, she's a good girl.'

'And I'm sure Penny's a marvellous help to you. She's wonderful with children. She's always said she'd like at least three of her own.'

'Abbie!' said a startled Chloe.

'Well it's true, isn't it?'

'Yes, but it's not for everyone's ears. Especially my boss's. What must he be thinking?'

'I'm thinking, Miss Penny Keeling,' said Santo with a warm smile that did things to her that should never be allowed, 'that there's a lot about you I don't know, and it will be my pleasure to find out.'

Penny glanced from Santo to her sister—saw the way Abbie's brows rose questioningly, and knew she'd soon be interrogated. Abbie had always said it was time she found herself another man and she might be thinking that Santo was an ideal candidate.

'I think not, Mr De Luca,' she declared. 'I'd prefer our relationship to remain purely professional.'

An eyebrow rose, dark eyes condemned. 'In that capacity then I insist you bring Chloe home immediately.'

'You can't do that,' she protested, anger rising inside her. 'She's enjoying herself. Surely you can see that?' They both looked across at where Chloe was peeping out from behind a bush, squealing and darting out of sight again when one of the others spotted her. 'She's having a wonderful time,' insisted Penny. 'What's she going to do at home with only adults for company?'

'I said ten minutes and those ten minutes are up,' he answered, his eyes clashing with hers. 'Chloe!' He called her name loudly and his daughter came running. 'We're going now,' he said, his voice more gentle.

Chloe looked across at Penny. 'Do I have to?' And she looked as though she wanted to burst into tears.

Penny couldn't go against her father's wishes, not in front of the girl anyway, so she reluctantly nodded, her heart aching when she saw Chloe's lower lip tremble.

When Penny looked at her sister she saw that Abbie also thought Santo was being too hard on Chloe. Was it her fault for daring to speak to him the way she had? The trouble was she was scared of the feelings he managed to arouse and biting back was her only defence.

'Are you coming too?' he asked Penny, causing her head to jerk back in his direction.

'If it's all right with you I'll stay and help my sister,' she said, 'but I'll be home in time to put Chloe to bed, you can be sure of that.'

Santo's eyes narrowed but he said nothing, walking away with Chloe's hand held tightly in his. The girl looked back over her shoulder and Penny smiled. 'I'll see you soon,' she whispered.

'He's a swine, isn't he?' questioned Abbie as soon as he was out of earshot. 'I know he's a killer in a business sense, and he's damn sexy-looking, but he hasn't got a clue when it comes to his own daughter.'

'I don't think he even knows what he's done,' sighed Penny. 'It's me he's angry with and I expect I shall hear about it when I get back.'

'But you can't be expected to answer to him all of the time. He's put you in charge of his daughter and as such you should be allowed to make decisions. His attitude stinks if you ask me.'

Penny didn't want to run him down so she said nothing. She had a secure, well-paid job now and didn't want to jeopardise it. Part of her knew that there was more to Santo's sudden arrival at the party and that it was a purely private part of his life. Besides Abbie had a habit of repeating conversations to her friends.

By the time all the children had gone home and Penny had helped Abbie tidy up, it was nearly seven o'clock. Santo was waiting for her when she got home. He'd changed into a pair of casual linen trousers teamed with a half-sleeved shirt. He looked gorgeous and Penny couldn't stop her blood warming up and pulsing rapidly through her veins.

'I'd begun to think you weren't coming,' he said, his voice rich and sexy, arousing her in an instant.

'I'd never let Chloe down,' she answered evenly, 'but if I might be permitted to say, I thought you were wrong in taking her away from the party. She was enjoying herself so much. It wasn't fair on her or her hostess.'

'Your sister complained?' he asked sharply.

'Of course not!' she declared. 'But it wasn't good manners. It wasn't as though you had a valid excuse. Top and bottom of it was that you didn't feel comfortable.'

'And you're an expert on my feelings?' he asked scathingly.

How she wished that she were. Not the sort of feelings he was talking about, but sensual feelings, ones that sent the body into spasm and demanded fulfilment.

The sort that she felt at this very moment!

'I wouldn't dare to be so presumptive,' she told him tightly. 'If you'll excuse me I'll go up to Chloe. Is she in her playroom?' On the top floor of the house he'd had a room decorated especially for Chloe to play in. It was a child's delight with every sort of toy imaginable. But she wasn't old enough to play for long periods on her own and in Penny's opinion it was a sheer waste of money.

'No, she's in bed.'

Penny looked at Santo in surprise. 'You put her to bed?' He nodded.

'And she's asleep?' She could hardly believe what she was hearing. But at least it was a step in the right direction so maybe he was heeding her words after all.

'I think so.'

Penny wanted to find out for herself and took the stairs quickly, half expecting him to call her back, relieved when he didn't.

She popped her head into Chloe's room, saw that she lay very still, and was about to leave when the girl's tiny voice called out to her. 'Penny.'

Swiftly she crossed to the bed. 'What is it, sweetheart?'

'Daddy doesn't love me.'

Her words struck a chill in Penny's heart. 'I'm sure he does, darling. What makes you say that?'

'He wouldn't let me stay at the party. And I wanted to wait up for you but he said I had to go to sleep. He doesn't love me like Mummy did. I miss my mummy. She'd have kissed me and held me until I went to sleep.' And she broke down in tears.

Penny lay down on the edge of the bed and cuddled Chloe against her, dabbing her eyes with a tissue. 'I'm sure your daddy loves you very much, darling, and he doesn't mean to be mean to you. He needs help from you, as well, you know. Don't forget he must be hurting too. He loved your mummy just as much as you did.'

'So why didn't he live with us?' asked Chloe, her eyes wide and questioning. 'I didn't know I had a daddy until he came for me when Mummy died.'

CHAPTER FOUR

PENNY felt as though all the breath had been knocked out of her body. She could hardly breathe. She had presumed Santo and his wife had still been living together when she died. Not that they were separated, maybe even divorced. She wished he had told her, it explained a lot.

Even so, it didn't account for the fact that he had never visited his daughter. Why had he ignored her, pretended that she didn't exist? Supposedly he'd had no feelings left for his wife, but his offspring, his own flesh and blood, his little girl, how could he have failed her like this? Chloe's psyche might be harmed forever more.

The man was obviously a callous, uncaring, insensitive swine, and she was going to tell him so. As she charged down the stairs in search of Santo Penny barely held on to her temper. But she couldn't find him.

She banged open doors, looking into each room in turn, finally finding him in his study, feet up on the desk, looking totally relaxed until she burst in. The surprise on his face would have made her laugh at any other time, but not today, not now. She was ready for battle.

He unfolded his legs and stood up. 'Is something

wrong?' He stood at his tallest and proudest, his initial smile of welcome fading abruptly, replaced by a frown.

Penny skidded to a halt. 'You can bet there is, Mr De Luca.' She drew in several steadying breaths, choosing her words carefully. 'Chloe's just told me something that's shocked me to the core.'

'Chloe?' His eyes widened in surprise. 'I thought she was asleep.'

'Then I guess she was pretending,' she flared. 'Thinking about it, though, it's hard to imagine how she could sleep when she feels her father never shows her any love!' Penny glared at him, angry on behalf of the little girl who only wanted his love. 'If Chloe didn't need me I'd walk out of here right now.'

Santo folded his arms, his eyes dangerously dark as he looked down the length of his nose. 'I'd be careful if I were you, Miss Keeling. You're overstepping the mark.'

'I don't care,' she riposted, even though the blaze in his eyes sent a faint shiver of fear through each of her limbs.

When Santo took a step towards her she stood her ground, blue eyes clashing with brown, all senses on full alert. She sucked in a deep breath, then wished she hadn't when he stood so close to her she could almost taste him. His cologne invaded her nostrils, reminded her that— No! *No!* She must not go down that road.

Move away, she yelled silently. Don't come near me!

But she remained where she was, not letting her eyes waver from his for one second.

'So, tell me what Chloe has said to make you so angry.' His accent had thickened, he was very much the Italian— volatile, proud, ready to defend himself to the core.

As far as Penny was concerned he had no defence. Abandoning his child was simply inexcusable.

She allowed herself the pleasure of staring into his eyes for a few seconds more, ignoring the wild beating of her heart, the rushing of blood through her veins. She was so angry she could have pummelled her fists against his hard chest and declared him the vilest man on earth.

'Tell me why,' she said in her coldest, most disapproving voice, 'why you never…' Then she stopped. 'No, something else first. Why did you give me the impression that you and your wife were still living together when she died?'

Her question clearly took him by surprise. His head went back, his eyes narrowed dangerously. 'Did I? I don't think I *ever* implied that, Penny. In any case my private life is no concern of yours—you work for me!' And he stood even taller, a cold gleam of disapproval filling his eyes, making them icier and more condemning than before.

'You've put me in charge of your daughter,' she declared strongly, 'and, as she's upset, it's my duty to try and put matters right.'

'Chloe's upset?' The news jolted him, his frown now one of a very different nature. Questioning, not condemning. Even concerned.

Which Penny didn't believe for one second, not after what Chloe had told her. Kids didn't lie, not five-year-olds anyway; they said exactly what was on their minds.

'I think she has every right to be when she believes that her father doesn't love her.'

'She said that?' He almost choked on the words.

Penny nodded, a little of her anger subsiding at his shocked reaction.

'And you believed her?'

'It doesn't matter what I believe—it's what Chloe believes. And why wouldn't she when you never went to see her once from the day she was born to the day her mother died?' Penny glared, daring him to deny it.

'You have no idea what you're talking about,' he snarled.

Penny watched the way muscles tensed in Santo's jaw, the way his fingers curled into fists, the way his body grew tenser, and she sucked in a deep breath. She'd better watch out. Goading him any further could end in disaster. He looked as though he was about to launch himself at her.

'Then tell me,' she demanded. 'Tell me exactly why Chloe believes such a thing and why she herself told me she didn't even know about you until her mother died.'

Suddenly something happened to his eyes. Anger was replaced by blankness, as though he was not looking at her at all, as though he was looking back into the past—and the memories were not happy ones.

Naturally. He had a conscience bigger than the Empire State Building!

It seemed like minutes before he answered, and when he spoke it was so quietly that she strained to hear.

'Because my wife never told me I had a daughter.'

There was such raw hurt in his eyes now, in his voice, that it took Penny's breath away.

'She was pregnant when she left me but I had no idea. She moved away. The divorce was settled through our respective lawyers. I had no more contact with her. Keeping Chloe from me was her last selfish act.'

Penny stood stock-still, lost for words. How could any woman deny her husband, or ex-husband for that matter, knowledge of his child? How could she? And now her heart went out to Santo. She was deeply sorry that she'd spoken to him the way she had. She felt as guilty as hell.

'I didn't know,' she declared huskily.

'How could you?'

'I'm sorry. I know it doesn't help, but I am. Truly.' And without even thinking she went to him, not quite touching but almost, lifting her face to look up into his pain-filled eyes. 'Truly.'

With a groan he pulled her hard against him. Penny dropped her head back, still looking into those deeply troubled eyes, and when his head bowed down to hers, when he took her mouth in a kiss that was both savage and furious, she knew that this was his way of ridding his mind of painful thoughts.

And because it was what she wanted too, because the coming together of their bodies had set off a riot of sensation, she returned his kiss, feeling it drugging her senses, filling her with an overwhelming desire to be made love to. And almost as though he'd read her thoughts Santo growled in her ear, 'Penny, sleep with me tonight.'

Penny knew that it wasn't because of any mistaken feelings of love. It was because he wanted to blot out everything that he'd told her. He could have got drunk, of course, that was one way of doing it. But instead he wanted to lose himself in her body, and heaven help her, she wanted him too.

Crazy, ridiculous, when she was dead set against getting involved with any man again. But this wouldn't be a true involvement. This would be a one-off, she would make sure of that. It couldn't do any harm, could it?

All these thoughts and more whizzed through her brain at the same time as she answered his question with a kiss so passionate that she couldn't believe this was really her. She had never done anything so dangerously impulsive in her life. And the odd thing was, she didn't even stop to wonder whether she would regret it.

Santo groaned deep in his throat and the next second she was swung up by a pair of strong arms, held against a hard, hot, throbbing body and carried upstairs as though she were no heavier than his daughter.

Penny felt his heart pounding against her, and the scent of his skin was almost suffocating. He was more male than any other man she knew, drugging her with his nearness, with the awareness of his arousal. It invoked an equal intensity in herself, in her needs, in her hunger to be satiated by this man.

Right from the very beginning she had felt drawn to him. Santo was the sort of man who could not be ignored. By anyone. Sexuality poured from him. No woman in her right mind would turn him down. And she was no different.

She needed him. Desperately. And she arched her back, lifting her head so that he could kiss her again. The kiss aroused, stirred emotions; sent excitement slithering through sensitised nerve-ends so that his lightest touch increased her need.

Penny wasn't sure what she expected when they reached his bedroom. Would he throw her down on the bed and take her immediately? Would it be swift and furious before he thanked her and let her go? Or would he take his time, lose himself slowly in her body, determinedly shut out all unhappy memories; insist she stay with him the whole night through?

As the door closed quietly behind them Santo relaxed his arms and she fully expected him to let her go. But instead he slid her deliberately and unhurriedly down the length of his hard, hot body—inch by excruciating inch, ensuring she knew exactly how much he wanted her.

His arousal was magnificent, it couldn't be ignored. The fierceness of it drugged her, excited her, made her own need so deep and painful and mindless that she pressed herself urgently against him, her arms linking around his neck, pulling his head down to meet her parted lips.

It was a fierce kiss, an erotic kiss, his tongue invading, touching, stroking, inciting. Triggering an even wilder response. Penny clutched at his head, lacing her fingers through his strong black hair, feeling herself being swept into a place she'd never been before, a place where nothing mattered except Santo.

The touch of his mouth on hers, the taste of his kisses, the masculine scent of him. Strong. So strong it was more intoxicating than alcohol.

Actually she felt drunk. Drunk with desire. A deep real need screamed through her body with the force of a cyclone. She felt compelled to cling to Santo in case she got blown away.

How it happened Penny didn't quite know, but one moment they were standing just inside his bedroom, kissing. More than kissing. They were practically devouring one another. And the next they were lying on his bed and all her clothes had been removed.

Santo's too. His long, hard, exciting body lay next to hers. Olive skin against milky pale. An exciting combination. His torso was well-honed, as were his legs.

She looked delicate beside him. Not that she wasn't fit, but against Santo she looked like a china doll.

His darkly mesmerising eyes locked into hers as long, sure fingers began an exploration that threatened to explode her senses. Penny had expected that he would take her urgently and masterfully without any preliminaries. How wrong she was. Fingertips traced and memorised each curve of her cheeks, her ever-so-slightly upturned nose, the fine shape of her eyebrows, the delicate curl of her ears.

When he reached her lips she was screaming with silent need and sucked his fingers hungrily into her mouth, touching his face too, discovering hard lines and jutting angles. A proud man, a fantastically handsome man. Arrogant, yes. Masterful, yes. But at this moment completely dependent on her.

He needed her. He wanted her to obliterate his unhappy thoughts. He wanted to lose himself in her, beside her, with her. And she was happy to oblige.

Somewhere deep down in Santo's mind was the knowledge that he was doing a very dangerous thing. He didn't want a relationship. He had no intention of getting involved with his daughter's nanny. What he did need was release from the torment in his soul.

It had almost crucified him to hear that his own daughter believed he didn't love her. And tomorrow he intended doing something about it. But for now he needed to immerse himself in a distraction of a very different kind. And so long as Penny knew how he felt, so long as she didn't expect something more from him, then it was the perfect antidote.

'You do know what you're doing?' he asked thickly against her mouth, his breathing deep and hungry.

Drinking from her lips was like tasting the most exqui-site wine, it was an aphrodisiac, making him want more, and then more again. In that instant he knew that this was not going to be a one-off.

It was more than dangerous. It was suicidal. Perhaps he ought to back out now while there was time? But already Penny was whispering her response. 'I know, Santo, and I can't help myself. I want you too.'

He sucked in a deep breath of air, feeling the taste of her on his lips. Feeling her supple body against his. Tantalising, beckoning, threatening. With a rough groan he claimed her mouth in another hot, reckless kiss that began the process of easing his pain.

Penny felt the sudden change in him, as though he'd freed himself of any doubts. And because he felt free, she did too. She abandoned herself to his kisses, re-turned them fiercely and hungrily, and when he left her mouth to explore the curve of her jaw and the slender column of her throat her head fell back against the pillow, her fingers returning to the wiry strength of his hair, clutching at the dark threads, accustoming herself to the shape of him, the feel of him.

But when his mouth moved even lower, when both his lips and fingertips found her breasts, discovered the hard nub that both protested and exalted when he teased it between thumb and forefinger, her hands flopped to her sides, her breath coming out in short gasps.

'Oh, Santo.'

At the sound of her voice he paused and lifted his head. His dark eyes were glazed and she wasn't even sure that he was focusing on her. 'You don't like it?'

'Like it? I love it!'

It was all he needed. He groaned and returned his attention to first one breast and then the other, suckling, biting, kissing, stroking, making her body arch with excitement, needing more—much, much more. Had she really said those words out loud? She sucked in deep breaths of air and closed her eyes to everything except the sheer exquisite pleasure of the moment.

Santo was an expert when it came to lovemaking. He knew exactly what would whip her body into a frenzy, what would make her curve herself into him, touch him too, run her fingers over his firm, warm skin, feel the strength of muscle, even the aching need deep down inside him.

When his mouth trailed a blazing line of kisses from her breasts to her navel, when his tongue explored, when she felt her skin prepare to ignite, when his fingers began to explore even lower, seeking the hot, moist heart of her, Penny could hardly breathe.

Her head moved from side to side on the pillow and she closed her eyes, conscious of nothing except this feeling of Santo being in charge of her body, instructing it to obey his commands, to burst into flames at a touch, to feel an explosion of sensation that she'd never felt before. Never!

It couldn't be the real Penny Keeling who was experiencing this serious metamorphosis. Things like this didn't happen to her. She was either dreaming or imagining it.

The Penny Keeling she knew would never have allowed herself to get into this situation. She didn't approve of affairs. One failed relationship had been enough. She was sensible, level-headed, careful…

Who was she trying to kid? Santo De Luca had somehow—she couldn't figure out how—deluded her into believing that she wanted him to make love to her, that it would be OK to give in to temptation.

And she didn't have the strength to rail against it. She'd known what she was getting into from the very start. She wanted Santo to make love to her. Now! This very minute. Deeply and furiously, assuaging the need that had built up and built up so that if he didn't take her soon she would turn the tables and climb on top of him.

'You're ready?'

Had Santo read her mind?

Penny nodded, then realised he wasn't looking at her face—he was too busy exploring other interesting areas of her anatomy. 'Yes.' It was more a squeak than a proper word but she arched her hips upwards and Santo groaned.

He moved away for the briefest of seconds while he sheathed himself and then he was inside her. So gently at first, so carefully, until he felt her fully relax—or was it when her hands clenched on his shoulders and she urged herself closer, repositioning her body, making it easier for him?

What happened afterwards was a blur of serious sensations, of nails digging into skin, of bodies bucking and gyrating, of primitive sounds escaping both their throats, of a final explosion that rocked and pulsated, bathing them both in a sheen of sweat, pounding hearts ready to leap out of their chests.

During the night Santo made love to her again—and again. He was a man who seriously needed to blot all other thoughts from his head, thought Penny. Not that she minded. This was a whole new experience. She had never been made love to so beautifully before, never been allowed to feel that her needs were important too.

After that first time he was a tender, considerate

lover and Penny couldn't believe that she was letting it happen. That the man she had thought was a hard, inconsiderate father was such a dream in bed.

Come morning, though, he had gone. The bed beside her was cold and empty. Immediately Penny felt guilt and shame. It spread across her like a rash. She had let him use her! She had let him see that she was his for the taking! Her stomach churned and anger and humiliation hit her full in the face.

She'd been incredibly stupid. How could she look him in the eye ever again? Perhaps she ought to leave before sleeping with her boss became the norm? Except that her duty lay with Chloe. She couldn't subject her to another series of nannies who revolted against the long hours Santo expected them to work.

By letting him take her to bed she had made a fool of herself but it wouldn't happen again, she would make sure of that. It would be strictly business from now on. She crept out of his room and towards her own, stopping to check on Chloe on the way. However, when she put her head around the door she saw that the little girl wasn't there.

Hopefully she'd be with her father. After what she'd told Santo he'd surely want to talk to his daughter, assure her that he loved her, that it was through no fault of his own that he'd never been around during those first years of her life.

Penny showered and dressed in double-quick time then, with her heart drumming, she went downstairs in search of them. She found Chloe in the kitchen with Emily, but no sign of Santo.

'Mr De Luca has gone to work,' informed the housekeeper.

'Did you see your daddy before he left?' Penny asked Chloe, and could hardly believe it when his daughter shook her head, her brown eyes revealing her disappointment.

Penny gave her a hug. 'He's such a busy man, I expect he didn't want to wake you. What are you having for breakfast?'

All day long Penny felt anger towards Santo. Not only for what he'd done to his daughter, but also because she'd made a fool of herself. He'd used her and she hated him for it. Except that he hadn't actually done that, had he? She'd been a more than willing partner. She'd wanted him as much as he'd wanted her, letting the sadness of the moment influence her.

When he didn't come home early enough to spend time with Chloe before she went to bed Penny was fuming, and it was almost ten before she heard his car on the driveway. She'd sat in silence, not watching TV, not playing music or even reading, she wanted to launch her attack the second he walked through the door. She knew his routine. He'd drop his briefcase in his study, hang his jacket on the back of a chair ready to take upstairs later and then move through into the smallest of the living rooms, where he'd pour himself a glass of whisky before relaxing in his favourite leather armchair.

He looked tired as he entered the room but Penny didn't care. She jumped up from her window seat and faced him. He smiled, unaware of the anger seething inside her. 'Penny. You looked so comfortable this morning that I didn't want to wake you. Hell, I've had a bad day.' He raked a hand through his hair, spiking it so that he looked younger than his thirty-six years, took off his tie, released his cuff-links and rolled back his shirtsleeves. 'How about you? What sort of a day have you had?' He walked over to her, looking prepared to take her into his arms. 'And Chloe? Is she in bed? I'd hoped to—'

'You'd hoped to what?' demanded Penny, unable to hold back a flood of anger.

'See her before she went to bed, of course.' He frowned and halted, sensing that all was not as he'd hoped it would be.

No doubt, thought Penny, he expected to carry on where he'd left off last night. If that was the case he was in for a big shock. 'That's very noble of you,' she shot fiercely, 'but she's been in bed hours. Do you have no idea what time it is? What was wrong with going in to work a little later this morning and talking to her before she went to school? Don't you care that your daughter thinks you don't love her?'

'Of course I care.' Confusion pulled his brows together. He clearly hadn't expected this attack.

'It doesn't look like it to me.' Penny's eyes flared fiercely into his face as she forget for a moment that she was his employee, that her livelihood depended on him. 'From where I'm standing you couldn't care less about Chloe. Find someone to look after her and she'll be all right; that's your maxim. You're not a father. You're simply a provider.'

His brow darkened. 'How dare you speak to me like that? You have no idea what I'm going through at this very moment.'

Penny lifted an expressive eyebrow. 'Perhaps I don't. But I know what Chloe's going through and she needs you more than your business does.'

Santo damned her with his dark eyes. All the passion and pleasure that she'd seen there last night was gone, leaving in its place a hard, cold man who didn't appreciate being told off by his daughter's nanny. After flaying her with another glance he strode across the room and poured himself a drink, taking a long swallow before facing her again.

'It's hard to believe you're the same woman who slept with me last night.'

Eyes that were black met her true blue ones, and Penny ignored the faint awareness that trickled through her veins. 'That's because I'm not the same woman,' she retorted. 'That woman was foolish. She gave in to emotional blackmail. She saw you were hurt and she wanted to help you through the pain. But this woman—' she clapped a hand to her heart '—sees the other side of you. The uncaring side. The workaholic. The man who puts his business before his family. I'm sure you'll agree it's not a pretty picture.'

CHAPTER FIVE

SANTO knew he ought to have spoken to Chloe before he went to work but he hadn't wanted to wake her at such an early hour. And because he'd been waiting for an international call, the time difference meant that he had made it home late. It didn't mean to say that he didn't feel deeply guilty; he did. He felt too awful for words. But what he didn't need now was a fire-breathing dragon telling him about it.

'You dare to criticise me?' Anger began to take the place of disbelief. No other employee had ever dared speak to him in this way. Not that he'd ever taken an employee to bed before! But this was a totally different person from the one who'd so fiercely fed his hunger last night.

Penny's chin rose and her eyes flared. 'I definitely do dare. You don't deserve Chloe. Perhaps that's why your—' A swift hand went to her lips and she stopped abruptly.

But Santo knew what she'd been going to say. And she was right; his work ethics had been one of the reasons his wife had left him. But he sure as hell wasn't going to let anyone else criticise his behaviour.

Nevertheless he couldn't help but notice how beautiful she looked in her anger. Her blazing eyes were more purple than blue, her cheeks flushed, her breasts rising and falling as her breathing deepened. She wore some ridiculously thin, silky, soft blouse and a swift surge of raw need raced through him.

He'd been looking forward to coming home. Penny had been an exciting lover last night and he'd wanted more of her. He'd never met anyone with such an incredible appetite, who seemed to know instinctively how to pleasure him, how to take him to the brink time and time again before finally tipping him over the edge.

'I'll ignore that comment,' he told her tersely, 'and if you've quite finished telling me off about my daughter perhaps you'd care to join me in a drink— perhaps we can talk this through rationally?' His male hormones were fuelled by the fire in her incredibly eloquent eyes. They damned him, but heaven help him, he wanted her in his bed again tonight.

One taste of Penelope Keeling and he'd become an addict. Normally when he was at work he never thought about anything except the job in hand. He kept the two parts of his life strictly separate. But today, even though the meeting was of paramount importance, he'd found his mind wandering.

Visions of long, wavy blonde hair spreading out over his chest and loins caused his breath to catch in his throat. Erotic images of her tempting little kisses getting ever closer to his manhood made him feel hard. He'd even thought he could still smell the heady scent of her on his skin.

Although he'd managed with a Herculean effort to banish such wanton thoughts, the feelings had returned with a vengeance as he'd made his way home.

Penny couldn't believe Santo's audacity. She stood and faced him, her breathing all over the place, wondering how she could have ever given herself to him. The man had no heart; he was driven by work. Pleasure was something to be squeezed in between. And as for his daughter—well, words failed her.

She would have thought that after losing out for so many years he'd want to spend every hour of every day with her. She couldn't weigh him up at all.

'You really think I'd have a drink with you after—after everything?' Penny curled her fingers into fists, ignoring the pounding of her heart and the heat filming her skin. 'You're unbelievable. I'm going to bed. Goodnight, Mr De Luca.' She spun on her heel and walked away.

'I think not.'

His words were a command. Automatically Penny stopped. And very slowly she turned around. 'You have no right to dictate what I do in my own time. I'm not employed to socialise with you. Or did I get the picture wrong?' she questioned, her voice full of sarcasm. 'Is that what you had in mind all along?'

'The hell I didn't and you know it,' he threw back at her.

'Chloe was your main concern?'

'Exactly.'

'Then you have your answer,' she returned fiercely. 'Chloe is my principal concern as well. Last night was a one-off; it will not happen again.'

And this time when she walked away he did not try to stop her.

Penny threw herself down on the bed and wondered at her temerity in speaking to Santo the way she had. It was a wonder he hadn't dismissed her on the spot.

But she wasn't sorry for what she'd said; she meant every word.

Through the window she could see an almost full moon, and as she hadn't bothered to switch on the light it bathed everything in cool silver, enhancing the elegance of the room. Penny knew she ought to feel lucky that she'd landed herself a job in a place like this.

It had been wrong of her to give in to temptation. One half of her still fancied Santo like mad and wanted to repeat the experience, the other half couldn't accept the way he behaved towards Chloe. She felt a fierce protective urge towards the child every time she thought about it, like a mother hen looking after its brood.

In the middle of the night Penny woke up and realised that she was still fully dressed. Quietly she slid off the bed and crossed to the bathroom—pausing when she heard the sound of voices.

It sounded like Chloe and Santo—in Chloe's room!

She tiptoed to the adjoining door and listened. Yes, it was definitely father and daughter. A faint smile curved her lips. She was tempted to go in and say something, but she didn't. She undressed and slipped back into bed instead.

All was quiet when she got up the next morning. She found Chloe downstairs in the breakfast room—with her father! The man who always left for work at seven…and it was now a quarter to eight! Penny walked in and smiled. 'Good morning.'

Chloe giggled.

'Do come and join us,' invited Santo.

Penny raised her brows at him. 'Thank you.' And took her seat.

There was not a lot she could say in front of his

daughter, but she let her approval show. And when he eventually said that he had to leave for work she nodded coolly. Chloe on the other hand gave him a big hug, and he kissed her on both cheeks, which was the first time Penny had seen him show such emotion.

'Did you know that Chloe breaks up for the summer holidays on Friday?' Penny had been enjoying the pleasures of the garden when Santo arrived home. It was one of those hot, sultry evenings when everything was still, when the perfume of the flowers hung heavy in the air, when even the birds were silent.

She'd found a bench by the lake—where already a fence had been erected—and was watching some squabbling ducks when Santo surprised her by joining her. His business suit was gone, replaced by a sky-blue shirt and a pair of casual trousers. His dark hair, still wet from a shower, looked as though all he'd done was run his fingers through it. Gone was the suave businessman, in its place was a relaxed, gorgeously handsome Italian who smelled exotic and sexy and set every one of her nerve-ends on fire.

'She does? Why didn't I know of this earlier?'

'I imagine you had a calendar at the beginning of the year,' she said, lifting her brows, wishing he hadn't sat quite so close. How could she possibly ignore him? How could she stem the flood of feelings that had begun to race through her body?

Santo's frown was almost comical. 'It was never passed on to me.'

And would you have remembered if it had been? wondered Penny. Santo was too tied up in his own world. He'd probably disposed of it in his waste bin.

'It means she'll be at home for six weeks,' said Penny.

'And—the reason you're telling me is?' he questioned. 'Surely you're not thinking of taking time off yourself?' A faint frown accompanied his words and Penny was fascinated by the two tiny furrows in his brow. She felt an urge to smooth them away with the tips of her fingers. She almost ached to touch him—which was crazy under the circumstances.

'Of course not,' she answered. 'But if you don't mind me saying so I would suggest that you take some time off yourself. Take Chloe away. A beach holiday somewhere; just the two of you. You need to bond with her and it would be an ideal opportunity.'

Penny held her breath as she waited for his answer. She expected an explosion. A 'who, me?' scenario. And she deliberately averted her eyes, went back to watching the ducks.

Not that she wasn't conscious of him; too much so. The very air around her had changed. It had thickened until breathing was virtually impossible. Santo's presence was everywhere. She would never have believed that one man could fill such a large space.

And when the silence between them lengthened, when she could wait for his answer no longer, Penny turned to him—and felt a shock wave rip through her. He was looking at her with such an intense expression in his velvety brown eyes that she couldn't breathe, couldn't even move.

'An excellent idea, Penny.'

Goodness. Had he really said that?

'You're right, we do need time together.'

So far so good!

'But there is one problem.'

Here we go! The excuse! The get-out!

'Chloe needs you as well.'

'What?' The word was out before she could stop it. Chloe needed her! More likely *he* needed her. An excuse to get her back into his bed.

'There are things you do for her that I'm no good at.'

'Then you'll have to learn,' she declared firmly, trying not to look into those magnetic eyes. Finding it impossible. He was so close, so vital, that she was trapped like a fly in a spider's web. 'If I come along it will defeat the whole objective.' And she glared at him, trying to feel nothing except contempt for his suggestion.

'And if you don't come along and I fail her, what then?'

'Are you blackmailing me, Mr De Luca?' Penny deliberately addressed him formally, seeing this as the only way she could keep their conversation on an even keel. Because, lord help her, she wanted him. And she was desperately afraid that it might show.

'Would I dare?' His lips twitched as he spoke.

He was different tonight, thought Penny. She was seeing a softer side to his character—or was it because he was after something? Because he wanted her back in his bed. Whatever, it was having an alarming effect on her senses. She ought to move, walk a few steps away; pull herself together.

But she didn't. She couldn't. She was immobilised. 'You're capable of anything,' she told him, and hoped he didn't hear the alarming tremble in her voice.

'That's something on which we both agree,' he told her, 'and at this very moment I do believe I'm capable of kissing my daughter's very attractive nanny.'

Even though he had warned her, even though she knew his intent, Penny still didn't move. She watched his face draw closer, saw the dangerous darkness in his eyes, inhaled the intoxicating male smell of him, felt excitement hurtle through her veins.

Ever nearer he came, stopping only when his mouth was millimetres away from hers. Penny held her breath and waited, locking her eyes into his. She knew what he was doing. He was tormenting her. Waiting to see whether she'd take the initiative or whether she'd back away.

Her palms grew sweaty and her heart pounded, and she wanted his kisses more than anything else, but common sense prevailed. From somewhere deep inside her came the strength to resist. She leaned backwards from the hips, blue eyes flashing. 'I think not,' she told him bravely, 'and if you think this is a good way of persuading me to join you on holiday then you're very much mistaken.'

To her annoyance he smiled and, with a faint you-win-some-you-lose-some shrug, he relaxed back against the bench.

Santo didn't know from where he'd found the strength to put distance between him and Penny. When he had arrived home and found Chloe asleep but no Penny he'd been disappointed, until Emily had told him that she was outside. And he'd come out here with one purpose in mind: to kiss her.

She had surprised him with the information that Chloe's school was closing for their annual holidays. He supposed that at some time he'd been told but he had completely forgotten about it. And his first thought had been thank goodness for Penny.

But when she'd mentioned taking Chloe away—just

the two of them—he'd not been happy. Yes, it would be a good way of bonding with his daughter, as Penny so eloquently put it, but coping with an active five-year-old on his own wouldn't be easy. He'd need help. And if Penny came too it would make all the difference. Penny in his bed every night would more than compensate.

Not that he expected she would fall easily into his arms. She'd been scared by the depth of her emotions during the night they'd spent together. Initially she'd wanted to comfort him—but who had enjoyed themselves the most in what followed afterwards was a moot question.

'It seems like I'll have to find some other form of persuasion,' he told her softly, stroking back a stray strand of hair where it clung to her cheek, allowing his fingers to linger, to feel the downy softness of her skin. He couldn't remember the last time a woman had got through to him like this.

Penny was different in every way to any other woman he'd known. It was a change for him to be rejected. Not that he wanted to take her for that reason alone. He wasn't that bloody-minded. But she was intriguing as well as a fantastic lover. She blew hot and cold and didn't mind telling him off. Something he'd never experienced before.

He'd had arguments with his wife but they had been different. They had been mainly about money—and how fast she spent it. Money didn't seem to be a factor where Penny was concerned. Yes, she'd needed the job, she'd been overwhelmed when he said how much he was prepared to pay her, but she hadn't tried to wheedle her way into his bed.

If anything it was the other way round. And he

wasn't succeeding. Which was proving to be something of a challenge. Especially when she knocked his
hand away from her face, saying crossly, 'Santo De
Luca, you're going the right way to make me walk out
of this job.'

He frowned then and drew back his hand. 'You don't
like me touching you any more?'

Penny closed her eyes and he saw the tussle she was
having with herself. 'What I like and what is proper are
two different things,' she said crossly. 'For one thing,
I'm in your employ and the way I see it there should be
no crossing over of loyalties. And also, I'm not interested in an affair—with any man.'

'Care to tell me who made you feel this way?' She
sounded so passionate, so vehement that he was intrigued. And he wanted to know who had done this to her.

But Penny shook her head. 'It's no one's business but
mine. It's not something I want to talk about, ever.'

'He hurt you that much?'

She lifted her slender shoulders. 'I guess.'

Santo felt a surge of anger that any man could take
advantage of such a warm, caring person. Warm and
caring? Where had that come from? Fire and brimstone
was a better description. Or was it the other side of her
that he was seeing? She was an intriguing combination
and he wanted to get to know her a whole lot better.

But more than that he wanted to pull her into his arms
and comfort her, except that he knew she'd take it the
wrong way. So he pushed himself to his feet and walked
to the water's edge, turning to look back at her. 'Care
to change your mind on the holiday idea?'

He made himself sound hopeful and wistful, slanting
her a wry smile. 'If I take Chloe I really could do with

your help—purely as her nanny, of course.' As for anything else, well, he'd see what happened. He was not looking for a permanent relationship—like Penny, once bitten, twice shy—but he didn't see why they couldn't indulge in an affair.

Penny found herself wavering. Of course she wanted to go. And more than anything she wanted to share Santo's bed again. But where would it lead? She didn't want to get hurt again.

On the other hand she wasn't sure that Santo was up to looking after his daughter full-time. Not on his own. Or was she being unfair? Doing him an injustice?

She looked at him for several long moments. He had a little-boy-lost expression, his gorgeous mouth turned down slightly at the corners, his eyes sad, and although Penny knew it was solely for her benefit she couldn't help but be won over.

What she wanted to do was smile widely, run over to him and fling herself into his arms, declaring that yes, she would join him. But that would be tantamount to declaring a willingness to indulge in an affair. And she knew in her heart of hearts that she wasn't capable of taking the pleasure and then walking away. It needed to be all or nothing.

And Santo was offering her nothing.

'I'm still waiting,' he said softly. 'If you can't do it for my sake then think of Chloe.'

Penny gave a wistful smile. He knew he'd get her on the Chloe issue. She gave the faintest of nods. 'For Chloe's sake.'

Immediately he grinned.

She'd not seen so much pleasure on his face before. Pleasure when they were making love, yes—but that had been entirely different. This was childish pleasure. It made her beam too.

'I think a celebration's in order,' he announced. 'Come.' And before she could object he took her hand and led her back to the house.

Penny wanted to snatch her hand away but felt it would be churlish, and when he almost ran across the lawns she started to laugh. Santo laughed too and when they burst into the house she half expected him to swing her around in his arms and kiss her.

But he didn't and she was glad because it would have ruined everything. This was a side to Santo she hadn't seen before, and she liked it. He was fun. And in the beginning fun wasn't a word she would ever have used to describe him.

He left her in the garden room, pushing the doors open wide to let in the pleasant evening air, returning a few minutes later with a bottle of champagne and two elegant crystal flutes.

Watching as he filled their glasses, Penny couldn't help admiring his long, slender fingers—fingers that had touched and excited every inch of her body, that excited her again now just thinking about the pleasure he'd given her! And she knew that she'd need to be careful and not drink too much or she'd end up in his bed again tonight.

And that would set a precedent for the holiday.

'Have you had any thoughts where you'd like to take Chloe?' Mentioning his daughter's name felt a safe thing to do. 'Somewhere in Cornwall would be nice. In Looe children sit on the harbour wall dangling crab lines into the water. She'd love that. And there are good beaches in the area as well.'

Santo handed Penny her drink and raised his glass to hers, waiting until she'd taken her first sip before answering. 'I'm going to take you somewhere—you and Chloe,' he amended quickly, 'where I used to go as a boy.'

'In Italy?' asked Penny quickly, not missing his slip of the tongue but choosing to ignore it.

He nodded. 'Have you ever been there?'

'No,' she admitted with a tiny rueful smile, 'though it's a place I've always wanted to visit, especially Rome.'

'Yes, Rome.'

He said the name with an odd inflection in his voice, and his beautiful accent deepened. It made him even sexier and Penny felt her throat tighten. 'Do you miss Italy?'

'Sometimes, but I love England too. My mother was English.'

'Was?' questioned Penny softly.

'Sadly she's no longer alive.' His eyes clouded over briefly. 'She was born and lived right here in London. She met my father here. But he wouldn't leave his beloved Italy. I had no such compunction. I studied at Oxford and have stayed ever since.'

'And your father—is he—?'

'He lives in Rome still and will until the day he dies.' A shuttered look crossed Santo's face before he continued. 'But enough about me and my family,' he said firmly. 'Let's concentrate on us.'

Us? Penny shivered inwardly, aware that she'd need to be on her guard while they were away. Nor could she help wondering why she'd given in to temptation in the first place.

Because, came the answer, Santo De Luca is one hell of a sexy man. How could anyone resist him?

But resist him she'd need to. She took another sip of her champagne, and then another, and before she knew it she'd finished the whole glass and Santo was refilling it.

'Please, no more,' she said faintly, but the alcohol was already beginning to take effect.

'We can't waste the bottle,' he declared. 'And the night's young. There's no rush.'

Penny sucked in a breath. What was he expecting?

CHAPTER SIX

A WHOLE week had passed since Santo asked Penny to join him and Chloe in Italy. Her emotions had seesawed; she'd gone from an absolute declaration that she wouldn't go to an out-and-out anticipation of the event that flooded her body with secret delight.

It was Chloe's enthusiasm that had clinched it for her. The little girl had been so excited after her father told her where they were going that she'd been physically sick and there were fears that they wouldn't make it.

Now they were flying over the Swiss Alps in Santo's private jet and Chloe was watching through the window. Each time she turned to look at them her eyes were as wide as saucers. There was no hiding her happiness.

'No regrets?' asked Santo quietly, one eye on his daughter but the other fixed firmly on Penny.

'None at all,' answered Penny.

Actually she was looking forward to the holiday almost as much as Chloe. She so wanted to see everything that she'd read about in history books or seen on television. This was going to be the real thing—and with a gorgeous Italian to show her around. What more could she ask for?

During the past week Santo had kept a respectable distance. He still maintained his long hours, though there had been a couple of occasions when he had surprised her by coming home early. He also tried to make sure that he saw his daughter before he went out to work each morning. He was making an effort and for that she thanked him.

When he did come home early they spent time together, usually outside, sharing a bottle of wine, and she knew that he was wondering whether he dared kiss her again. She tried to give him no encouragement, except that it was hard with her emotions running high!

She had only to catch sight of him to feel a rush of desire, a trembling in her limbs and an unbearable heat in her lower abdomen. It was sometimes more than she could bear and it was all she could do to hide her feelings. At least she hoped that she did. There had been a time when she'd caught Santo looking at her strangely and realised that she was in grave danger.

'I'm eternally grateful that the agency sent you to me,' he'd said softly, his voice little more than a throb.

'You mean I'm better at my job than the others?' she had asked, deliberately misunderstanding.

'That too,' he'd agreed.

But it was the words he didn't say that had made Penny's heart spin.

Nevertheless they'd made it through the week without him attempting to kiss her, or even touch her again. Not that he hadn't made love to her. His eyes had seduced and her body had erupted traitorously. Not once but several times. It was something she would never have thought possible, not in a million years.

The plane had surprised her, though it shouldn't

have. She'd never actually thought about it; if she had she would have guessed that the likes of Santo De Luca had their own private jet.

The cabin was as sumptuous as a king's palace with deep leather armchairs and a marble-topped table. One would be spoilt for choice from a well-stocked book-case, and in a corner was a computer console so that business could be conducted throughout the whole flight. There was even a bedroom.

Penny's mind had balked when Santo had shown her; she'd taken one swift look and backed out again.

An eyebrow had risen and she knew exactly what he had been thinking. Had they been alone it went without saying that the whole flight would have been spent ex-ploring its possibilities. Thank goodness for Chloe!

This was Chloe's holiday, not hers, not to be spent enjoying herself with Santo, but ensuring that his daughter had a good time.

And he needed to do that too. She had frequently told him so and it looked as though he was finally taking her at her word. He'd ensured that Chloe had a good stock of toys to keep her occupied when she tired of travelling, and he'd talked to her a lot about what they planned to do.

'Do you know,' he said, interrupting Penny's thoughts, 'I haven't had a holiday for as long as I can remember? How about you? When was the last time you went away?'

Penny smiled. 'Last year actually. I went to Corsica with a group of friends.' And when he raised a question-ing brow, she added, 'It was a hen party.' And thought she saw relief on his face.

In reality it shouldn't have bothered him who she holidayed with. Except that she sensed Santo had a proprietorial air about him these days. And it scared her. Making love with him had been a big mistake. She could never look into his face again without remembering those magical, heart-stopping moments. The link had been created; it would be impossible to break. Only time and distance could do that—and she was reluctant to leave her job, even though she knew it could well come to that.

'I'm looking forward to Rome,' she said, needing to rescue the situation.

'Rome?' His eyes widened. 'I didn't say we were going there. We're going to a place in the Bay of Naples. Chloe will love it.'

'But—don't you want to go and see your father? I thought he lived in Rome,' she asked gently, knowing that this was a subject Santo didn't like talking about.

'No, I do not.' A deep scowl darkened his brow, making him look stern and forbidding. 'In fact I'd rather we didn't talk about him. Please don't mention him again.'

Penny knew she had hit a raw nerve and thought back to other times she had tried to broach the subject of Santo's family. She realised that she knew hardly anything about the man seated next to her and the subject of his father clearly upset him. Penny couldn't imagine what it would be like not to want to spend time with your father. Surely his father would need him more than ever, since his mother had died? But if Santo didn't want to go and see him, or even talk about him, then who was she to argue?

Penny had loved both her parents dearly, and could never imagine falling out with either one of them. And now that they were gone she was glad that they'd never had cross words. It must be uncomfortable to know that you were a sworn enemy of the person who had pro-created you. How could it be? How could anything be so bad that you didn't even want to talk about him?

'Look, aeroplanes,' cried Chloe, pointing out of the window.

Penny gave a faint sigh of relief when she looked down and saw that they were almost at their destination.

The heat met them as they alighted from the aircraft, but in no time they were whisked away in a chauffeur-driven, air-conditioned car.

Chloe insisted on sitting between them, which was something of a relief as far as Penny was concerned because the long hours sitting in Santo's company had sizzled her senses. She was more aware of him than she'd ever been—and even began to wonder whether it had been wise to suggest this holiday.

Except that she'd done it in all good faith. Not for one moment had she anticipated Santo suggesting she accompany them. But he had, and she was here, and a whole week lay ahead of them—maybe longer—and she didn't know what he expected of her.

There was little chance of conversation, Chloe did all the chattering, pointing out everything that was fasci-nating and different, until finally they pulled up in front of a pair of electronically operated gates that opened on their arrival. Once out of the car they were whisked upwards in a lift set into the hillside to an amazing open terrace. And right in front of them was the villa.

Penny could only stand and stare. 'This is where you holidayed as a child?' Not only was it huge, with windows and balconies overlooking the turquoise waters below, but its architecture was stunning also.

White walls that dazzled, arches, pillars, even some castellation. It was truly magnificent. 'Does it belong to your family?' she asked in awe.

Even Chloe was lost for words.

'It's my grandfather's—or was; he died last year. My father owns it now but he doesn't come here himself. He keeps it for any one of his relatives or friends who wishes to use it.'

So he had at least been in touch with his father, thought Penny, though wisely she said nothing. 'It's out of this world.'

Santo smiled. 'I'd actually forgotten how splendid it is. When I was a child I have to confess it seemed much bigger. I expect Chloe thinks it's enormous, don't you, *mio bello*?'

Chloe smiled from ear to ear and nodded. 'Is it a fairy castle?'

'It's everything and anything that you want it to be,' he agreed. 'Shall we explore?'

Chloe nodded energetically and took Santo's offered hand.

Penny felt a glow of satisfaction. It looked as though this holiday was going to be the turning point in Santo's relationship with his daughter—exactly what she had hoped for.

The villa had more rooms than they would ever use, more bathrooms, more of everything in fact; three terraces, two with swimming pools, both fenced, she was pleased to see. They even had their own private beach.

There was also a maid and a cook, and a handyman who looked after the gardens and the pools. It was sheer luxury and nothing like Penny had expected.

Tired after their long journey, Chloe had climbed on her bed and immediately fallen asleep.

'I suggest a drink,' announced Santo as they left her room. 'We'll take it on the terrace and discuss the view.'

'I need to unpack.' Penny felt her heart give a sudden jerk. She knew what view he meant.

'The maid will do it,' he assured her, 'that's what she's here for. What is wrong? You do not want my company?'

There was a faint sound of irritation in his voice and Penny shook her head. 'I can't help but remember that I'm your employee. It's not proper that I should spend so much time with you.'

'So what would you propose you do?' he enquired, an eyebrow raised, eyes closely watching her reaction.

Penny shrugged.

'There, you see. You have nothing to do but keep me company. It is both my wish and my pleasure. Come.' He took her elbow and led her outside, where they sat in wicker armchairs beneath a huge canopy. The ocean was a mixture of delicate blues and greens, dotted by the occasional white sail, and on the horizon she could just make out the shape of a liner.

All was tranquil except for the fast beat of her heart. Bougainvillea trailed over a low wall and hibiscus grew in tubs. It was the fairy-tale palace Chloe had claimed. Never in a million years had Penny ever dreamt that she would one day holiday in a place like this.

'It's very beautiful,' she said with a faint smile.

'I thought you would like it.'

'And you haven't been here since you were a boy?'

'No.' He allowed himself a faintly nostalgic smile. 'Life got in the way. University, building my business.

I had no time for holidays. And I wouldn't be here now if it wasn't for your insistence.'

Her smile widened. 'Then I'm glad I pushed you.' And her heart did amazing somersaults when he flashed his white teeth in an answering smile. Even his eyes softened, looking at her with something near to tenderness.

'Your drinks, Signor.' The maid appeared silently at their sides.

Penny was glad of the interruption and watched the girl as she slid a jug and two glasses onto the low table in front of them, together with a dish of olives, and then disappeared as quietly as she had come.

Santo leaned forward and filled her glass with the delicious-looking fruit juice and Penny was glad it wasn't anything stronger. It would be so easy to drink too much here in this place of blazing blue skies and fantastic surroundings—to say nothing of the company!

But when she tasted the juice Penny found that it wasn't what she'd expected. There was a definite taste of alcohol. She looked at Santo with a frown chasing across her normally smooth forehead.

'You don't like?'

'What is it?'

'Fruit punch, I think you would call it. Made to an old family recipe. It is very refreshing.'

'And intoxicating,' she accused.

'Too much and it will go to your head, I agree,' he said. 'But is that a bad thing? We have had a long day; we deserve to relax and enjoy.'

Penny picked up an olive and bit it in half, looking at the piece that remained between her fingers as though it was of paramount interest. Anything so she didn't have to look at Santo. 'You make it sound as though you and I are here on holiday together, not as employer and employee.'

'Is that how you want it to be?' asked Santo, a sudden edge to his voice. 'You do not want to be friends?'

Penny dared to look at him and saw the frown slashing his brow. She felt a rush of unease. Of course she wanted more. That one taste had caused a hunger that only he could assuage. But brief affairs, because that was all it would be, were not for her. She couldn't give her body to any man who wasn't seriously interested in a long-term relationship—ideally marriage. And she knew that Santo had no intention of ever getting married again.

She ignored the tiny voice in her head that said she had already given herself to him. That had been a one-off, never to be repeated. If anything had been dangerous it was that. A foolish error of judgement. She had only wanted to comfort him.

'We can hardly help being anything other than friends, can we,' she said, 'when we both have Chloe's best interests at heart?'

'I love my daughter,' he acknowledged, his gorgeous brown eyes terrifyingly watchful on hers, 'and I know you're very fond of her already. But we both have a life outside Chloe.'

'Naturally,' agreed Penny, 'I'm here as Chloe's nanny. You're her father. That's it, that's what we are.'

'So if I said that I want you in my bed again you'd refuse?'

It was the way his voice had seductively lowered that sent the shivers through her body. The way his eyes made love to her. And she knew that she was doomed. It was going to be impossible to resist this totally gorgeous Italian.

And when he spoke again in his own language, when the words sounded so romantic and exciting, Penny knew that she was lost. Nevertheless she spoke firmly. 'It was a mistake I'm not likely to repeat.'

But there was no conviction behind her words and Santo knew it. She could see the speculation in his eyes, the knowledge that he was going to enjoy the chase as much as the capitulation.

Santo was well aware of the fact that he'd insisted Penny accompany him and Chloe because he wanted—no, correction, because he *needed* her company. He thought about her constantly, his body demanded fulfilment, and having her at his side but knowing that he could not reach out and touch, and take, was driving him crazy.

It was early days but he hoped that the ambience here, coupled with the beautiful weather and the fact that he'd be her constant companion, would bring to him again the fantastically uninhibited woman who had shared his bed. If they'd gone to his father's place then he might as well have left her at home. There was nothing there that was conducive to romance.

His lips thinned for a moment as memories he'd tried to bury rose once again to the surface. Determinedly he dashed them away. He wanted nothing to destroy their pleasure. One day he might let them take hold. But not now. 'Drink,' he ordered, gesturing towards her glass, and he was pleased when she took a sip, and then another.

'You like?'

'It's lovely,' she agreed, 'but I'm not going to forget that it's alcoholic.'

'Just a little,' he declared with a careless wave of his hand. 'Nothing to worry about. You won't get drunk.

Tell me more about yourself, about your childhood. You say your father died when you were—how old?'

'Five,' she said.

'Chloe's age. That is sad,' he acknowledged.

'And it's also why I'm urging you to spend more time with your own daughter,' said Penny urgently. 'They are such important years. You want her to remember every one of them with pleasure. My father and I did some wonderful things together. He always seemed to be playing with me, taking me out, buying me little treats—not that we had much money. But I'll never forget them.'

She spoke with such sincerity, such earnestness that Santo could picture in his mind Penny as a little girl with her father. He could see love and joy, friendship and fun, and the hurt deep down inside that Helena had denied him Chloe for the first years of her life grew excruciating.

Penny had opened his eyes to the fact that his daughter, his very own flesh and blood, was crying inside because he didn't know how to love her.

All of a sudden he wanted to rush inside and fold Chloe in his arms and tell her how much she meant to him. When she woke, yes, he would… Now, though, he had the beautiful Penny to keep him company. Beautiful and exciting.

Simply looking at her sent his male hormones into overdrive. He wanted to make love to her *now*! His whole body was sensitised, as though it was ready to explode at any minute. He'd never had to work so hard keeping himself in check.

'It sounds as though your father was a wonderful man.'

'He was,' she admitted easily. 'My mother went to pieces when he died. It was a car accident. He was there one day, gone the next. She never had time to say goodbye, to tell him how much she loved him. She instilled in me and my sister the importance of telling a person you love them. We said it to each other every day after that until—' Penny's eyes filled with tears '—she too died. She was ill a long time, so it wasn't unexpected, but even so it was hard. I still miss her.'

Santo couldn't help himself. In a heartbeat he closed the space between them and, kneeling in front of her, he took her into his arms.

Strong arms, thought Penny. He was comforting her the way she had comforted him—and look where that had led! But she didn't push him away. She allowed herself the pleasure. She drank in the clean masculine smell of him, letting it wash away her sadness, bring back to reality the fact that he was the most exciting man she had ever met.

When he let her go and returned to his seat she was surprised. She had expected it to lead to a kiss, perhaps something more, and contrarily was disappointed. But what he didn't do with words and actions he did with his eyes. Velvety brown eyes made love to her. They undressed her and made love to her. She could feel it in every part of her body.

Half-hidden by lowered eyelids, they searched and found each intimate area. Her nipples hardened and stung so much that she wanted to protect them with her hands, every one of her sensitive spots was on high alert, and when her groin grew unbearably responsive, when she couldn't help wriggling in her seat, she knew she had to create a diversion.

A drink, a long drink, she thought, and to hell with the fact that it was laced with alcohol. To her horror her hand shook so much that she knocked the glass over. Mortified—she hadn't wanted to create that kind of distraction—she lifted the glass, only to have Santo's hand close over hers.

'Leave it,' he said, his voice low and gruff. 'Isabella will clean it up.'

As if the maid had been hovering she appeared on silent feet, taking the glass away and bringing another, mopping up the spilt drink. Penny was embarrassed, Santo on the other hand acted as though nothing untoward had happened.

Did he know, she wondered, that her clumsiness was a result of his mental lovemaking? That her body was achingly aware of him and if she didn't get away soon she would end up in his bed? Heaven help her if this torment was going to last the whole holiday.

'I'd like to explore,' she said, dismayed to hear how husky her voice sounded. She felt as if she was enclosed in a prison of her own making. There was no air to breathe, no space to move. Only Santo! All around her. Consuming her, feeding her, sensitising her. Doing everything in his power to entice her into his bed.

She was weak, treacherously so, and she wanted time to herself but it wasn't to be. 'Good idea,' declared Santo, jumping to his feet. 'Come, I will show you the delights this place has to offer.'

He held out his hand but she ignored it, trailing alongside him instead. At the other end of the terrace was a dining area with a table for up to eight people. Would they entertain? wondered Penny. Or would it be just the three of them the whole time?

Through a gate and down some steps was another terrace where a large kidney-shaped pool sparkled invitingly in the sunlight. At its side was an impressive array of sun beds. But more tempting still was a hydro massage tub. Penny could just imagine sitting in it enjoying the view while her body was stimulated and relaxed at the same time.

Santo saw her eyeing it. 'Shall we?' he asked softly.

Together! The two of them! Penny shook her head. Too intimate, too everything. She needed distance from Santo, not intimacy.

But intimacy was what she got when he pressed a button in the wall, a door she had not noticed slid open and he stepped back for her to enter.

'What's this?' she asked suspiciously.

'A lift down to the beach. I thought you might enjoy a walk along the shore, we might find a sea breeze there. It can be stifling on the terraces.'

Penny nodded. 'It is hot.' The doors closed silently and they were entombed in their own private space. She forgot to breathe. She held herself rigid against one of the cool metal walls and closed her eyes.

'You don't like lifts?' Santo's concerned voice entered her consciousness.

'No, I was stuck in one once for three hours.' It didn't bother her any more and she hadn't even thought about it before he asked. But at least it was an excuse.

Immediately his arms came around her and she was held firmly against him. 'You should have said, there are steps. A lot of steps, admittedly—it's a long way down—but…'

Penny wasn't listening, at least not to his voice, but to the strong beat of his heart against her. To her own throbbing in unison. She prayed they'd arrive quickly. It suited her to let him think that she was panicking because of the lift; she didn't want him to know that he was the one who'd dealt her senses such death-defying blows.

But when his mouth claimed hers Penny knew that she was lost.

CHAPTER SEVEN

ON A SCALE of one to ten Santo's kiss rated about thirteen. Penny forgot where she was, aware of nothing except the taste of his lips, the feel of his hard, exciting body against hers, the way the blood raced through her veins as though someone was in hot pursuit. She actually found herself urging her hips closer, returning his kiss with an abandonment that she knew she would regret later.

Was it the confined space that made her act like this? The knowledge that no one could see them? Up until now she'd been determined not to repeat the kiss that had shown her exactly how deeply Santo could affect her senses.

He was an undisputed expert in the kissing stakes. He made her feel special. He was sending her mindless with desire. The scent of him was all-enveloping in this tiny vacuum, it flooded her senses, invaded and controlled.

Her arms laced around his neck, fingers threading through the thickness of his hair, pulling his head even closer, her lips parting beneath the onslaught. Their tongues danced around each other, touching, tasting, teasing, until Penny's body screamed out for more.

Even when the lift stopped, when she sensed that they were no longer falling in space, she didn't struggle for freedom. It was crazed insanity but there was something inside her that refused to let go.

'You're safe now.' Santo's voice broke the spell— plus the fact that the lift doors opened and a blast of hot air swept in.

Feeling dazed after the intensity of her emotions Penny backed out of his embrace and took a faltering step forward. Immediately his arm steadied her. 'I'm sorry,' said Penny.

'For what?' One corner of Santo's mouth curved upwards in amusement. 'For kissing me or for feeling afraid in a lift? The way I see it, if the kiss took your mind off your fear then it did its job and you have nothing to apologise for.'

'I shouldn't have let you.' It had been a bad mistake. One that could have disastrous consequences. It had told him how easily she could be manipulated. And she was afraid that this one kiss might lead to something more.

Santo was irresistible, there were no two ways about it. And here in this magical place it was going to be incredibly hard pretending indifference. Would she even want to? He was the sexiest man she had ever met; he did things to her that should never be allowed.

Crazily she hadn't wanted the kiss to stop, she had wanted more. She had wanted to feel his hot kisses on other parts of her body; she had wanted to touch him, to feel his need, to feed the hunger growing inside her, to bring it to its ultimate, mind-blowing conclusion.

She felt bereft now, as though she'd been given the taste of a golden prize and then had it snatched away. She felt strangely uncoordinated, her legs not carrying her as steadily as they should. Her mind searched for something to say, something to take her mind off this torment.

'Chloe,' she said urgently. 'What if she wakes? She's in a strange place; she'll—'

Promptly Santo stroked a gentle finger over her lips, stemming her flow of words, but in so doing creating a fresh flow of desire. 'You need not worry; Isabella will keep an eye on her.'

Penny sighed gently. She liked the feel of him, the taste of him, and she wanted to touch her tongue to his finger, she wanted to suck it into her mouth, to keep alive those feelings that had not yet gone away. But she didn't. Common sense prevailed. She moved away from him instead and began walking across the white sand. The beach was tiny and crescent-shaped and one half of her revelled in her fortune to be in such a wildly beautiful place, while the other half was deeply disturbed at the way her feelings were running out of control.

The azure ocean lapped gently at her feet and she kicked off her sandals and let the sand and water drift through her toes. She had an urge to throw off her clothes and swim naked in the warm waters. Of course she didn't, but she promised herself that one day she would sneak down and do just that.

The beach was private, backed by sheer cliffs clothed in green shrubs and trees that she felt sure must have a very tenuous hold. She couldn't even see the villa from here. It was like being alone in the world; a magical place.

'What are you thinking?'

Santo's gruff voice was close and she whirled around to find that only inches separated them. He too had taken off his shoes and socks and rolled up the legs of his light cotton trousers. He looked carefree; he had a very different persona from the dedicated businessman who found it difficult to spare time for his own daughter.

'How beautiful this part of the world is. You're very lucky.' And she ignored the racing of her heart, tried to pretend that his nearness hadn't once again affected her breathing.

'I'm lucky to have found you—for Chloe's sake,' he added. But his sensational dark eyes told her differently. They swept over her with amazing thoroughness, not missing an inch. Causing her to suck in her breath and attempt to ignore the hardening of her breasts and the crunch deep down in her belly.

It was hard though. How could you ignore a man as damningly sexy as Santo De Luca? Especially here in his home country, where he had become even more Italian. His accent had deepened and he seemed so at home with his surroundings that Penny couldn't understand why he had ever chosen to live in London.

'If this were mine,' she said with a wide sweep of her hand, 'I'd want to spend as much time here as possible.'

'Time is money as far as I'm concerned,' was his response.

'But everyone needs a holiday at least once a year.'

'Maybe if I'd had you for company,' he said softly, 'I'd have been persuaded before now.'

A fiery heat returned to fill her body with burning passion. 'Mr De Luca,' Penny drew herself up to her full height, still failing by several inches to match up, nevertheless doing the best she could to look imposing, 'I am your daughter's nanny, nothing more, and I'd appreciate it if you'd remember that.'

His gorgeously shaped lips twitched as he fought to hide a smile and Penny couldn't fail to acknowledge that a few minutes ago, seconds even, they had been staking a claim on hers. So beautifully. So intimately and heart-stoppingly. Therefore how could she expect him to take her comment seriously? And how could she pretend that it was otherwise?

She had placed herself in a damning situation and she couldn't see her way out of it.

'I think,' he said, stroking a strand of hair back from her face, 'that while we're here we ought to forget the employer-employee relationship. Think of us as just you and me, friends, Santo and Penny, together, enjoying a well-deserved holiday.'

'And Chloe,' she amended swiftly. 'How could you forget your daughter?' The trouble was she had liked the way their two names had rolled off his tongue. They sounded as good together as Tristan and Isolde, Romeo and Juliet. Star-crossed lovers. Was that them? Were they destined to meet only for life to thrust them apart?

'I've not forgotten her,' he said firmly, 'have no fear. But when Chloe's in bed, when she doesn't need me, then the only person I want is you.'

He didn't touch her but their eyes met and held and Penny couldn't have moved if she'd wanted to. She was gripped by something far too strong to deal with. In the end it was Santo who turned to the ocean and looked out.

Penny studied his profile. His thick dark hair was swept back from a strong, proud forehead, his nose was long and straight, his lips, those beautifully sculpted, infinitely kissable lips, were slightly apart, his chin was firm and jutted only slightly. It was a strong face with silky brows over dark, unreadable eyes, eyes that had the power to melt her bones and make her into someone she wasn't.

And that someone was hungry for another kiss. This wasn't the sensible Penny, this was her wanton alter ego. She had become two persons since meeting Santo and she wasn't sure that she liked the side of her who had fallen under his spell. Yes, it was exciting, it was the most exciting thing that had ever happened to her. But it was something that couldn't last and was therefore wrong.

'I don't think we should stay out long,' she said quietly.

'Because you're afraid?'

Yes! Very much so, yes. But she reigned in illicit thoughts and smiled brightly. 'I have nothing to be afraid of. But I'm neglecting my duty.'

'Chloe's still asleep,' he reminded her.

'You cannot know that. How will she feel if she wakes and finds only strangers?' And how will I feel if I allow myself to have a full-blown affair with my employer?

The question was answered immediately. She would hate herself. It would be totally unprofessional.

'If you are so worried then feel free to go back up,' he answered. 'I intend staying here for a while.' He turned to look at the cliff face. 'There are steps over there. One hundred and sixty-two of them to be precise. There is a hand rail but do be careful.'

To Santo's dismay Penny walked away without another word. He had thought she would balk at the thought of all those steps, and he had known she wouldn't take the lift on her own. He wanted her, he needed her; he couldn't get enough of her.

Earlier in the lift she had returned his kiss as though she'd needed it as badly as he did. He'd soared with the angels. Not that he intended embarking on a serious relationship. He couldn't offer her that. But having Penny share his life and his bed for however long a period it took for him to get her out of his system felt like heaven.

And now she was walking away from him, giving him a clear indication that she had no intention of indulging in an affair. She had kissed him because she couldn't help herself but she didn't want to take it any further.

Except that she'd done it before!

So there could be another time!

He smiled and watched until she disappeared from sight. Then he turned back to contemplate the warm, translucent water that circled his feet, and on an impulse he stripped off his clothes and waded out until it was deep enough to swim.

By the time Penny reached the top she longed for nothing more than a long cold drink and somewhere to sit. But it wasn't to be because Chloe came running towards her. Isabella was hovering a few steps away. 'I was looking for you,' Chloe said. 'Where's my daddy?'

Pleased that Chloe seemed to be happier with her relationship with her father, Penny stooped down to her level. 'He's on the beach, my darling. I've just been there, but it's a long, long way down.'

'Can we go?' asked Chloe excitedly.

'Another time, I need to sit down for a while,' answered Penny. 'It was a big climb up and my legs are very tired.'

'But I want my daddy.'

'And I'm sure that if he knew you were awake he'd have come back up too. He won't be long, I promise.'

But Santo was much longer than Penny had anticipated and by the time he did arrive Chloe was in tears.

Afterwards, when he'd consoled her and she'd finally run away for something to drink, Penny said,

'She was waiting ages for you. What were you doing?' Though actually she didn't need to ask; his hair was wet and his feet still bare and it was obvious he'd been swimming. As she could have done if she'd stayed! The sea had been so inviting, so gloriously warm and clear.

'I didn't think she'd be awake yet.'

'That's the trouble, you never think,' she retorted, and went in search of Chloe.

It was late evening before Penny saw Santo again. She'd spent time playing with Chloe while he disappeared somewhere in the villa's interior. He reappeared when Chloe was being put to bed and insisted on reading her a bedtime story.

He'd certainly made strides in his relationship with his daughter, but to Penny it was still not enough. This holiday was supposed to be about him and Chloe spending time together and getting to know each other better—not about Santo trying to persuade his daughter's nanny to have an affair!

She was determined not to let him kiss her again. Things had gone far enough—too far, in fact. She had foolishly given him encouragement and it was asking for trouble. From now on she would remain entirely vigilant; under no circumstances would she allow him through her defences.

And who was she trying to kid?

It would be practically impossible.

However, for the next few days Santo turned his attention to entertaining Chloe; they went swimming together—the girl was a good swimmer for her age, totally fearless in the water—and they played all sorts of silly games. It did Penny's heart good to see Santo letting his hair down and Chloe so at ease in his company.

Chloe clearly no longer thought that her daddy didn't love her. She was forever flinging her arms around his neck and kissing him. At first Santo had looked a shade uncomfortable from so much affection but it wasn't long before he was kissing her back and telling her how much he loved her.

Just occasionally Chloe would ask how her mother in heaven was, and the first time Penny had held her breath as she had waited to hear what Santo would say. But he told her that she was watching over them all the time, that she saw everything they did, and wished with all her heart that she could be with them now.

It was when Chloe was in bed that Penny and Santo spent time together, dining outside usually, the cooler evening air very welcome after the heat of the day. Sometimes he'd be called to the telephone and never return. At others Penny would hurry away to her own room before anything intimate could develop between them.

She was aware of Santo's disappointment but it worried her how close they were getting. She didn't want to be hurt again and the only way she could prevent that happening was by keeping him at arm's length. And it worked until the night he told her he was taking her out to dinner.

'We can't leave Chloe,' she protested. 'What are you thinking?'

'Isabella will be on hand in case she wakes. It is time for you and me to enjoy ourselves.'

You and me! He made them sound as if they were already a twosome. Panic rose in her throat. 'I can't,' she declared, and heard the fear in her voice. Oh, heavens, she mustn't let him think that she was afraid of him, or know of the feelings he managed to evoke. 'It wouldn't be right,' she added defensively.

'So you keep saying.' A frown dragged silky black brows together, lowering them over eyes that were dark with anger. 'Forget whatever it is that's troubling you. You're joining me. I've been patient long enough.'

'Since you put it so delicately, how can I refuse?' Whether he heard the sarcasm she couldn't be sure.

He didn't smile, he simply inclined his head. 'We're leaving in half an hour.' And he stalked away.

What would he do if she dared to ignore his request? Would he drag her out screaming? Or would he go anyway—and find another woman to keep him company? This last thought sent Penny scurrying to her room.

But what to wear? She didn't even know where they were going. Undoubtedly it would be somewhere expensive, and she didn't have one suitable dress in her wardrobe. What she did have was a black camisole and a long, floaty black skirt, normally worn separately but together, with a silver belt and her silver sandals, they should meet with his approval.

She brushed her hair back, fixing it loosely in her nape with a silver clip, and after applying a stroke of mascara, a smudge of eye-shadow and a touch of lip gloss she was ready. She found Santo waiting on the terrace and when he turned to look at her Penny's breath caught in her throat.

He wore an ivory jacket over a black shirt and trousers. She had never seen a man look so amazingly handsome, so devastatingly sexy. Her heart beat so strongly it felt as though it would burst out of her chest. She didn't want to go out—she wanted to go to bed with him! Now! Forget the clothes—rip them off; let him seduce her, let them make love all night long.

But outwardly she was serene, smiling faintly.

He studied her too, his incredible brown eyes taking in every detail.

'Will I do?' she asked softly, horrified to hear how husky her voice had suddenly gone.

'You look stunning.'

No man had ever said that to her before. A fresh river of sensation danced through her, making her want to twirl and display herself for his benefit. She felt good in her own skin, more beautiful than she had ever thought she could be.

'We should be going.' His voice had deepened too, gone even lower than normal, triggering a fresh surge of awareness. And she knew, before they'd even begun their evening, that danger was in the air. It was all around her, teasing, tormenting; washing over her in unstoppable waves.

Santo wondered whether he'd made the right decision in deciding to take Penny out. He'd told himself that it was because she deserved more than to be constantly in charge of his daughter. But was that the real reason? Wasn't it himself he was thinking of?

He was the one who wanted escapism. Much as he was enjoying getting to know Chloe, much as he lapped up the love she was now unconditionally giving him, he needed something more.

And that something was Penny.

He needed exclusive female company. He had sworn to himself that he would remain the perfect gentleman, but seeing her now, he wasn't sure whether he'd be able to do that. She was beautiful in black, it suited her

English rose complexion, and with her amazing blonde hair taken back from her face she looked so young and innocent, so tempting in every way, that he knew he was lost.

Leading her outside to a waiting car, Santo wanted to take her elbow, but he knew even that small courtesy would trigger an unstoppable desire to kiss her, to hold her against him and smell the sweet, fresh scent of her skin. And from there it would be a simple step to saying to hell with the evening, let's go to bed.

And so he didn't touch her, he didn't even speak, he simply opened the car door for her, settling her in before walking round to the other side.

'A new car?' she asked with a slight lift of one fine brow as he slid in beside her.

'You don't like?'

'I do,' she admitted, 'but I assumed you were always chauffeured.'

'It depends on where I'm going and who I'm with.' He hadn't wanted a third party getting in the way tonight. 'You needn't fear for your safety, I have no intention of drinking too much.' He wanted to remember every tiny detail about this evening. He wanted it to be romantic and perfect. And hopefully by the end of it she would agree to sleep with him.

That one night she'd spent in his bed lived in his mind. He had recreated it time and time again. He had discovered a side to Penny that she rarely showed and he wanted it again. There'd been glimpses of it since but that was all. Always she withdrew back into the safety of the cocoon she'd wrapped around herself.

He was taking her to a restaurant that belonged to someone he knew. It was built into the cliff face and the views were awesome; if they were lucky they would catch a spectacular sunset. Penny couldn't fail to be moved by it.

She was silent on the way and he wondered what she was thinking. She didn't really want to be out with him, that was for sure. 'Forgive me if you feel I've bullied you into this,' he said, slanting a glance in her direction, 'but I'm sure you'll enjoy it.'

'I'm sure I will,' she answered, and her tone was so cool that he wanted to stop the car right where he was and kiss her until fire ran through her blood, until she could no longer control herself.

But of course he didn't. He would play it her way— for now. 'The restaurant isn't too far away.'

No answer.

'Are you hungry?'

A shrug of her shoulders.

'The food is superb. You do like authentic Italian food?'

'Sometimes.'

He was beginning to lose patience. 'And would to-night be one of those times?'

She turned her head finally and looked at him. 'Santo, I am here under sufferance. How do I know what I will like until I see the menu?'

Santo gripped the wheel until his knuckles whitened and hung on to his temper—just. 'I'm sorry you feel like this. Maybe I will turn the car around and take you home. Then I will come out again and dine on my own. But I tell you, you will be missing a treat.'

Penny finally relented. What was the point in antag-onising Santo any further? He had taken so much trou-ble to arrange this evening and she was behaving like a spoilt child. In truth she was afraid. So very afraid.

Already her hormones were creating havoc. In the close confines of the car, with his hand only inches from hers whenever he changed gear, he filled every one of her five senses.

Sight. She was afraid to look at him because he had never seemed more broodingly Latin and electrifying than he did at this moment. Every inch of him excited her.

Smell. He had a special scent that was his alone. Not just his cologne, tantalising though that was, but a clean male smell that would for ever remind her of him.

Hearing. That incredible deep voice that shivered through her veins and damaged her nerve-ends. Rich and baritone, so sexy that she could listen to it for ever. So sexy that she went weak at the knees every time he spoke.

Touch. His hands on her body the night they had made love. Expert, gentle, tormenting. Stroking her into life, encouraging, arousing. Finding sensitive areas she hadn't known existed.

Taste. The taste of his mouth on hers, always clean and fresh. The taste of his skin as she had nibbled her way over it. A male taste. A taste exclusive to Santo.

And she wanted to taste him now, this very minute. She wanted to take his hand and press it to her lips. She wanted to kiss his fingers, suck them into her mouth; create fresh fantasies.

Dared she do it?

CHAPTER EIGHT

'IT'S WONDERFUL! It's totally amazing! It's out of this world!' Penny couldn't find enough superlatives to describe her first impressions. When they entered via the main door it had seemed like any other Italian restaurant. It was not until they were led through that it took her breath away.

They were on a balcony jutting out of the cliff face—practically suspended in mid-air. Leaning over the pretty white railing, she could see a village far below on the shoreline. And either side of them, nestling into the cliffs, were a few elegant villas. Santo pointed along the coastline. 'Just around that headland is where we are staying.'

Penny wished he wouldn't stand so close. His hand was on her shoulder and the heat of him, his individual male scent, was far too invasive for comfort. She turned away, missing the disappointment in his eyes.

She hadn't dared take his hand earlier for fear of showing him how desperately she wanted him, then their passion would have overtaken them and they wouldn't have made it here. It was essential that she keep everything light-hearted; getting drawn into a relationship could only spell unhappiness.

A hovering waiter pulled out a chair for her at a table far enough away from the other diners to give them a degree of privacy. And when Santo said something to him in Italian he inclined his head and disappeared.

'Santo!' A small, slim man suddenly beamed his way towards them. 'Long time no see, my friend.' The two men shook hands and clapped each other's backs.

'Now you must introduce me to this beautiful young lady. An English rose, no less. Who is she? What does she mean to you?'

Santo grinned. 'Too many questions. This is Penny. Penny, meet an old friend of mine, Enrico. We went to school together but rarely see each other these days.'

'Because you insist on living in England,' countered the other man, kissing Penny on both cheeks as she got to her feet. 'Can you understand him,' he asked her, 'when we have such beauty here?'

'England is beautiful too,' she declared. 'Have you ever been there?'

Enrico shrugged and shook his head. 'Sadly no. I do not have time. I run my restaurant, I have a large family. It is—' he held out his hands '—all I want. I am a happy man. I want for you two to be happy too.' He looked at them both questioningly.

Penny wanted to say that she was not Santo's girlfriend but Santo forestalled her.

'We are—new friends, Enrico. We are just getting to know each other.'

'Ah!' The Italian nodded knowingly. 'I leave you, then. *Buon appetito.*'

Once he had gone Penny glared indignantly. 'You let him think that we—'

'It is best,' cut in Santo. 'Enrico is an incurable romantic. He loves love. He will be happy.'

Penny wanted to protest that she was not happy about the deception—except that she knew it would do no harm. She was overreacting; they were not likely to see Enrico again. So she lifted her shoulders and then the waiter returned.

As they sipped their drinks and waited for their meal the sun, in all its golden glory, sank lower and lower in the sky until it finally disappeared. There followed a pictorial display of colours that took Penny's breath away. It was an extravaganza *extraordinaire*.

She had always enjoyed the aftermath of a sunset and was not disappointed. The sky was streaked with every colour imaginable, oranges and reds, purples and blues, all reflected in the almost still waters of the sea. There were oohs and ahs all around them. And her eyes were shining as she looked at Santo.

She was surprised to find that he was watching her instead. 'Wasn't that out of this world?' she asked with a great big smile on her face, trying not to show that the way his eyes were claiming hers triggered an immediate response.

'We were lucky.'

'It was incredible.'

'I'm glad you enjoyed it.'

Polite conversation, but Penny was well aware that they could have watched this same sunset from the villa and she wouldn't have felt the same. It was special here. There was a whole different atmosphere. Each of the tables were occupied by couples, all intent on each other, all watching the sunset and then turning to their partners and holding hands across the table and kissing.

As she wanted to kiss Santo! As she wanted him to kiss her!

The spectacular solar display had generated a response that craved fulfilment. Disastrously she was falling in love with Santo. But he didn't want love, he didn't want a serious relationship, and under those circumstances it would be impossible to continue working for him. She felt quite ill at the thought that it might become necessary to hand in her notice.

Actually Santo was the man of her dreams, as far removed from Max as it was possible to be. He made her feel good about herself, all woman, sexy and beautiful, and she wanted to spend the rest of her life with him. It wasn't possible, of course. He'd made it very clear that he never intended marrying again. Love didn't enter the equation. Not as far as he was concerned anyway. And if she wasn't in love with him now she soon would be.

Their first course arrived and as darkness surrounded them candles were lit on the tables and the atmosphere heightened. It was difficult not to give in to temptation, let herself be swept along by the tide. Santo's eyes were ever-watchful on hers; he saw the mixture of emotions she was putting herself through. And if he ever found out exactly how she felt he would take advantage and it would be her undoing.

The risotto was followed by roast sea bass, then later ice cream. Santo chose a Soave to drink with their main course, though, true to his promise, he limited himself to one glass.

There was a hint of dark shadow on his strong jaw and a proud tilt to his head. It was almost the face of an aristocrat. But his eyes, those incredible, velvety dark eyes that if he so wished could melt her bones in a second, gave nothing away.

Santo hated to admit, even to himself, that Penny was getting through to him the way no one had since his wife walked out. She was as different from Helena as it was possible for a woman to be. She was caring and thoughtful—and concerned not only for Chloe's well-being, but his own as well. She was one in a million. Despite this fact, though, he was still wary of letting anything serious develop between them. He couldn't afford another mistake.

So what was he doing leaning towards her, lifting her chin with one finger, allowing his eyes to blaze into hers as his lips found their target?

As soon as he tasted her all hell broke loose inside him. This had been the real purpose behind their evening. He had been almost certain there would be a spectacular sunset and he had known that it would excite her and hopefully entice her into responding to him.

Her lips quivered beneath his, he felt her soft sigh, he tasted her sweetness and he deepened the kiss, groaning low down in his throat as he did so. His other hand slid behind the back of her head, securing her, making sure she couldn't escape. Except that delightfully she didn't want to. She returned his kiss with a passion that excited him.

He traced the outline of her face, he trailed fingers down the line of her throat, exploring the throbbing pulse before continuing his journey. Her camisole was made of some soft, silky material and he could feel her breasts rising and falling beneath it, his suspicion that she was not wearing a bra proving to be true.

'Let's get away from this place.' The growl came from deep in his throat.

And so that Penny wouldn't have the opportunity to change her mind, once they were in the car he took her hand and placed it on his thigh, keeping his own over it except for when he needed to change gear. He couldn't be sure, but he thought her fingers were creeping slowly towards the part of his anatomy that was on high alert.

If they touched it would be his undoing. 'Save me,' he whispered.

Penny chuckled and it was the most beautiful sound he had ever heard. 'From whom—yourself?' she teased.

He muttered something in Italian, his voice thick and incredibly seductive, renewing the urgent need that was building inside her. Without a word being spoken Penny knew that she was going to spend the rest of this evening in Santo's bed. And, safe in that knowledge, everything she had been thinking earlier forgotten, she took delight in tormenting him, in increasing his hunger, making it almost impossible for him to hold back.

She wanted him to make love to her, splendidly and heart-stoppingly. All night long. She wanted memories to carry with her for the rest of her life. Santo had known what he was doing when he'd taken her to that particular restaurant; he'd known that it would appeal to the sensitive, romantic side of her. And how! She was his for the taking.

Just one tiny part of her brain sent out warning signals but she ignored it. Her body ached to be possessed, she wanted to feel Santo's hands exploring and discovering all her intimate spots, inciting deeper hunger, making her writhe and twist beneath him.

Even thinking about it created fresh shivers of need and she leaned across and impulsively kissed his cheek.

Santo groaned. '*Mio Dio!* Do you know what you're doing? We'll have an accident if you're not careful.'

Reluctantly Penny sat back in her seat, closing her eyes, letting her mind take her wherever it wanted. Her hand remained on Santo's leg, her fingers stroked and teased and she delighted in the power she had over him. She was able to forget that he was her employer, she saw him only as a man capable of torturing her soul. Making her crave fulfilment.

They couldn't reach home quickly enough as far as she was concerned, and when Santo led her straight to his bedroom, her hand tightly enclosed in his, it confirmed that his needs were as deep as hers.

Once there, though, his urgency left him. 'The night is ours,' he said in his deeply erotic voice. 'There's no need to rush.' He wasn't touching her, he was letting his eyes do all the work. They stripped her naked, saw the way her nipples were tight and hard, the way she kept moistening her lips, the way she couldn't keep a limb still because the very heart of her ached with a need so great that it hurt, forcing her to dance on her toes.

'I want you, Santo,' she told him, her throat dry, her words husky and sexy, and just for a moment she felt embarrassed that she was giving so much of herself away.

'How much?' Deadly dark eyes burned into hers.

'Too much,' she admitted.

'Impossible.'

'Too much for my peace of mind.'

'Ah! You still think it is wrong to want to make love with your employer?'

Penny nodded, wishing he hadn't put it into words. She was so desperate for him and yet he was making it sound all wrong.

'Don't you think there's something dangerously erotic about forbidden love?'

It was the way he spoke, his thickened accent, that sent her over the edge. Forbidden? Yes! Wrong? Yes! Did she still want him? Yes! *Yes, yes, yes!*

'I like danger. I like erotic,' she declared and sashayed towards him, propriety now forgotten, raw need taking its place. She pressed her body up against his, linked her arms around his neck and, lifting her chin, she claimed his lips. She kissed him with such passion that she knew she would feel ashamed at some later date.

Santo needed no more encouragement. He clasped her head between warm firm hands, his kiss as fierce and demanding as her own, parting her lips, exploring, tasting, teasing, fuelling fires already alight.

And when his hands began an exploration of their own, when he slid down the straps of her camisole and palmed her naked breasts, when thumb and forefinger teased and tortured her sensitised nipples she threw back her head and thrust her hips against him. The strength of his arousal sent a shock wave through her, and the next second she felt herself being carried towards the bed.

By this time her mind had drifted away into a world of its own. Nothing else mattered except pleasure, except the release of feelings that threatened to explode any second.

Santo disposed of her camisole and skirt in one swift movement, his own clothes following. He pinned her to the bed with his body, his eyes blazing into hers, and Penny felt all the air rush from her. Her mouth went dry, her lips were dry, she ached for him so much that it hurt.

'Santo!' she whispered.

'Penny!' he growled.

'Daddy!'

They both stilled at the same time, listening hard, hearing it again. 'Daddy! Daddy!'

'Don't move,' he told her. 'I'll be back.'

CHAPTER NINE

PENNY couldn't lie in bed and wait for Santo to return. She scrambled into her clothes and followed him into Chloe's room, desire quickly replaced by concern. There had been real panic in the little girl's voice, but the positive thing about it was that she had called for her father. Santo had to feel good about that.

Chloe was sitting up in bed, her eyes wide and scared. Santo had her cradled against him, stroking her hair, saying something in Italian that neither of them understood. But whatever it was it seemed to have a calming effect on Chloe. Penny saw her visibly relax, her eyes returning to normal, even a faint smile turning up the corners of her mouth.

All Santo wore was a pair of boxer shorts that he'd pulled on quickly, and Penny found it profoundly moving to see Chloe held against his bare chest. He was no longer afraid of his daughter, his feelings now came naturally and there was no awkwardness. It was a scene that warmed her heart and she actually felt as though she was intruding.

But when she turned to leave Santo beckoned her towards him. 'Come and join us,' he said softly.

And so she climbed on the bed too, sitting the other side of his daughter. 'Was it a bad dream?' she asked gently.

Chloe nodded.

'But you're feeling better now?'

The girl nodded again and put an arm around each of them. 'Will you sleep with me?'

Penny looked at Santo and knew he was thinking that this wasn't how he'd envisaged spending the night. Nor had she. But Chloe needed them. It actually felt as if she was inviting Penny to take the place of her mother. She could never do that, ever, but as a stand-in, in Chloe's eyes, for tonight, Penny fitted the bill.

She smiled at Santo over his daughter's head. He rolled his eyes, but it was good-naturedly. 'I think we could do that, *mio bello*.'

Chloe smiled and wriggled back down the bed.

Penny bade goodbye to a night of passion and settled beside her.

Santo followed suit. Never in his life had he been interrupted when he was on the verge of making love. He knew that if anyone had disturbed him in the past he would have been extremely angry. Surprisingly he was merely aggravated. Penny would wait. The pleasure would be there whenever he wanted it. He was sure of that now. But his daughter was a different matter. He'd learned to love this little bundle of joy and her peace of mind was his main concern.

He drifted into sleep at his daughter's side and was shocked to find it daylight when he awoke. Penny was gone and Chloe giggled as she tickled his nose.

'You snore, Daddy.'

'I do not,' he declared strongly.

'Yes, you do, like this.' And she made a tiny sound in the back of her throat.

He tickled her then and the two of them were rolling on the bed in laughter when Penny came to find them.

'It's time you were up and dressed,' she said to Chloe.

Santo thought Penny had never looked lovelier. She had showered and changed into a short white skirt and a T-shirt. Her hair was still damp and curled in long tendrils over her pert breasts. He wanted to touch, to stroke her beautiful hair away, to reacquaint himself with this most tempting part of her body.

Tonight, he thought. Tonight he would take her to his bed and he wouldn't let her go until daybreak. Preferably he would like her in his bed now. His testosterone levels had rocketed the moment she entered the room.

Why not let Isabella see to Chloe?

He squashed the thought the moment it arose. For all these years he'd only ever had himself to think about, but there was his daughter now. He couldn't hand her over just because he wanted to make love to her nanny.

It was actually getting harder to think of Penny as Chloe's nanny. He felt that she belonged to him. Their positions had radically changed. He no longer saw her as one of his employees. She was Penny, his lover.

He'd been excited when she had lost her inhibitions last night and made a move on him. It had been unexpected and erotic and he couldn't wait to get her into his bed tonight.

'I don't want to get up yet,' said Chloe, 'I'm playing with Daddy.'

'Daddy's going to get up too,' he told her. 'But after

breakfast, if you're very good, we'll go swimming in the sea. Would you like that?'

Chloe nodded emphatically. 'Penny as well?'

'Penny too,' he agreed, looking across at her. She tried to hide the fact that she still hungered for him but he saw it and smiled, his smile widening even further when she turned away and led Chloe from the room.

It was mid-morning before they went swimming. A phone call had taken Santo away from them and they'd spent their time exploring the garden, watching a swallowtail butterfly glide from flower to flower, looking down at the turquoise waters of the Mediterranean, Chloe impatiently asking when her daddy was going to be ready.

At last he joined them and they went down in the lift to the beach. Chloe was filled with excitement and couldn't stand still for one second, but Penny noticed something different about Santo. He seemed slightly withdrawn and she wanted to ask him what his phone call had been about. It had clearly upset him. But it wasn't her place—it was probably to do with business anyway—so she did her best to ignore his mood and pretend that everything was well.

In the water Chloe was in her element and Santo was so good with her that Penny stood for long moments at a time just watching them. Whatever it was that had been bothering him earlier he had shrugged it off and made sure that his daughter enjoyed herself—for which Penny was grateful.

They spent all day playing with her and after Chloe had gone to bed they dined outside. The sun had gone down, the air was cooler and the lights on the terrace cast interesting shadows. It was a night made for lovers. As had every night been since they came out here.

'You do know that I want you in my bed tonight?' His voice was no more than a low throb, even the air seemed to be throbbing.

Penny drew in a painful breath and nodded. She knew that if she tried to speak nothing would come out except a breathy whisper. Besides, saying that she didn't want to share his bed wasn't an option. The very thought of it made her heart race, sent red-hot blood shooting through her veins, made her want to dance and sing, filling her with a longing so intense that it hurt.

'I love playing with Chloe, but a man needs more.'

His fantastic dark eyes never wavered from her face and Penny didn't want him to wait until bedtime. She wanted him now, this very minute, this very second. 'I need more too,' she declared huskily.

Whether it was the way that she said it, or the desperate plea in her eyes, but he groaned and almost knocked over the chair in his haste. Strong arms lifted her and held her close. His scent invaded her nostrils, as powerful as any drug. Santo was making her his own; she was submitting to him without sensible thought.

Santo's lovemaking was as spectacular as Penny had known it would be. They moved into a world apart from other humans, reaching heights unimaginable. Their bodies were completely attuned with one another, each knowing what the other wanted, needed….

It felt as if she had merely existed before, waiting for the right man to wake her, to release her from her inhibitions. She was alive, soaring high, reaching levels of sensuality that threatened to melt her bones.

At the back of her mind was the knowledge that it would one day inevitably end. It had to. But for the moment she preferred to forget that. She wanted only to greedily take what he offered.

They touched and tasted, they explored and enticed, they took and they gave. It was a night filled with passion. Sleep came and went. Each time they started afresh it was like being with a new man. Never had her body been used so much. Never had it enjoyed such intense pleasure, such deep fulfilment. She didn't want the night to end. But eventually she sank into a sleep so deep that it was mid-morning before she awoke.

The bed beside her was empty and as memories swiftly returned she felt embarrassed over her wanton behaviour. Santo must have thought he'd died and gone to heaven. She'd held nothing back. Her cheeks flamed and she jumped out of bed and raced for the shower.

Santo watched as Penny approached. She looked amazingly shy, her head down, her cheeks flushed, glancing at him cautiously from beneath lowered lashes. God, she was lovely. She'd been a siren in bed and now she was tempting him again. And how he needed her, there were things going on in his mind that called for distraction.

'I'm sorry, I overslept,' she said as she reached him. 'I've not seen to my duties this morning. Who got Chloe ready?'

'Why, her father, of course,' said Santo, surprising himself by how easily he had said that.

They played ball games in the pool before lunch, and later in the day, when the air had cooled a little, he suggested they go for a walk to explore the surrounding countryside.

Penny had felt all morning that Santo wasn't in the best of moods—nothing she could put her finger on, just the occasional irritation that gave him away—so she was delighted when he suggested a walk together. She imagined that he was getting fed up. That work beckoned him. Their lovemaking had helped but he wasn't used to taking this sort of holiday. Relaxing and playing with a child had certainly never been part of his lifestyle.

He probably jetted here, there and everywhere, staying in top-class hotels, having people wait on him hand and foot. Theatre visits and a round of social soirées were probably more in his line.

Actually the more she thought about her previous suggestion that they go to an English seaside town, the more she realised that he would not have not fitted in. She couldn't see him sitting on the beach building sandcastles, popping into a crowded café for lunch, or enjoying an evening meal in a local pub.

Not that she was complaining about his standards. She appreciated the places he took her to, the quality of the villa they were living in, his own private aircraft! She could most definitely get used to this kind of lifestyle.

On their walk they discovered a tiny village nestled into the hillside. It had a central *piazza* and a beautiful church that Penny explored on her own while Santo kept his eye on Chloe. There were children playing in the square and his daughter was quickly welcomed into their midst.

Penny was pleased that Chloe had found someone to play with and when she finished her exploration she joined Santo where he sat outside a café. He bought them each a *gelato*, and every one of the children as well. They must have thought all their birthdays had come together, mused Penny.

But he remained quiet and lost in thought and Penny couldn't sit there any longer without knowing what was wrong with him. 'Is something bothering you, Santo?' She posed the question gently, knowing it was none of her business but unable to sit and pretend that there was nothing wrong.

'Why do you ask?' His eyes were sharp and defensive as he turned to look at her, sending out a very strong message that she was out of order.

But Penny wasn't going to give in. 'Because you've gone very introspective all of a sudden.'

'And a man's not allowed to sit quietly, is that what you're saying? You're not the centre of my universe—'

'Santo! Of course not,' declared Penny immediately, her blue eyes very wide and hurt. 'I'm not thinking of myself.' Well, not much anyway, though she would have liked some of the warmth and interest she'd gotten used to. For heaven's sake, she'd spent last night in his bed— and now this! Almost ignoring her. What was she supposed to think?

'Do you think I'm not giving Chloe enough attention—is that it?'

'No, you've been wonderful with her,' she said quickly, 'she's enjoying herself. But it's clear you have something on your mind. Are you anxious to get back to work? Are you beginning to resent your time here?' Or was he regretting starting an affair with her? Afraid she might want more from him than he was prepared to give? He needn't fear, she knew exactly where she stood.

'You're way off the mark, Penny.' His dark eyes blazed into hers and he got to his feet. 'Yes, I do think about work; it's my lifeblood—why shouldn't I? But there are other things that concern me—and they're none of your damn business.'

Which put her firmly in her place! 'I'm just not used to you being this quiet,' she said softly, getting up too, facing him bravely. She wanted to reach out and touch his cheek, she wanted him to kiss her, to reassure her. She wanted to feel the bond that had been so strong between them last night.

For some reason he had erected an invisible barrier that she was not allowed to cross. She hoped, she really hoped that it was not going to last for the rest of the holiday. If so they might as well pack up and go home.

'Maybe you should get used to it,' he answered sharply. 'A man needs space for his thoughts sometimes.'

Penny drew in a deep breath and looked away. Now that there was nothing else left for them to say it had gone very quiet. Too quiet! Even the leaves on the trees had stopped rustling. To her horror she realised that all the children had disappeared.

'Where's Chloe?' she asked sharply, her heart beginning to hammer in her breast.

Santo swept his eyes over the deserted *piazza*. 'Weren't you keeping your eye on her?'

She couldn't blame him. It was her job to look after his daughter. 'Didn't you see where they went?'

'If I had I'd have called her back. It's as simple as that,' he declared cuttingly, striding around the square, peering along the streets leading off it.

Penny called her name to no avail. There was simply no one in sight, no one to ask. Her heart lurched painfully.

'We'll search each street in turn,' he declared, his voice rough with worry. 'I'll start this side, you take that.'

'There is the consolation that they're all together,' said Penny. 'She'll be perfectly safe wherever they are.'

'And how do we know that?' he barked. 'She may very well have wandered off on her own once the others got fed up of playing. She could be anywhere.'

Penny felt physically sick as they parted company. She could hear him repeatedly calling Chloe's name and then she heard him talking to someone in his native language. She looked back to see that a woman stood on one of the doorsteps.

Santo called to Penny. 'There's a group of children in the woods behind the church. I'm going to search there. You keep looking down here.'

Penny would have preferred to go with him. This was all her fault. If she hadn't started their silly conversation they would have seen which way Chloe had gone. She ran up and down the streets, calling and peering, seeing curtains pushed to one side, people staring out to see what was happening. But there was no sign of Chloe.

And then Santo came back from the woods, his face pale, his eyes haunted. 'She's not with them.'

If Penny had felt sick before she felt even worse now. Her stomach twisted into hard knots, her throat felt raw and tight. 'Are they the same children she was playing with?'

He nodded grimly.

'So where did she go when they went to the woods?'

'They assumed she'd run back to us.'

Penny's eyes were as wide as saucers. 'What do we do next?'

'Call the police,' he declared vehemently.

'Don't you think it's a little soon for that?' There was hesitation in her voice.

'Do you have a better idea?' he snapped.

'Are there any other play areas? Somewhere that might have caught her eye? Is there a swimming pool for instance? You know what she's like where water's concerned.'

'I don't think so,' he said, 'but we'll ask,' and without further ado he pounded on the nearest door.

An excited conversation followed, none of which Penny understood. But she guessed by the constant shaking of the woman's head that there was no pool in the area. She had never felt so dreadful in her whole life. She blamed herself entirely for not keeping an eye on Chloe. Tears sprang to her eyes and blurred her vision.

Then just at that moment, just as she thought that this was the worst day of her life and that she would probably lose her job, Chloe came into sight. She and another girl about the same age came strolling around the corner hand in hand.

When Chloe saw them she smiled widely and came running over. 'Daddy, I've found a new friend. Her name's Pia and she says I can come and play with her any time I like. I've been playing with her new puppy.'

Relieved that his daughter was safe and sound, Santo gathered her up in his arms. 'I've been so worried about you, Chloe. I didn't know where you were. Penny and I have looked everywhere for you. Next time,' he added sternly, 'you must come and ask me. You can't just go wandering off.'

'I'm sorry, Daddy,' Chloe said and her thumb went in her mouth.

'Just don't do it again, *mio bello*. Penny and I were very worried.' He kissed her before putting her down.

'Say goodbye to your new friend because we're going home now.'

He looked at Penny then, who had stood silently at his side while he told Chloe off. 'I shouldn't have shouted at you. I'm as much to blame.'

She nodded and turned her head away and he knew that there were tears in her eyes. Relief that Chloe was safe? Or because he'd upset her? It was the first time since he'd found out that he was a father that he'd experienced this awful feeling in the pit of his stomach. He was responsible for another little person and he'd failed her. So he'd lashed out at Penny, blaming her, when it wasn't her fault.

He'd had other things on his mind as well and he'd not been in the best of moods. Penny had been trying to help. She'd been concerned for him. And this was how he'd repaid her!

Gently he took her by the shoulders and turned her to face him. With gentle thumbs he wiped away the tears still damp on her cheeks. 'I'm sorry. It wasn't your fault. Forgive me?'

He turned his lips down at the corners and put on his most pleading face, and eventually Penny smiled and nodded. He touched a kiss to his fingers and touched them to her lips. 'Friends again?'

'Friends,' she acknowledged.

Because that was how he saw her these days. Not as Chloe's nanny, but as his friend.

That night she shared his bed again. She hadn't needed much persuading and Santo felt that their lovemaking had reached a new level. Penny gave herself to him so fully, so eagerly, with no holds barred. She was a woman in a million and he felt humble that she had come into his life.

The next day he suggested they go into Naples. 'It's perhaps not quite as delightful as Rome,' he told her with some pride, 'but you shouldn't miss it.'

Penny discovered that the old part of Naples had three parallel streets across the centre with small, narrow, interesting streets connecting them. There were street markets, there was washing strung high overhead, there was absolute chaos with pedestrians and cars and motorcycles all sharing the same space.

She loved the noise and the ready banter, even though she couldn't understand any of the language. She kept Chloe's hand held tightly in hers and the little girl looked in wonder at everything that was going on around her.

They popped their heads into a church where by contrast all was peaceful and quiet—and they took the *Funiculare Centrale*—funicular railway—to the top of a hill with fantastic views over the whole of Naples. In the distance they could see Mount Vesuvius and Santo told his daughter the story of how it had erupted nearly two thousand years ago and covered Herculaneum with mud and Pompeii in ashes. 'I'll take you to Pompeii one day when you're older,' he promised.

'To see ashes?' she asked, looking at him in surprise.

'Ah, but you see,' he explained, 'people have dug away the ashes and you can see what is left of the buildings and streets. It will be good for you to see it.'

Penny thought he was going way over the top of Chloe's head, but his daughter nodded wisely. 'Then I will enjoy it. Thank you, Daddy.'

By the time they reached home that evening Chloe was dead on her feet, and after she was bathed and tucked up in bed her eyes closed before either of them could kiss her goodnight.

'It's been a good day,' Santo said with some satisfaction.

Penny nodded. By now they had both showered and changed and were sitting outside sharing a bottle of wine. 'Tomorrow we will rest,' he said, 'and then we will go to Rome. We'll spend a few days there.'

She looked at him in some surprise. There was no pleasure on Santo's face and she knew that he was doing this for her sake. 'Are you sure?' Perhaps this was what had been on his mind yesterday.

'*Naturalmente.* You cannot leave Italy without seeing it. It is your dream, I know that, I have been selfish.'

Penny wanted to ask whether he had changed his mind about visiting his father while they were there, but wisely kept her mouth shut. Santo had become more Italian, she felt, since arriving here. He seemed at home in this environment, and she failed to understand why he had turned his back on his country. He and his father must have had a very big row. She couldn't imagine anything being serious enough for him to boycott both his parent and his place of birth. It was a bizarre state of affairs.

She would have liked to know more about his family, whether he had brothers and sisters for instance. Santo was very much a private man; it had been with reluctance that he'd told her about his wife. It was as though he compartmentalised his life, opening each door only if the necessity arose. Hoping that it wouldn't.

And as though he knew what she was thinking, and was afraid she might voice her thoughts, he turned the tables and said instead, 'Why don't you tell me about the guy who hurt you?'

Penny was reluctant to admit that she'd been taken

in by someone just like Santo. Rich, handsome, charm-
ing, a real ladies' man. And the thought struck her that
she was in danger of doing so again. She was playing
true to form. A cold shiver ran down her spine and she
took a long swallow from her glass. The only good
thing about it was that this time she knew the risk, and
therefore could avoid it.

By not falling in love!

Except that she was already doing it. Or was it
simply Santo's body that she enjoyed? A no-strings-
attached affair, one that she could walk away from at
the end of the day?

Penny didn't care to delve too deeply into her mind
in case she came up with an answer that displeased her.
So she swirled the last drops of her wine round the
glass, watching it closely, as though it were of the
utmost importance, before taking a breath and looking
at Santo. 'Where shall I begin?'

'Isn't the beginning always a good place?' He picked
up the bottle and refilled her glass. Then he sat back in
his seat, his eyes watchful on her face.

'Before I became a nanny I had an office job. Max
worked there too,' she admitted reluctantly and slowly.
She didn't tell him that he was one of the bosses, and
that she'd fallen for him as had plenty of others before
her. Or that she'd thought he saw her in a different light.
That would be far too humiliating.

'How long were you together?'

'A few months. I was deeply in love. He made me
feel beautiful and special.'

'So what happened?'

'He dumped me,' she answered harshly. 'Suddenly,
without any warning. Prior to that he'd told me that I

was the only one. He bought me jewellery and clothes. I felt glamorous and loved and I wanted to spend the rest of my life with him.' She paused for a moment before adding bitterly, 'He went on to someone else, feeding her the same pack of lies.'

Unaware that her voice had risen, that her resentment was coming through when she'd been determined not to show any emotion, Penny was surprised when Santo declared loudly, 'I'd like to get my hands on him.'

'I was the fool,' she declared, 'for being taken in by him. It taught me a lesson—to never let myself get that close to a man again.'

They were in the same boat, thought Santo. Neither feeling they could trust. Neither wanting a serious relationship. Somewhere in the back of his mind was the faint niggle that he was already in deeper than he'd have preferred, but he ignored it. They both knew what they wanted—a relationship they could walk away from with no regrets.

At this moment Penny needed comforting. She'd opened her soul to him and now he had to make sure she was all right, that she didn't go on thinking about her disastrous affair. Actually he wanted to throttle the man who'd done this to her. She didn't deserve it.

He jumped to his feet and pulled her up too, then he held her close where he could feel the rapid beat of her heart dancing against him. She was hot and slightly breathless as though she was panicking, and Santo murmured words in Italian, stroking her hair, her sweet-scented hair, waiting for her breathing to return to normal.

'Is there anything you want?' he asked softly.

And was stunned when she said, 'I'd like you to take me to bed.'

It wasn't what he'd meant or what he'd expected, he'd always been the one to do the inviting. Nevertheless he didn't hesitate. Within the space of a heartbeat he swung her up into his arms and carried her into the villa.

CHAPTER TEN

AS THEY got ready to leave for Rome, Santo couldn't help wondering whether he was doing the right thing. He actually preferred not to think about it. There were so many bitter memories inside him that he felt irritable every time they raised their ugly heads.

He'd phoned his brother earlier and had discovered that his name was never mentioned in the family home. Not once, apparently, had his father asked about him in all these years. It was as though he'd cut him out of his life altogether, as though he'd never existed, making Santo wonder whether taking Chloe to see him was the right thing to do.

But Chloe deserved to meet her grandfather. And his father should know about her. Whether it would help to heal the rift, God only knew.

Chloe had no other grandparents, his ex-wife's parents had died before she was even born. And soon she would begin questioning him and it wouldn't be nice for her to discover that he had fallen out with his father. It didn't make him a very good role model.

It was time to try and put the past behind him and move on. Penny had shown him that he could have true happiness—when he had thought it would never be possible again. She was an unbelievable woman.

Penny's eyes were wide when they reached the hotel. Despite being in the heart of the city it was surrounded by lush greenery. 'They call this part of Rome the green lung,' said Santo. 'It's actually the Villa Borghese Gardens. As far as I'm concerned it's the only place to stay.'

The hotel was out of this world but Penny was surprised to discover that Santo had booked them separate rooms. She wanted to ask why but the guarded expression in his eyes told her that bad memories were haunting him and it would be wise to hold her tongue.

Chloe was their saving grace. They couldn't keep her out of the swimming pool. It was bordered by gardens and trees and felt almost tropical, and the rest of the day was spent playing with her in the water or relaxing at its side. By evening Santo seemed a little calmer and they dined on their own private terrace. But if Penny had had any thoughts that he might change his mind and invite her into his bed she was very much mistaken.

He didn't even kiss her goodnight. He had retreated into himself, deep in thoughts that had nothing to do with her. He even retired before she did.

Penny spent most of the night lying awake, wondering what was going on in his mind. She guessed it had something to do with his father, who must surely live near by. She wondered again why Santo refused to visit the man and wished he would share it with her.

The following day they visited the Vatican City. Penny was in awe as she stood in St Peter's Square—it was a much larger area than she had imagined from seeing it on television. And as they looked up at the Basilica Chloe asked who lived there.

Santo's accent was deeper than she'd ever heard it. He was truly Italian. More gorgeous than ever. He even lapsed into his native language.

'What are you saying?' she asked. It had sounded romantic and beautiful and even though there was no smile on his face she knew that he had spoken from the heart.

'It is nothing,' he snapped.

Penny flinched. 'I'm sorry,' and devoted her attention to Chloe, who was running around chasing pigeons. She wished again that Santo would share his feelings with her. Surely they were close enough by now? Instead he was shutting her out, keeping all his unhappy thoughts to himself. If she had known how badly it would affect him returning to his home city she would never have said that she'd like to come.

His unhappiness was spoiling what could have been a very beautiful time spent together. He knew so much about Rome and its history that he would have made an excellent tour guide. Instead he said nothing. She and Chloe stood and looked and wondered and marvelled, while he remained broodingly silent.

The queues were too long to go into the Basilica itself. 'Another time,' Santo promised, though she knew he didn't mean it. There wouldn't be another time. He was here under sufferance because she had told him she had wanted to see it. And now she felt truly dreadful.

They made their way to the Trevi Fountain, where Chloe and Penny threw coins over their shoulders. 'It means we'll come back here another time,' Penny told her conspiratorially. Afterwards they rested on the Spanish Steps and from the top Penny admired the view across Rome. Then it was back to their hotel, which was surprisingly close, and by this time Santo had lapsed into complete silence.

Another night spent alone in her bed and the next morning they piled into the car again, but Santo didn't tell them where they were going this time. If anything he seemed in an even worse mood and they hadn't gone far when he pulled up outside a property with amazing views over the hills.

Penny looked at him questioningly.

'My father's house,' he said, almost under his breath.

She would have been ecstatic if Santo's attitude had been different. He was obviously not happy about being here and Penny understood that this was the reason behind his behaviour over the last few days.

'Are you sure you want to do this?' Penny asked and gently touched his arm.

Santo looked out into the distance and released a deep breath before speaking. 'Me? No, I don't want to do this, but for Chloe…I will do anything.'

Penny understood then. He was here because he felt that it was the right thing to do. Not for his own sake, but Chloe's. In one respect Penny was pleased and admired him for it, but if things didn't go well, how would it affect Chloe?

Penny wondered whether Santo had really thought this thing through and began to feel decidedly nervous. Her heart pitter-pattered as she followed him along the winding path to the house and she held Chloe's hand tightly in hers.

The little girl had no such qualms. 'Whose house is this, Daddy?' she asked curiously.

'This is where my father lives, Chloe,' answered Santo.

'You have a daddy too?' asked Chloe. 'Oh, goody, I want to see him.'

Santo felt his heart thudding loudly against his rib-cage as he waited for his knock to be answered. In fact he was praying that his father wouldn't be home. This was not going to be easy. How many years had it been since he'd last set foot in this house? Nineteen? Twenty? He might not even get invited in. And how would that appear in front of Penny and his daughter?

Finally the door opened and a strange woman looked at him. 'Yes?' she asked in Italian. 'What do you want?'

'Is my—is Signor De Luca at home?'

'He is. Who shall I tell him is calling?' The woman looked curiously at Penny and Chloe.

'I'll tell him myself.' Santo brushed past her and stepped inside, ignoring her startled expression. He couldn't risk his father stating that he didn't want to see him. Not now he'd come this far.

Penny and Chloe followed, Chloe's hand still held tightly in Penny's. He found his father sitting reading in the large living room. At first he was unaware of their presence and Santo was able to observe him. He was shocked by the change. His hair was white, his skin sallow, and he'd lost weight. In fact he didn't look well.

'Father,' he said in Italian.

Antonio De Luca looked up and his expression was comical, except that Santo did not smile. 'You!' the man exclaimed. 'What are you doing here?'

'I can go…' declared Santo. He should have known it was a waste of time. There was no welcoming greet-ing, even after all these years. Not a smile. No pleasure on the old man's face. 'I thought you might have had a change of heart in your old age and been pleased to see me. My mistake.' And he spun on his heel.

There was real alarm in Penny's eyes and he wished now that he'd not brought her or Chloe with him. This was something he should have done alone, tested the waters before he introduced them.

'Wait!'

Very slowly Santo turned. He found himself looking into a pair of eyes that were identical to his own. Funny, he'd not noticed it before. He'd always thought his father's eyes were hard and cold; he'd never really looked at their shape or colour. Now he saw that they were the same shade of brown, and the same thick eyelashes fringed them. It was almost like looking into the mirror he used each morning as he shaved.

'You simply wanted to find out whether I was dead or alive, is that it?' sneered the old man, his lip curling derisively, his eyes flaming into life. 'So now you know. Satisfied?'

This was everything and more than Santo had feared. There was no welcome for him in this house. There never would be, even when his father was on his deathbed. The old man had cast him out of his life, disowned him; couldn't care less about him.

But before he could turn round again and usher Penny and Chloe outside his father spoke again. 'Who is this you've brought with you?'

Santo closed his eyes briefly, wishing he didn't have to explain, not now. Coming here had been a big mistake. He drew in a deep breath and held his hand out to Chloe. 'This is my daughter. Chloe, meet your grandfather.'

For several long seconds the only sounds Santo heard were the somnolent ticking of a clock and his own heart beating. Chloe gripped his fingers hard and stuck her thumb in her mouth. It was like a scene out of a play when someone had forgotten their lines.

Antonio De Luca's harsh words had scared Chloe and all she could do was stand and stare. Santo smiled at her reassuringly and picked her up. 'It's all right, *mio bello*,' he whispered.

She flung her arms around his neck and turned her back on the older man, looking at Penny instead over her father's shoulder.

'I have a granddaughter I know nothing about?' roared Antonio, clearly shocked. 'May the devil take your soul, Santo.' And then in English, 'And this is your wife, I presume. You never even thought to tell me that you were married.' His voice was thickly accented but perfectly understandable.

'Actually this is Chloe's nanny,' declared Santo harshly. 'My wife died. And I can see now that it was a bad idea coming here. I wish I hadn't bothered. We will leave you in peace. Come,' he said to Penny, both his voice and his face dark with anger.

'Wait!' declared the older man. 'Don't go....please. It has been a long time... Join me for dinner tonight.'

Penny held her breath as she waited for Santo's answer. She was annoyed that he clearly hadn't warned his father that they were coming, and even more exasperated that he'd not told her what he'd planned to do. Not for her own sake but for Chloe's. The girl was clearly upset. Antonio De Luca was nothing like a child's idea of a grandfather.

Grandfathers were gentle and loving and fun. This man was harshly forbidding. He was enough to frighten an adult, let alone a child.

'Impossible!' Santo's eyes were hard as he looked at his father. 'Chloe goes to bed early. I cannot leave her at the hotel.'

Antonio's eyes swivelled towards Penny and she realised that he expected her to stay with Chloe. Which was only right, considering her position. Except that she found it hard to think of herself as just a nanny these days. And she didn't think that Santo saw her in that light either—not any more. Was she wrong? Was he just playing with her? Or was the introduction purely for his father's benefit?

Despite the fact that they were lovers he had never once said that he loved her. Which could mean, she guessed, that nothing would ever come of their relationship. Which she should have known, of course. Perhaps she did. Perhaps it was wishful thinking that it was getting more serious.

She hadn't wanted seriousness. Not ever again. So why was she feeling a little miffed that Santo had introduced her as Chloe's nanny?

'Nor would I dream of leaving Penny and Chloe on their own in a strange country,' declared Santo firmly.

'Then you shall all stay here,' declared the older man. 'The matter's settled.'

There was such clear enmity between them, thought Penny, that surely Santo would find it impossible to accept his father's offer.

Two pair of brown eyes clashed and held. Both men were as strong as the other. The silence was broken by Chloe turning her head and looking shyly at the older man, slowly her thumb came out of her mouth. 'Are you really my grandfather?' And then it shot back in again.

Antonio nodded gravely. 'Yes, my child. I am your grandfather.'

Moving slightly so that she could see Santo's face Penny knew the exact second he decided to agree to his father's suggestion. A strange sort of resignation crossed it, and some of the harsh lines disappeared. Chloe had made up his mind for him. 'Very well,' he announced gruffly. 'We'll stay. I'll fetch our cases from the hotel.'

'Thank you,' said Antonio quietly.

As soon as they'd walked back out to the car Penny spoke to Santo. 'Why didn't you tell me we were coming here?'

'Because it's none of your business.' His dark eyes flared into hers and a muscle worked furiously in his jaw. His whole body was so tense that it looked as though it might snap in two at the lightest touch.

'But you don't really want to stay, do you?' she asked, adding more quietly, 'And don't you think Chloe will pick up on the tension between you and your father?'

'You have no idea why I'm doing it,' he snarled as they jumped in the car and headed for the hotel.

Once they were back and their bags unpacked Santo took Chloe out to the swimming pool. Penny followed slowly because there was nothing else for her to do. She couldn't sit in her room and she didn't fancy facing Santo's father. Besides, Santo wouldn't approve of her chatting to him, he'd made her position very clear.

She guessed that their brief affair was now over and felt sad because this holiday had been her idea. Conversely it had now ruined their relationship.

Penny swam a few lengths and then hauled herself

out, dropping onto a lounger near to Santo. 'Why do you think your father asked you to stay?' she asked hesitantly.

'Because the old dog wants to get to know Chloe,' he growled. 'It's certainly not for my sake. My brother, Vittorio, and his wife, Rosetta, have no children yet. He wants a grandchild to spoil before he dies.'

Penny was interested to hear that he had a brother. Finding out anything about Santo's family was like extracting teeth with a tooth pick.

'He likes little children,' Santo added with a harsh laugh. 'He was always good to us when we were Chloe's age because children do as they're told. It's when they get older and he can't control their minds that he finds it hard; that's when the bullying begins...'

Penny was saddened to hear this. Life was so short, why make it unhappy? What was wrong with the old man that he'd treated his family like this? Her mother had been so wonderfully kind and supportive over the years that Penny had assumed all parents were the same. 'Do you think Chloe will like him?'

'Once she gets over her shyness. Actually, look at her...' They both turned their heads and watched Chloe slowly making her way towards the house. The thumb was in her mouth but she didn't falter. 'She kept asking me if he really was her grandfather. She's intrigued. She wants to talk to him even though she's a little afraid.'

'Should I go with her?' asked Penny.

Santo swiftly shook his head. 'She'll be safe with my father. I loved him too when I was her age.'

Penny sighed. 'It's a shame things change. And I truly never realised how traumatic it would be for you coming here.'

'I always swore I never would.'

'But you put Chloe's needs before your own?'

Something shifted in his eyes and he turned his head away. And before she knew it he'd dived back into the pool. Penny watched his long lazy strokes for a few seconds and then turned to see where Chloe was—just in time to see her entering the house through the terrace doors.

They led into Antonio's living room so she strained her ears in an effort to listen to their conversation—but she was too far away. She knew Chloe well enough, though, to realise that if the girl wasn't happy she'd come running back out.

'Why don't you join me?' Santo halted in front of her, shaking the water from his hair and eyes.

Penny wanted to swim with him more than anything. She longed to slide her body against his, to tease him, to have him grab hold of her and kiss her. Even thinking about it caused a serious disturbance in the pit of her stomach. But she remembered the way he had introduced her. 'It's not proper for a nanny to swim with her employer,' she protested, lifting her chin and trying to look outraged.

'*Touché*,' he agreed, 'but what did you expect me to tell my father? He's a stickler for propriety.'

'And if he saw us swimming together he'd have a fit, is that it? I have no wish to cause any more friction between you. Although—' she said with her fingers mentally crossed '—I would like to know why you fell out. It might help me understand your situation better.'

Santo drew in a harsh, ragged breath and his eyes flashed fierce unhappiness. Penny thought he was going to tell her that it was no business of hers, but after a few anxious moments he hauled himself out and sat on the edge of his sun lounger, facing her.

Long seconds passed. Water dripped from his hair down his face, pausing on his beautiful, long eyelashes, glistening like diamonds. It ran in rivulets down his chest and she wanted to touch, she wanted to trace each line with gentle fingertips. What she really wanted to do was arouse him, set fire to those strong male hormones and enjoy lovemaking right here in the sunshine.

She didn't like seeing him unhappy. He needed to lay his ghosts, yes, but she'd never dreamt that it would be this hard. And she wanted to do something to ease the situation. But how could she if she didn't know all the facts?

Finally he spoke. 'My father wanted to control my life. I would not allow it. It's as simple as that.'

'Is anything that simple?' she asked, thinking about her relationship with Max. That had seemed simple in the beginning. She had grown up a lot since then. 'How did he want to control it?'

Santo's eyes grew as hard as bullets. 'I can see you won't rest until I tell you.'

Penny nodded briefly. It would probably have been for the best if she'd suggested they forget it. But there might not be another occasion to ask these questions and she really did want to know what was behind his falling out with his parent.

'My father is a control freak.' A long sigh followed, together with a few moments silence. Penny could see his mind going back over the years. 'He manipulated everyone, including my mother. I don't know why she put up with him for so long. Actually, yes, I do. She did it for our sake. Mine and my brother's. As soon as

Vittorio and I were of an age when we no longer depended on her, my mother left. She returned to her beloved England. She had never been truly happy in Rome.'

Santo closed his eyes for a few seconds and Penny knew he was reliving that scene. Her heart went out to him and she wanted to throw her arms around him, make him feel better—but remembered in time that his father might be able to see them.

'My father was furious, I have never seen anyone before or since in such a rage. I could not stay there or I would have hit him. I decided to join my mother.'

'And your brother, what did he do?' she enquired softly, hating to see the look of pain in his eyes.

'He stayed. He's weak. He let my father walk all over him.'

'Do you have contact with your brother?'

Santo nodded. 'I phone him occasionally. Vittorio and his wife actually lived with my father for the first few years of their married life until he finally plucked up the courage to leave. The old man doesn't deserve loyalty. He didn't even attend my mother's funeral.'

It was a sad story and compulsively Penny reached out. 'I'm sorry.'

Santo held her hand tightly between both of his. She saw the hurt and sadness behind his eyes and wished there was something that she could say or do to make him feel better.

'What does your father know about your—personal circumstances?' She posed the question carefully, fearing that she might be going too far again.

'Nothing.'

'Not that you're a very successful businessman?'

'Let's say I have not told him,' declared Santo tersely.

'But since you're world-renowned it's a possibility?'

'I guess so.'

'And you've not been in touch since the day you walked out?'

'I've tried,' he answered, his eyes flashing with fresh anger. 'But not once would he take my call, not even when my mother died. And if it hadn't been for you I wouldn't be here now.'

'I'm sorry,' she said quietly.

'Don't be; it's probably for the best,' he said, letting go of her hand and standing up. 'I have to be the best father I can be to Chloe—you taught me that. Chloe needed to know that she has a grandfather. And by the time she's grown up, well, I guess he'll no longer be around, so she'll never see the harsh side of him. She'll have happy memories. Come and join me for a swim.'

And this time Penny didn't refuse.

CHAPTER ELEVEN

IN HEIGHT, Santo's brother, Vittorio, was the same as Santo, but otherwise they were as different as it was possible for two brothers to be. Whereas Santo's face was all hard angles and his body perfectly honed, Vittorio was fleshy around his jowls, suggesting that he liked his food too much—and consequently he carried more weight.

But it was in his manner where their differences were most apparent. Vittorio was loud and didn't care what he said, and he was hurt that Santo had never let him know that he had a daughter.

'Why did you not tell me?' he asked petulantly, like a child quizzing his parent.

They were seated at the dinner table in a room overlooking the hills leading to Rome. Santo sat at Penny's side and his brother was directly opposite her.

She felt Santo stiffen and when she darted a glance at him his face was totally impassive. 'Do you think that I'm proud of the fact that my child didn't even know she had a father? Or that I knew nothing about her? Why would I want to sing it from the rooftops? It's hard enough to bear as it is.'

'What did you do to Helena to make her hide her daughter away like that?'

Santo drew in a deep breath and paused a long moment before answering quietly, 'I didn't need to do anything. Helena was a law unto herself.'

'I always wondered why she left you.'

'And you'll have to go on wondering,' returned Santo evenly. 'I do not discuss my private life with anyone— not even my brother.'

Penny admired his self-control but Vittorio wasn't finished. 'It seems to me that you have something to hide. All this secrecy.'

'And you, dear brother, would do as well to keep your mouth shut or I won't answer for the consequences.' Santo's eyes blazed with fury; he was unable to keep his emotions in check any longer.

'He's right, darling.' Rosetta, beautiful Rosetta with her scarlet lipstick and nail polish to match, and her heavily made-up eyes, tapped her husband on the arm. 'I'm sure Santo will tell you when he's good and ready.'

'Which will be never,' snapped Santo, his eyes daring Vittorio to say anything more.

All their father did was sit at the head of the table and watch the drama unfold. He was enjoying it, realised Penny, but she wasn't. Even though she knew it wasn't her place to say anything—she was actually surprised that she'd been invited to dine with them at all—she knew that she had to, she hated the way Vittorio was questioning Santo.

'Tell me, Vittorio,' she said, 'what you do for a living?'

It was a perfectly ordinary question as far as she was concerned, it never occurred to her that it could inflame the situation further.

Vittorio's face went a fiery red and she thought he was going to bang his fist on the table.

'My husband's health doesn't let him work,' answered Rosetta for him, her hand on Vittorio's arm as she looked fondly into his eyes.

'In other words he's a kept man,' declared Santo. 'He's never done a decent day's work in his life. I'm surprised he ever found himself a wife.' He scraped his chair back from the table. 'I need some air.'

Penny excused herself and hurried after him, not even caring that it might seem strange. 'I wish you'd told me more about Vittorio. I've really put the cat amongst the pigeons, haven't I?'

'Why should I have said anything?' he asked harshly. 'I'm not proud of the fact that he's sponged off my father all his life and I'd like to bet he's still doing it to his wife. Rosetta works but she doesn't bring in enough to fund his lifestyle. He gambles and drinks—he's a complete waste of time. I thought marriage would change him, but he's still the same as he ever was. You can see now why I didn't want to come here. I've no love left for either my brother or my father. Thank God for you,' he groaned. 'One little bit of sanity in an insane world. I can't do without you any more. Will you stay with me tonight, Penny?'

It was a totally unexpected question here in this house where he had introduced her as Chloe's nanny. Even thinking about sharing his bed turned her bones to liquid. Santo was such a fantastic lover that she would never tire of him. It wasn't that simple, though. 'What will your father think?' she asked, hearing the unease in her voice.

'Who cares?' he demanded harshly. 'He's probably

already guessed anyway. Didn't you see the calculating way he looked at us earlier? I need you, Penny.'

But only to take his mind off his present unhappy state of affairs. Making love was a good problem-blocker but it didn't resolve it. He'd invited her into his bed before; he would very likely do it again. Was she foolish to let herself be used like this?

The answer was yes, she probably was, but how could she help herself when her body was attuned to his so closely that she sometimes felt a part of him? When his kisses rocked the heavens and even the lightest touch of his fingers sent her spinning into space?

And so in bed later Penny held nothing back. She took the lead, kneeling over him, stroking and kissing, trying to ease the tension in his limbs. Today had been so hard for Santo that she knew he wouldn't relax immediately. With fingers and tongue she explored and tasted, slowly and sensually, from his throat down to his navel, tempted to go further but knowing that it was too soon yet. She sucked and gently bit his nipples, exulting when he groaned deep in his throat, when he grew hard and excited.

She lay over him, moist and ready, and knew exactly what she was going to do—until suddenly Santo turned the tables. She was beneath him now. And he didn't waste time. He was hot inside her, fiercely demanding. Her muscles closed around him and she lifted herself up to meet his fiercely hungry demand.

Her fingernails dug into his back and she rocked with him until suddenly he lost all control. Seconds later Penny reached her own earth-shattering climax and for long moments they both lay on the bed, spent.

'You are some woman,' he said gruffly.

'I aim to please,' came her demure reply. Except that inside she felt anything but demure. Santo made her feel like a princess, beautiful and needed, and aroused emotions far deeper than she had ever thought herself capable of. When Santo made love to her it was as if she was in a different world where only senses mattered. Each time it was a different mind-blowing experience. And even though she knew he had only used her tonight, somehow it didn't matter.

When he was asleep she lay curled against him, her head nestled into his shoulder, her arm across his chest, the scent of him continuing to tantalise her nostrils. The feel of his skin beneath her fingertips made her want to trace every inch of his body, to feel again the exciting hardness of him. She wanted to be with him for ever!

It was such a crazy, impossible thought that tears squeezed from her eyes and when she finally went to sleep she dreamt that she and Santo were out walking on a cliff top that suddenly fell away beneath their feet. She managed to hold on to a small bush that had amazingly remained anchored, but Santo fell to his death. And she knew it was her subconscious preparing her for the fact that one day it would be all over between them.

She woke to find Chloe snuggled in the bed, sandwiched between her and Santo. 'I like my grandfather,' she declared, 'he's funny. What are we going to do today, Daddy? Nonno says he will swim with me. Can old men swim, Daddy?'

Santo smiled indulgently. 'Of course. My father was one of the best swimmers in Italy. He taught me to swim. But I actually wanted to show Penny some more of the sights and I was hoping you'd come with us.'

Swift tears welled in Chloe's eyes. 'But Daddy, I want to stay here. I want to swim. I don't like old buildings.'

'I'll talk to your grandfather,' he promised.

'I'm not sure it would be wise letting her stay,' said Penny, once Chloe had run out of the room. 'Your father might have been a good swimmer in his time but is he capable of looking after Chloe? What if anything happens? He's not quick any more, is he? And won't he think it strange if I go off with you?'

'I have fears too, but I didn't want to spoil Chloe's happiness. I'll talk to him.'

In the end it was decided that Signora Moretti, the housekeeper, would invite her daughter, who had a child about Chloe's age, to come and keep Chloe company. Santo and Penny waited for them to arrive and reassured themselves that Chloe would be in safe hands before departing. Chloe herself was in her element.

Even so Penny still felt faintly anxious. It didn't feel as though she was doing her job properly. Santo on the other hand didn't seem to have any such fears. 'Italians love children; nothing will happen to her. She will be treated like one of their own.'

They both lapsed into silence on the drive into Rome. Penny was getting a pretty good picture of what Santo's life had been like: a father who detached himself from his family, and a brother who was consumed by jealousy because Santo had made something of his life. She could see how this had moulded Santo into the private person that he was. And why he had found it difficult to bond with Chloe. There had been no love in his family—even his wife had walked out on him.

She had no idea what his mother had been like, but she had the feeling that she'd been sparing with her love also. It had probably been knocked out of her by her bullying husband.

She felt sorry for Santo. Not that he would appreciate sympathy. He'd become a tough, hard-working man who'd pushed everything unhappy out of his mind. He would be horrified if he knew she was thinking that she would like to spend the rest of her life making it up to him.

An impossible dream, but it was unfortunately true.

'We'll do the touristy things first and the shops later,' said Santo as soon as he'd parked.

'Shops?' queried Penny.

'Do not all women like to shop? There's everything here—Versace, Valentino, Armani.'

'And way out of my price range,' she pointed out. 'But I suppose it won't hurt to look. At least I can press my nose to the windows.'

She missed the curious look he gave her, and hummed happily to herself as they walked once again to St Peter's Square. She discovered to her surprise that Santo had arranged a private tour.

Their guide told them that the Vatican Museums were originally meant for the sole enjoyment of the pope; that there were two thousand rooms stretching over nine miles, and it would take them twelve years to look at every item.

Penny gasped and he laughed. 'Do not worry, we are just going to look at the highlights today.'

The decorations, the paintings, the statues, the ornateness of it all took Penny's breath away. She couldn't speak she was so overwhelmed. And she wished that she'd thought to bring her camera. The Sistine Chapel was stunning. She'd seen it on television but to actually be there and look up at the amazing ceiling, to wonder how anyone could paint such exquisite pictures, was beyond her.

And then the Basilica itself. There was so much marble and the size was so vast that Penny found it difficult to comprehend. 'It's claimed to be built over the tomb of St Peter,' their guide told them, 'and is the largest Catholic church in the world.'

Penny felt tiny in comparison and she took hold of Santo's hand as they looked up as if it would somehow make her feel more secure.

'You're enjoying it?' he asked softly.

'I feel totally insignificant,' she answered. 'I had no idea it was so large or so beautiful.'

Once outside again in the bright sunlight, they crossed St Peter's Square, which was now packed with people and found a small, quiet back-street café, where they had a sandwich and ice cream, and then it was on to the shops, to Via Condotti, where most of the designer boutiques were.

Santo insisted on taking her inside one of them, where she tried on a variety of dresses and skirts and fancy tops especially for his benefit. The assistants bowed and scraped, unable to take their eyes off him, almost ignoring Penny so eager were they to please him.

'So which ones are you having?' he asked finally.

Penny knew that he had to be joking. These were way out of her league. 'If I could afford any, which I can't, of course,' she said, 'I'd have the black cocktail dress, the tan skirt, and the blue one, I think, as well as that delicious little lacy top. Oh, and probably that slinky pink suit as well. I felt a million dollars in that.'

She missed the gesture Santo made to the manageress and was stunned when she came out of the dressing room and discovered that everything she had mentioned had been packed into bags and was ready to take away.

'Santo! You can't do that!' she exclaimed. 'I thought this was a game.'

'I don't play games,' he told her.

But his generosity worried her and on the way back to the house Penny continued to tell Santo off for spending so much money. 'You shouldn't have done that. It's not right,' she insisted.

'Aren't they what you wanted?' he asked.

'I love them but—'

'Then the matter's closed,' he said quietly.

It had been a perfect day, thought Penny as they pulled up outside. She'd seen so much of historic interest, so much wealth and beauty, that it still continued to awe her, and as she took her new purchases upstairs she couldn't stop smiling.

Santo had thought that spending the day with Penny, seeing her pleasure when she tried on outfit after outfit, would lift the depression that had overtaken him. But it had done no such thing. The instant he set foot in his father's house it was back again, hanging over his head like a thundercloud.

He had hoped, he had prayed even, that his father might have mellowed over the years, that he might actually have been pleased to see him. But no. There was no softening of the old man's heart. He was still very much the oppressor.

At least he hadn't hurt Chloe—in fact he'd welcomed his granddaughter; he'd given her love and affection, which should have pleased Santo—and did in a moderate sort of way. But Santo knew that beneath the surface his father hadn't changed. He enjoyed conflict, he enjoyed power over people, to such an extent that he had no friends.

It would be interesting to know what his father thought about his success. Penny was right; he probably did know—Vittorio would have told him—but not once had he mentioned it and Santo himself had no intention of saying anything. Ironically he had his father to thank, because if he hadn't left home, if he hadn't needed to support himself, he might not have got where he was today. It had been sheer drive and determination that had made him do it.

All this made Santo treasure the daughter he'd never known about. He loved her so much that it hurt. He would never treat her badly. He would love and cherish her to the end of his days.

Penny had had such a lovely day that she was disappointed when Santo changed as soon as they got home. He withdrew into himself; he didn't sit and talk to his father as any other son would have done. He wandered out into the garden instead and stood for ages looking out over the countryside. The void between them was too big to ever be bridged. A lump lodged in Penny's throat every time she thought about it.

Dinner was uncomfortable again. She did her best to break the silence, but conversation became monosyllabic and eventually she gave up. Once it was over Santo shut himself in his bedroom and she didn't dare follow.

It was all she could do to fight down tears. When she thought of all he'd spent on her, of the lovely time they'd had when she tried on the dresses and paraded and flirted in front of him, it was hard to believe that he was now letting the enmity between him and his father ruin it.

Surely he could have made an effort? Didn't he realise how awkward it was for her? How it would affect Chloe if he carried this on tomorrow? Or was he planning to go home then? She really had no idea what he was going to do. All she knew was that she'd never before found herself in such a difficult situation.

The next morning, however, the whole affair faded into insignificance. What was happening between Santo and his father was nothing compared to what was happening to her.

CHAPTER TWELVE

SHE was late! And she was never late. Her monthly cycle was as regular as clockwork.

When the appalling truth hit her Penny felt sick. In the stark light of morning she stared at her shocked face in the bathroom mirror. She looked truly awful—dark circles beneath her eyes, every trace of colour drained from her cheeks. Haunted, a picture of sheer fright. Her normally pretty blue eyes were wide and traumatised; she felt as though she would never be able to look at herself again.

When she thought back there had been only one occasion when Santo hadn't used protection—when they'd each been too desperate to even think about it.

And that was all it had taken!

One tiny mistake to ruin her whole life.

All they'd thought about was pleasuring each other's bodies, pleasuring themselves; nothing else had been in their minds. Just each other. Just the joy of giving and receiving, the intense excitement, the serious sensations that had screamed through every vein, every artery, every limb—until the ultimate release. A powerful, mind-blowing moment that had left them writhing on the bed, entirely unaware that in those few seconds a new life had been created.

She had not even thought about it since, not until she opened her diary and realised what the date was. Now she sat on the edge of the bath and dropped her head in her hands. She'd have to tell Santo, of course, it was only right that he should know. She couldn't walk out on him as his wife had done and not let him know that he had fathered another child. But she pitied the poor baby who'd be born into a family where father and grandfather were estranged, where an uncle lived on handouts from his parent. Where there was no love.

Oh, God, what a mess!

It took an effort to shower and dress and accept that she had to face Santo and pretend for the moment that nothing was wrong. She needed to be sure they were completely alone when she told him; she dared not risk being disturbed because she knew there would be tears and recrimination. Tears were close to the surface even now. She couldn't believe that she'd been such an idiot.

On the other hand, looking on the bright side, perhaps she wasn't pregnant. Perhaps she was worrying for nothing. Admittedly she was never late but then again she'd never had so much excitement in her life. This visit to Italy was one of her dreams come true, and to be treated like a princess by an exciting, gorgeous man had to have an effect on her.

And who was she trying to kid? Hadn't she felt nauseous the last few mornings? She'd put it down to a change of diet. But it was no good believing that morning sickness didn't happen until a few weeks into pregnancy because her sister had suffered the very same symptoms. Yes, she was pregnant all right.

She found Santo and Chloe on the terrace eating breakfast. Chloe was still in her pyjamas and she had jam all round her mouth. She was jigging up and down with happiness and it did Penny's heart good to see her. It worried her, though, how Santo would take the news that he was about to become a father for a second time. She didn't believe he was ready for it. He'd already had one child launched on him, interfering with his busy work schedule. How would he adapt to another?

'Ah, you're here at last,' he said, his eyes meeting hers briefly. 'Chloe's all yours now—I'm going out.'

And before she could ask him how long he would be, he'd gone.

Penny had been apprehensive about seeing him, hoping he wouldn't question her pallid skin and lacklustre eyes, ready with the excuse that yesterday had worn her out, that it felt like an anticlimax. He'd barely glanced at her; he'd seen none of her torment.

Food was the last thing she wanted but she managed a glass of fruit juice and a bread roll before the housekeeper came to clear the table. The rest of the morning was spent entertaining Chloe. They swam, they walked, they explored, but on their own. The child was disappointed that her father had disappeared and kept asking when he would come back.

They ate lunch with Antonio and when he announced that he was going to take a siesta Penny put Chloe to bed as well. Their morning activity had worn her out—Penny too, if the truth were known.

She sat outside on the terrace. There was plenty of shade and a gentle breeze whispered through the foliage, so even though the temperature was high it didn't feel uncomfortable. She tried to read a magazine but the words merely danced in front of her eyes. There was no way she could concentrate when so much was going on in her mind.

Eventually Santo put in an appearance and she smiled tentatively. 'Where have you been?' she asked. 'Chloe missed you.'

His eyes were hard as he looked at her, his brow furrowed. She'd rarely seen him look this fierce before. Even his lips were grim—which didn't bode well for what she had to tell him.

'I had something to take care of,' he answered a little harshly. 'Where is she?'

'Asleep. Your father's taking a siesta too.'

'Good, because we need to talk.'

'I want to talk too,' she said quickly, 'there's something I have to tell you.' She needed to do it straight away, before she lost her nerve. It wasn't a particularly good time with Santo in this mood, but when would it be? She didn't want to wait…she couldn't; she couldn't bear the thought of carrying this secret around for any longer than necessary.

But Santo had other ideas. 'Whatever, it will wait,' he declared impatiently, dropping onto the chair opposite her.

Penny would have preferred him at her side, where he couldn't see her face so clearly. It would be purgatory trying to hide her emotions. 'Santo, I—'

But before she could get any further he butted in. 'Is this about Chloe?'

Penny frowned. 'No.'

'Is it about my father?'

'No.'

'Then I don't want to hear any of your problems, I

have enough of my own. Dammit, Penny, you're forgetting your position here.'

Penny felt as though he'd slapped her hard on the face. She felt as if she was an insect that had been trodden on by someone's big boot. She felt as insignificant as an ant. And without a further word she got up and ran to her room.

Santo had just made it stunningly clear that their relationship was over! And it hurt as nothing else had ever hurt in her life. What she ought to have done was stood her ground and asked him what the hell he meant instead of scuttling away like a scared child. She guessed it was her hormones playing up because normally she would have done that. She would have faced any situation. Had Santo forgotten all their time spent together? The hours in each other's arms making love? He'd needed her then; he hadn't been able to get enough of her. So what had happened to turn it around?

She wondered whether it was to do with his father. There was no sign of a reconciliation. Had Santo gone out because he couldn't bear to be in the same house? Even so, why take it out on her? What had she done? And how was she going to tell him that she was pregnant with his baby when he was in such a bad mood?

In her heart of hearts Penny knew that such a delicate subject should be discussed only when they were at ease in each other's company. Perhaps she ought to leave it until tomorrow? Or maybe she could creep into his room tonight, sneak into bed with him; use her body to coax him into a good mood. She knew exactly what it took to arouse him, to make him groan and gather her close, to make him lose himself inside her. It would be an excellent time to bare her soul.

Santo was well aware that he ought not to have spoken so harshly to Penny but, dammit, he was so filled with rage and frustration that anyone who came near him was in the firing line. He'd spent most of the morning on the phone to his London office and, boy, had they received the harsh edge of his tongue when he discovered there was a problem they'd been unable to solve.

It had been a bad idea coming here. He'd given his father one last chance and it hadn't worked. There'd been no welcome for his long-lost son, nothing but more of what he'd endured all those years ago. Antonio could go to hell now as far as he was concerned.

Of one thing he was very sure; he would never treat his daughter the way his father treated him. Not ever, not as long as he lived. He would treasure her and guide her and give her every support possible. She would grow into a beautiful, well-adapted young woman with no harsh memories of a father who didn't love her.

Tomorrow they were flying home. He was needed at the office—and would he be thankful to get away! But first, he supposed, he ought to seek Penny out and apologise. Except that in all honesty he was in no mood to do it.

He went for a swim instead, punishing himself, length after length, powering his arms through the water until he was exhausted. And it worked. Some of his bitterness and anger faded and when he saw Penny walking towards him he was ready to talk.

She'd said that she had something to tell him and he'd rudely cut her short. What if it *had* been about Chloe? Perhaps his daughter wasn't well? She was asleep apparently but she didn't always take an afternoon nap. Was there something wrong? Alarm bells began to ring in his head, especially as Penny looked pale and drawn, desperately worried about something.

He too began to feel fearful and he spoke as soon as she reached his side. 'Is Chloe all right? Is she still asleep?'

'Your daughter's fine,' Penny answered quietly.

'So what is wrong? Is it you who's not well?'

Penny closed her eyes briefly. 'I'm OK, but there is something I need to tell you. May I sit down?'

'Of course. Would you like a drink—some water perhaps? You look a little pale. Has the sun got to you?' He felt guilty now for scaring her away earlier. She had turned wide, shocked eyes on him and run like a rabbit for the safety of the house.

'Water, yes, thank you.'

Penny took a few deep, steadying breaths while Santo was away. From her bedroom window she'd seen him swimming and recognised that he was chasing his demons. He looked calmer now and she kept her fingers mentally crossed that he wouldn't slip back into his rage when he heard what she had to say.

When he returned with her drink he had donned a pair of cotton trousers and a T-shirt and he even smiled as he filled her glass from the jug. 'This heat is unforgiving, you know. You need to be careful.'

Penny drank deeply before setting the glass back down on the table. 'It's not the heat that's affecting me.'

'So what is it? The tension between me and my father? I'm sorry about that, and I've—'

'No!' declared Penny at once. And, since there was no way she could wrap up her confession in pretty words, she blurted it out. 'I'm pregnant, Santo.'

The silence that followed was unending, and deafening. Penny avoided looking at him. She didn't want to see the horror, the disbelief, the shock, the denial.

When he did finally speak there was recrimination in his voice. 'It is impossible. You are mistaken.' His accent was deep and there was nothing but harsh shadows across his face.

'No, I'm not,' she declared, trying to keep her voice level, to not let him hear any tremors. 'Believe me, I know how I feel. I'm carrying your baby.'

'But when, how?' Dark eyes were still disbelieving. 'I've always taken precautions.'

'Except once,' she reminded him firmly. 'Maybe you don't remember, but I do. Naturally, when we return to England I'll be handing in my notice. I won't deny you access to the baby, but—'

'The hell you won't!' Santo's roar rent the air. It seemed to echo around them and everything stilled. Even Penny's heart stopped beating. 'If—and I won't accept it until you've seen a gynaecologist—you are pregnant, then you're going nowhere.'

Penny's eyes flared a vivid blue. 'Do you really think I'd let a man who finds it so hard to love that he can't even make it up with his own father bring up my child? A man who spends more time at work than he does at home? Not in your wildest dreams.'

Her heart beat so fiercely that it hurt and, fearing that she had gone too far, Penny stood up with the intention of fleeing again, but Santo was having none of it. Eyes hard he unceremoniously pushed her back down. 'We haven't finished.'

An icy shiver ran down the length of Penny's spine but there was no way she was going to let him intimidate her. This was her baby—he hadn't asked for it, he didn't want it. It broke her heart to think that she had to walk away from him, but what choice was there? 'I don't think there's anything left to say.'

'You really think I'd let you go?'

'Other than locking me up, how can you stop me?' she challenged.

'You could marry me.'

Silence! Complete and utter silence. Even the birds stopped singing.

'Marry you?' she whispered eventually. 'Just because I'm carrying your baby? You really think that would work?' She shook her head. 'You're out of your mind.' And she was out of her mind because just for one crazy second she had thought about saying yes. And how stupid was that when he'd only proposed because she was pregnant? She was useful to him, yes—she was good at looking after Chloe, and she'd be good with the new baby, and she might even feed his sexual desires occasionally, but as for anything else…

Santo was definitely not marrying material. Not since his first marriage had ended in disaster. He didn't trust women, full stop. He might even believe that she'd gotten pregnant deliberately in order to trap herself a rich man.

'I'm perfectly serious,' he told her, 'and I cannot see why—'

'Daddy, Daddy, you're back.' Chloe came running out of the house and flung herself into his arms. A sigh of relief whooshed from Penny's lungs and she quietly slipped away while he was chatting to his daughter.

For the rest of the day she carefully avoided Santo. And that night over dinner with his father he announced that they were leaving early the next morning. 'I need to get back,' he announced tersely.

'Or is it that you've had enough of me?' barked the old man.

Santo glared. 'I would have thought it was the other way round. At least you've been kind to my daughter, I'm grateful to you for that.'

'And I wasn't kind to you, is that what you're claiming?' The cold glint in Antonio's eyes revealed exactly how much enmity there still was between the two men.

Penny shivered.

'Why do you think I walked away from you?' challenged Santo.

'Because you were a mummy's boy and wanted to be where she was,' sneered Antonio.

Santo shook his head. 'You're so wrong, Father. But I refuse to sit here and argue. I've finished.' And he scraped back his chair.

Penny pulled a wry face after he'd left the room. 'I need to pack, if you'll excuse me.'

He didn't try to stop her, and for a brief moment she felt sorry for Antonio. On the other hand he deserved everything he'd got. He wasn't a very nice father. There was such bitterness inside him, such anger. Penny could suddenly see that this old man had affected Santo terribly.

She couldn't marry him, she couldn't. She had to get away, away from all of this.

As she carefully packed the beautiful new clothes that Santo had bought her, she realised that soon she wouldn't be able to wear any of them. And would she want to anyway? They would for ever remind her of this disastrous holiday.

There was silence on the plane journey home. Even Chloe was silent. It was as though she'd picked up on their vibes and was afraid to speak in case she got into trouble.

And once they were cleared through the airport Santo announced that he was going straight to the office. 'There's a problem which no one seems capable of dealing with.'

A problem bigger than seeing that his precious daughter got home safely, or bigger than discussing your unborn baby? thought Penny bitterly as she climbed into the chauffeur-driven car he had provided for them.

Chloe slipped her hand into Penny's on the journey home. 'Is Daddy cross with me?'

'Of course not, my darling,' said Penny, feeling her heart lurch. 'Daddy has problems at work that he needs to sort out.'

Wide eyes were plaintive. 'Will he be home to kiss me goodnight?'

'I'm not sure,' answered Penny gently, 'but I'll be there. Don't you worry about that.'

'I miss my mommy.'

It was a cry from the heart and an ice-cold shiver slid through Penny's veins. Chloe hadn't said this since the early days of her coming to live with her father. She'd learned to trust and love him and now she felt that he was letting her down again. And if Penny gave up her job, as she desperately wanted to do, she would be letting Chloe down as well.

How could she stay, though, under the circumstances? She needed to be loved too, not be used as a bed partner whenever Santo felt like it, not just as a nanny to his daughter. She wanted more, much more. She'd fallen irreparably in love with Santo and she wanted to spend the rest of her life with him. It was an impossible dream, though.

They were both in bed when he came home. Penny heard his footsteps coming up the stairs and she held her breath, praying he wouldn't come to her and demand they finish their conversation. They needed to talk, yes, they needed to sort things out, but she wanted to wait until he'd had time to calm down, accustom himself to the situation.

She worried for nothing and the next morning he left before she and Chloe had breakfast. They went for a walk, took bread to feed the ducks on the river, and on the way back Penny popped into a chemist and bought a pregnancy-testing kit. Not that she needed proof, not in her own mind, but Santo did and she'd be happy to provide it. She wasn't going to see one of his fancy gynaecologists, that was for sure. She'd see her own doctor.

The only problem about leaving Santo was where was she going to live. She'd shared a flat with a friend at one time, but there wasn't room for her now. She could, she supposed, lodge with her sister for a while, she didn't have much room since they'd had the new baby, but she'd make do.

The test proved positive and although she had known that it would, it was still a shock to her system and she broke down in tears. Nevertheless when Santo came home early, she had herself well under control.

Chloe was delighted to see her father and Penny was pleasantly surprised when he supervised her bath and put her to bed. Once she was asleep, though, he sought Penny out. 'It is time we talked.' There was grimness both in his voice and in the set of his mouth. And when he looked at her Penny shivered all over. It was hard to imagine that they'd made this baby together, that their bodies had become one and she'd felt special.

'There's not much to say.' Penny made an effort to meet his eyes. They were dark and forbidding, with nothing at all like the soft sensuality she had seen when he was making love. 'I did a home test today—it proved positive.' As far as she was concerned it was evidence enough.

Very faintly he nodded. 'In that case, if it is true, then we have arrangements to make.'

'Such as?' queried Penny, conscious that her voice had risen sharply, even though she wanted to remain calm. 'If you're going to ask me again to marry you, forget it. It's out of the question.'

'Because?' he snapped.

'Because we don't love each other,' she returned equally sharply. 'Because we wouldn't be happy together. You're a workaholic, while I believe a man should make time for his family. There are infinite reasons. I won't deny you access but I'm definitely bringing this child up on my own. And I'm quitting my job.'

'What if I say you're a liar?'

Penny frowned. 'On which count? I am pregnant. I am giving up this job. I am bringing this child up on my own.'

'But you're lying when you say you don't love me.'

Her heart did a swift shuffle and her throat jammed. She tried to swallow but nothing happened. He was trying to sweep her into a corner from which there was no escape. Not for his sake, but for the children's. He wanted her to continue looking after Chloe, and ultimately this baby who had been conceived of their passion. He couldn't cope on his own and he'd found no other suitable person.

'Love you?' she echoed, hearing the wild fear in her

voice. 'I've enjoyed having sex with you, Santo. But I have no intention of falling in love ever again.'

She heard rather than saw the harsh breath he drew, but she did observe the thinning of his lips and the way his eyelids lowered over his eyes until they were almost but not quite closed. 'And that's all it was, sex? I've had sex with women before, and it was nothing like what you and I experienced.'

'What are you saying?' Penny lifted her chin and eyed him coolly, hoping he would believe that his words didn't bother her. He was making it sound as though the whole experience had meant a lot more to him than she'd suspected. And if that was the case…

'I think that you've fallen in love with me. I think you're running scared. I think you believe that I'm like Max and will drop you like a red-hot coal when I find someone better. But how could that be, when I've found the woman I want to spend the rest of my life with?'

Penny's blue eyes widened dramatically, turning into huge, wide, disbelieving orbs. She shook her head, unable to believe what he was saying.

'You think I'm not telling the truth? Why would I lie about something so important?' He took a step closer, close enough for her to feel the warmth of his body, his fresh breath on her face. 'I'm asking you again, Penny; will you marry me?'

'You actually mean it?'

'*Mio dio*, what does it take to convince you?'

'But—but you don't love me. You're doing this for the baby's sake. I could never marry you for that reason.'

'Do you love me?'

Penny didn't answer. How could she, when he'd never actually said that he loved her?

'Perhaps this will persuade you.' Without warning he took her face between his palms and kissed her, deeply and satisfyingly, and it wasn't long before Penny returned his kisses, urging her body closer, exulting in his hardness, and the fleeting thought passed through her mind that marrying Santo might very well be worth the risk.

Perhaps in time he would learn to love her as she loved him. Could she do it? Dared she do it?

He eased his lips away from hers, gentle fingers tracing her eyebrows, the line of her nose, the curve of her ears. 'There was only one reason I went to see my father.'

Penny couldn't see what this had to do with him suggesting they get married, nevertheless she waited patiently for him to continue.

'I wanted to introduce you as the woman I intended marrying. As my fiancée.'

Penny's mouth fell open. 'You did?'

'I thought he might have changed. I thought he might be pleased for me. But no, his behaviour was as appalling as it's ever been. I couldn't do it. I couldn't force him on you like that. There's no saying how he would have taken it, what he would have said. He could have hurt you so much.'

'You were going to declare that I was your fiancée without even asking whether I wanted to marry you?' Penny's thoughts ran riot. He'd had this in his mind all the time. He'd braved his father for her sake— Chloe's as well—but he'd actually been going to tell Antonio that he'd found the love of his life and planned to marry her.

And Antonio had ruined it…

No wonder he'd been in such a foul mood. No wonder he'd never spoken to his father unless it was absolutely necessary.

'I knew you'd agree to marry me,' he said with a wide smile that revealed his beautiful, even teeth. 'You love me, Penny. Go on, deny it. Tell me you don't and I'll let you walk away.'

'Oh, Santo…' Such happiness as she had never felt before swept over her, filled her, warmed her. Tears welled at the thought that this man, whom she had been going to desert, loved her enough to face his hostile parent. He'd wanted to tell him that this was the woman he loved; he'd wanted to show her off.

Instead his father's welcome had been hostile. It was only to Chloe and herself that he'd shown any warmth, and perhaps that hadn't been genuine. 'I really had hoped that you and your father would make up,' she said.

'I'd hoped so too, for your sake and for Chloe's. But since it's not to be let's forget him and concentrate solely on us. Do you love me enough to marry me? Or do you need a little more persuasion?'

'Maybe a little,' she answered with a mischievous smile.

His kiss melted her soul. She clung to him as though she never wanted to let him go, as though she was afraid that this moment wasn't real, that it was all a dream and she would wake to find that Santo didn't want her after all.

But he was still there, smiling down at her, his eyes full of love and tenderness and a promise of things to come. 'So it's a yes, then?'

'With one proviso.'

'Anything for you, *cara*. Anything.' It was spoken from the heart.

'I don't want a workaholic husband whom I never see. I want you to delegate, hand the reins over to someone else. Isn't your home life more important?'

'It never has been,' he said with a wry twist of his lips. 'I guess it's a throwback to the years spent under my father's thumb. I needed to escape. And work was the only way out. But for you, *il mio tesoro*, anything. You have no idea how often I've wanted to race home to you. I was afraid of scaring you away, though, I wanted you so much.'

'As I wanted you, my darling,' she breathed against his lips.

'I love you, Penny. I never thought I'd fall in love again. You're a very special person.'

'And I love you too, Santo. I will love you for the rest of my life. I promise you that.'

Penny and Santo got married almost immediately. Chloe was their bridesmaid and she was as proud as punch when they presented her with a baby brother seven months later.

'We must take him to see my Italian grandfather,' she declared importantly.

Penny and Santo looked at each other and because they were both feeling sentimental Santo nodded. 'One day, my little love, we will. We'll visit him again.'

Penny smiled inwardly. She hoped they did. She hoped that Santo would make one further attempt to heal the rift between him and his father. The man wasn't getting any younger. Nor would it be right for him to die before he'd seen his new grandchild.

Later that year they made the visit. By this time

Penny was pregnant again and they'd debated whether to wait until the baby was born, but Vittorio had phoned to say Antonio was ill.

They made it just in time. Penny's lasting impression was of father and son holding hands. Chloe kissed her grandfather and introduced her little brother before Penny ushered them out of the room.

When Santo came to find her he had tears in his eyes. 'At least we made our peace.'

Penny nodded. 'I'm proud of you, Santo. And I love you so very, very much.'

'As I love you, my darling, with all of my heart. For always.'

* * * * *

THE ITALIAN COUNT'S
DEFIANT BRIDE

BY
CATHERINE GEORGE

Catherine George was born on the border between Wales and England, in a village blessed with both a public and a lending library. Fervently encouraged by a like-minded mother, she developed an early addiction to reading.

At eighteen Catherine met the husband who eventually took her off to Brazil. He worked as chief engineer of a large gold-mining operation in Minas Gerais, which provided a popular background for several of Catherine's early novels.

After nine happy years, the education of their small son took them back to Britain, and soon afterward a daughter was born. But Catherine always found time to read, if only in the bath! When her husband's job took him abroad again she enrolled in a creative-writing course, then read countless novels by Mills & Boon® authors before trying a hand at one herself. Her first effort was not only accepted, but voted best of its genre for that year.

Catherine has written well over sixty novels since and has won another award along the way. But now she has come full circle. After living in Brazil, and in England's the Wirral, Warwick and the Forest of Dean, Catherine now resides in the beautiful Welsh Marches—with access to a county library, several bookshops and a busy market hall with a treasure trove of secondhand paperbacks!

To rugby players of all nationalities,
with a special dedication to the men
who wear the red shirt of Wales.

CHAPTER ONE

THE atmosphere in the city was electric. Alicia Cross felt it tingle in her veins as she joined the Welsh rugby fans streaming into Cardiff's Millennium Stadium. As always they had arrived in their thousands to support their heroes, with the added excitement that today a victory against Italy would mean a step forward towards the holy grail of the Six Nations contest, the grand slam; victory over all five of the other teams. Wales were now level with England on wins.

After weeks of travel and hard work to organise parties and press events, Alicia had begged a couple of hours off duty this afternoon to watch the match with friends. Earlier she had checked the arrangements for the sponsor's lunch at the stadium, then hurried back to Cardiff Bay to ensure that all was ready in the hotel chosen for the party later that night. But now at last, instead of joining the sponsors in their hospitality box, she was on her way to her seat in the stands, and she was cutting it a bit fine. In her rush she almost bumped into the man who stepped in front of her, barring her way. She opened her mouth to apologise then snapped it shut, the colour draining from her face. In a knee-jerk reaction she flung away, but he was too quick for her and seized her hand. Conscious of curious glances beamed in their direction, she forced herself to stand still, her heart thudding against her ribs as she looked up into the handsome, unforgettable face of the man who had once changed her girlhood dreams into nightmares.

'Alicia,' he said in the voice that had not, to her intense disgust, lost the power to send shivers down her spine. Eyes locked with hers, he held her hand captive.

She returned the intent, heavy-lidded gaze for the space of several, deliberate heartbeats, then wrenched her hand away and turned on her heel.

But Francesco da Luca caught her by the elbow. 'Alicia, wait. I must speak with you.'

She stared at him in silent disdain, refusal blazing in her eyes as a crowd of late arrivals surged through the turnstiles to jostle them, and with a smothered curse he let her go.

'Do not think you can escape me again so easily, Alicia!'

The hint of menace in the deep, husky voice sent her racing up after the other fans as though the devil were after her. She shot into the cauldron of noise and music in the famous arena, and dived down the steep steps at such breakneck speed that Gareth Davies leapt up from the end of a row to seize her by the arm.

'Steady on, you'll break your neck.'

'Where have you *been*?' demanded Meg indignantly, as her brother thrust Alicia into the seat between them. 'The teams are just about to come on— Hey, what's up?'

'Big rush.' Alicia leaned across to smile at Meg's husband. 'Hi, Rhys.'

'Are you all right, love?' he said, reaching to pat her hand.

'Fine.' Or she would be in a minute.

'You don't look it,' Gareth told her.

Alicia's reply was drowned by the roar from the Italian supporters as their team ran onto the pitch. Then the entire arena erupted as Billy Wales, the famous ram mascot of the Welsh Guards, was led out from the players' tunnel. The big Welsh captain came next, holding a tiny red-shirted boy by the hand as he led his team to line up for the royal presentation.

The smiling prince went along the line, shaking the hands of players on both teams, saying a word here and there. Once he was escorted back to his seat the band of the Welsh Guards